D1524418

Grace in Love

A Novel about
Grace Woodsworth

by Ruth Latta

Grace in Love

Printed by
Du Progrès Printing

Published by:

Baico Publishing Inc.
E-mail: info@baico.ca
Web site: www.baico.ca

Acknowledgements

It is always a pleasure to work with Ray Coderre and Stephanie Bertrand of Baico Publishing. Thanks once again for your help.

Thank you, Lorna Foreman, author, columnist and member of the Cornwall Writers' Group, for reading an early version of *Grace in Love* and offering wise and helpful suggestions.

Thank you, Jo-Anne Ward, lawyer, avid reader and book club member, for editing a later version of the manuscript so carefully and insightfully.

Thank you, Roger, for too many reasons to list here.

Chapter One

On a warm October afternoon in 1928, with the fragrance of chestnut trees in the air, a petite young woman got out of a taxi at 18 rue Cler in the 7th arrondissement of Paris. Her hand trembled slightly as she paid the driver. She gazed up at the house, hoping it would be a good place to spend the next six months.

In the summer, while in the Loire Valley, she had placed an ad in a Paris paper requesting accommodation for a woman student taking the course in French Civilization offered to foreign students by the University of Paris, and the best reply she had received was from a Madame De Bussy who lived here.

The taxi driver carried her two suitcases to the door. She thanked him in competent French, and he answered, *"Bonne chance."*

She looked up at the house, saw a lace curtain twitch in a window, and a young voice saying, *"C'est la Canadienne."*

The door was opened by a stout grey-haired woman in a blue denim apron, her hair in a bun.

"Oui?" she inquired.

"Je cherche Madame De Bussy."

"Suivez-moi, s'il vous plait."

The maid picked up one suitcase and Grace, taking the other, followed her into a small foyer. The parlour door opened and two ladies, flanked by a girl of about twelve, came out to greet her.

"*Merci, Hubertine*," said the younger of the two ladies. The maid bowed and retreated down the hall.

"*Bienvenue, Mademoiselle.*"

Madame de Bussy looked kind but tired, with greying brown hair pulled back from her face in a chignon. She introduced her mother, Madame Hamel, a stout grey-haired woman wearing a dark figured dress with jet beads, and her young daughter, Edith. As Grace smiled and shook their hands she was relieved that they looked plain, ordinary and safe.

The introductions were entirely in French; the household spoke no English. Grace had studied French in high school and at a convent, and had majored in that language at the University of Manitoba, from which she had just graduated. She welcomed this immersion to increase her fluency and vocabulary.

Twelve year old Edith, in her school uniform of black tunic, white blouse and dark stockings, gazed at Grace with big dark eyes and asked her if she played the piano.

"*Un peu*," Grace said. "I'm sure you do, since your name is De Bussy."

Edith's mother laughed.

"Alas, my late husband was no relation to the famous Claude, and Edith has a long way to go before she rivals that great composer."

After some mental acrobatics to select the right words, Grace said that she loved music but was out of practise on the piano. During her summer and fall in the Loire Valley, Grace and her friend Isabel had spoken English when they were alone, a counter-productive thing to do, because it led to thinking in English. Though Grace thought she spoke French fairly well, her recall and vocabulary tended to break down when she was nervous and tired, as she was today.

Edith was saying that they should try some duets sometime.

"I would like that. I have a brother at home who likes music. He is twelve. His name is Howard." Saying his name brought on a stab of homesickness.

"Mademoiselle, you must be tired and wanting to see your room."

"Please, call me Grace."

"Please follow me, Grace. Hubertine will bring up your luggage."

Madame went to the door and called, "Hubertine!" Quickly Grace went out to the foyer, grabbed the handle of the heavier suitcase and started up the stairs.

On the second floor, her landlady pointed out Grace's room, which was across the hall from the bedroom shared by Madame Hamel and Edith. Down the hall was Madame's room, and across from it, the *chambre* occupied by their other boarder.

Grace hadn't realized there was to be another boarder. She felt a pang of concern, that the grandmother or granddaughter had to double up to free another room to rent out. The threadbare carpets and shabby furniture made it pretty clear that the family needed the income.

"You will meet our other paying guest at dinner," Madame told her. "He is a young man from *Australie* who is also taking the *Course de Civilisation Française*, so you will have that in common."

"All the way from Australia!"

"*Oui*. If you study together, you must leave the door open at all times."

"But of course," Grace assured her.

"The toilet is down the hall and the bathtub is in the *salle de bains* off the kitchen, naturally, since the water tank is heated by the stove."

Grace nodded. When her landlady opened the door to her room, she gasped with delight, for the window framed a city scape that featured the Eiffel Tower in the distance.

Madame De Bussy smiled. "Yes, we are within walking distance of the Tour Eiffel and also of the Sorbonne; that is, the *Université de Paris*."

"That's perfect."

Opening her purse, she paid Madame the agreed-upon rent, and her landlady departed, informing her that dinner was at 6:30 p.m.

As her footsteps faded, Grace looked around at the single bed, the dresser, the washstand with china pitcher, basin and slop jar, and, under the bed, the chamber pot. There were hooks for hanging clothes, a small writing desk and book shelf, and two chairs, an easy chair to relax in and a straight wooden chair uncomfortable enough to keep her awake while doing her assignments. In one corner was a tiny stove.

Leaning her elbows on the window frame, she looked out at the Eiffel Tower. Holiday time was over. Tomorrow she would go to the university and find out the location of her classes and the required texts. At this thought, her hands began to tremble and her stomach churn, so she left the window and opened her suitcases.

"You should be ecstatic," she scolded herself. "You're in Paris."

From the age of thirteen, when she first started studying French in high school, Grace had longed to go to France, but had never really expected to do so.   Back in 1918, the Great War was still going on, and as well, her parents didn't have the money for foreign travel. Captivated by photos of the Louvre, the Eiffel Tower and Versailles, in books, she'd kept the idea of France in the back of her mind. Then, in her final year at the University of Manitoba, when she'd learned about the French government scholarships, she knew she had to apply, though the odds against being awarded one were great. Now that this dream had come true, she would drink in every sight, sound and sensation of Paris.

"You're used to change," she told herself. Indeed, her life so far had been one of making friends, then having to say good-bye when her family moved, and then forging new friendships all over again. The first move was in 1917, when she was twelve, and her parents moved their family of six from wintry Winnipeg to a beautiful British Columbia coastal village, Gibson's Landing. The sheltering mountains, mysterious woods, balmy weather, proximity to the sea, and best of all, their new friends, had made Gibson's like the heaven that their father spoke of from his pulpit.

The next move was to Vancouver in 1920. After breaking with the church, Father had worked on the Vancouver docks and then became a spokesman for the labour movement. As a result of his involvement in the Winnipeg General Strike of 1919, he, like some other strike leaders, had been arrested and briefly jailed. To everyday working people, however, the strike leaders became heroes. By 1920 he was based in Vancouver, lecturing and teaching for the labour movement, so the family moved there to join him.

Then came the move to Ottawa, Ontario, in 1922. In 1921, Father had been elected Member of Parliament for Winnipeg North Centre, and found the national capital very lonely until the family joined him there. Grace, then sixteen, had just completed her first year at the University of British Columbia. In Ottawa, she had to put university on ice for a while, as the University of Ottawa didn't admit female students, so she had polished her French at a convent school and had taken teacher training at the Ottawa Normal School.

She'd just finished her first year of teaching in a one room country school at Dunrobin, outside Ottawa, when the family moved back to Winnipeg in the summer of 1925. If all six children were to go on to higher education, it was necessary that they live at home, to save expenses, in a city with a university, one open to women.

Grace's younger sister, Belva, started in the new B.Sc. Home Economics program, a five year course at the Manitoba Agricultural College, and Grace returned to university too. She completed an Honours B.A. in French, and won the prestigious scholarship to the Sorbonne. So far, she'd handled every move well, so why shouldn't she succeed in Paris?

Leaving her unpacking, she got out her stationery and fountain pen and began a letter to her parents to let them know she was now at her Paris address. No sooner had she written "Dear Mother and Father" than the full force of homesickness descended upon her. She put her pen down and thought about what they might be doing.

In Winnipeg it would be seven in the morning. Mother would be downstairs in the kitchen, having tea and a few moments to herself before the younger family members got up. Soon she would be making school lunches, boiling water for porridge and probably thinking about her two chicks who had left the nest.

If Parliament was not in session, and Father was home, Mother would slip out of bed quietly, so as not to disturb him. As one of two Independent Labour Party Members of Parliament, he was always on the go, speaking with labour and other progressive audiences about the need for a party of the democratic left to help everyday Canadians.

Belva would be in her dorm room at the Manitoba Agricultural College getting ready for a day that involved a range of courses from Organic Chemistry to Home Nursing. Ralph, Bruce and Howard would be at home, asleep in the room they shared, unless one of them had taken over Charles's room. She pictured their clutter of birds' nests, science experiments, Ralph's wood carvings, and novels by Zane Grey and Ralph Connor. Ralph's and Bruce's school books would be on the dining room table where they often did their homework with the girl next door. Grace had asked Ralph whether the young lady was his girlfriend, or Bruce's, and with a wicked grin, he'd replied, "We're sharing her."

When she thought of her nineteen year old brother Charles, Grace's homesickness faded a little. Charles wasn't an ocean away; he was just across the English Channel on a scholarship at the London School of Economics. They would see each other at Christmas.

What would Charles be doing? Leaving a lecture, looking up a book in the library, chatting with friends in a common room, or practising his violin. Grace remembered, with a smile, how Charles used to say, "Don't let anyone touch my violin." "Anyone" meant Howard. As a little boy, her youngest brother loved to get his hands on the instrument, imagining that you could produce beautiful strains from it if you sawed on it hard enough with the bow.

Christmas with Charles was a comforting thought; closer to the festive season she would find him a place to stay. A mischievous child, often in trouble, he'd grown up clever, good-humoured and self-confident. In his last letter he'd asked her, jokingly, if a "Frenchman in a beret had stolen her heart away."

"Alas, no," she'd replied.

She was twenty-three, and no one had stolen her heart. Her best friend from British Columbia days, Kathy, had met the love of her life at university but Grace hadn't found "the one." Since her parents had met at university she'd imagined that she would meet someone special there, too, but she hadn't. Now she wondered if she should have tried harder to get to know young men. In class discussions she'd listened respectfully to all opinions, but never shied away from polite disagreement with her fellow students, no matter what their gender, if she thought they were wrong. She'd been friendly but reserved to the young men, including the one who had asked her out for ice cream and to the movies a few times. She'd kept him at arm's length because she felt absolutely no animal magnetism toward him and couldn't imagine him being part of her future.

Perhaps her strength on the debating team had frightened away "Mr. Right" without her recognizing him, but anyone who was so easily intimidated wouldn't have been "Mr. Right" anyway. Still, she worried that her take-charge nature was off-putting. As the eldest in her family she'd often been responsible for her younger siblings, especially when her mother had gone back to teach and her father was working on the Vancouver docks, and sometimes she'd had to lay down the law about chores. As a teacher in one-room schools, she'd been kind, effective and entertaining, but she'd made it clear to the children that she was boss. Her mother said that she would eventually meet the man for her life, and in the meantime, she should develop her own potential, which she hoped to do in Paris.

Hearing a knock, she looked up and saw a young man in the doorway. Neatly dressed in a brown suit, he was slight and slender like her father and Charles, and had light brown hair combed in a cowlick, with a few strands escaping onto his forehead. His hazel eyes, the same colour as hers, were magnified by his glasses.

"*Bonjour,*" he began. "*Je m'appelle Andrew Hallett.*" His Adam's apple bobbed as he talked. He extended his hand and she shook it, introducing herself, in French, as the student from Canada.

"And you must be the student from Australia," she continued in French.

"I am," he said, in French. "From Sydney."

"I imagine that your first language is English, as is mine," Grace added, still in French, "but out of respect for our landlady and her family, and because we're here to enhance our ability in French, I suggest that we stick to that language."

"*Une bonne idée,*" he agreed, then asked if she was from Quebec.

She shook her head. "No, though our family rented a cottage there one summer when we lived in Ottawa."

"I know nothing of Canada, really," he said, "except that Quebec was once New France and that French is spoken there."

"That's true. And where in Australia do they speak French?"

He laughed. "In grammar schools and universities."

"Then do sit down and tell me how you became so fluent in the language." She indicated the easy chair and sat on the bed.

The rest of the afternoon passed quickly, as they exchanged autobiographical notes. Surprisingly, some details of their backgrounds were similar. Like Grace, Andrew had graduated from university that spring. His mother, formerly a French teacher, like Grace's mother, had started teaching him that language at her knee.

Both he and Grace had taught school to earn money for their studies, he in an outback school where the board cared little about formal qualifications, but just wanted someone who could teach the "three Rs".

There were differences, of course. Andrew's maternal grandparents had moved from France to Australia for a fresh start after the Franco-Prussian War; that explained his mother's competence in French. Grace's mother, of Irish Protestant ancestry, had grown up in the rural heartland of English-speaking Ontario but had shown an aptitude for French in high school. Andrew's father was the principal of a grammar school. When Grace said that her father was a Member of Parliament, Andrew seemed impressed.

Grace had sailed for France on a tour organized by the Overscas Education League in order to have the support of a group, a guided introduction to London and Paris and a placement with a suitable French family, before starting at the Sorbonne. Andrew had travelled all alone from Australia, on a lengthy voyage with many interesting ports of call. On board he had met another "Aussie", Mr. Taylor, who was taking the advanced French Civilization course. Grace liked Andrew's suggestion that the three of them get together for coffee sometime.

Disembarking at Marseilles, Andrew had looked up distant cousins of his mother in Nice, where he had been staying until coming to Paris. The Nice relatives had invited him back for Christmas, warning him that the coming cold months in northern France would be a harsh experience for someone who had never known winter.

"Actually," he said, "I'm looking forward to seeing snow for the first time."

Grace laughed and said she was hoping not to see snow that winter, or perhaps just a flake or two that would melt before it hit the ground. When she described the typical high snowdrifts of a Canadian winter, he accused her of fibbing, though his smile showed that he'd read about the Canadian climate.

They spoke of future plans. Andrew thought of aiming for the headship of a secondary school French department, but was also considering the civil service. When Grace suggested that he might become a representative of Australia in foreign countries, he said that it would more likely be in Indo-China than in France. His scholarship was a wonderful stroke of luck, a once-in-a-lifetime opportunity, and he was determined to make the most of his stay and work hard on his French.

Grace said she planned to teach French, though she was afraid she lacked the teacherly dedication that she had found in her mother and the nuns at the convent where she had studied the language. Her father sometimes hinted that she should enter politics, following in the footsteps of Miss Agnes Macphail, the first woman elected to the House of Commons. Elected in 1921, the same year as he was, she was part of the informal caucus of cooperating independent M.P.s, the "Ginger group", which her father headed.

Although Grace knew and liked Miss Macphail, and had enjoyed watching Parliamentary debates from the Gallery during the Ottawa years, she couldn't imagine undergoing the press scrutiny that Agnes had to endure. Journalists had a field day with her appearance and her social life. They kept asking her about women's issues when her major concern, as a United Farmer representative, was rural poverty.

Hubertine's call to dinner interrupted their conversation. The food, *pommes de terre au gratin*, *jambon* and *salade* was excellent but in very small portions. The ladies' kindly questions made Grace relax.

"Living here, close to the Sorbonne, we have the world coming to our doorstep, and it is so interesting for us to welcome young foreigners and get to know them," Madame Hamel remarked.

"We enjoy our paying guests," added Madame De Bussy.

Young Edith wanted to know all about kangaroos, koala bears and other exotic animals of Australia; the adults were interested in hearing about the aboriginals hunting with boomerangs. Then attention turned to Grace. Was Canada much as depicted in *Rose-Marie*? Grace was at a loss, for she had never seen this musical theatre production, though she had certainly heard some of the songs from it. It had been a big hit in North America and, she gathered, had been running for several years in Paris. She promised to go and see it as soon as possible and then tell them if it was an accurate depiction of Canadian life.

Striving to be succinct, she started telling them about the parts of Canada where she had lived. Winnipeg, her birthplace, was a bustling heartland industrial city, Canada's Chicago. There, when Grace was young, her father had run a community centre/ settlement house for the Methodist Church. The ladies looked confused, seeming not to understand the concept, until Grace explained that it was something like the St. Vincent de Paul Society. When she mentioned having attended the Sacred Heart convent school in Ottawa their eyes flickered with recognition.

"Then you are Catholic?" asked Madame De Bussy.

Grace shook her head. "No. Protestant. Like the Hugenots. My father used to be a Methodist pastor. I attended the convent school for six months to improve my French."

As they nodded vaguely, Grace decided not to elaborate about her family's religious and political beliefs. She especially wouldn't mention that her parents were socialists, considering Monsieur Fuchs' shocked reaction to that information back in Cinq-Mars-la-Pile during the summer.

When they asked about the Canadian climate, she told them that Winnipeg, her home town, was nicknamed "Winterpeg," but the joke did not translate. The ladies turned back to Andrew and asked about his family.

"There are just my parents and myself."

"An only child, like me," little Edith piped up.

Andrew nodded. "I had an older brother, but he was killed in the Great War."

The ladies looked solemn.

"In what theatre of war?" asked Madame Hamel.

"Gallipoli. He was only seventeen."

"I understand your sorrow," said Madame De Bussy. "My husband, Edith's father, was killed in the *guerre* not long before the Armistice."

Grace was relieved when Hubertine came in at that point to clear the first course, because it saved her from having to speak of her family's views of the Great War. In her parents' view, Gallipoli had been an Allied military blunder, a costly sideshow which had taken the lives of a quarter of a million men, including ten thousand Australians and New Zealanders. Grace wasn't sure whether her table companions looked upon the Great War as a glorious cause or a tragic waste of human life, but it was certainly a topic to avoid.

Later, over coffee in the salon, while Edith played the piano, Grace nodded off during Brahms' *Lullaby*, and was roused by the others' applause. Embarrassed, she rose and said goodnight.

Andrew stood up, too. "Shall we go together to the university tomorrow?"

"That would be nice. What time?"

As they agreed on 8:15 a.m., Grace noticed the ladies' approving looks at this exchange. Clearly they were glad the young boarders were making this arrangement out in the open, in front of the family, rather than alone upstairs. Grace had to smile. If the ladies could read her mind, they would know there would never be anything improper between herself and Andrew. He was very nice, but her feeling toward him was what she felt for her brothers, nothing more. Still, she thought he would be a good friend.

Although she was exhausted and her bed was comfortable, Grace couldn't sleep. When her thoughts turned to home, she immediately blocked them with a firm "No." She couldn't risk being sleepless from homesickness. Speculation about her course at the Sorbonne needed to be set aside, too; there was no point in trying to anticipate what her classes would be like.

Then, in her mind, she heard a gruff voice saying, "You'll be fine," and she pictured Monsieur Fuchs when they'd said goodbye at the station at Cinq-Mars-la-Pile on her departure for Paris.

Despite their differences, she'd seen in his eyes that morning, and in Mrs. Fuchs's too, the unconditional affection of grandparents for a grandchild.

They had made tentative plans that, next summer, Grace would return to Cinq-Mars-la Pile, bringing her sister who planned to come to Europe in the spring of 1929. "See you next summer!" Madame Fuchs had called, as Grace waved from a window of the train. Grace knew, though, that if she ran into serious difficulties in France, and needed their help in the meantime, the Fuchs would welcome her back.

Last July, on arriving in Paris with the Overseas League, Grace and the other girls had a whirlwind tour of the "city of light" that had left her thrilled but exhausted. She was glad when the Paris phase of the tour was over and she and her university pal Isabel left the group to board for a couple of months in a village in the Loire River valley.

On the train to Cinq-Mars-la-Pile, Grace and Isabel were glued to the windows, gazing at the passing scene. The chateaux in the distance were magical, but nature even more so. Grace's eyes feasted on the fields, cattle, fruit trees and vineyards. Truly this was the garden of France. According to the guidebook, Cinq-Mars, a sleepy hamlet of fewer than a thousand souls, had two tourist attractions, an ancient chateau a few kilometers away and a red stone tower, the "pile", just outside the village, which was thought to mark the burial site of a Roman official, back in the days when Gaul was a Roman province.

At the station they were met by their host family, or rather, couple, who looked like two storybook characters. Their name "Fuchs" was pronounced something like "Foosh" in English. Monsieur Fuchs was a dignified man in a worn three-piece black suit, a shirt without a collar, and a watch chain. He leaned on a cane, his plume of white hair ruffled by the breeze. Madame was rosy-cheeked and grey-haired, wearing a dark cotton-print dress that came almost to her ankles. Embracing Grace and Isabel, she declared that she was looking forward to their company, that she had always wanted daughters but, sadly, never had any. The girls heaved their suitcases into the farm cart that the Fuchs had hired to pick them up, helped the old couple in, and waved to passersby as they went down the main street to the outskirts and the Fuchs' home.

Grace was charmed by the beauty of the summer, the scent of clover and the glimpses of the river, the Loire, shining in the distance. The Fuchs' stone house reminded her of the Georgian stone houses that she had first seen on arriving in Ontario years ago. Coolness rose from the stone floor. A narrow staircase led to their room under the eaves. Grace loved the painted wooden furniture, the hooked rugs, and the crocheted coverlets on the two beds. Later, when it rained, the rhythm on the roof would sound like a mother's heartbeat.

Isabel raised her eyebrows at the china pitcher and basin and shook her head at the chamber pot under the bed.

"No indoor plumbing," she commented.

Grace shrugged. She'd spent summer holidays in rustic cottages with outhouses, where the lake was the bathtub.

Though the girls were on holiday, to learn French, they offered to help Madame with the cooking. It turned out that cookery was her passion; she hired a local woman to come in and clean so that she would have time to create great meals. Mornings, the girls accompanied her to the village, taking turns carrying her shopping basket, observing her selections of produce and meat, and enjoying the conversations with the neighbours, who were curious about the girls and happy to correct their errors in pronunciation.

Back home, Madame taught them some of her recipes. In fine weather, they ate outdoors at a table under a tree. The food was varied and delicious; for the first time in her life, Grace tried rabbit, eel, goat cheese, and pork cooked with prunes. Dessert was usually fruit, sometimes greengage plums and often melon with cream, frequently served with a liqueur that Monsieur brought up from his "cave." He also brewed the coffee, convinced that only he could do it properly.

The Fuchs never tired of answering the girls' questions, whether about viniculture or the nuances of spoken French. The first evening they were there, Monsieur set out for a walk, as was his custom, and Madame suggested that the girls go along. Tired after her shopping, she was happy to sit. Eventually Isabel begged off these walks to stay and sit with Madame or write letters to her family; at the end of her stay at Cinq-Mars she would be joining her mother in Italy for the winter. Grace was happy to continue the evening strolls with Monsieur, to practise her French, and also because he limped badly and if he fell, he'd need someone to help him up or go for assistance.

Their walk took them past a vineyard, one of many in the area, and Monsieur told her that the grape harvest would take place in early September and that the whole village pitched in.

"Old folks like my wife and I are excused, and of course nobody expects you young ladies from Canada to participate," he said. When Grace said that she would like the experience, he warned her that the work was backbreaking.

On these walks, Monsieur and Grace talked of modern history and current affairs. In 1914, at fifty-one, he'd been too old for active service in the Great War, but he alluded obliquely to the horrors he had seen as a civilian. His hatred of "Les Boches" was profound. He maintained that the western allies should not have negotiated peace with Germany but should have invaded that country as far as Berlin so that the Germans would have realized that they'd been defeated. Gloomily he predicted that it would take another war to curb the German threat to France. When Grace mentioned the League of Nations, Monsieur Fuchs voiced complete disbelief that the member states would ever come together to curb an aggressor nation.

Grace's father had been a pacifist since his student days in England. At the time, the drums were beating in support of the Boer War in South Africa. Working class men were being recruited to put their lives on the line to protect British mining interests. When the Great War broke out, he saw the conflict as a catastrophic culmination of imperialist rivalry, a war caused by ruling elites in which powerless men were ground into cannon fodder. His views had cost him an administrative position in a social service agency. Later, he'd left his pastoral charge in British Columbia because some of the congregation wanted him to beat the drum for war from his pulpit.

She told all this to Monsieur Fuchs, expecting admiration and approval, and was shocked at his reaction. In his view, pacifism was folly when it came to the Germans. He had much to say about the Franco-Prussian War, which had been fought when he was just a child. Grace had studied this war in history class, and had been particularly interested in the seige of Paris and the Paris Commune, the workers' government which had ruled Paris for sixty days in the spring of 1871. In this context, she happened to mention that her father and she were socialists, not realizing that she was waving a red flag in front of a bull.

Monsieur Fuchs stopped in the middle of the road and began to rant against Bolshevik Russia. When he waved his cane at her for emphasis she was aghast, and angry, then terrified because without its support he wavered and almost toppled over. She reached for his arm to steady him, wishing she'd kept quiet and not agitated him.

They walked home in silence. Finally he said, "You're young yet."

Where Madame was concerned, the girls could do no wrong. She asked a neighbour with a car to take her and the girls to see several chateaux in the area, marvellous storybook castles with elegant manicured gardens. Grace took many pictures with her Brownie box camera.

At home, one of her greatest pleasures was the river. Madame urged the girls to use water from the rainbarrel for washing; she claimed that the soft water made one's hair silky and manageable. With the river so near, however, basin washes seemed an unnecessary bother. Every second day the girls put on their bathing suits, packed up their shampoo, soap and towels, grabbed their bags of laundry and wandered down the path to the shady banks of the Loire. In the sun-warmed water Grace floated beneath willow fronds, waving away schools of minnows, feeling as close to nature as the little green frogs on the banks. After their swim, she and Isabel shampooed their hair, then washed their clothes. They laughed at each other's bedraggled appearance and took each other's pictures.

As the days passed, Grace saw signs that summer was drawing to an end. The grape leaves had changed from bright green to dark green to yellow, and the oats and barley were golden. When the grape harvest began, she and Isabel showed up at the neighbouring farmer's home, each in a pair of Monsieur Fuchs' old trousers, with their hair under bandannas. They were given secateurs and basic instruction in their use, and were told not to waste any grapes, but to pick up any that happened to fall to earth.

Back in Grace's churchgoing days, she'd been interested in the many Biblical references to vineyards, and now she was about to labour in one. The first day, however, she found out how much work it was. She skinned a finger and was convinced that she would have a permanently hunched back. That night she and Isabel didn't bother washing off their dust and sweat but fell into bed with their clothes on. The following day was easier, though, and when the last grape was picked they felt proud of themselves, especially when they heard someone say, "Those Canadian girls are tough." The farmer invited them to help with the fall pruning, but Grace said, with genuine regret, that soon she would be leaving soon for Paris, and Isabel for Rome.

Now her thoughts drifted back to the Loire and the silky water on her skin. She dreamed of peaceful days under a clear blue sky beside a river that flowed on and on.

Chapter Two

Grace appreciated Andrew's company during their first weeks at the Sorbonne. As they familiarized themselves with their courses and their part of the city, she developed an affection for him, though nothing more. When they learned that students in the Course in French Civilization could complete the program between November and March if they chose, they decided to tackle the program as a crash course so as to have the spring and part of the summer for sightseeing and travel before going home.

It was good to have Andrew just down the hall to consult about obscure phrases and usages in some of the texts. Often, around 9 p.m., he would come to her room, or she would go to his, to have a chat, always with the door wide open.

After classes they often stopped at a café for a snack, in order to discuss things that they didn't want members of the household to overhear. Andrew confided that when he'd asked about taking a bath in the *salle de bains* off the kitchen, Hubertine acted as if she'd never heard of such a thing, and Madame Hamel, who happened in on the conversation, told him to be economical with the water because of the cost of heating it. Grace, too, felt frustrated about hygiene. A dip in the Loire had been fine in summer but in a major city, having to be presentable every day, it was hard to resign herself to basin washes.

The cost of sending out their laundry was another concern. They ended up buying a thick bar of yellow laundry soap which they shared, and each washed out small items in the evenings and hung them to dry on their iron headboards.

While at 18 rue Cler, they were careful not to say anything derogatory about France, but privately they discussed things that grated upon them. Grace told Andrew about her visit to the famous food market, Les Halles, during her first week in Paris. Grace and the other young women on the Overseas League tour rose early one morning to see this vast, colourful market which sold everything from eels to eggplant, and although it was as spectacular as reputed to be, they'd been unpleasantly surprised by the bold male vendors, who had called out, "Dolls. Little wax dolls. English ladies." Some tapped the girls on the shoulders, others tickled them under the chin with celery leaves, and many tried to pinch their bottoms.

Andrew said that these men sounded rougher than the denizens of the Australian outback. If she ever decided to brave Les Halles again, he would go with her and see that no one laid a hand on her. He hadn't seen much of Paris yet, and like Grace, was watching his pennies, so together they talked of free or inexpensive entertainments. She recommended Notre Dame Cathedral. The immensity and space, and the sunlight breaking into rainbows through the windows, had filled her with awe.

"Have you read *The Hunchback of Notre Dame*?" she asked. "You can see the spot where Claude fell to his death, and the staircase where Quasimodo shouted, *Aside, Aside*!"

Andrew had read it and was eager to go up to the towers where one could see Paris from all directions. From on high, Grace told him, one realized that the city was in a river valley with the land gently sloping up from the Seine. The two hills, Montmartre and Montparnasse, were plain to see, and at the top of Montmartre you could see the white dome of Sacre Coeur Basilica.

Andrew wanted also wanted to see Versailles, a longer and more expensive excursion which she had taken with the tour group. When he asked her impression of it, she said "amazing." She had been amazed and appalled. To her, the palace was a big heap of gilt, too ornate to be beautiful. Looking at it, one saw that the French Revolution had been inevitable. She had particularly disliked the Petit Trianon, given by King Louis XVI to Queen Marie Antoinette. There the queen had built a miniature hamlet where she and her court play-acted at rural life. Meanwhile, peasants and workers had been living in abject poverty. But she went along with Andrew, because she wanted his support and companionship as she braved the August atmosphere of the Sorbonne, where she knew no one. At least Andrew knew Mr. Taylor, who was in the advanced course.

There were fifty-four students in Grace and Andrew's program, with the largest national group from the United States, followed by Britain. Others came from Poland, Germany, Norway, Russia, Czechoslovakia and Australia. Grace was the only Canadian. She and Andrew joined the group that went for coffee after classes, but a couple of weeks into the course, Andrew decided that he would rather go straight home after class to take a nap, clear his head, and get on with his studying. Grace liked sitting on café terrasses, in the open air, keeping warm near the charcoal-burning heaters, watching the passing scene. She accepted an invitation to join a group of girls who met for a social hour after classes. Though she didn't have a lot to say, she enjoyed the company.

During her first couple of years at the University of Manitoba, she'd felt like a fish out of water, not academically, but socially. Most of her classmates were the children of wealthy Winnipeggers who had opposed the workers in the 1919 General Strike. Grace had been radicalized by the events of the strike, particularly her father's arrest and brief jail stint, and felt that she had nothing in common with her wealthy classmates.

Worse, many of the girls regarded university as a finishing school. She'd been particularly irritated by one young woman who had the money for travel. Whenever a faraway foreign place was mentioned in literature or history, this girl would pipe up, in a stage whisper, "I've been there!"

Feeling isolated yet superior, Grace had focused on her studies. Then, in her final year, things changed. The frivolous girls had dropped out by then and the serious ones decided that Grace was worth knowing. They began inviting her to their homes for tea, or to the motion pictures, and Grace warmed to them. That year, for the family Christmas annual, she wrote a self-mocking essay about having grown younger rather than older. She'd realized that it was relaxing and fun to talk about popular music, film stars and clothes. She'd begun to powder her face and raise her hemlines. She learned to dance. She liked all the girls in her class and although she hadn't lost her "puritanical independence" – to quote her brothers – she was willing to concede that some of the boys were all right, too.

Grace liked the girls in her Sorbonne class too. The British and European girls seemed reserved but the Americans were open and gregarious. They liked to get together at one of the cafés near the intersection of Boulevards Montparnasse and Raspail. The Dôme had chairs and tables outside, in rows which extending as far as the Coupole terrace next to it. Across from the Dôme and Coupole was the Café de la Rotonde which had trays of hors d'oeuvres which the young women dipped into.

Sitting outdoors, the girls watched the passersby, hoping to spot celebrities like Ernest Hemingway, Scott Fitzgerald, and the model, Kiki, who lived with the photographer Man Ray. Their conversation ranged widely. They were surprisingly open about personal matters, perhaps because it was safe to confide in people you'd be parting from in six months' time. It wasn't as if you were sharing your secrets with somebody you'd be living next door to for a lifetime.

The American girls seemed quite socially advanced and sophisticated. Some of them had gentleman callers back home but weren't ready to settle down yet, and eagerly anticipated the freedom they'd have in Paris. To hear some of them talk, college had been one big party culminating on graduation night. On that special night, one girl, from upstate New York, had gone skinny-dipping with friends. Another had danced till dawn at a big hotel, and another had got drunk on apple jack at a party in a farmer's field. Grace's graduation had been celebrated at a family afternoon tea with ice cream and cake.

Grace had little to say until the conversation turned to life back home. When asked about Canada she spoke of the places she knew; the mild and mysterious Sunshine Coast of British Columbia; beautiful Banff in the spectacular Rocky Mountains, where she and her sister had waitressed one summer; train-trips through seas of golden prairie wheat; the lofty Peace Tower on Parliament Hill in Ottawa.

Several American girls had heard of Agnes Macphail and were interested that Grace knew her personally. A bright, fun-loving former school teacher, Agnes had been a frequent visitor with Grace's family in Ottawa.

"Is she married?" the girls asked. "Does she have a fiancé?"

Grace shook her head. She'd heard Agnes Macphail say that although she liked men, she would never marry because she could not subordinate herself to a husband. Rumour had it though, that she'd had several romantic involvements and was currently seeing a fellow United Farmer/Progressive Member of Parliament, one from Alberta.

"But they aren't living together and don't pool their finances," Grace added.

"It must be hard to balance marriage and a political career," someone remarked. Another young woman asked if Miss Macphail believed in free love.

Grace laughed and said that having one steady partner, as Agnes had, wasn't the same as free love. Someone wanted to know if free love was common in Canadian socialist circles.

"Not in my parents' circle. Canada is a staid, conservative country and socialists have to be above reproach."

"Free love only leads to heartbreak for the woman," one of the girls contended. "To quote Lord Byron: *Love to man is a thing apart, but a woman's whole existence*."

Several girls took issue with the quote, but when talk turned to birth control, they agreed that it needed to be legal if women were to develop their full potential and participate fully in society.

In the United States, the laws about contraception varied from state to state, but in New York city the billionaire John D. Rockefeller had helped to fund a women's clinic established by Margaret Sanger. In Canada birth control devices and information were against the law, but Grace was pretty sure birth control was practised. Her mother had belonged to a group studying this matter and had made Grace aware of Marie Stopes' books on the subject, but the topic hadn't seemed relevant to her at the time.

Here in France, a law passed in 1920 had made birth control information and devices illegal. Condoms were the exception, on the grounds that men needed to protect themselves from disease. The church and government declared that contraception was immoral. Parents of large families received tax breaks. Government maternity hospitals would give a free meal to any pregnant woman who came to their doors, no questions asked. Grace and her friends recognized that France was trying to build up its population after its losses in the Great War, but at the expense of women's well-being.

Grace listened closely. When she was a little girl, her mother had explained to her where babies came from and how they originated. Grace supposed that when she met her own true love, the two of them would come to a *modus vivendi* about their intimate life together.

Ever since she'd first begun to have womanly feelings, she'd hoped to find someone and have a marriage like her parents', who were still devoted to each other after almost twenty-five years. She remembered sitting out on the back steps one spring night in Ottawa, hearing the strains of a violin in the darkness. The quality of the playing far surpassed that of her brothers. The notes surged with love, expressing exactly what she hoped to experience someday. She wished she could meet the violinist, whoever he was, who would understand all the passion bottled up inside her. Then she realized that his playing expressed the feeling he already had for someone, and she'd crept back indoors.

When one of the girls in the café asked about her "love life" she laughed and said she didn't have one, that she was fancy free and open to new experiences, within reason.

"Being a modern girl is quite a challenge," she said. "We're supposed to be stylish, have sex appeal, find love and build a career as well."

The others sighed in agreement. Someone remarked that the fast-living flapper, the subject of much moralizing in newspapers and magazines, was a myth.

Early one November evening a mixed gang of students, including Grace and Andrew, went for supper at the Brasserie Lipp on Boulevard Saint-Germain, for *pommes a l'huile* (potato salad) and *cervelas* (sausages with mustard sauce.) While they were having coffee, afterwards, two young men entered and came over to their table. One clapped Andrew on the shoulder and greeted him warmly as a fellow "Aussie".

"Taylor! Salut!" Andrew stuck to his French-only rule.

The man with Taylor made Grace catch her breath. Six feet tall, broad-shouldered, with curly blond hair, he looked like a Viking. He was movie-star handsome, with a friendly open face. Greeting them in faintly-accented English, he introduced himself as "Willem Van Aarden, with three A's."

"*Doctor* Van Aarden," Taylor corrected, and the Viking god turned red. "At only twenty-six years old, he has a shiny new Ph.D. in history from the University of London."

"My brother is studying at the London School of Economics," Grace said in French. For a moment Mr. Van Aarden's blue eyes met hers, then switched to someone else who'd asked where he was from.

"South Africa," he said.

"And what brings you to Paris?" someone inquired.

"A fellowship to further my studies in France and Germany. Also, the lower cost of living, the food, and the *joie de vivre*. It's quite different from England."

"Do join us," said Andrew, in French.

The newcomers pulled up chairs and Andrew went around the table, introducing everyone by name and country. When Andrew introduced Grace as "notre Canadienne", Mr. Van Aarden smiled at her, and every nerve in her body came alive. She began fiddling with her hair. She could hardly take her eyes off him, though she took no part in the conversation, which was mostly about England. The others joked about the rain in England, the reserved English personality, the cuisine, or lack of it. Someone said that the English kill their lamb twice, once when they slaughter it and again when they cook it.

Dr. Van Aarden refrained from these English jokes. As a Dutch boy who had spent most of his life in working class Capetown, he'd never expected to win a scholarship to a university in England, and felt privileged to have had the opportunity, so he wouldn't say a word against the country. Then he excused himself, as his landlady had invited guests that evening and wanted him to meet them.

Grace watched him leave. If only he were taking the course in French Civilization! But he wasn't and if they ever crossed paths again he probably wouldn't remember her. He must be a genius to have completed a Ph.D. at his age. It was silly to have a crush on him. She was an ordinary mortal; he belonged on Mount Olympus.

One afternoon a few days later, when Grace was returning from classes, Madame De Bussy popped out of the salon. "May I have a word?" she said.

"Certainly." She followed her landlady into the salon and took a seat, noticing that Madame De Bussy's face was grave.

"Grace, you have been going out at night," she began. "A respectable young woman just doesn't run around like that. It isn't proper. What would your parents think?"

Grace's eyes widened. Apparently Madame and her family were bourgeois in their attitudes if not their finances. They were still caught up in the era in which a respectable young woman was chaperoned, and received "gentleman callers" under supervision.

"I have my parents' permission to go out," she said. "I know Paris is a big city compared to those in Canada, but I feel quite safe with my new friends from the university."

Madame looked pained. "I felt it my duty to mention it."

A week later, Andrew and Grace went to a café after class to work on an assignment. Looking out the window, Andrew remarked that on dull grey days like this he missed sunny "Oz."

"You have Nice to look forward to," she reminded him.

"True." He brightened and described that city's wide streets, ornate Edwardian houses, the blue of the sea, the bathers and little yachts with white sails. When a shadow fell across their table and a faint, pleasant vanilla scent wafted past her, she looked up, and tingled all over. It was Dr. Van Aarden, beaming down like the sun.

"Did I startle you? I'm sorry." He spoke in French, not as fluently as she and Andrew, but competently. Reintroducing himself, he asked for a moment of their time. Grace said, "Of course", and Andrew got him a chair.

"Last week when we met, I made a mental note to seek out you two," he began, "so when I glanced at the window and saw you here, I couldn't pass up the opportunity to ask you about a rather ticklish issue. You see, my subject is British colonial history."

"We'd be glad to help if we can," said Grace.

Willem Van Aarden explained that his Ph.D. thesis, soon to be published as a book, dealt in part with the exploitation of South Africa's black population as a cheap labour source in agriculture and mining. The race issue in his homeland deeply troubled him. When he heard that Grace and Andrew were from Canada and Australia, respectively – two other former British colonies – he saw an opportunity to hear about the condition and status of the native people in their countries.

Andrew spoke well, if reluctantly, about aboriginal people's resistance to European settlement in Australia, and their suppression and plight. Grace didn't feel qualified to talk about the situation of indigenous people in Canada. The official consensus was that they should be assimilated, mainly through agricultural training, but this didn't seem right to her. When her turn came she said that their situation varied in different parts of Canada. Back in the 19th century there had been armed resistance by Metis and Indians, in 1869 and 1885, when settlers encroached on their lands. She mentioned the sophisticated culture of the west coast native people, and wound up by admitting that she was not as well-informed as she should be.

"You've been very informative," Dr. Van Aarden said. "Liberals like myself are a minority back home, and I don't know if I should go back there to teach, or not. Would I be a progressive voice, or one crying in the wilderness? In any case, thank you for filling some gaps in my knowledge. Now, may I treat you both to dinner tonight?"

Grace was about to say "Yes!", but sensed Andrew's reluctance. Both of them were swamped with assignments to complete before he left for Nice and before Charles's arrival. Andrew explained that they were both trying to complete the course by April.

At the look of disappointment on Willem's face, Grace added that she was expecting her brother at Christmas and was trying to accomplish as much as possible before then.

"Perhaps we could all get together for a meal after he arrives," she suggested.

"An excellent idea. The more the merrier." He bowed and left.

Andrew glanced at his watch.

"Do you suppose Hubertine has lit the fires in our rooms yet?" he wondered.

"We might make more headway at home." Grace gathered up their books.

"Dr. Van Aarden probably knew everything we told him, from his reading," Andrew remarked, as they left.

Then why had he approached them, she wondered. Was it possible that this brilliant young scholar was interested in her?

Chapter Three

Careful not to disturb the Christmas wreath in the window, Grace peered out from behind the lace curtain. She spotted a dark-haired slender young man walking jauntily along the sidewalk. Did he have a violin case as well as a suitcase? Yes. She rushed to the foyer and opened the door.

"Charles!" She threw her arms around him. "I hardly recognized you. You look like a man."

He laughed. "I am a man. You look well."

"I'm so happy to see you. Here, let me take your violin and show you your room."

"Shall I meet your friend Hallett?"

"He has left already for Nice. You're in his room."

Having Charles here made it feel like home for the first time. They had just finished unpacking his things when the chiming clock downstairs reminded Grace that the De Bussy ladies had invited them both for wine and hors d'oeuvres in the salon before their evening meal. They hurried downstairs, where Madame Hamel, Madame De Bussy and young Edith were waiting. Charles turned on all his charm. In careful French, for he was less fluent than Grace, he talked of his Channel crossing. The chairs were arranged in a semi-circle around the tea table. Madame De Bussy poured wine and as she raised a glass and proposed a toast to Charles's good health, Hubertine entered with a plate containing six radishes, some cheese and crackers, and six sardines, which she placed on the table in front of Charles.

"*Merci*," he said politely, as he seized a radish and devoured it. Grace waited for him to pass the plate, but instead, he took another radish and two sardines and downed them. In dismay, Grace realized that he thought the entire plate was for him and that the others' plates would be coming. She knew better. The ladies had carefully calculated one radish and one sardine per person. Having eaten his share, and Grace's, he was poised to take someone else's, until Grace picked up the plate and passed it to Madame Hamel. The ladies pretended not to notice his faux pas, but Edith's lips twitched with mirth.

"My brother has a Canadian appetite," Grace murmured.

After dinner, which Charles found good, though in ridiculously small portions, they went up to her room and caught up on things. When he asked how her course was going, she said that she was doing all right, that her professors' main criticism of her compositions was that she was too tentative; she used too many qualifiers, like "perhaps" or "possibly."

"I guess I should be more assertive."

He chuckled. "You're assertive at home. I'm sure you'll sail through as you always do."

They were interrupted by a knock on the door. Hubertine presented Grace with a letter that had come earlier, and had been left on the hall table for her. In her excitement, she'd never thought to look for mail.

The return address was Auteuil, a neighbourhood in the 16th arrondissement. She knew no one there. She opened it and found that the Winnipeg grapevine, or network, had reached out on her behalf. Friends of Grace's parents had visited Paris a few years earlier and had stayed in Auteuil as the paying guests of a delightful woman on the left of the political spectrum. On hearing that Grace was spending a year in Paris, they'd given this woman her address. Now this woman, Madame Emilie Simon, the widow of a university professor, was inviting Grace to her Sunday afternoon salon.

Grace and Charles looked at each other and said, "Why not?"

Auteuil, known for its race track, had once been a separate village but was now part of Paris. It had many Haussmann-style apartment buildings dating from the mid-1800s, and they soon found the one where Madame Simon lived. They were greeted by an effusive woman who might have been in her late forties, but had the verve and enthusiasm of someone much younger. Her hair, bobbed short, was dyed a brilliant henna, and on her it looked dashing, not outrageous.

"*Bienvenu*! Oh, you've brought a gift. Mandarins! You shouldn't have, but how lovely. We will enjoy them for sure. Now, come and join the group."

Fifteen men and women ranging in age from early twenties to sixties were chatting in both French and English. As Grace scanned the group she caught her breath. Over by the fireplace, talking to Andrew's friend Taylor, was Willem van Aarden.

"Grace!" A young blonde woman named Kay, from her class in French Civilization, sprang up from a love seat to greet her. "Great to see you. Is this your brother? Any party can always use another handsome man. Aren't you going to introduce us?"

As Grace introduced Charles to Kay, the other Kay in the course, who had brown curly hair held in place by a headband, came over to say hello. Another classmate, "Brandy" joined them. Easing away from the cluster around her brother, Grace strolled toward the tea table and pretended to be very interested in the sandwiches, hoping Willem would notice her and come and say hello. She lingered over the radish roses until she felt a hand on her shoulder. She turned and smiled up at him.

"Oh, hello, there."

"Grace! So nice to see you again. Come and join Taylor and me. He has a suggestion for this evening."

Taylor, leaning on the fireplace, said that it was nice to see her again. He'd heard from Andrew that her father was a socialist member of Parliament. He and Willem were going to a meeting of young French socialists this evening and wondered if she and her brother would like to come along.

"Oh, yes, very much, and I know Charles will be interested too." She looked across the room, where Charles was deep in conversation with the girls.

"Let me ask him," said Taylor.

As he started across the room, Willem turned to Grace.

"So your father is a cabinet minister in Canada," he began.

Grace shook her head.

"No, he's just a Member of Parliament. The Independent Labour Party has only two seats in Canada's Parliament – right now."

His brow furrowed. "But someone spoke of your father as a 'minister'."

She laughed. "Oh. Not a cabinet minister, but a preacher, a minister of the Gospel. He was a pastor until he broke with the church in 1918 over the Great War."

He studied her, smiling. "I'd never have taken you for a daughter of the manse," he told her.

"Well, thank you, I guess. Why not?"

"You don't have the look of a good Christian woman, if you don't mind my saying so," he declared, with a twinkle in his eye. "They tend to be plain and drab, as if it's insincere to look anything but their worst. You look thoroughly modern and very chic, particularly your haircut. The bangs accentuate your eyes."

She laughed. "I'll bet you say that to all the girls. And you're not fair. Some of my relatives are good Christian women."

"Maybe my observations don't apply to Canadian church women, seeing as my experience is in the Dutch Reformed Church, or, as I call it, the Dutch Deformed."

"I sense that we're both freethinkers," she said. "When I was eighteen I spent six months polishing my French at a convent school run by the Sisters of the Sacred Heart. I did well and made a good impression, and after several months one of the sisters approached me to talk about spiritual matters. Over tea in her office she asked me what I believed, and the more I told her the more shocked she became. She found my beliefs such a blend of pantheism and socialism that she cut the interview short, probably for fear that I would shake her faith."

Willem was much amused.

"Come, let's sit down. I want to hear more about you."

When he put his arm around her to guide her to the sofa, she realized how much she had been wanting him to do that. He put a cushion behind her, and glanced at her empty teacup.

"First I'm going to refill my glass," he said. "Would you like some cognac?"

"Oh, no thank you."

Leaning back she watched his progress across the room, greeting people, and worried that he would get diverted and not return. But no, he came back with two snifters of brandy and presented her with one.

"Please, a little vice," he urged. It tasted like delicious fire.

"Tell me something about yourself," she said.

He was happy to do so. He was a British subject, but also a Dutch one, born in Holland. His father had gone to South Africa to seek his fortune during the gold rush, and during the Boer War, he was imprisoned by the British for a few months. On being released, he went back to the Netherlands to get married. When Willem and his brother were young the family returned to South Africa, where his father worked on the railway.

Growing up in working class Capetown, Willem had gotten to know native people and was troubled that they were denied human and civil rights. The prevailing view was that the "kaffirs" were childlike, ignorant and fit only for manual work, but he had never believed it, and at the University of Johannesburg he'd found liberals who believed in racial equality. After earning his B.A. in History in 1922, he'd done a Master's under the supervision of a progressive, liberal historian, who had encouraged him to apply for scholarships to pursue his studies in England. Both the professor and Willem were elated when he was accepted at the University of London.

"The English climate took some getting used to," he told her, "but that was a small price to pay for being among the world's greatest thinkers."

After completing his Ph.D., he had received a fellowship from the University of London for a self-designed program of study abroad in France and Germany. His Ph.D. thesis was soon to be published in book form.

She congratulated him and asked him where he hoped to teach.

"I've applied to the University of Capetown but haven't heard yet."

"Maybe you should try North American universities," she suggested.

When he asked her about her university experience, she explained that her post-secondary education had been on-again, off-again, for financial reasons, with her first year at the University of British Columbia and the final three at the University of Manitoba. Without scholarships and bursaries, neither she nor Charles would be studying abroad.

"Ah, your brother is looking in our direction. Introduce us."

Grace beckoned to Charles, and, as she'd expected, he and Willem hit it off right away, with Charles as eager to attend the young socialists' meeting as she was. The De Bussy ladies had warned her against going out at night, especially to certain streets and sections of the city, but with Willem, Taylor and her brother, she would be perfectly safe.

They left rue de Verneuil at five o'clock and made their way to the meeting in a working class café where they ate bread and cheese, drank wine and listened to the speakers. In the discussion, Willem impressed her with his insightful questions. Good looks, a fine mind, a sense of humour, the ability to carry on a conversation without leaving it all to the girl – he was perfect. Normally Grace would have asked questions, too, but she was too busy dealing with the excitement coursing through her. In Latin class she'd translated poems that spoke frankly of erotic attraction, and now she understood them completely.

After the meeting no one seemed in a hurry to leave, so the group hung around and talked. Eventually Willem saw Grace and Charles back to rue Cler.

"Tomorrow evening is Christmas Eve," he remarked. "What are you two doing to celebrate?"

"We haven't decided," Charles said.

"Then please, join me for tea at my place and perhaps we can plan an adventure."

"I'm game," said Charles.

"Let's," Grace agreed, trying not to sound too eager or to levitate with joy.

Chapter Four

The following morning Charles slept late while Grace worked on her assignments, and wondered what the evening would bring. She went through her limited wardrobe and selected her rose wool dress with the black border pattern. Her American friends had told that, in Paris, only prostitutes went around bareheaded, so she had bought herself a new chapeau which made her look stylish, even wicked and futuristic. A hairdresser had thinned her hair over her ears in a neater style which made her face seem less round, more oval.

Willem was waiting for them at 11 rue de Verneuil where a small fire took the edge off the chill. He greeted them warmly, insisted on first names, and mentioned that his landlady's family were out. When he asked Grace to "be Mother" and pour the tea, she did so self-consciously. He inquired about Charles's studies and soon they were deep in conversation. Though pleased that her brother could talk on the same level as a scholar of twenty-six, with a Ph.D., she felt left out, for they mentioned places in London and professors of whom she knew nothing. As if sensing her feelings, Willem changed the subject to his sixtyish landlord and landlady and their thirty-something daughter.

"I'm treated like a son," he said, "and by that I mean that sometimes they ignore me, sometimes they ask my help, usually to lift heavy things, and they don't hesitate to boss me around, like the time they kicked me out of this easy chair I'm in now, because it's the old man's favourite. They also feel free to comment on my personal life. Tell me, Grace, is this typical of a French household or just my bad luck?"

"My landlady disapproves of me going out at night, though I'm always with friends."

"Well, this family hints that I break all the Ten Commandments." He chuckled. "I keep a sense of humour, but if I were in an English boarding house and subjected to such remarks, I'd have no alternative but to give a week's notice."

Grace and Charles laughed.

"It's really good fun. I'm never at a loss for a laugh, or for the stimulation of a good quarrel. I argue like a Frenchman now, I never mince words or spare feelings, and after a day my remarks are all forgotten. But there's one aspect of my situation on which I could use some advice."

"Do tell," Charles urged.

The thirtyish daughter of the family, said Willem, was kind, charming and well-read. If he showed off by quoting a line of poetry, she would finish the verse and cite other similar poems. Occasionally they'd gone walking, and she'd shown him little houses on hidden streets where revolutionaries had lived over the centuries, groups ranging from the Fronde to the Communards. She also knew all the amours of the French monarchy and nobility down through the ages.

"She sounds like the perfect companion for an historian," Charles commented slyly.

"And that's what she thinks," Willem said wryly. "Her situation isn't happy. She's the daughter designated to look after her parents in their old age. They married off the other children and now she's the housekeeper here, and may yet be the nurse."

"It seems a waste of her talents," Grace remarked.

"A woman so knowledgeable about the love intrigues of historical figures is probably living in a dream world, imagining their adventures as her own, because she doesn't have any. She doesn't welcome spinsterhood, and now, things have changed for her."

"You arrived on the scene," Grace supplied.

"Well, there's more to it than that. I've been friendly and paid her polite compliments and she has taken them as meaning more than they do. Then one Sunday dinner with the extended family, her brother criticized her and she burst into tears and said she felt like a lonely captive. Everyone felt stricken and helpless."

"So you've offered to marry her?" Charles teased.

Willem shuddered. "Absolutely not. I'm in no position to marry. But her outburst shocked her parents, and they've made plans."

"Involving you?" asked Grace.

Willem shook his head. It turned out that the parents had a woman friend with a brother in the colonial administration of Madagascar who was back in France on holidays. Matchmaking was going on. Willem considered the man ineligible, since his way of life on that remote island would be completely different from what the Frenchwoman was used to. On top of that, he'd brought with him his young daughter, who was of mixed race.

"The result, said Willem disapprovingly, "of his unashamed excess with a native woman. Imagine how hard it will be for this Parisian woman to leave her home and her cultural activities and go off to the jungle with this man and bring up this girl and whatever other offspring he may have!"

The matter had come to a head the previous week when the parents broke the news of this marital opportunity to their daughter. She wasn't pleased and didn't want to meet the man. Soon after that, she came up to Willem while he was reading and asked, "Est-ce que tu m'aimes?" Willem said yes, he did like her, but when it became clear that she thought he was seriously in love with her, he'd immediately poured out the many reasons why he was not the answer to her problems.

"So now she isn't speaking to me," he said.

"Is the arranged marriage still on?" queried Grace.

"I don't know but I'm sure to find out, and I'll keep you informed. One thing about living here, it's never boring." He smiled ruefully.

"Is the woman pretty?" Charles's eyes twinkled.

Willem rose and got down a photograph from the mantel. "What is your opinion?"

"I'd say of average good looks, but of mature years."

"I agree," said Willem. "Not as pretty as present company."

Grace blushed.

"I would like to take your photograph." Willem's blue gaze was upon her. "You look something like the film star Louise Brooks. Maybe a little like Kiki."

She gasped. "I'm definitely not going to pose like Kiki." Kiki was famous for posing nude.

"Oh, certainly not, something more tasteful." Willem rose from his chair, pulled it into the light from the window, and invited her to sit in it.

Confused yet flattered, she shook her head.

"Oh, come on, Grace," Charles urged. "It's only a photograph. He's not going to capture your soul."

Reluctantly she sat down as Willem went to get his camera.

"Very nice," he said, as he prepared the flash. "Now, lean toward us. Let the wings of your hair fall forward and accentuate your cheekbones."

She smiled the shutter clicked.

Talk turned to film stars, and eventually Willem mentioned a movie, *Midnight*, which he'd heard about. It was playing not far away, and immediately Charles wanted to go.

"What is it about?" Grace asked Willem.

"An introduction to the underside of Paris," he said with a mischievous smile.

"It has been banned in Canada," Charles announced.

"Then let's see it!" exclaimed Grace. Her ready-for-anything tone hid her misgivings. She didn't want to be a poor sport, but she was tired. Also, it was Christmas Eve, and although her family no longer attended church, Christmas retained some of its holiness for her. On Christmas morning she and Charles had planned to go to Mass at L'Eglise Sainte-Marie-Madeleine, popularly known as the Madeleine. Had he forgotten? And what would Madame De Bussy say if they disturbed the household coming in late on Christmas Eve? But the chance to be out with Willem was more important than all these considerations.

She and Charles went back to rue Cler for dinner, and Willem called for them at eight. The film turned out to be about the various forms of vice in Paris. Before Grace's departure for France, one of her parents' acquaintances had expressed shock that they would let her go alone to Paris, a very wicked city. Grace's mother had replied calmly that all cities had their dark underside and that Grace was as capable of looking after herself in Paris as in Winnipeg. Now, viewing the movie, Grace thought it was just as well it was banned in North America, for if this very conventional friend were to see it, her worst fears would be confirmed.

Then, beside her, she heard a chuckle.

"Sensational tripe," Willem whispered. "It's not racy, just stupid."

"I agree," she said.

Out on the sidewalk after the movie, Willem asked if they would like to see the real night life of Paris.

"How about Montmartre?" he proposed.

"Lead on!" Charles' cheeks were flushed. Grace had her doubts, but before she could speak, Willem had seized her arm.

"We must stick together crossing this street," he said. With Charles, they dashed across the thoroughfare among automobiles and pedestrians. Being guided by a strong man was new for her and she liked it. As they climbed higher and higher up into bohemia, she took Charles's arm, and was glad her purse was in the inner pocket of her coat. They passed brasserie doors swinging open and shut, from which couples burst out, laughing, holding each other up, stumbling on the cobblestones, and in a couple of cases, throwing up in the shadows. Raucous jazz poured out of cafés and clubs, music that would normally make her feel like dancing, if she were less on edge. Scantily clad women on street corners tilted their pelvises and tried to make eye contact with men.

Grace, Charles and Willem joined a small crowd which had gathered to watch a sidewalk acrobat doing handstands, cartwheels and other gymnastic feats. His cap, on the sidewalk, held only a few coins. As he concluded his routine and bowed to the applause, a few more people put money in his hat.

"And now my daughter will sing for you," he said.

A tiny girl, in threadbare clothing, stepped out of the shadows. Her big dark eyes beneath her bangs were red-rimmed and sadly worldly-wise. She stood as tall as she could, opened her mouth, and in an astonishing voice, full of range and resonance, she began to sing the *Marseilles*.

Grace knew that the French national anthem had originated with the poor people of Marseilles rising up against the monarchy in 1789. The child's song arrested the crowd, as they paused in collective memory of the Great War. France's losses were still obvious ten years later. So many men with missing legs and arms. So many beggars. So many widows and orphans like Madame De Bussy and Edith. The sight of this little girl, like a tiny sparrow, turned Grace inside out. At this time of night on Christmas Eve the poor kid should be tucked up in a clean bed dreaming of sugar plums. Grace drew out her pocket book, found money, and threw it into the father's cap, hoping he would buy the daughter something to eat. Willem looked surprised, but Charles, who understood his sister, took her arm.

They continued their stroll, caught up in waves of loud music and laughter coming from a cabaret with a neon sign flashing over the door. Photos of young, beautiful bare-breasted women were posted outside. Embarrassed, Grace pointed to an arcade down the street saying, "Win me a kewpie doll." Both men tried a game of marksmanship but neither won, and they grumbled that the game was rigged.

Then Willem declared himself famished, so they found a café, bought sausage and cabbage sandwiches, and ate them on the terrace.

But Charles's attention was still on the cabaret with its alluring flashing sign and blaring music.

"Let's go there and see the show," he suggested.

What would her parents say? And was he even old enough to go in?

"It's late," Grace said. "We should go home."

"Oh, Grace!" he sighed. "Don't be such a Puritan."

"Madame De Bussy won't like it if we come in late and disturb the house."

Willem looked from Grace to Charles.

"You go ahead," he said. "Grace and I will have dessert and coffee and wait for you here. We'll get to know each other."

Charles didn't wait to hear more from Grace, but took off.

Willem summoned the waiter and ordered coffee and pastry. Sitting across from her, he leaned toward her and smiled.

"It must be hard to give up the elder sister role," he remarked.

She smiled wryly. "It is. I've always looked out for my brothers. Our family's politics meant that we were usually in the minority wherever we were, and we've stuck together."

"You must be proud of how Charles has turned out," he said. "He's young to have won a scholarship to the L.S.E. and he's living successfully on his own far from home."

"I am proud. He used to be the most headstrong of all of us, the one most likely to get on Father's nerves. He has grown up a lot, and I'm glad."

Willem smiled and sipped his coffee.

"When your father left the church, did it make a difference to your way of life?"

"Financially, yes, for a while. Father went to Vancouver to work on the docks and Mother went back to teaching. Now he gets a decent salary, but that could end with the next election."

"I meant in terms of behaviour. Did you stop attending church?"

"Pretty much, except for weddings and funerals. When they left the church, Mother and Father wrote out this odd but sweet declaration that they were rededicating themselves to love, humanity and service."

"It must have been a relief for you to quit churchgoing. I imagine a pastor's children are supposed to behave in an exemplary way."

"That's true, but leaving the church meant no great change for us. My parents have high expectations of us, but they have always explained things and have always listened to our point of view."

"They sound ideal. They must be happy that you're broadening your horizons in Paris."

"Their letters are always supportive and encouraging. But enough of me. I'd rather hear about you."

Willem spoke of his brother, who was interested in science and technology rather than liberal arts, and who had been his staunchest supporter all their lives.

"He'll make a fortune one day, while I'm eking out a living as a professor, but that's the way the world works," he said. In response to her questions he talked about the African landscape, and said he missed it. Caught up in his story, Grace did not notice that time had passed until she felt a hand on her shoulder. Charles was back. It seemed as if he'd just left, but over an hour had gone by.

"How was the show?" Willem asked.

"Revealing. I'll have plenty to dream about tonight."

As they left, Grace felt Willem's arm around her again, guiding her across busy streets, catching her when she caught her toe on a stone. At rue Cler, he wished them a Happy Christmas and said he would drop by to see them the following evening if they were free.

"Please come," she said.

Settling down to sleep was impossible for Grace, so she lay in bed and reviewed her conversation with Willem, savouring his every word. Then she realized that actually, he'd been criticizing her in a gentle, subtle way, drawing her attention to her character flaws. She hadn't realized it while it was happening, but now she saw that, with the kindest of questions, he'd suggested that she was a wet blanket, an overbearing eldest child grown large. Willem didn't regard Charles as an irresponsible youth who had to be kept on the straight and narrow. Though he'd never said so directly, he heartily agreed with her brother that she was being a prude in a city that he considered refreshingly free. On several occasions, her mother had told her she was too critical of her brothers, and Willem had detected that same unpleasant tendency. He probably despised her for being weak, for wasn't it weak to shy away from new experiences and to try to make others do the same, when the unknown might be harmless and amusing? Willem had seen the timidity that her professors had found in her essays, and he didn't like it.

She wept in her pillow for a while, then got up and wrote in French in her journal:

"I am nothing compared to him, but if someone like that would let me be by his side and learn from him, it would help me take courage. Ever since coming to Paris I've been afraid. I'm afraid all the time. I have nothing solid in my life. I am all alone and feel weak."

Back in bed, fatigue blotted out these thoughts. She woke to sunlight, with someone knocking at her door. It was Charles. It was 10 a.m.

"Merry Christmas!" he called.

When she opened the door she found him dressed and ready to experience the Mass at the Madeleine. Hurriedly she washed and dressed and they were soon out of the house in the crisp morning air.

Charles had expected a Gothic cathedral, so when they reached the 8th arrondissement and approached the church, he was surprised that it was neo-Classical. Grace, who had already been there, explained that it was a relatively new building, designed to honour the Emperor Napoleon's army. They entered through the famous bronze doors cast with illustrations of the Ten Commandments, then stared in awe at the mural on the domed ceiling, the altar with the statue of Saint Mary Magdalene, the enormous pipe organ, and the lovely blue stained glass windows.

In the middle of the service she whispered to Charles that partaking of the communion wafer was only for Catholics. When he whispered, "I know", she realized that again she was giving guidance where none was needed. As the music swelled, she promised to try to be a better person. The singing was so beautiful that it made her weep.

"What's wrong?" whispered Charles, offering her his handkerchief.

"Nothing," she murmured, as her tears continued to flow. She promised to be stronger and braver, to make the most of the good fortune that had come her way, to rise to the occasion and stop being afraid.

Back at rue Cler, they dipped into the box of chocolates that Andrew had left for her, and opened their cards and gifts. She gave Charles a scarf and a copy of *Capital*, in perfect condition, that she had bought at a bookseller's stall on the Quai de Montebello. He gave her a compact with pink pressed powder and a copy of a new book, *The Intelligent Woman's Guide to Socialism and Capitalism*, by George Bernard Shaw, and she laughed and thanked him for the compliment. Then they opened the cards and letters they had saved for the occasion. Everyone in Grace's family had written. Mother and Father had sent a bank draft with a note saying that they wanted their two chicks who had left the nest to enjoy their Christmas. Kathy, Grace's girlhood friend from Gibson's days, sent photographs.

After a late Christmas lunch with the landlady's family, a delicious but small roast chicken, Grace and Charles went to the Odeon to see the motion picture *L'Avare*, then dropped off a gift of mandarin oranges to her classmate, Miss Brandsome, nicknamed "Brandy", who was ill with a bad cold.

That evening they sat for a while in the parlour, talking about Christmases past with the De Bussy family, while Grace listened for a knock at the door. But Willem didn't come. She hoped he was having a good time wherever he was. Possibly Madame Simon was having a party. Knowing that Charles and Grace hadn't seen each other for a while, he probably didn't want to intrude. Or maybe he'd decided she was too judgmental and puritanical to associate with.

Starting on Boxing Day, Grace and Charles developed a holiday pattern. He slept later than she did, so while waiting for him to get up she studied or wrote in her journal. On Boxing Day afternoon, they went to the Rodin Museum. "The Thinker" was impressive, and if she ever saw Willem again, she intended to tell him so, for he had urged them to see it. Charles's irreverent comments on some of the sculptures made her relax and quit obsessing over Willem.

The following morning, while Charles slept, Grace went to the Latin quarter to visit one of her most interesting new acquaintances. A month or so earlier, in the Dôme, one of the girls had announced that she'd asked a friend of hers to join them.

"She's a sculptor, a real one," the girl added. Grace grasped her meaning. So many foreigners in Paris pretended to be artists of one kind or another but never got around to producing anything. This woman, however, sounded like the genuine article. Her name was Batia, she was a student at the Academie des Beaux Arts, lived frugally in her studio, and was working on a series of figures showing the range of human emotions. Grace had never met a sculptor before.

Batia was a striking woman with dark hair, a few years older than the girls in Grace's course. She was very direct. When introduced to Grace, she informed her that her hairdo enhanced her cheekbones.

"I'd be interested in sculpting your head, if you'd sit for me," she said.

Stunned, Grace managed a "yes", and they agreed that she would drop by Batia's studio sometime in the week between Christmas and New Years.

Batia greeted her, invited her in, wiped clay from her hands on her apron and offered her hand.

"You've come at the perfect time, because I need a break," she said, lifting the whistling kettle from the stove to make tea. "You're Canadian, aren't you? I've never met a Canadian before, although some of my distant relatives have settled in Canada. Come and let's exchange autobiographies."

Cosy in the heat of the small stove, Grace learned that Batia was twenty-eight years old, and one of four sisters born in the Ukraine to Jewish parents. In 1910, she and her mother had immigrated to Palestine, where she started studying sculpture. The further training she needed could be found only in Europe, though, so she went first to Rome to study at the Academy of Art. But when riots broke out in Rome, she returned to Palestine and joined a kibbutz, a socialist community based on the principle, "from each according to his abilities, to each according to his needs." All material possessions were common property to share. Grace was fascinated. Batia said that although she admired the community's goals and felt at home there, she realized that her calling was in the arts, so she left again, for Berlin, where she studied for three years. In 1927 she had come to Paris to continue her education.

She was interested in Grace's labour/socialist background, and in hearing about members of Winnipeg's Jewish community who had been on labour's side during the 1919 strike.

After tea, she showed Grace her work. Her sketches showed joy and pain on the faces of everyday people, and her miniature, table-sized sculptures made the sketches three dimensional. The figure of a grieving woman with her fist raised drew Grace's attention.

"It's called *Agony*," Batia told her. "I believe I'll call your sculpture *Pensiveness*. You seem to have a lot on your mind. Will you sit by the window and let me sketch you?"

Grace took the chair she indicated.

"You may talk," Batia told her. "Is something in particular bothering you?"

"Well, yes." Grace hesitated.

"A man?"

Grace sighed.

"Yes. He seemed to be interested in me, but now it seems that he has changed his mind, and I'm sorry, because I really like him."

Batia made rapid strokes in charcoal on her pad. "Maybe his interest will rekindle."

"I don't know. He thinks I'm a prude and a wet blanket."

She found herself telling Batia about Christmas Eve and asked her opinion.

"Well, your brother is old enough now to make his own decisions without your permission," Batia said in a kindly tone. "Even so, he should have considered your feelings. You were tired, and I imagine you would have preferred Christmas Eve elsewhere, since it's one of the holiest days on your calendar. Your historian friend was kind but condescending, and he put your brother's whim ahead of your feelings." She paused. "Why not put the incident out of your mind and tell me what you and your brother will be doing for the rest of his holiday?"

Grace had arranged with her landlady for the use of the parlour for afternoon tea on December 31st, so that her friends could meet Charles. She invited Batia, who said she would love to come. As they talked about entertainment and sightseeing, Batia kept drawing, then closed her book and wiped her fingers.

"May I see?" asked Grace.

"Not just yet, but soon you will see yourself in clay."

That afternoon Charles and Grace went for a walk in the Bois de Bologne. Grace loved the old trees green with moss. They rented a boat and went rowing on the lake until fog started to roll in. Rain followed, and by the time they arrived back at rue Cler, late for their evening meal, they were soaked, and grateful that Hubertine had kept their dinner warm in the oven. As they ate together in the kitchen, Grace asked Charles if there was any place in particular that he'd like to go that evening.

"Yes, but you won't approve," he said. "I'd like to see the Folies Bergère."

"All right."

He gulped in astonishment. They had both heard of the famous music hall, and of the director who promised lavish costumes and sets and "small nude women." They'd seen reproductions of Manet's famous painting, "A Bar at the Folies Bergère", and they knew that Josephine Baker, the African-American singer-dancer, had appeared at the Folies two years earlier, in a costume consisting of jewellery, a short skirt made of bananas and nothing else.

"Josephine Baker isn't currently performing at the Folies," she told Charles.

"Let's go anyway."

"All right. I won't mention it in my next letter home, though."

After midnight, emerging from the show, Grace felt bedazzled. Even if she were to write home about it, any description she attempted would fall short of the reality, for it had been amazing in so many ways. The dancers were supple, athletic and delicate, their acts beautiful, exotic, and often amusing.

"Mesmerizing," she said to Charles.

"I hope you weren't too shocked."

"I wasn't shocked at all. The human body is beautiful, and, after all, it's 1928."

Chapter Five

The following day when Grace and Charles were out, they were caught in a sudden downpour. They dashed into a café, where they settled at a window table and watched others hold newspapers over their heads, unfurl umbrellas and take shelter in doorways. Over coffee, as she and her brother talked, she realized that he had grown up a great deal in the past five months. He spoke of his ambition to be a journalist, like the popular new author, Ernest Hemingway, who first came to Paris as a reporter for the *Toronto Star*. After completing his course at the L.S.E., Charles intended to go home to Winnipeg for a semester and then travel to Japan, where their uncle, a university president, lived with his family. He intended to fund these travels by writing articles for the Winnipeg *Tribune*, where he had worked part time. She praised him for thinking it all through. Though she wondered if he'd be able to settle down to university after he came back, she didn't raise that concern. She was so pleased that he was confiding in her that she didn't mind that the conversation was all about him. She didn't have any plans other than the general intention to teach, though occasionally she thought of studying for a Master's in French literature. Lately she'd been imagining a future with Willem Van Aarden, which was foolish, as he'd lost interest in her.

When the rain let up they went back to rue Cler where Grace found a letter on the front hall table. She caught her breath. It was addressed in Willem's handwriting. He was planning a New Year's Eve party and wanted her and Charles to come.

"I warn you," he wrote, "that I'm no cook and that my guests must pitch in." After dinner, he added, they would dance to the gramophone. If she and Charles were interested, would they drop by that evening to join in the planning?

That evening they found Willem, Taylor and McGrath sitting in the salon near the fire, with no family present. Willem greeted Grace warmly, then handed her a pencil and notepad and appointed her secretary of New Year's Eve planning. As they discussed the party, she made notes about food to be purchased. Walking home with Charles, she felt that 1929 was going to be a very good year.

The following day they went to Notre Dame Cathedral, where the sun illuminated the famous stained glass windows in a blaze of sapphire, ruby and emerald. That evening they went to Café des Princes to dance. The air was blue with smoke and the ladies were painted like movie stars. Grace enjoyed dancing with Charles; they executed some clever moves and smiled proudly at each other. Then Grace almost stumbled, because a tall blond figure was watching them.

"Ah, there's Willem!" said Charles. They joined him, found a table and ordered wine.

"Grace, your name suits you," Willem told her. "You're a graceful dancer."

They sat and talked, but when the band played the opening notes of *Stardust*, Willem rose and held out his hand to her. In each other's arms they moved in perfect synchronization. Later, when he proposed going back to Place Pigalle to see more of the night life, she felt that she was being given a second chance, and took it.

"So you do have a spirit of adventure!" he exclaimed.

That evening she was neither depressed nor amused by the street corner buskers, drunks, pimps and prostitutes; they were all just there, just backdrop, with Willem in the foreground as the star. Though the *poules* of Montmartre were the most aggressive in the city, they didn't accost Willem and Charles, perhaps because Grace was walking between them with her arms linked in theirs. They bought roasted chestnuts from a vendor and, as they perched on a low wall to eat them, two couples in formal attire strolled past. One of the women, in a sable coat, glanced at them and remarked to her companion, "Some typical bohemians of Montmartre."

"See, Grace, we fit right in," Willem said, and the three roared with laughter.

Grace was prepared to go to a cabaret if Charles and Willem wanted to, but they didn't suggest it, so instead they went to a club, drank wine and danced some more, then linked arms and made their way back to rue Cler. Willem urged them to come to a gathering at Madame Simon's the following evening, then clapped Charles on the shoulder and brushed a kiss on Grace's cheek. That night, in bed, she caressed the spot his lips had touched. Would he have kissed her on the mouth if Charles hadn't been there?

At dinner the following evening, Grace's landlady opened a bottle of Chablis given to her by her employer. It was delicious, but couldn't make up for the tough chicken which was the basis of the meal. Grace ate little, and realized, as she and Charles left on the metro for Auteuil, that she was a little tipsy. When they arrived, Willem opened the door for them. As he took Grace's coat, his hand lingered on her shoulder, and she saw that his blue knitted vest was the same colour as his eyes. In the parlour they met the usual guests and a few new faces. All the seats were occupied, so Grace took the ottoman, while Charles asked Madame Simon if he could look at the art on her walls.

Brandy asked what Grace and Charles had been doing lately, so Grace attempted to describe *Les Folies*. Words like "magnificent", "hilarious", "daring" and "magical" spilled out of her, though normally she didn't speak in superlatives. She couldn't seem to shut up. Charles, now perched on the arm of Brandy's chair, was staring pointedly at her, so she paused for breath.

"How gratifying that one of our national institutions is so appreciated," Madame remarked, with a chuckle. Everyone laughed and Grace turned red. Willem came and knelt beside Grace's ottoman and handed her a piece of cake.

"Please, have something to eat," he urged, sitting down on the floor beside her. His attention gave her a delicious shiver.

As she and Charles were leaving, Grace invited everyone present to come to tea with her the following afternoon. Madame Simon thanked her but said she had other plans.

"I'm off to bed," she announced. "Goodnight all. Willem, when everyone leaves, will you turn off the lights and lock the door behind you?"

Shopping at the *patisserie* the morning of the 31st, Grace made her selection carefully, wanting everything to be perfect for her guests that afternoon.

The landlady and her family had left early to visit friends, but they had offered Hubertine's services, and she was a great help. She got out Madame's Limoges tea service and lace tablecloth, helped Grace arrange the fruit, canapés and little *gateaux*, and kept the kettle boiling and fresh tea available.

Brandy was the first to arrive, bringing a bouquet of roses, her parents' Christmas present, which she wanted to share with everyone.

"You look wonderful," she said, as she hugged Grace. "All these late nights gadding about with your brother, and you're fresh as a daisy."

"The night air agrees with me."

Next to arrive were the two Kays. Charles, now up and dressed, was at his most charming and Grace was proud of him. Batia arrived in good time, in a beaded sequined black dress and a crimson necklace. Each time there was a knock at the door, Grace hoped that it was Willem, and finally he arrived. Grace introduced him to Batia, and, as she had hoped, they struck up a conversation. Grace was sure that he would impress Batia. Both in their mid-twenties, they were the two oldest people there, and the ones who had found their life's work.

It was the kind of party Grace liked, everyone talking, some in French, some in English, others nimbly switching back and forth. She felt like a little girl who had just opened her birthday presents and had a grand celebration to look forward to. When Willem and Charles left early for 11 rue de Verneuil, her excitement grew, for she knew they were going to prepare for the festivities.

Soon Batia departed, as she had New Year's Eve plans with the Beaux Arts crowd.

"Well?" inquired Grace, as she helped Batia on with her coat.

"He's interesting. We'll talk next time you come to pose."

The blond Kay and Brandy left too, but the brunette Kay stayed to help Grace and Hubertine clear up and pack up the leftovers and the roses, to take to the New Year's Eve party chez Willem. Then, after some primping, Grace and Kay took a taxi to rue de Verneuil, arriving at 7 p.m.

Madame Simon was nowhere to be found, and it was just as well, as the salon and the dining room were being transformed by McGrath and a couple of girls into a bower of paper streamers and Chinese lanterns.

"Just the woman I need," Willem declared, as he took Grace's coat. "Could you possibly wash some plates? Ah, this will come in handy," he added, seeing the basket of goodies. "And roses for the centrepiece too."

She followed him down the passage to the kitchen where Henning and Taylor were making sandwiches and Charles was washing and slicing *crudités*. Willem grabbed a checked apron from a hook, slipped it over Grace's head and tied it around her waist.

"Are you aware," he whispered, "that this is the last day of *l'année bissextile*?"

"Oh, you mean Leap Year. Yes." As she plunged her hands into soapy water she smiled. The dying year, 1928, had indeed been a leap year, with twenty-nine days in February. Was he referring to the old tradition that women may propose marriage in leap years? Was he telling her she had only a few hours left? Possibly he liked saying "*bissextile*" because it had "sex" in it.

New people kept arriving. She heard McGrath say, "It's Texas!" and wondered what he could possibly mean. When

Willem, who was setting the table, came in for more plates, she asked, "Texas?"

"McGrath's girl from America. She has come all this way to visit him."

Leaving the dishes to air dry, Grace joined the gang in the salon. "Texas" was pretty and elegantly dressed; her fringed skirt said "high fashion", not "frontier". She spoke in a charming drawl that made Grace want to hear what she sounded like in French, but the conversation was in English.

At nine o'clock Willem called everyone to the dining room. By that time everyone was badly in need of food. He held Grace's chair for her, and claimed the one next to it. In the hum of voices, punctuated by bursts of laughter, he asked her questions to draw her out, starting with New Year's customs in Canada. She spoke of the annual fireworks display on Parliament Hill in Ottawa. When he politely turned to talk to the girl on his right, Grace turned to Taylor, but she felt inexplicably sad. Then when Willem turned his attention back to her she felt absurdly happy. "It must be the wine," she thought.

After the meal, Willem announced that he and Grace would do the dishes while McGrath, in the salon, would explain the games he'd planned. With Willem by her side, drying, reminiscing about a wild New Year's Eve during his university days in South Africa, she could have washed dishes forever, although it was her least favourite chore. When the last cup was returned to its hook he grasped her hand.

"I hear Charles's violin," he said, "and I really want to dance with you. Let's see if he can play something danceable."

Though Charles played well, his repertoire of popular dance tunes was weak, but fortunately Texas had brought with her a satchel of 78 r.p.m. records. She wound up the gramophone and put one on.

"It's *Let's Fall in Love*," she announced, "or, as I call it, *Birds do It*."

Willem grabbed Grace's hand and pulled her into the centre of the salon. As they danced she felt like a glamorous new version of herself. Soon, everyone was up dancing. An hour later, however, first one couple, then another, had pleaded exhaustion. All were sprawled on the furniture and the floor.

When pealing bells all over Paris announced that it was now 1929, Willem looked into Grace's eyes and silently asked a question. Wordlessly she answered; then he pulled her into the passageway, pressed his lips on hers, and transported her to another plane of being.

Time stood still, but only for a moment; then someone brushed by them in the passageway, rushing to the toilet to be sick.

"Time to put coffee on," he said, drawing away from her.

Alone in the kitchen, they kissed again. When eventually they brought coffee into the salon, they found one of the girls sitting on the floor in a corner beside Charles, stroking the bow of his violin. Four of the company had linked arms and were singing *Auld Lang Syne* as a barbershop quartet. McGrath and Texas were discovered behind the sofa on the floor in each other's arms. Blonde Kay, looking green, declined coffee. She and the other Kay slumped against each other.

Grace and Willem exchanged glances.

"They're in no shape to go home," she whispered.

"I'll give them my bed," he said. "I'll sleep on the sofa." The girls accepted his offer gratefully and, supporting each other, left the salon.

Everyone else seemed capable of getting home safely, and the gang gradually dispersed, with hugs and exclamations of "Happy New Year." McGrath and Texas suggested that the five of them should all go to the Dôme. Suddenly full of energy, Grace had no objections. As they left the house, Charles walked with McGrath and Texas, and she was alone with Willem a few steps behind them, quietly happy.

The Dôme was pulsating with life. There, Texas soon gave up on her café au lait, folded her arms on the table, and rested her head on them.

"Time to get you home." McGrath draped her coat over her shoulders, helped her up, and half-carried her out the door.

"Let's walk by the Seine," Willem proposed.

The night was magical. All over Paris horns blared, music played, and fireworks lit up the night. An embracing couple sheltered by the arch of the Pont Neuf made Grace half-wish that Charles were not there, but of course, without him she wouldn't be walking by the river in the wee small hours with a man she was just getting to know.

When Willem patted back a yawn she suggested that she and Charles walk him back to rue de Verneuil. Once they'd seen him to his door, Charles was reluctant to call it a night.

"Let's stay up and watch the sun rise," he said, and since she wasn't particularly tired she agreed. They retraced their steps to the banks of the Seine, walking in silence. Then Charles said, "You like him."

"Of course." She felt her cheeks grow hot. "Everybody does. You like him too, don't you?"

"I've never met anyone quite like him – a liberal from South Africa. That's pretty rare. If his thesis makes clear that he regards black South Africans as equals, then he probably can't go home again. You can't help but respect someone with that much strength of conviction."

"I agree."

They watched the rising sun's rays gleam on the water.

"Don't get hurt," Charles said, out of nowhere.

"I won't."

After breakfast, alone in her room, Grace turned to her journal.

"Nineteen twenty-eight has been the best year of my life," she wrote, in French, *"but something tells me that 1929 will be even*

better. This past year brought so many gifts, like the friendship of the other girls in my graduating class, after two years of being on the margins. And now I'm in Paris. New horizons are opening up before me, and I have more faith in myself. What will 1929 bring? I'm happy to wait and see. I've never felt more alive than now."

Chapter Six

Grace woke and stared at the clock. 2:30. Morning? Afternoon? It had to be afternoon, because the sun was shining. She washed, dressed and found Charles reading alone in the salon, the warmest room in the house. The De Bussy ladies weren't home, and the fire was so inviting that she decided to study there, too.

Lost in her book, she was jolted back to the present by a knock at the door. Charles sprang up to see who it was, and found on the threshold Willem, McGrath and Henning, who had been out for coffee and had come to return Charles's violin which he'd left at 11 rue de Verneuil.

Willem, who looked pale, sank into a chair and said he hadn't had a wink of sleep. On returning from their early morning walk he'd tried to settle on the sofa in the salon, but it was too short for him, so he'd stretched out on the floor with a cushion under his head. He fell asleep around 7 a.m and was awakened an hour later by his landlady, shouting at him. She'd looked into the salon, found him there on the floor, and accused him of passing out drunk. Then, as if on cue, the two Kays emerged, dishevelled, from his room. Madame thought the three of them had shared a bed, and as yet, hadn't been convinced otherwise.

As Grace and Charles laughed, Willem managed a smile, then held his head in his hands. Groaning, he said he'd have to find a way to make amends. The family had been very good about welcoming his friends to their home. As Taylor and McGrath talked to Charles about London, Willem smiled at Grace, but for once seemed too tired to talk. She wanted to take him in her arms, but instead urged him to go home and sleep.

"You could have waited to return the violin," she murmured.

He whispered back, "I wanted to see you."

She put her hand on his arm. "Go and rest," she said.

On January 2nd, Grace went to Batia's to pose and to hear her impressions of Willem. The visit began in silence because Batia was concentrating on capturing one particular expression of Grace's and needed her face to be still. Over tea, later, Batia thanked her for a very pleasant afternoon two days ago, and, casually, Grace asked what she thought of Dr. Van Aarden.

"He is very handsome if big blond men are your type," Batia replied. "He's well spoken about his field of scholarship. Someday he will head the history department of some world-class university. I can tell by your expression that you agree with me and that your friendship with him is on again."

Grace nodded and waited for more.

"You want me to say that he's your *basherter*, but I have no way of knowing whether or not he is."

When Grace asked her what "*basherter*" meant, Batia explained that "*bashert*" was Hebrew for "destiny". A woman's "basherter" was the man who was her divinely foreordained soulmate – the one who was meant to be. According to the Kabbalah, God divides a soul at birth into male and female, and when two people marry they each recover their missing half and become whole.

"I'm not an authority on this matter," Batia added with a smile. "But I can tell you all about the process of casting a sculpture in bronze."

Grace was interested in the process, and their time together was soon over. She returned home to find a note from Charles that he had gone to the YMCA to work out. He'd also shifted the furniture in her room, and she approved, as the desk now got more light from the window. Shivering, she wished she had a fire in her room, but she didn't like to ask as she knew Madame was hard-up. Several weeks earlier she had returned from class to find a couple of burly men in grimy clothes carrying baskets of briquets made of coal dust into the *salle de bains*. The claw-footed tub was now a storage receptacle for winter fuel; all tub baths were over for the season, except for bird baths in the baby-sized tin tub, the "*bain sabot*" that hung in the kitchen.

Grace's classes resumed on January 3rd while Charles was still in Paris. She completed her assignment that morning and when called upon in history class, expressed herself well. Whether answering in class, studying or hurrying home in the cold, she had Willem on her mind. When would she see him again?

When she got home, Charles suggested asking Willem to come with them to see *Rose-Marie* that night at the Theatre Magador.

"From the reviews I've read, it includes everything Canadian," he said with a grin. "The Rocky Mountains, the Mounted Police, gold prospecting, and the legend of the Indian Love Call. It will present all of Canadian history to him in capsule form."

Since there was no way to contact Willem in advance, they stopped at rue de Verneuil on their way to the show to see if he was free. When his landlady's daughter came to the door and said that he was out, Grace hid her disappointment. As they walked briskly in the cold, Charles hummed *Rose-Marie, I Love You*. The show had premiered in New York way back in 1924 and its songs were well-known all over.

Twenty-minutes into the performance, Grace was glad Willem wasn't there, because the plot was ludicrous. Granted, the production was lavishly staged and the mountain vistas were triumphs of art; Madeleine Masse was excellent in the role of Rose-Marie, and Robert Bernier, a baritone, was splendid as her lover, Jim, but their talents were wasted in something so silly. Grace recognized nothing of the Canada she knew; the story seemed set in some melodramatic, imaginary realm.

The following day, Andrew came back from his holidays suntanned and cheerful, and had no problem with Charles sharing his room for the rest of his stay. The following evening Willem dropped in and the young people and the landlady's family sat in the salon and conversed entirely in French. Because young Edith was studying early explorers at school, talk turned to great European adventurers who had gone to the far corners of the world. Grace mentioned the courageous French explorers who had established New France until Willem interrupted with the statement that no nation had produced such intrepid, practical adventurers as the Dutch, a tiny nation which had built a remarkable empire. Judging from the ladies' expressions, he went on a bit too long in this vein, but Grace enjoyed every word he uttered. When Charles and Grace saw him to the door, he proposed that they go out the following evening, just the three of them, to see *Chicago*. Grace promptly said yes.

Since his holiday was drawing to a close, Charles decided he had to see Versailles and set out the next morning when Grace went to classes. That day she received a high mark for one of her assignments and felt that 1929 was starting out right. The evening, however, was less than stellar. *Chicago* was mediocre, and afterwards, in a café, Willem directed most of his conversation to Charles, as if she were a knot in the table. Conversations in her parents' circle weren't male-dominated; the women always participated and often led the discussions. Perhaps he was just being nice to her brother, whom he wouldn't see again soon.

Saying goodbye to Charles made Grace sad, but he reminded her that it was just "au revoir", for they would be meeting in the spring. After he'd left, Grace concentrated on her studies, visited with Andrew, and wished Willem would write or call. One evening after dinner he stopped by to invite her to a gathering of socialists, and without hesitation she threw on her coat and went out with him. It was a stimulating evening, and the icing on the cake was when, on the way home, he asked her out to dinner and a motion picture the following evening.

The film, *La Madame de la Rue*, sounded racy, but Grace hardly noticed one way or the other, because, when the lights went down, Willem reached for her hand and held it as if it were the most natural thing in the world. As her eyes adjusted, she realized that hand-holding was pretty tame in this milieu. Couples around them were glued together at the lips and moaning softly in the dark. She sat beside him, delighted to be in his presence, knowing now that their passionate kiss on the 31st had meant more than "Happy New Year."

On the way home Willem said he was sorry if she felt left out on Charles's last evening. He'd seized the opportunity to converse with her brother, who was so bright and had a fresh perspective on many topics. Willem also confessed that he'd been in a bad mood lately.

"Is your landlady still angry?"

Willem said no, that she had forgiven him. He was revising two scholarly articles for a history journal and it was tedious, arduous work. Also, he was worried about what the editors might be doing to his book.

"Imagine having one's thesis published in book form! You must be very proud."

He smiled. "I am, to be honest, and only hope the editors aren't butchering it."

He was down in the dumps because he hadn't heard from his family during the holidays. Grace, who felt honoured that he was sharing his concerns with her, suggested that he send them a telegram wishing them a Happy New Year and asking what was new. The cost would be considerable, but worthwhile for his peace of mind. He brightened.

At her door, he made a date to see her in three day's time. She said yes. Just when she thought he wasn't going to kiss her goodnight, he brushed a soft kiss on her lips that promised more in the future. Once inside, she did a dance step for joy. They were "going together", as people said back home. On the hall table was a letter from her mother, full of news and encouragement. Should she tell Mother about Willem? It was early days yet.

Their next evening together was in a cosy café. There, Grace asked him to elaborate on historiography, specifically, the "Whig interpretation of history?" She knew of two approaches to history. One, which she'd learned about through reading, was Karl

Marx's, about one period leading to another, culminating in an ideal state of communal sharing and equality. The other, which she'd studied in school, was about heroes, great battles, and steps toward constitutional monarchy.

Pleased by her question, Willem explained that "Whig history" took its name from the early days of the party system in Britain, when the Whig party was on the side of Parliamentary power, versus the Tories who supported royal power. Whig historians, exemplified by historians like David Hume and Thomas Babington Macaulay, saw history as events marching forward to the goals of liberal democracy and constitutional monarchy.

The term "Whig interpretation" now referred to any version of history which postulated the march of progress toward a goal, with every event regarded as either an advancement or a setback.

Grace recognized the approach she'd learned in school. Perhaps it applied to Marx as well.

"I was taught two forms of this kind of history, the British version and the Afrikaaner version," Willem said, with a smile. "What I really learned was that history is subjective. In my own work I try to follow the example of Leopold Von Ranke."

"Do go on," said Grace, always eager to learn something new.

Apparently this 19th century German historian held that historians must understand the past on its own terms, for its own sake, from the viewpoints of those who lived it, rather than evaluating it as a precursor of what came next. Von Ranke rejected speculation in favour of facts obtained from primary sources, such as government documents and authentic eyewitness accounts.

"My other inspiration is one of Von Ranke's contemporaries, Friedrich Hegel," he continued. "He held that history concerns the development of the human spirit's consciousness of its own freedom."

Grace had heard of Hegel, who had influenced Karl Marx in his concept of stages of history. She asked Willem if Marx fell into the category of "Whig historian" because of his belief that economic production had developed in stages with each one leading to the next: primitive communism, slave-based societies, feudalism, and capitalism, the stage in which they were living. The final stage was socialism.

Willem was looking at her with surprise.

"I haven't met many young women who are interested in ideas. Since you ask, I think of Marx as a political economist."

Willem liked Hegel's view that history is a struggle for freedom because of his own concern about the oppression of black South Africans. His own task, as a scholar, was to conscientiously and rigorously examine primary sources, like British government documents on colonial policy. He also had to bear in mind that his interest in any aspect of history was the result of his own background and upbringing. He had to delve for facts, see connections, distinguish between causes and effects and write as objectively as possible.

Listening to him was pure pleasure for Grace, because of his dedication to his profession. She envied him. To what was she dedicated? Teaching? Drawing out children's innate abilities? Creating an environment for learning? Normal school had emphasized these noble goals, but to be honest, they weren't what she cared about most. Right now, she didn't know what her "calling" was.

"That's my lecture for tonight," he said, smiling, as the waiter approached to ask if they wanted anything else. "You're the best of students."

"Thank you," she said, smiling. "I wish you'd been my history professor at the University of Manitoba."

Actually, if he had, she'd have been too enthralled to learn anything at all. And that night, back at rue Cler, when his lips met hers she trembled and hated to see him go.

In the evenings that followed, however, she had more to say, and occasionally disagreed with him. One evening he remarked that he'd made up his mind, when young not to live the life of his railway worker father.

"Early on, I saw there had to be more to life than days spent stoking a locomotive boiler and evenings in the pub," he said.

Grace winced. She wondered if he'd had to fight his father for an education? Perhaps that was the reason for his attitude; otherwise, what he'd just said sounded like contempt for those who did manual labour. When he asked her what was the matter, she said as much.

"My father worked for a while on the Vancouver docks to support us," she said. "It was hard work for such a slight man, but it was one of the best experiences of his life. He found a brotherhood among the workers that he'd never known in the church. The men looked out for each other because a runaway barrel or a malfunctioning crane could wipe them out. Certainly, some of them drank. Who could blame them? Father respected his co-workers. He is convinced that the so-called ignorance of ordinary people is a myth."

Willem raised his eyebrows. "But your father moved back into the middle class," he said, with a mischievous smile. "He wasn't stuck doing physical labour all his life."

"True, but now he understands from direct experience how other people live. Now, Willem, I do sympathize with your decision not to live your father's life. It's the same thing as me and my mother. I'll never be as good as she is in running a household and nurturing children, but helping her with the housework and my younger brothers was good for me. I didn't always enjoy it, but I learned how hard it is and I respect her choice to do that with her life. But I won't live my life exactly like hers."

That led to a discussion of the changing role of women. Willem expressed the opinion that now, in 1929, women in the western world were emancipated and enjoyed equality with men. The legal and social barriers to their advancement had been largely removed, and they had more opportunities than ever before in history.

Grace was shocked to hear him say this. She shook her head.

"We're a long way from equality."

She reminded Willem that back in May, the Italian Duce, Benito Mussolini, had taken away the franchise from Italian women. In England, the law had been changed only recently to permit women to vote at age twenty-one, as men did. Prior to that women had to be thirty. Here in France, women didn't have the vote, and, in the realm of education, the Sorbonne had only recently admitted women, and only nine had graduated, with the ninth, a young woman named Simone de Beauvoir, graduating this past spring.

She paused for breath. Willem smiled.

"Grace, you're a feminist! You're like those ten women who stormed the French President's palace back in August."

Grace felt her face getting hot. She'd read of this demonstration in the Paris papers while she was at Cinq-Mars. Ten leaders of the women's movement, from several different countries, had picketed the palace where the French president was entertaining male world leaders who had gathered to sign a pact renouncing war as an instrument of national policy.

"If world leaders can agree to a peace pact," she said, "they could make a similar pact guaranteeing women's rights in all the signatories' countries."

Willem's eyes widened. "I would never have pegged you for a feminist, Grace. For one thing, you're too pretty. For another, most feminists are middle class. They're liberals, not socialists."

"Beauty is in the eye of the beholder," she told him, "and liberal reforms like the vote and equality before the law, and admission to the professions and governing bodies are important and necessary. Socialists support those things, but we want to go beyond them, to social and economic equality for everybody."

"But surely you agree that women now have more opportunities than ever before in history," he insisted.

"We're getting there."

Why, when she liked him so much, was it so vital that she win arguments with him?

"I wonder why women are so slow to embrace their opportunities," he continued. "So many women want to marry and be supported by a man and have children."

"Well, to adapt a quotation from Marx, I think that family is the heart in a heartless world. Women are at such a disadvantage in the work outside the home that naturally many prefer to spend their energies on their own family life. Society doesn't do much to encourage women in the workplace. In Canada during the war there were a few crèches – child care centres – where women could leave their children while they worked, but these folded once the war was over."

She paused, wondering if she should add something more, even though it might make her look "fast."

"The laws against family planning prevent women from taking control of their own lives," she added. "So if women are less adventurous and less independent than you'd like – those are some of the reasons."

Willem said she'd given him food for thought. That night, at her door, she was the first to hold out her arms for a goodnight embrace, to show him that she was open to the adventure that they seemed to be embarking on.

That night she wrote to her mother about Willem. She praised his academic achievements, his good looks, charm and sense of humour, and said she was thrilled to have him as a friend and to see him every other day.

"I never expected to form a friendship of such intensity," she wrote. "Friendship is too weak a word, really. I have a lot of faith in your opinions, Mother, and I know you may be thinking that the feelings he and I have for each other are magnified and enhanced because we're far away from home in Paris. If you think my heart is over-ruling my head, and that it's advisable to break off with him, I will, although it will be hard."

Chapter Seven

Grace and Willem met every second day for a meal or coffee, and fell into intense conversations and passionate arguments about current events. On the subject of the recent international pact renouncing war, they had different opinions. Grace thought that any step toward peace was positive. She was also pleased that the former British colonies which were now self-governing, like Canada and South Africa, had asserted their independence in foreign affairs by signing the pact. Willem shook his head. The Kellogg-Briand Pact might reflect the good intentions of the U.S. Secretary of State and the French foreign minister who had initiated the agreement, but he didn't think it would hold up if put to the test. He saw it as another sign of France's fear of Germany. When Grace claimed it worthwhile to try to establish international rules, he merely shrugged, filling her with indignation.

Occasionally, Willem made remarks that were beneath him. One evening they were talking about British politics and the possibility that Ramsay MacDonald would lead the Labour Party to victory in next year's general election. She asked Willem's views, because he had been living in England and knew more about the political scene there than she did.

"The bastard is in trouble in his own constituency," Willem declared.

When her jaw dropped, Willem laughed and said, "Well, he is one, you know. I'm sorry to have shocked you."

Grace shook her head. She knew that the Labour Party leader was the child of unmarried parents; the opposition had made much of that when he'd first entered politics.

"When you use that word, Willem, you show how conventional you are about marriage and social proprieties," she told him. "And does it matter, really?"

Willem turned red, and hastily spoke of MacDonald's difficulties with the radical miners in his Welsh constituency.

Another time, discussing his future plans, he said that McGrath had encouraged him to apply to teach at several American universities, not those in the Ivy League, but in the great heartland. McGrath thought they would be so excited to have a faculty member with a Ph.D. from a British university that he could forcibly deflower a co-ed and get away with it.

Grace couldn't believe her ears. She sat very still for a few minutes, then got up and walked out of the café. Willem soon caught up with her.

"Grace, I'm sorry. I thought you'd find it funny."

She turned and glared at him. "How could you imagine that I'd find that funny?"

"It was McGrath who said it, not I?"

"But you thought it was worth repeating. You should be ashamed of yourself. I'm disgusted with both of you."

"Then please help me to be a better person." She kept on walking and so did he, until she had reached rue Cler. When he asked to see her again, she said she didn't know.

He said he would be at their favourite café the following evening, and hoped she would forgive him and join him there.

The following evening she did. Things started out well enough. He asked about her courses; she spoke about the realist tradition in French literature. He listened for a while, then began talking about realism in English literature, declaring that Dickens was the consummate proletarian writer, exposing the social injustice in Victorian England.

Grace found herself contradicting him, declaring that Dickens's novels demonstrated a middle class outlook. She knew she was being prickly about something unimportant. She didn't know why she felt compelled to assert her view, but she did.

Shaking his head, Willem mentioned the character Stephen Blackpool in *Hard Times*; was he not an industrial worker? Grace said yes, but that the novel's message was merely that employers should be more generous, not that workers should organize.

"Dickens wanted a kinder society but had no plan as to how to get there," she said.

"Is it necessary that a writer prescribe as well as describe?"

She thought he sounded condescending.

"If he or she is a proletarian writer, yes. Have you read much of Dickens?"

Her guess that he hadn't was confirmed when his face turned crimson. He turned and summoned the waiter to bring more wine. Grace wondered why she'd become so passionate over Dickens, a writer she didn't particularly like. And why had he become so angry? Then it dawned on her that the passion they felt for each other, having no other outlet, expressed itself through anger.

She declined wine and asked for coffee instead. They sat in silence for what seemed an eternity. Then Willem snapped his fingers at the waiter for the *addition*.

"We need a walk to cool off," he said.

In the cold starry night they walked side by side, their breath steaming in the frosty air. Music poured like molten lava from the doorway of a night club. He grabbed her arm and propelled her inside, hauled her to the dance floor and took her in his arms. He twirled her around, then jerked her to him, in time to the wild music. Then when the band switched to *I'm Confessing that I Love You*, he took her in his arms and they clung together, swaying to the slow song. She was completely caught up in the experience.

"I should get you home," he said.

They didn't speak. Then, at her door, he mentioned a movie he would like to see. He had revisions to complete, but would be free in two days time, if she wanted to go.

"I'd like to see it too," she said. He bent toward her and they kissed.

Up in her room, sponging off in cold water, she thought about where they were headed.

The movie was playing in a seedy neighbourhood. The run-down theatre was half-empty. William chose a shadowy corner, dim even before the lights went down. He heaped their coats in an empty seat beside him and put his arm around her shoulders. She snuggled in the curve, their upper bodies touching. When the film got underway he drew her to him, and their lips came together. The tip of his tongue in her mouth felt exhilarating yet completely right. The feelings she had been trying to suppress surged up inside her. Vaguely she hoped that the elderly usher wouldn't start wandering around with his flashlight, but that concern was lost in the thrill of Willem's kisses.

Then Willem's large warm hand guided hers, gently, downward, and she came suddenly out of her erotic blur. Fear seized her. She understood instinctively what he wanted, and it seemed natural, but not here. Surely such an intimate act deserved a better, more private environment.

"No," she whispered. She drew away, smoothed down her blouse and gazed at the screen, with no idea what the movie was about. When it was over and they had left the theatre, Willem apologized for getting carried away.

"I am sorry I offended you," he said.

"How can I not be offended? We were in a *theatre*, Willem, *surrounded by other people*! And what those other people might have been doing doesn't influence me."

"It's hard to be restrained when I'm with you. Next time we'll sit decorously and not even hold hands."

"If I ever go out with you again, we'll definitely hold hands, so that I can keep yours under control."

"I'm sorry. I'm so attracted to you. I would like to make love to you properly."

"You're moving too fast for me."

They walked along in silence.

"I know you're a sweet girl from a good family. But you're in Paris, Grace, a city where anything goes, and you're here for a limited time. Don't you want to have experiences to look back on?"

"Yes, of course, but I have to be careful about experiences that lead to consequences. It's late and I don't want to talk about this now, but we must talk."

"Then we will. Shall we have coffee Tuesday afternoon? I'll come and meet you in the great hall after classes."

She nodded. He took her face in his hands, bent and kissed her.

* * *

"Come in," said Batia. "Your head is like John the Baptist's, on a platter."

Grace laughed and entered Batia's studio. On the table she saw her head in clay.

"You captured my facial structure perfectly, but do I really look so dejected?"

"Occasionally. That's the look I need for my series on human emotions. But today you look full of anticipation."

The kettle on the pot-bellied stove whistled and Batia lifted it off and made tea. Handing a steaming mug to Grace, she asked, "How are things with your historian?"

"He's well. He thinks I should be more open to experience."

Batia raised her eyebrows. "Does he know yet where he will be teaching this coming autumn?"

"Not yet."

Grace admired Batia's ability to grasp a problem and put it in a nutshell. As they talked about their work, she wished she dared ask Batia for some advice, but she was too much in awe of her, and to ask would imply that Batia was a woman of experience, and she might be offended.

Back at rue Cler, there was a letter from Winnipeg in a long white envelope. She opened it and mulled it over, wondering how she should reply.

On Tuesday after class, with butterflies in her stomach, she went down the stairs to the great hall, and spotted Willem the same instant he saw her. As he came toward her, smiling, yearning coursed through her, but it was tempered by resolution.

"You're brimming over with happiness," she told him.

"In the café I'll tell you the good news."

He'd finished revising his chapters for the *Cambridge History of the British Empire*, and had been asked to come to England for meetings with the editor and publisher over a two week period.

"So you're being published in two books, one based on your thesis, and also the *Cambridge History*? That's amazing, Willem. Congratulations."

He reached across the table and seized her hand. "I'll miss you. I wish you could come with me to England."

Thrilled to be asked, she reluctantly said that she had to study.

"I hope you'll write," she added.

"Of course."

"When do you leave?"

"Tomorrow."

"So soon?"

"I'm afraid so."

"I've had some news too," said Grace. "The Winnipeg school board has offered me a position for the school year 1929-1930, teaching French."

He looked startled. "Will you accept?"

"I think so. If my plans were to change before September, I could always withdraw."

How horrified her parents would be if they heard her speak so casually about withdrawing from such a good offer – a position in a city school and in her area of specialization, too!

"Wouldn't it be more satisfactory to complete a Master's Degree in French Literature?" he asked.

"I'll need to earn some money before I can even think of it."

He studied her. "You impress me, Grace. So pretty and fragile-looking, yet so practical. Have you thought any more about – er – us? About taking things further?"

"Of course I've thought about it. I feel the way you do about your meeting in England."

He looked confused. "How so?"

"Honoured and excited to be asked, but wanting to be clear on terms and arrangements, and what is expected."

He gripped her hand, his blue eyes boring into her.

"I want to know you completely. Are you saying 'maybe'?"

"We can talk about that when you get back from England."

"I don't leave until tomorrow," he said softly.

"But you have to get your things together. I'll be here when you return."

Chapter Eight

The following morning Grace plunged into her work, an essay on "The Lion and the Fox" from the *Fables of Lafontaine*, a book she and her mother had read together.

When she thought of Willem, at least once every hour, she felt both desire and confusion. Going all the way was a huge step. She wasn't prepared, in a practical sense, and there was also the problem of where. It was just as well that circumstances had forced them to take a breather for two weeks. When he came back they would discuss it.

Meanwhile, it was relaxing to talk to Andrew, who had been working furiously on his assignments because he was taking a few days off to escape the cold weather and go back to Nice. He never asked her why she was missing evening meals at rue Cler, but the morning that Willem was scheduled to leave Paris, he asked her to have coffee with him after class. This invitation was a surprise, since usually he went right home to study.

Over coffee, he said that he wanted to grouse about the food at 18 rue Cler. He liked the various potato dishes that Hubertine cooked, and had no quarrel with macaroni and cheese, but he felt starved for protein. Grace felt guilty about dining out with Willem so often and leaving Andrew to the repetitive bill of fare at rue Cler. At least, in her absence, there would be more food to go around.

Andrew suggested a trip to a butcher shop to see if there was some meat they could afford. If so, perhaps they could go fifty-fifty and buy enough for a meal for the entire household, presenting it as a gift from both of them, so as not to hurt Madame De Bussy's feelings.

Grace thought that any hurt feelings would fade in the appetizing aroma of roast chicken or broiled pork chops. Together they went to the market, where they examined the poultry, pork and beef, but to their dismay, the prices for enough of anything for six people would make a serious dent in their budgets. Then Andrew pointed at some fresh lean steaks that, incredibly, were affordable.

"Do you suppose they made a mistake in the price?" he whispered in French.

Then Grace spied a sign obscured by another tray of meat. She nudged him, pointed at the word on the sign, and mouthed it. "*Cheval*."

They looked at each other.

"We've eaten *escargots*," he said. "Also *ragout de lapin*."

"Frogs' legs, too, and eel."

They left with six horse steaks tied up in butcher paper, one for each member of the household, including Hubertine. Back at rue Cler, they found Madame De Bussy with Hubertine in the kitchen.

"Andrew and I wanted to provide a treat," Grace said, presenting the package.

"How thoughtful of you! Meat! Steaks?" Eagerly Madame unwrapped the package. Then she and Hubertine stared at the steaks.

"What are they?" she inquired.

"Cheval."

Madame winced visibly.

"I am afraid we in the family would find them too troubling to our digestions," she said, "but you two must try them. Hubertine, put them on to broil."

With a look of distaste, Hubertine did so.

At dinner time Andrew and Grace cut into their meat with firm resolve, aware of four pairs of eyes upon them waiting to see if they gagged. Grace didn't mind the meat but would have liked it more if she hadn't known what it was.

"Well, we tried," Andrew said, upstairs, on the threshold of his room.

Grace giggled. "We have the other four steaks to look forward to."

That night they worked independently on different projects, with their doors open in the hope that heat from downstairs would rise to their rooms. Grace was lost in the "bishop's candlesticks" section of Victor Hugo's *Les Misérables*. Then Hubertine called from the bottom of the stairs that Grace's gentleman friend was here. Dropping her fountain pen, she tore downstairs. It was Willem, wearing a blue scarf that matched his eyes.

"My trip has been postponed for two days," he said. "I came by to invite you to see *The Golden Age* at the Palais Royale tomorrow evening."

"That would be lovely. Here, let me take your coat."

"I can't stay, though I wish I could. I'll pick you up tomorrow."

Back upstairs she recaptured her fountain pen before it made an ink stain on the rug. Although she tried to concentrate, her emotions were on a roller-coaster.

Next day, a Saturday, an unexpected snowfall turned everything white. Snow was commonplace back home, but here in Paris it seemed a novelty. She set out in a blur of snowflakes to Brandy's to help her with the Victor Hugo assignment. That afternoon, Edith invited her to come and play duets with her in the salon, and she was glad to do so, so as not to get too jazzed about seeing Willem.

By evening the snow had lightened; flakes floated singly down like silver dust on the lamp posts. Walking to the theatre, holding Willem's hand, she was content. During the entertainment, a satirical review, he was a perfect gentleman, holding her hand lightly. Afterwards, walking home arm in arm, they paused to kiss at intervals, but didn't talk, not wanting to shatter the magic snow globe which enclosed them.

"I'll miss you," he said. "I'll write to you as soon as I get there." His lips were soft and warm on hers.

"*I hope I will make him happy,*" she wrote in her journal that night. "*I have no right to try to shape our friendship according to my ideas. I must try to act like a girl living in the twentieth century.*"

The first thing to do was to make up for neglected studies. She started putting in five hours a day with her books in addition to class time and meetings with tutors. She and Andrew worked together part of the time, always with the bedroom door open, and when he left for Nice on February 10th, she promised to take careful notes to share when he returned.

Between classes one day, Taylor and Henning hailed her and told her that, after the regular Sunday afternoon social at Madame Simon's, they were going to a gathering of French socialists to hear a woman speaker. Would she like to come along? Grace begged off the visit at Madame Simon's; without Willem there she knew she would feel uncomfortable, though she wasn't sure why. She told Taylor and Henning that she needed to study on Sunday afternoon, but would like to hear the socialist woman, so they offered to come to her house and take her with them.

The woman was a powerful speaker and the audience enthusiastic. Grace summoned up the courage to ask her a question, which was well-received. She enjoyed the discussion in a café, afterwards, with Taylor, Henning and some of their crowd.

Back home around 9 p.m. she found the ladies out, at a wake, with Edith having hot chocolate with Hubertine in the chilly kitchen, usually the warmest room of the house. They offered her some, and the mug warmed her icy fingers.

"Hubertine, let's have a fire in the salon," she proposed. "Please join us there."

This was a bold request. The briquets stored in the bathtub were dwindling; it was her landlady, not she, who decided how much of the house to heat, and when. Hubertine complied and built a fire, but sat in the kitchen. Warm for the first time since arriving home, Grace talked about Lafontaine's fables to Edith, and when they got drowsy, they went off to their chilly beds. Grace doubted that anyone would reprove her about the fire. The ladies would return and think that Hubertine had built it for their comfort.

The weather got colder. The newspapers reported record low temperatures of minus 13 Celsius, a figure that would be considered balmy in February in Manitoba. Back home, though, Grace would have worn her thick coat with layers of sweaters, knitted legwarmers, a touque and sturdy boots. During the Canadian winter, life consisted largely of dashing between heated classrooms, the students' union, and cosy homes heated with coal furnaces. The coat she had brought along was not her warmest, and here in Paris there was no central heating. Since she didn't have classes for two days, she stayed at home, studying in her room with a blanket over her feet and legs and with her coat on, because the tiny stove didn't produce much heat.

A letter had arrived from Willem, full of news about what he was doing, with endearments at the end praising her beauty and kindness. Its tone of balance and good sense was reassuring. Shivering in bed at night, bundled up in the blankets, with her coat on top of her, she thought how cosy it would be to cuddle close to him on such a cold night. But if she knew Willem, cuddling would be just a preliminary.

She was pretty sure that respectable girls didn't discuss precautions with their beaux, but took care of the matter by themselves. She tried to remember what Marie Stopes had said on the subject in *Wise Parenthood*.

There was a rubber cap, also called a diaphragm, which a woman could insert to shield the womb from sperm, but it wasn't something a virgin could use the first time she had sexual relations. Before she could be fitted with one, a woman had to have some experience; things had to be stretched a little. The cap was academic anyway because there was no way she could obtain one.

Some women calculated their fertile days in each cycle, but Dr. Stopes had warned that it was not an exact science. Shielding methods were best, she wrote, but they made Grace feel squeamish. Stopes had mentioned a small sponge with a string attached, treated with powdered soap. What if the string broke and it got lost? Stopes had also mentioned cotton wool pads treated with vaseline and borax – again, what if they got lost? There were, apparently, soluble pessaries of quinine and cocoa butter which were commercially available – maybe at Dr. Stopes' clinic in London.

According to Stopes, a woman could make her own pessaries using quinine and either cocoa butter or gelatine. The notion made Grace cringe. It was ludicrous to think she could cook up this mixture in her rented room, especially since cocoa butter had a strong scent. Hubertine came in to sweep, dust and change the sheets, and possibly she snooped. Madame de Bussy, if she ever found out, would evict Grace immediately.

Also impossible was douching in a solution of vinegar and water, or salt and water, as Stopes had mentioned. She couldn't imagine bringing the necessary equipment to a rendez-vous with Willem. Grace could see why *Wise Parenthood* was addressed to married people. It wasn't so much a matter of morality as of practicality. A woman who was using these messy and complicated techniques, and perhaps preparing them for herself, would want to be in her own home with a cooperative and understanding husband.

If she and Willem were to go all the way, it would be easiest if he used a condom. Coitus interruptus, according to Stopes, relied too much on timing and control. But could she speak of such things to Willem? Not without seeming "fast."

A deeper concern nagged at her. Shouldn't they be more committed to each other before taking this big step? If the most careful precautions failed, a woman would need a man to stand by her, and to be honest, she had no idea if Willem would. His future was up in the air. She didn't know if he'd applied to any North American universities. He'd spoken of "having experiences to look back on," but he didn't say they'd look back on them together.

After two days at home with her books, brooding about this matter, she was desperate for a change of air and thought, so she bundled up as best she could and left the house for her phonetics class. Later, she went to Batia's studio.

The sculptor, bundled in sweaters, opened the door with a finger pressed to her lips. When Grace stepped inside, Batia pointed to her bed at the far end of the studio, where a young man was sleeping.

"A fellow art student," she whispered. "There's no heat at his place. Let's go out and visit my Russian friend."

After a brisk walk in the cold they arrived in a poor neighbourhood and climbed the stairs to the friend's flat. Grace had expected someone Batia's age, but the friend turned out to be a middle aged woman who shared the apartment with her daughter, who was at work, and her young grandchildren. Batia presented the woman with a bag of croissants which she said she would save for their evening meal. Though the furnishings were makeshift and shabby, the fire was burning brightly. The two preschoolers were shy but friendly, and the woman eager to talk. Unfortunately, she didn't speak either English or French. While she and Batia talked in Russian, Grace found some peppermints in her pocket. With a nod of approval from the grandmother, she offered them to the toddlers and won their hearts. The baby, who was crawling, wrinkled her nose in distaste at the peppermint her brother offered her. Sitting down before Grace, she held out her arms to be picked up. Grace took her on her knee, stroked her fine hair and remembered her brother Howard, the youngest of the family, now twelve. She'd been eleven when he was born, and in a way he'd been her baby, as she'd helped take care of him from infancy. The memory made her eyes prickle with tears. She patted the baby's back and held it close, wanting it to be warm and well.

Chapter Nine

The weather continued cold. On Valentine's Day she received a card from Willem, asking her to meet him on Sunday at Madame Simon's salon. They would go from there to dinner and then to the Recamier Theatre.

"I can't wait to see you," he wrote.

The message warmed her heart but the rest of her was shivering. At the university, no one could talk about anything but the cold snap. After class, she and some friends spent a pleasant hour in a warm café, then braved the minus 8 degree Celsius temperature and hurried home.

Back at 18 rue Cler she found her room so icy that she could see her breath. Hubertine had not lit a fire in her tiny stove, no doubt counting on her being out late. It would take forever to get the room warmed up. Grace went back downstairs, knocked on the door of the salon, and asked if she could come in and sit with the family.

"But of course," said Madame Hamel. Madame De Bussy went out and spoke to Hubertine and an hour later when Grace went upstairs to study, the fire had been lit and the room, while not warm, was at least warmer than the outdoors.

Settling down to work, she was glad she hadn't just put up with the cold of her room. She also felt satisfaction at having gone out and seen people during Willem's absence. He was such a large personality, and she was so crazy about him, that other friends got short shrift.

She was eager to see him, though, and when their Sunday date got off to a bad start she felt terrible. When she arrived at Madame Simon's in Auteuil, he opened the door and gave her a quick kiss in the foyer, then brought her into the salon to join the company. Several people greeted her, but Madame Simon barely acknowledged her presence, though to everyone else there she was bubbly and charming. Why was Madame giving her the cold shoulder? Did she disapprove of her relationship with Willem? Surely she didn't know anything about it, unless she read minds. Furthermore, Madame Simon liked young people and seemed the sort to approve of young love. Right now she was flirting with Dr. Adams, the American-born professor of American history, praising his beret, thin moustache and heavily accented French, telling him it was so nice to meet a francophile.

Mystified and irritated, Grace was glad when Willem wanted to leave. Once out of the house, walking along with him, hand in hand, she forgot Madame Simon, and eagerly listened to his account of England. The editors and publishers were enthusiastic about his articles for the *Cambridge History*, and the book based on his Ph.D. thesis was about to be published. Now that this long-awaited day was approaching, he had mixed feelings about it, including nervousness about his family's reaction. He might not be able to go home again.

"Parents love you no matter what," she told him, as they sat across the table from each other. "I can't imagine my parents rejecting me over anything."

Saying this, she thought of one thing that she might do, accidentally, that would cause them great anguish and embarrassment, though they would love her just the same.

He grasped her hand. "You're so encouraging," he said. "You're my Egeria. Do you know who she was?"

Grace laughed. "Of course I do, King Numet."

Just in case she didn't grasp the reference fully, Willem explained that King Numet, or Numa, elected king by the Roman Senate in 715 B.C., had loved a nymph, Egeria, who taught him to be a wise legislator and prepared him for a battle of wits with Jupiter."

"Egeria sounds wonderful, but please explain exactly what a nymph is," she teased.

"A beautiful nubile young maiden who dances, sings and loves freely. It's a compliment."

"Thank you," she said. Later, in the theatre, with his arm around her, she felt perfectly happy.

That evening she found a letter from her mother on the hall table.

"My own Darling," Mother began,

"Your letters are such a comfort to me because you tell me so wholeheartedly about what you are doing. I love you for telling me all the details about your friendship with Willem. He must have much force of character to have accomplished so much in a mere twenty-six years of life. Bless you, my darling, for saying that if I need you to break it off you would do so, though it would be hard. I don't need you to do that, Dear, to be easy in my mind. Friendships are among life's choicest gifts and if each of you is true to the highest you know, you must just be left to work it all out in your own way.

I always feel that one must not put to sleep one's good judgment, or, shall I say, one's instinct that makes one know whether new friends are true and genuine. Wouldn't it be nice if we were near enough for you to "have him in" to your own home. It must be very pleasant to have such a friend in Paris, especially one with a sense of humour.

You mustn't be too impatient with your landlady who lectures you about staying out late. She thought you were out alone, and after all, she knows more about Paris's untoward side than you do – but not more than my imaginings could conjure up if I let them, which I don't.

I know your natural instincts and common sense will guide you in all of your friendships. When you get home we'll devote an entire day to each other and talk.

I'll send your letter on to Father in Ottawa, as you did not say it was for me alone. I know he would love to read it. It seems to bring you so very near me."

The rest of the letter was family news. Belva was studying hard and looking forward to joining Grace in a couple of months. The boys were all well. Father had received Christmas greetings from across Canada, from friends, acquaintances and strangers, among them a card from the Vancouver councillor who intended to run as an Independent Labour candidate in the 1930 federal election.

Grace pondered the letter. She too wished she could bring Willem home; that paragraph reminded her how far she was from her people. Here she was rootless. She was sure Willem was true and genuine; he revealed both the bad and good about himself. But were they being true to the highest they knew? And what if natural instinct and common sense didn't coincide?

* * *

While walking home from the university the following day, a neat but shabbily dressed middle-aged woman stopped her and asked her for some money.

"I can't find work," she said. "If you give me two francs and fifty pence, that will buy me a lodging for the night."

She looked so gaunt and worn out, and sounded so genuine, that Grace immediately reached into the inner pocket of her coat and gave her the money.

"Thank you!" The woman was close to tears. "You are so kind, Mademoiselle. You are a darling. I will never forget you. Tonight I will pray to Our Lady of Victories for your happiness."

Grace wished her well and walked on, twinging with guilt. The encounter brought her back to earth, after her day in the rarefied atmosphere of the Sorbonne. Lately, if she noticed needy people at all – homeless people, war amputees, hungry children, beggars, people selling their bodies – she had ignored them as just part of the scene, not taking time to feel for them. Somehow she had let herself become desensitized. She was no better than the other foreigners who had flocked to Paris for a rip-roaring good time without much regard for the concerns of the Parisians.

Of course, this wasn't her country, so there was nothing much that she could do. Back in Canada, her father and others in the labour movement were trying to draw the government's attention to social ills. And where was she? Enjoying a year of exceptional privilege. Graduation from her course at the Sorbonne would count a great deal if she were to pursue an advanced degree in French, but honestly, if her goal was to improve her fluency and vocabulary, she could have done so in Canada. Back home, she might do something effective for humanity, though she wasn't yet sure what.

When she met Willem, as prearranged, at the Luxembourg Gardens, she tried to talk to him about the destitute woman and the thoughts the encounter had stirred in her. As they strolled the gravel paths, he listened, then suggested some wine at the restaurant. Sitting across from her, he told her that while her concern for the needy showed her humanity and sensitivity, she was wasting her emotional energy, for there was little one individual could do. "Often the most useful thing we can do for humanity," he said, "is to look after ourselves."

Then, as if he'd dealt with that subject, "case closed", he changed the subject to an area of historical inquiry that interested him. Maybe she could help him with it. While studying in England he'd become aware of a body of correspondence between Lord Carnarvon, Secretary of State for the Colonies, from 1874 to 1878, and the Marquess of Dufferin, who had been Governor General of Canada during that time frame.

As an historian from South Africa, which was relatively new to self-government, he was interested in the process through which other former colonies had passed in attaining dominion status. His impression, from a cursory glance at some of the letters, was that Lord Dufferin had been a master diplomat, performing a remarkable balancing act between the emerging nationalism in Canada, and imperial authority.

In history classes, Grace had studied Canada's progress from colony to nation, but she honestly couldn't remember this particular governor general, or whether he'd been a help or a hindrance. He dated back to the era when her parents had been tiny babies. Vaguely she recalled something about Lord Dufferin supporting Prime Minister John A. Macdonald, a Tory, through a railway corruption scandal in which Macdonald was implicated. After Macdonald and his party were turfed out of office, Dufferin had been very interventionist in the new Liberal administration.

She shared this impression with Willem, adding that Lord Dufferin hadn't been of major importance in Canadian history. Willem's eyebrows arched and he suggested that she didn't fully grasp the importance of the colonial period. Grace's collar began to feel hot. She informed him that research into this correspondence sounded tedious, elitist and possibly irrelevant in the third decade of the twentieth century.

He laughed.

"You've become more argumentative while I was away. Forgive me. To someone in another discipline it probably does sound tiresome. I tend to take refuge in research plans when I feel discouraged."

Instantly she was concerned. "Discouraged? Why?"

"When I got back from England I found a letter from the University of Capetown, turning down my application."

"Well, don't despair," she said. "With your degrees and publications you'll be in demand everywhere. How about Great Britain?"

He shook his head. "An overwhelming number of applicants apply for a very few academic positions there. And in England, I'm an outsider, a colonial, who knows the history and politics of an outpost of Empire and can write a book about it, but who isn't really 'one of them.'"

"What about some other part of the world?"

He sighed. "Well, I'm sure I'd be hired at a university in India, but the political situation there is unstable. If the nationalists secure Home Rule, then English-educated professors like myself won't be wanted."

"How about the American universities?"

"I'll look into them. They seem so remote, though, and so foreign to my experience."

"A man with a Ph.D from a British university would be considered a catch by any Canadian university, and probably any American one too. Also Canadians and Americans are less reserved than the English. You could fit in and make a good life there."

"That's my Egeria," he said, patting her hand. "So encouraging. You're wonderful. You restore my faith in women."

What an odd thing to say! Perhaps it was a joke.

Then out poured a story about a girl in England, a professor's daughter, with whom he'd been "very close". Then, in the middle of last year, she'd broken things off with him to accept a proposal from a young man she had known since childhood.

"Did you want to marry her?" asked Grace.

He hesitated.

"I wanted a lover and a comrade, and thought she wanted the same thing. She knew that my future plans were indefinite. She seemed to be enjoying our time together, but suddenly she wanted a tame civil servant husband who came home every evening at six."

"Well, I guess you wanted different things," Grace said briskly. "I'm sorry for your disappointment but I'm glad she broke things off or we wouldn't be here together now."

"I'm glad of that too," he said.

The waiter chose that moment to interrupt, to Grace's disappointment. She'd been hoping Willem would add that he now knew what real love was and wanted her in his life forever. But the moment passed, and he didn't say it. Nevertheless, the rest of their afternoon together was happy and she enjoyed being with him.

Back home, she wrote in her journal.

"Will he continue to open up to me? I believe I love him but am afraid he doesn't love me with the same intensity. Our days together are numbered unless we come to a decision to stay together and make a plan to that end."

Chapter Ten

Although the examinations were fast approaching, Grace spent the next evening with Willem. At a club, they danced to *You Were Meant for Me; You Brought a New Kind of Love to Me, If I Had You*, and other songs that expressed her hopeful longings. Back at rue Cler, neither wanted to say goodnight, so she took a chance that the household would be in bed, and invited him into the parlour, where he stayed until 1 a.m., sitting on the floor by her feet, talking as she stroked his hair. Somehow they got onto the subject of language teaching, and he talked about teaching Afrikaans, the Dutch dialect that was the lingua franca of South Africa, while in Rhodesia working on his Master's thesis. He spoke of his brother and how they'd always had each other's backs. Grace thought about introducing the topic of their relationship and how far they were going to take it, but hated to interrupt his confidences. She would wait.

When the clock struck one he got to his feet.

"I know you have examinations starting next week and that you need your rest and study time," he said, "but could you spare time to see *La Foule* at the Vieux Colombier?"

Grace was delighted. This experimental theatre, in the sixth arrondissement, was all the rage. Apparently no props, machinery or scenery were used, so that the audience would focus on the play and its author.

"I've been wanting to go there!" she said.   He smiled at her enthusiasm.

"Pick you up at seven o'clock then," he said, and bent to kiss her goodnight.

Grace had another reason for being happy about the theatre date. It wouldn't be like going to the movies, where petting was permissible and where their feelings would be inflamed; it would be decorous and he would do no more than hold her hand. Soon though, she wanted to have that personal talk with him.

"I long for a future with him," she wrote. *"With him by my side I could do anything."*

The theatre evening, which stimulated an animated discussion of the "aesthetics of the bare stage", was their last date for awhile. They agreed not to see each other on the weekend because her examinations started the following week. Two big tests were looming up in her life, she thought. Her examinations at the Sorbonne were the culmination of all her work. The second test was the conversation that she must have with Willem.

The examinations were stressful enough in themselves, and were made more so by the unpredictable scheduling. She wrote Classical Literature from noon to 2:30 one day, then waited until 5:30 p.m. for the professor of Modern Literature to be ready for her oral examination. When he finally summoned her to his office she had a sinking feeling, and although he praised her last essay as one of the best he had ever read, and although she expressed herself well in the oral, she left feeling wrung out like a dishrag.

The following morning, in her oral on Paul Verlaine and the Symbolists, she surprised herself with her fluency. Then she waited around for hours until her oral with Professor Guignebert, who showed up late. At five o'clock, when she was leaving, she found Willem waiting, wondering if she would like to go out to dinner. His kindness touched her heart, and soon they were walking rapidly toward a restaurant in a slight sprinkle of rain. While they were eating, the rain intensified, and by the time they were ready to leave, it was pouring.

"We'll get soaked to the skin if we go to rue Cler now," he told her. "Let's go to my place. It's closer, and everyone else is out this evening."

Huddled together under his umbrella, they leapt over puddles and raced back to rue de Verneuil, slightly damp. He led her to the sofa in the salon and took her in his arms. As raindrops pelted the panes, they kissed and caressed each other.

"When will the family be back?" she whispered.

"Late, probably."

Grace drew away. "We can't risk it."

Sighing, he got up and helped her on with her coat.

Back in her room, she sat up late studying, and arrived at the Sorbonne next morning for her 8:30 exam, only to find the examiner busy with students trying for the higher level diploma. After two and a half nerve-wracking hours going over her notes on Louis XIV's regime, she was called by the examiner and awarded her A. Drained of energy, she arrived back at rue Cler to find Hubertine waiting with hot chocolate, bread and cheese. Upstairs she slept for two hours, then rose and studied phonetics. That was the final test; tomorrow afternoon the results would be announced.

Up at dawn, she reviewed her notes, then went for a walk on the Champ de Mars, admiring the limbs of the Eiffel Tower against the blue sky. The fresh air and sunlight banished her fear, and when the time came to recite for Professor Pernot, she did fine. He said her recitation of *La Chèvre de Monsieur Séguin* was one of the best he'd heard in some time. What a relief! She took out her handkerchief and mopped her face. Now she would receive her diploma with honourable mention.

There was no point in going home, so she decided to go to the Café de Sorbonne. On her way she noticed a fashionably dressed young woman from her class slumped against a wall, sobbing. She went over and touched her shoulder.

"Julia? What's wrong?"

"Everything."

Grace insisted that she join her in the café. There Julia dried her eyes and confided miserably that she had botched her exams. She hadn't studied enough, because she was in love with a young

French Canadian jazz musician, and had been seeing a lot of him. A New York girl, she'd met Luc on holiday in Montreal. Her parents didn't know about their romance and were quite unaware that she'd applied for the scholarship to the Sorbonne in order to join him in Paris.

"They'd like me to marry a stockbroker," she said. "They would hate Luc because he has no money and his clarinet is his life."

"Couldn't you redo the assignments and take the exams over again in a few months?" Grace asked. "Cramming the program into six months isn't for everyone, and your parents probably expect you to be away for the summer anyway." As Julia brightened, Grace found herself offering to help her with some of her essays.

"Would you? You're a dear!"

A couple of hours later they went back to the university to hear the results. First came those for the higher level diploma. Out of 150 candidates, only three received their diplomas, among them Mr. Taylor. The girls then held their breath, for it was time to hear the results for the regular diploma program. Out of 54 candidates, only 26 received their diplomas, with Andrew Hallett coming first. Grace looked across the crowded room, caught his eye, smiled and waved at him. Julia felt better about flunking when she realized that over half the class was in the same boat.

With a score of 88 out of a possible 125, Grace came sixth.

Julia hugged her and cried, "Congratulations!"

Back at rue Cler, Madame Hamel, Hubertine and Edith were waiting for Grace and Andrew with a celebratory snack of hors d'oeuvres, tartes and wine.

"How did you know we would pass?" asked Andrew.

"From the intensity of your studying," said Madame Hamel. When the family heard that Andrew had come first and Grace sixth, they were elated and drank to their brilliant futures. In the middle of this toast there was a knock at the door.

It was Willem. He congratulated both of them, accepted a glass of wine, and invited them to see *The Foolish Virgin* at the Avenue Bosquet cinema, his treat. Andrew thanked him but said no; he intended to go to bed and sleep for days.

"How did you know I'd passed?" Grace asked Willem as they sat waiting for the film to start.

"I had confidence in you," he said. "Also, I ran into Taylor and he told me."

Then, as the lights went down, he put his arm around her and with his lips against her ear, whispered, "You are wonderful."

She'd have preferred three other little words, but felt confident that he would speak them soon, and she snuggled close to him.

Chapter Eleven

Back home, Grace slept for twelve hours. She awoke feeling grubby, and decided that she couldn't face another bird bath in the washbasin, so she went downstairs in her robe and asked Hubertine for the tin tub and some hot water, in front of Madame Hamel, who was in the kitchen at the time.

"Now that the coal is almost gone and spring is coming, Hubertine," the old woman said, "you must soon clean out the big bathtub in the *salle de bains*. We'll all need baths soon. Grace, are you sure you want the tin tub when it's still so chilly?"

"Yes, please."

Grace promised to bail out the tub and put the used water down the toilet at the end of the hall. She carried the *bain sabot* upstairs while Hubertine brought a bucket of water, and returned, grumbling, with a second one. First Grace washed her hair, then she sat in the tub with her legs over the side and sponged her body. She emerged cleaner than she would have with a basin wash. Towelling her hair dry, she told herself to be thankful that the house had a normal toilet. Old Paris apartment buildings in the poorer section often had squat toilets on each landing, with cleated cement treads where you put your feet when you squatted over the hole.

She tidied up her room, because she was expecting the two Kays and a new girl, Tess, who had just moved into their lodgings. They arrived with a bag of tangerines, bubbling over with plans for their upcoming trip to Italy. Tess, an American, was soon to start the Course in French Civilization, and eager to see some sights first. Her priorities were Chartres Cathedral and Versailles, both involving train trips out of the city. The Kays were busy getting ready for Italy so Grace offered to accompany Tess.

After they had left, Julia arrived with her failing-grade essays in a satchel. Grace glanced through them and thought that the main problem was carelessness about accents and lack of thoroughness. Julia wasn't interested in studying, though, preferring to talk about her jazz musician. They loved each other, but he hadn't a sou, and had no idea when, if ever, he would be going back to Canada.

As Julia chatted, Grace couldn't help but compare this relationship to her own with Willem. She got the impression that Julia and her musician were already intimate and that the practical details of that closeness posed no problem, as Julia seemed mainly concerned about whether her parents would cut off her allowance. Grace urged Julia to repeat the Course in French Civilization, to have a reason for staying in Paris to give her relationship with Luc more time.

"Maybe you can convince Luc to come back and play jazz in North America," she said. If only Willem would choose North America too.

That evening Willem took her to a Polish restaurant featuring Hollywood-style posters about gold miners in Canada. "Completely unauthentic," she said. Willem talked about the common European misconception of Africa as all sultry jungle. When he talked about lions on the veldt, Grace thought that he was like a lion himself, golden and splendid.

Then he changed the subject. "Now that your exams are over and my work largely completed, we should see as much of France as we can. Have you been to Saint Cloud?"

She shook her head.

"It makes a good day trip, they say."

He particularly wanted to see this village, nine miles from the heart of Paris, because it was the site of Napoleon Bonaparte's coup d'état, his seizure of power from the Directory. He was also interested in visiting the park around the ruins of the Chateau de Saint Cloud; the chateau had been destroyed in the Franco-Prussian War.

"Let's go tomorrow," he suggested and she agreed.

In the hazy weak sunshine of the March morning, she met Willem on the Carrousel Bridge and together they took the tram to Saint Cloud. Though the air was nippy, Grace enjoyed the open air market. Gradually the sun melted the ice on the puddles, which seemed like a happy omen. They strolled around admiring the villas with odd names, and the porcelain cats on the housetops. Next they explored the church and park, and had lunch in a quaint restaurant. When they were returning to the transit station, the sky darkened. Grace suggested that they take a short cut across the rails and try to get to the bank of the Seine before the rain began, and Willem agreed. They had just started out when they heard shouts. Halting, they turned and saw an employee frantically waving his arms at them.

"The rails are electrically charged!" he bellowed. "If so much as your coat touches them, you'll be electrocuted!"

Grace froze.

"We've gone so far we might as well go on," said Willem, taking her hand. On they went, very cautiously. Finally they made it to the other side. Once safe, Grace sagged against Willem, thankful to be alive. In his arms, she felt his body quivering, tensed for action.

"We defied death!" he exclaimed, laughing. Grace found his reaction amazing. She was still shaking, and felt extremely lucky to be alive.

Exhausted, she trudged back to the seventh arrondissement, leaning on him. The sky was threatening, the walk interminable. Willem suggested that they go to his place first, as rue de Verneuil was nearer than rue Cler. Once they had their second wind, he would see Grace home.

"Tonight the family is meeting the Madagascar suitor again," he said. "They'll be back late."

Once there, Grace collapsed into an armchair while Willem made a fire. Then he stretched out on the floor in front of the hearth, putting a sofa cushion under his head. After a while he held out his arms to her.

"Come over here and get warm."

Grace sat on the floor beside him. He shifted his head and rested it on her lap.   "That's more comfortable," he said, with a happy sigh, smiling up at her. She began to stroke his hair.

"What a terrific day!" he remarked. "You're the perfect comrade, with a real sense of adventure. You can't be comfortable sitting here, though. You should stretch out too."

He sat up, put his arms around her and drew her down beside him. Her body, though tired, seemed to reach out to him with a will of its own. It was heaven to lie so near him. Then he grew hard against her and his hand made an unambiguous move. Grace drew away and sat up.

"I'm sorry. We can't," she said. "We're not prepared."

"Oh, Grace, I'll be careful."

"I can't take that chance." She stood up and straightened her clothes.

He propped himself up on one elbow. "I thought you wanted to."

"I like being near you, yes, but we never had that talk."

"Don't you trust me?" He sounded hurt.

"It isn't about trust. I trust your good intentions, but it's playing with fire."

"You underestimate me," he said, looking sad.

"I shouldn't be here. I'll go home." She got up and reached for her coat on the back of a chair. "No, you don't have to come with me. I'll be fine."

She thought he would insist on seeing her home, but he didn't.

Back at rue Cler, Andrew's door was closed, and she was glad, because she didn't want to talk. She slumped in her easy chair, feeling like a fool. Stupid for not anticipating what might happen if they were alone together. Cowardly for not having initiated the contraceptive conversation immediately after his return from England. Foolishly shy, for not daring to ask the advice of her women friends. Weak-willed for having lain down beside him and letting things get as far as they had this afternoon.

But she didn't regret saying no. Willem wanted the kind of woman who could love freely with no strings, and although it was painful to admit it, she wasn't that kind of woman. Maybe someday she'd evolve into one, but she wasn't there yet.

She had no regrets about getting involved with him; she couldn't have resisted any more than a moth could turn its back on a flame. She knew now how it felt to have every atom of her body come alive. Loving him had forced her to confront real, adult feelings and problems, even though she wasn't dealing with them very well.

It would be very hard to lose Willem, but then, she'd never really had him. She loved him; he liked her. She'd wanted a soulmate, but he was not exactly that. Brilliant, personable, articulate, with a great sense of humour, he was wonderful, yet he lacked something fundamental. Empathy, she guessed.

She lay down and her exhaustion took over. Then, at 3 a.m., her eyes flew open and she sat up, thinking, "It can't be all over between us. It just can't."

Empathy could be learned, couldn't it? Love could grow. He needed her as a confidante. Closed up in himself, he would never become the great man he could be, and she could help him with that.

At 7 a.m. she changed her mind again. The modern girl, she knew, was supposed to thrive on casual relationships, but she wasn't a modern girl, so it was unkind of her to keep tormenting Willem. The only solution was to stop seeing him. If he contacted her again, she would have to break things off with him.

The thought was excruciating. How could she live without him? Maybe it would help to see more of her other friends.

The opportunity to do so presented itself at breakfast. Andrew, at the table, was eating nothing. Sipping tea made him wince.

"Toothache?" she asked.

He nodded. He had cracked a tooth and was going to the dentist that morning.

"Would you like me to go with you?"

"Would you?" He looked so grateful that she was glad she'd offered.

The extraction was tricky, bloody and painful. Andrew emerged into the waiting room dopey, with a red-stained handkerchief pressed to his mouth. Grace summoned a taxi to take them home. Leaning on her, he made it up the steps and into the foyer.

Madame Hamel emerged.

"Oh, you poor boy!" she exclaimed. "I'll send Hubertine for some ice. Here, come into the kitchen and sit down before you climb the stairs."

Turning to Grace, she pointed to a letter on the hall table.

"Dr. Van Aarden hand-delivered this letter while you were out. He looked upset." The old lady chuckled. "Apparently both men in your little ménage are suffering."

Grace stopped in her tracks and just stared at her. Concern for Andrew, confusion over Willem, now this remark! She knew the phrase "ménage à trois" and all that it implied, and she was incensed.

Just then Hubertine stuck her head out and summoned them to lunch.

Grace picked up her letter and looked coldly at Madame Hamel.

"I'm not hungry, thanks," Grace stated. "Andrew, if you're not eating and want to try going upstairs, I'll follow right behind you."

He nodded, with a grateful look.

In her room she opened Willem's letter. It was an invitation to the movies the following evening. No endearments, no apologies, no reference to the previous afternoon. Its casualness exasperated her. She wrote him a brief note explaining that she and Tess were going to Chartres and Versailles that day and that she would be too tired to go out in the evening. She would put it in the mail later.

As she left to meet Tess at the Montparnasse Station the following morning, to embark on the sixty mile train trip to Chartres, the sky was a grim slate-grey. Leaving Paris, the train went through the zone of slums where the poorest Parisians subsisted. Awareness of human need descended on Grace like a damp wool sweater. The hour ride to Chartres, and Tess's high spirits lifted her gloom, however, and once in the medieval town, the fresh air and the climb to the thirteenth century cathedral made her feel better. Inside, the blue stained glass windows, the unique shade of "Chartres blue" took her breath away.

But they had happened upon a funeral. They sat silently at the back, observing the catafalque, the mourners, the pomp of the Mass, the sad but majestic music. It was a unique experience but a somber one. Tess summed things up when she said it was a joy to see the cathedral, but a "sober joy."

"Life is fleeting," thought Grace. "Those with courage seize the day."

At lunch they tried the local delicacy, soft crushed cheese wrapped in chestnut leaves. Then they caught another train, to Versailles. Tess gasped with amazement at the magnificence of the palace and couldn't seem to take enough photographs. Grace had been wondering if her initial dislike of the place had stemmed from fatigue and sensory overload during last summer's whirlwind tour. But again she was filled with distaste at the extravagance of the *ancien régime* at the expense of the common people. For her, the best parts of the afternoon involved nature, a white swan swimming in an icy lake, birds chirping in the naked trees, and a crimson sunset through the woods behind the Trianon. These simple things, and Tess's pleasure in the excursion, made Grace feel that it had been a worthwhile day.

As part of her resolve to keep busy, she set out the following day to visit Batia. On her way through the Latin Quarter, floats of young people in medieval costumes passed by her. It was the time of the annual arts ball. She'd heard that the students danced through the streets nude, except for masks and body paint, and, at Batia's, asked if that was true.

"Absolutely," said Batia, without a trace of a smile. She pointed to a tigress mask hanging on the wall. "I'm wearing that mask and painting myself gold."

Was she joking? Grace couldn't tell.

"And how is Dr. Van Aarden?" Batia inquired.

"All right, I guess. I haven't been seeing him lately."

"Oh."

Batia showed Grace her sculpture, which was coming along. Over tea, she remarked that Grace's time in France was drawing to an end and that she would miss her. With a pang, Grace realized that what she said was true.

"I'd like us to keep in touch, but I don't know where I'll be next year, and perhaps you don't know where you'll be," Batia continued. "So why don't you give me your parents' address and I'll give you my mother's."

Grace felt honoured at this suggestion. As she wrote out her parents' address in Winnipeg she asked Batia if she would like to meet her sister, who would be arriving in a few weeks.

"I'd love to. We must all go out together."

As part of Grace's effort to forget Willem, she called upon Julia the following afternoon to help her with her assignments, but Julia didn't feel like studying on such a fine day, and proposed a walk in the Luxembourg Gardens instead. There was a hint of spring in the air, and the park was busy. Every bench was occupied, so they strolled and talked about Luc. He'd asked Julia to move in with him. Should she?

Just as Julia asked her opinion, Grace spotted a bench that was being vacated by a stout mannish woman, her petite dark companion in a frilly dress, and their little dog. The girls rushed to take their spot.

"I want your honest opinion," Julia persisted. "Should I move in with him?"

She was living in an upscale apartment belonging to wealthy friends of her parents, who would soon be returning to Paris after wintering in the south of France. Luc lived with some fellow musicians in a crowded attic which Julia described as a dump. With her allowance she could rent something decent, but would that hurt Luc's pride?

"Moving in together is a big decision," Grace said. "Have you considered the possible consequences?"

"Oh, I won't tell my parents or their friends," Julia said firmly. Then, glancing at Grace's face, she laughed.

"Oh, you're talking about me getting in a jam. I'm not worried about falling *enciente*. Back in New York I got myself fixed up at a women's clinic. I'm more worried that my parents will pay me a surprise visit and then all hell will break loose, and they'll cut off the money."

Grace didn't know what to advise, but it didn't matter, because she knew that Julia was just using her as a sounding board.

Over the next few days she kept busy with social activities. She and Andrew went to a concert featuring movements from *Tristan and Iseult* and Beethoven's Ninth Symphony. The music spiralled heavenward, taking her sadness with it.

Another diversion was the new boarder at 18 rue Cler. Madame De Bussy had shuffled the sleeping arrangements to accommodate the new girl until Andrew and Grace vacated their rooms at the end of March. Now the three De Bussy women were crowded into the one bedroom.

Gunvar, the newcomer, was Norwegian, tall, blonde and beautiful, the sort of girl who often considered herself superior because of her looks. But Gunvar turned out to be down-to-earth, friendly, and eager for advice about the Course in French Civilization. She was delighted when Grace suggested a walk in the Bois de Bologne and pleased when she offered to show her around the Sorbonne. In late afternoon they arrived back at rue Cler to learn that Willem had been at the house looking for Grace.

"Your fiancé?" inquired Gunvar.

"No, just a friend."

When Willem reappeared fifteen minutes later, her vow to stay away from him evaporated. She invited him into the salon where they could talk privately. There, he apologized for what had happened, or almost happened, after their return from Saint Cloud, and asked her to go with him to a restaurant where they could talk. Grace got her coat.

They found a quiet little place with unintrusive waiters, and chose a table in a secluded corner. They ordered, and then his blue eyes met her hazel ones across the table. He leaned toward her.

"Again, I am sorry about the other night. You stir such strong desire in me. Believe me, if one thing had led to another no harm would have come to you. No consequences. But I know now that you're not ready."

"I have strong feelings for you, too, but we haven't talked about my concerns."

"I've been waiting for you to open that conversation."

"All right. May I begin by telling you two experiences from my childhood?"

He nodded.

"When I was little my mother often had young women from the mission to help with the younger children and do light housekeeping. Each of them left rather suddenly, and a new one would come in her place. For a while I didn't notice this coming and going. I was just a little kid, and we always had a lot of visitors from among the mission's clientele. When I was around seven, though, I became attached to one young woman named Emma, and when she disappeared I asked where she had gone. My mother said she had left to have her baby. I hadn't realized that Emma was expecting one, and asked about the baby's daddy. Mother said he wasn't around because he wasn't ready to have a family."

She paused.

Willem raised his eyebrows. "Nowadays," he said, "Emma and her beau would be better informed and there wouldn't be a baby."

"Who knows? Maybe so. Now, for the second experience. I have vivid recollections of a talk about love and marriage that Father gave to young people during his days as a pastor. Nothing was more worthy of celebration, he said, than a young man and woman falling in love, becoming life partners and establishing a home together. But growing boys and girls, he said firmly, were not ready to form a home."

"Well, not everyone is, for various reasons," said Willem. "But I'm glad you shared your memories with me because I understand you better now. I too know the fetters of religious training. Sometimes I fall into the thought-mode of the fundamentalist pastors of my boyhood and feel guilty for no logical reason."

He reached for her hand. "Whatever you decide about the nature of our relationship will be all right with me. And I promise not to lead us into temptation."

"I have another anecdote, if you can bear with me," said Grace. Then, without mentioning any names, she told him about Julia and Luc. He didn't know them, so she was not betraying a confidence.

"I'm not as sophisticated as she is, and I haven't been as resourceful as she has," she told Willem. "I thought my education here would be confined to the French language. I never dreamed it would extend to intimate matters. I'm a foreigner here in a country where birth control is against the law. I don't know of any women's clinic."

"That's no problem," he said, his eyes twinkling. "I can be resourceful for both of us."

She gripped his hand with relief. He was wonderful. He understood completely.

"I thought things were over between us," she said, "so I've filled up my calendar, to try to stop thinking of you."

He grinned. "Has it worked?"

"Of course it hasn't. But I do want to go out with my friends again before it's time to say goodbye."

"Naturally you do. I have farewells to say, too. But if you have any free time, pencil me in on your calendar and I'll come at your command. Now, just for tonight, let's forget about goodbyes and enjoy each other's company."

That night they walked by the Seine, with lights rippling in the water and the moon beaming down at them. If only time would stand still, she thought, like the scene on the Grecian urn in Keats's poem. It was too soon to know if they would have a future together. Nothing was decided yet. They'd write. But a little voice in her head said, "It's going to end soon."

Her mother had urged her not to worry about the future or review the past, but to live in the present, and Grace tried to do so during the next few days. She saw the two Kays at the Foyer; spent a morning in the Tuileries Garden with Brandy; took Gunvar to the Sorbonne and out for coffee at the café *Place de Sorbonne*. With Andrew, Taylor and a couple of Taylor's friends, she went to see *Prince Igor* at the Russian Opera.

Then a note arrived from Willem. The author's copies of his book had arrived, hot off the presses, and he wanted her to see it. She hurried over to his place. There, he handed her a copy bound in a rich wine-coloured cloth.

"Another tome for the boredom of students," he said, but he glowed with pride. She raised the book to her nose, inhaled its fresh print fragrance, and stroked the gold lettering that spelled out the title and his name.

"What a wonderful achievement!" she said.

She turned to the introduction by a well-known historian, then to the dedication to his parents, next to the acknowledgements where he had thanked his mentor and expressed gratitude to his brother, who had helped him in various ways.

Turning to the first chapter, she read the opening paragraphs aloud. It was as if she were speaking in Willem's voice. Amazingly, he had avoided academic jargon and had written an informative, serious, scholarly work in the same friendly tone in which he talked. Standing on tiptoe, she pressed a kiss on his cheek.

"It's perfect!" she said.

"I'll admit it, I'm awfully proud of it."

Carefully he put it back in the box with nine others. Grace had thought he was going to autograph a copy and give it to her, but no matter. Others who had helped him had a greater claim than she on a free copy. It was enough, really, to share his happiness.

"Let me take you out to dinner out to celebrate," she said. "Tonight it's on me."

On the metro, en route, she wondered jokingly if the other passengers sensed that they were in the presence of greatness. He laughed and embraced her right there in front of everyone, despite her protests.

"When in Paris, do as the Parisians do," he declared. That night, when he kissed her goodnight at her door he whispered that she was a beautiful girl with a beautiful soul.

"And you are too – I mean, you have a beautiful soul."

He laughed. "Till tomorrow."

The next day, when they met for coffee and croissants, he took the *Times* of London from under his arm, and opened it to a glowing review of his book. The icing on the cake, he said, was that a peer of the realm had actually read part of the book in the House of Lords during a debate on Britain's Africa policy.

Grace was delighted for him. She also shared some news of her own. Charles was spending his spring vacation in Germany and wanted her to meet him on April 5th in Heidelburg.

Willem's face lit up.

"I want to do some research in Heidelburg. Let's go there together."

Grace took a deep breath. "We could go there on the first of April, and spend a few days on our own before meeting up with Charles."

His eyes widened. "Are you saying ..."

"Yes. I'm thinking of throwing my bonnet over the windmill. Isn't that what you Dutch people say?"

"Is this to celebrate my book being published?" he inquired mischievously.

She blushed. "Yes, partly."

"Wonderful. Are you finished your coffee? Then, let's go for a walk while I let this stupendous news sink in."

They strolled arm in arm in the Bois de Bologne. Whenever a passer-by glanced at them, Grace wondered if they could read on her face her excitement at what lay ahead. Then Willem drew her under an old tree in new leaf, and covered her face with kisses.

Later, alone in her room, she got out her journal.

"He is too great a man for me," she wrote, "but maybe one day my achievements will be in harmony with his."

Chapter Twelve

The following evening, after dinner, Grace went up to her room and changed, and came down in her best dress.

"Where is the Netherlander taking you tonight?" inquired Madame Hamel.

"Tonight I'm going out with Andrew. We're off to the Opera, to see *The Magic Flute*."

"Ah, Mozart!" the old woman said, as Andrew, in his good suit, came downstairs.

The evening was fantastic, the music graceful and melodious. Afterwards they had coffee with friends and didn't get back to 18 rue Cler until 2:00 a.m. To her surprise, when they said goodnight, Andrew bowed and kissed her hand.

Next morning, when Grace was in her room looking through her clothes, he knocked on the door.

"Do you want to sort through the photos we've taken this year?" he asked in his flawless French. "If there are any of mine you want, I'll give you the negatives and we can have prints made before we leave."

"What a good idea!" Grace gathered up her dresses from her bed and they spread out the snapshots. As they relived memories, sadness came over her. She would miss Andrew. He'd been a perfect friend, unfailingly kind and considerate. He'd never said anything to wound or shock her.

They discussed their immediate plans. Andrew's friends in Nice had arranged for him to visit friends of theirs in Switzerland. Grace mentioned that she would be meeting Charles in Heidelburg, and then later would meet up with her sister, who was leaving Canada for Europe on March 28.

"I'd like to see Charles again," said Andrew. "Perhaps I could accompany you to Heidelburg and the three of us could go sightseeing. Then I'd go on to Switzerland later."

Grace froze.

"Oh, my God!" she thought. "I'm a character in a French farce."

Her mind raced. Nothing could interfere with her plans with Willem. Then she spoke.

"Charles hasn't been definite about his plans," she lied, "so I don't know yet exactly when and where we'll be meeting. I'd hate to let his uncertainty spoil your holiday plans. Since everything is up in the air, probably you should stick to your original plan and go to Switzerland."

As she spoke, she was amazed to see his face break into a grin.

"You've violated our pact, Grace!" he exclaimed. "You're speaking English."

She gasped. "So I am."

"Well, school is out, so I guess we can go back to our mother tongue."

Now she stared at him. In French, he had no Australian accent, but in English he sounded very Aussie, and comical to her ears, for she had expected his English to be like that of the British royal family.

"You have a perfect Parisian accent when you speak French," she said.

"In French you sound very polished, too," he told her. "The way you say some words in English, like 'aboot' for 'about' is very Geordie. There must be many Scots in Canada. "

Grace was stunned. Then she giggled.

"An accent? Moi?"

"Maybe we should go back to speaking French," he suggested.

"Let's. Do you want to see that musical about Napoleon III?"

"Yes. I want to absorb some culture before I leave Paris."

Before I leave Paris. Her throat constricted. Fumbling for her handkerchief, she wondered why, if she had to fall in love with somebody, it couldn't have been Andrew, so good and considerate. But the special spark just wasn't there.

"Please don't cry," he said, in French, "or you'll set me off."

"I'm sorry." She dabbed at her eyes. "You've been a wonderful friend, Andrew. I'll never forget you."

"Nor I, you," he said. "Now, I want to say something. From the moment we met, I've been attracted to you, and not just as a friend. But our homes are a world apart. I knew I'd be going back to Australia and you to Canada, and it didn't seem right to start something. That's why I've never made a move – though I've wanted to."

Grace was stunned. If he was speaking honestly, then he was a model of self-control. "You're so wise and sensible, and such a good person!" she exclaimed. "Shall we write, after we go back to our separate worlds?"

"I'd like that."

She wondered, silently, "Why can't a girl love the one who is best for her?"

* * *

That evening she accompanied Gunvar to the British Festival at the Foyer for an evening of charades and English songs. Singing along, her throat got hoarse, and that night her nose was so plugged up that she didn't sleep. Nevertheless, the following evening, she went with Andrew and Taylor to the Napoleon III musical, wishing she were with Willem, who, as an historian, would have enjoyed it. Taylor jokingly complimented her on her sexy voice, and she told him it was merely husky.

That night when she and Andrew walked home it was under a moon so clear it might have been part of a stage set. If only she were with Willem! But she would be seeing him the following evening, meeting him at the Odeon at 7 p.m. for dinner, then a talking picture, the very first either had seen.

The following day she woke up sweating; a cold was coming on. But it was just a common cold and if she went about her plans, she might shake it.

That didn't happen; she arrived at the restaurant feeling worn out and plagued with chills and found Willem in a buoyant mood. He had been to Cook's, the travel agent, and had made arrangements for their trip.

She smiled approvingly "It sounds as if you've taken care of everything."

"I have, and I will," he said meaningfully.

She shivered.

"What's wrong?" he asked. "Second thoughts?"

"No, I'm very pleased at the prospect. I'm just tired."

He frowned. "Don't tell me that timidity and Puritanism are taking over?"

"No, I'm just not feeling very well. I'm getting a cold."

He sighed. "There's always something."

She lost her patience. "It's a common cold, Willem. It takes three days to get it, three days to have it, three days to get over it. It will be long gone by the time we leave for Germany. Someday even you may catch a cold, so instead of talking about timidity, try to show some understanding."

"Forgive me," he said, summoning the waiter. "I'm feeling impatient and frustrated."

They ate in unaccustomed silence, and in the theatre they sat up straight, decorously holding hands. Grace didn't mind watching the movie, for a change, as she was eager to see what a "talkie" was like. She wondered if Willem was keeping his distance to avoid catching her cold. She missed his arm around her shoulders.

Afterwards, she wanted badly to go home and lie down, but when he suggested coffee, she thought she should make an effort, and said yes. They agreed that the talking picture had been wonderfully lifelike and that "talkies" were the wave of the future, but she could tell that he was still irritated with her. When they'd finished he said he'd walk her to the metro.

"You're not seeing me back to rue Cler?"

"I need to be by myself. Take the metro; you'll be fine."

She didn't feel fine, she felt weak, and it was 1:30 a.m. She was too proud to admit how awful she felt, though, and didn't want to be called timid again. When they reached the metro station he tried to embrace her, but she drew away. She got back safely to 18 rue Cler on her own and fell into bed.

Overnight her cold worsened. She got up for breakfast but felt queasy and went back to bed, where she dozed, feverishly dreaming – mostly happy dreams in which Willem played a major role. For the next while she was vaguely aware of anxious faces looking down at her. Gunvar put cold cloths on her forehead; Hubertine brought her boiled rice; Andrew sat beside her, gave her sips of water and held her hand. Finally she moved out of her dream world into the real world again and learned that three days had passed. She decided that she needed fresh air.

She asked Andrew to take her to a small sidewalk café around the corner, and, frowning, he agreed. Leaning on his arm, she ventured out, wobbling and dazzled by the sunlight. By the time they got to the café she was glad to sit down and let Andrew go inside to order hot chocolate. Closing her eyes, she leaned back and let the sun warm her face.

"Grace?"

Was she dreaming again? She opened her eyes. There stood Willem.

"You look awful," he said, sitting down beside her. "You should be in bed. What are you doing here?"

"Getting fresh air. What are *you* doing here?"

"I was on my way to see you."

Andrew came out then, followed by the waiter carrying the hot chocolate on a tray.

"Hello, Willem," he said politely. Willem greeted him and they shook hands.

"You and Grace probably have things to talk about," Andrew said. "I'll leave you two alone, but Willem, you must keep her out only a short time, and walk with her back to rue Cler."

"Oh, Andrew, please stay," she implored.

"Yes, do. Sit down, have your chocolate," Willem insisted.

Andrew shook his head. "It's yours if you want it. See you later, Grace."

Smiling cheerfully, he set off down the street.

Grace squinted after him. "There goes a gentleman," she remarked.

"How do you feel?" Willem asked, taking her hand.

"Tired and dull. According to Madame Hamel, I had *la grippe*. Mental fogginess goes with it. Supposedly it will pass."

"I should have seen you home the other night." He sounded contrite. "I didn't realize how ill you were. Also, I think you had things you wanted to ask me."

"Right now I'm too weary and discouraged to remember."

"Don't make any big decisions until you feel better," he said.

Tears welled up in her eyes. She leaned toward him. "I truly want to go on that journey with you. These past few days I've had the sweetest dreams about you. By your side, I could help you achieve your goals, and you could help me become all that I can be."

He started to speak, hesitated, then stroked her hand.

"Sometimes I'm convinced that you're the woman for my life," he said, "but my future is so up in the air. Also, we've gotten to know each other in a rather artificial situation. This holiday is our opportunity to get to know each other in every way."

She nodded. He was being honest and patient. She tried a sip of hot chocolate but was put off by its sweetness.

"I should be home in bed," she said. "May I lean on you?"

"Of course."

Supported by his strong arm, she made it home with no trouble.

"If you're well enough, how about dinner tomorrow evening, to go over our plans," he suggested, as he helped her over the threshold.

"If I'm well enough," she said.

"I'll come to your place and see how you are."

"All right. No, don't kiss me. I'm full of germs."

"I have a strong constitution," he said, ignoring her protest.

Chapter Thirteen

Grace spent the following day resting and writing in her journal. She reconsidered her feeling that Willem lacked empathy, because he'd been so kind yesterday. She wrote:

"He wants a courageous, intelligent woman comrade and he's open to the possibility that I may be that person. He doesn't want to make promises that he can't keep. He's looking at the big picture, being realistic."

What would be the next step after their tryst in Heidelburg? It depended on how well their romantic interlude went. She prayed that he would be a good teacher and she a fast learner. Or perhaps instinct would take over and all of her secret imaginings would culminate in a marvellous experience. Sometimes she burned with so much longing for him that she thought there would be no afterward, that they would together burst into flames and their ashes rise to heaven.

At the restaurant that evening, they reviewed their plans. Willem had reserved them a room in a secluded guesthouse as Herr Doktor and Frau Van Aarden.

"I have our tickets and everything else we'll need," he said meaningfully. "What's the news on Charles?"

"He has reserved a room for me at the guesthouse where he'll be staying, but he expects me five days after you and I arrive in Heidelburg," she replied.

"Good. And after our honeymoon in Heidelburg we'll meet him and the three of us can explore the city."

She raised her glass. "To our adventure."

"To our adventure," echoed Willem, and they drank.

Grace was thinking about what would come after that. It was all rather vague. She would sightsee with Charles, then return to France to meet Belva. Meanwhile Willem would visit some German universities, as provided for by his scholarship. Then he would return to Paris to await replies from history departments and there, at some point, they would meet again. By then he might have been offered a position at a North American university, maybe in a city that was a short train journey from Winnipeg.

"I wonder if Charles will suspect anything," she mused. "There's an old saying that two things cannot be hidden – love, and a cold."

Willem laughed. "He won't care. If anything, he'll be glad his sister has abandoned her Puritanism."

"I don't know what Mother and Father would say about this."

Then she turned red, because she had spoken this thought aloud.

William looked quizzically at her. "Do they need to know?"

"No, and I hope that if Charles figures things out he'll be discreet. They're generally advanced in their thinking, but maybe not about this."

Having a thrilling secret made it easier for Grace to say goodbye to her friends. She said she was leaving to meet her brother in Germany. Brandy was leaving Paris for Denmark, the Kays for Italy. Grace paid a final visit to Batia's studio, where they admired Grace's head cast in bronze.

"When you are famous and a catalogue of your work is published," Grace told her, "I'll boast to people that I knew you back when, and that I am *Pensiveness*."

"And when you are famous, I too will boast that I knew you," Batia said."Here, I want you to have these."

She handed Grace the preliminary sketches she had made.

"Me, famous? It will never happen."

"You will make your mark," Batia insisted. "You just haven't found the right vocation yet. Now, no tears. We'll always be in each other's hearts."

Grace wanted to say goodbye to Julia, and wish her well, and was pleased when a note came from her inviting her to tea at her parents' friends' apartment. There, with sparkling eyes, she said that she and Luc were moving into a two room apartment together on June 1st. When Grace confided her plans with Willem, Julia hugged her and congratulated her.

"Are you nervous?" Julia asked.

"A little, and I wish I felt more alluring. You know the hot water situation at 18 rue Cler. My hair badly needs washing."

"Wash it here!" Julia exclaimed. "You can't go away for an erotic holiday with dirty hair!"

Immediately she led Grace to the modern, well-appointed bathroom and told her to take her time. Grace luxuriated in gallons of warm water, scented shampoo and soap and thick towels. As they towelled her hair dry, the girls talked about the event that had recently occupied the news and thrown France into mourning. Maréchal Foch, the Great War hero who had stopped the German advance on Paris in the second Battle of the Marne, and who had come up with the strategy that had won the war for the Allies in 1918, was dead.

The ladies at 18 rue Cler could talk of nothing else but the loss of this national treasure. They explained to Grace that Foch had wanted peace terms that would have made it impossible for Germany to pose a threat to France again. He'd wanted the Rhine River to be the boundary between Germany and the rest of Europe, but at the Versailles peace conference, Clemenceau, Lloyd George, and Woodrow Wilson had overruled him. Of the Versailles Treaty, Foch had said, "This is not a peace. It is an armistice for twenty years."

Grace was sure that Monsieur Fuchs in Cinq-Mars would agree.

Julia didn't know what to make of this prediction of another war with Germany, but didn't think the United States would get involved in another European War; public opinion was very isolationist.

When the girls said farewell they exchanged addresses. Walking home, Grace thought ruefully that Julia would probably never get around to writing.

The next day, Grace, Gunvar and Andrew set out for the Arc de Triomphe to see the field marshall's catafalque, but couldn't get anywhere near it because of the crowds. Back home she was touched by the ladies' grief for their hero, and mentioned it, and Foch's prediction in a letter to her father.

The day before the state funeral, Grace devoted herself to Andrew. First they went to Notre Dame Cathedral to buy souvenirs. Then they had their photos taken. Then, since he'd never been to *La Coupole*, they sat sipping coffee for a couple of hours and discussed his vacation plans. That evening they went together to the Comédie Française to see Racine's *Athalie*. Grace felt that the music expressed perfectly all the hope and longing in her heart. It swept her away.

"Magnificent," Andrew remarked, on the way home. "Here in Paris I've had a cultural feast that I'll never experience again in my life."

Next morning the entire household at 18 rue Cler got up at 6:30 a.m. to get good seats on the sidewalk on the Esplanade to see Maréchal Foch's funeral procession. The crowds wept and cheered. Several princes and heads of state were in the cortège; they included Prince Albert of Belgium; Prince Louis of Monaco, and Edward, Prince of Wales. The one who interested Grace most was the Polish president, the great composer Paderewski.

On Wednesday, there was another farewell ceremony, this one harder for Grace to bear. The ladies put on a gala luncheon in honour of Andrew, who was leaving that afternoon. They toasted his health and prosperity. Young Edith presented him with handkerchiefs on which she had embroidered his initials, and when he thanked her she burst into tears. After the meal, Grace gave him a quick hug goodbye, then rushed out of the house so as not to see him leave. Later, she returned, went to her room and slept for four hours.

On March 30, a radiant spring day, Grace and Willem met for lunch. They were leaving on April 1st. She felt shy, and when he overturned his wine glass she realized that he was nervous too. They agreed to spend the following day apart, tying up loose ends.

On March 31st she slept late, then went walking in the Bois de Bologne with Gunvar. They made plans to meet again in a few weeks' time when Grace was back in Paris with her sister. That afternoon, Grace finished her packing and that evening Hubertine served one of her favourite dishes, *boeuf bourguinon*. The ladies were interested in Grace's holiday plans with her brother and sister. They asked to be remembered to Charles and looked forward to meeting Belva.

That night, too excited to sleep, she turned to her French journal and discovered only three pages left.

"I'm going to end this book," she wrote, "by being as honest as I have throughout. What is my future with Willem? Lately he has been all I could dream of. At other times he has made me feel that, to be the one for him, I must develop infinitely more as a person . One thing is certain, I have matured from contact with him. He has been instrumental in my transition from a schoolgirl to a woman. He has the potential to be a great man – perhaps he is one already – and I am proud to have met him and proud that he has shared his thoughts, feelings and triumphs with me. Whether or not we have a future together beyond these next four days, I know I am going to enjoy our adventure."

Chapter Fourteen

When her Grace's taxi pulled up at the station, Willem was waiting for her, and lifted her suitcase as if it were full of feathers. He'd only brought one suitcase for himself. After Heidelburg and Berlin, he'd return to Paris, his home base, to await the offer of an academic position.

As the train left Paris, she asked him about the latest between his landlady's daughter and the man from Madagascar. Willem said that they'd actually come to a sensible plan. The woman was going to Madagascar with him, but unmarried, to see whether she could live there. Her return passage was guaranteed if she didn't. To Willem's surprise, she had no problem about the little daughter of mixed race, and had made friends with her.

"I admire her for considering a totally new way of life instead of flatly refusing to consider it," he said.

Grace grinned. "You had a narrow escape, Herr Doktor."

He laughed and put his arm around her. Nestling against him, completely happy, she dozed. In her dream they were at Madame Simon's. Hennaed, vivacious, their hostess circulated among her guests, flirting, laughing unrestrainedly, full of the joy of living. Then suddenly Emilie Simon turned red as her hair and flew into a fit of rage at Willem, in a staccato of French too fast for Grace to make out.

She woke, trembling, and looked up at Willem's sleeping face. Why, when she was so happy, would she have such an unpleasant dream? True, Madame Simon had been aloof and unfriendly of late, for no apparent reason.

Unless there was a reason.

She studied his face. A handsome face, and one she loved. But he wasn't ready to be faithful to anyone. "I've been deluding myself," she thought. "There is none so blind as one who will not see."

His eyes flickered and he smiled. "I'm hungry. Are you?"

They got out the baguette sandwiches, oranges and Willem's thermos of red wine, and he picnicked as France rolled past their windows. Grace nibbled; she didn't feel like eating. As Willem told her about Heidelburg, the home of Germany's oldest university, she felt sad. He wanted to stroll on "Philosophers' Walk", a path along the mountainside where scholars had walked and shared big ideas for centuries. It was in Heidelburg, too, that Martin Luther had defended his Ninety-five Theses that touched off the Reformation. Also, her old friend the philosopher Hegel, who had influenced Karl Marx, had studied and taught there.
All she could think was that, when she saw these sights, it would be just with Charles.

"You're far away," Willem remarked. "A penny for your thoughts."

She didn't know how to tell him. "Just thinking of Charles."

"It will be nice to see him again – in a few days." He grinned.

"What do you hear from your family?" she asked, to buy time.

"They're pleased at the offer I got from the American midwest," he said. "They don't worry that I'll get lost in the cornfields. After all my efforts, to end up there!"

Grace was thinking that the state university he mentioned was just two states south of Manitoba. It might be possible... But no...

"There'll be little intellectual stimulation there and no chance for me to do research in British colonial history. I don't know what I'll do with myself there. I'll have to take refuge in pleasures of the flesh."

This casual remark confirmed in her mind that she shouldn't waver. But the coach was crowded; this was no place to tell him she wasn't going through with it.

"In Heidelburg, let's find a café before we do anything else," she said.

"All right. We're close now. Getting nervous?"

She didn't reply.

In a café near the train station, he suggested some wine instead of coffee. She shook her head.

"Lovely Grace, you look worried again."

"This is awful of me, Willem, and you may call me any name you like, but I can't go through with it."

He looked stunned. "Why this sudden retreat to conventionality?"

"For you, it's just another experience. For me, it's such a big step."

"I wanted us to have a wonderful time that you would always remember."

"But we aren't going to stay together, are we?"

"Who knows what the future holds? I won't make promises that I can't keep. But having you wouldn't be just another experience; it would mean a great deal to me."

"As a wonderful way to say goodbye. We're going to say *adieu*, not just *au revoir*, and I know I'll miss you terribly. If we part as friends, I may be able to handle it. But to be lovers, and then part, well, I couldn't bear it. It would break me."

Her lips trembled.

"Grace, it's all right." He reached across the table for her hand. "You're a wonderful girl with a beautiful soul and it's an honour to have you as a friend. We've had great times together that I'll never forget, and who knows, we may meet again. I hope you will write to me, long letters, sharing what's important to you. All right?"

She nodded. "Would you mind taking me to Charles's guest house?"

"All right."

As the taxi crept down the street to the address Charles had given her, she prayed that he would be there.

"I don't imagine, under the circumstances, that you want the three of us to go sightseeing together," he said, "so I'll see you settled and then go."

"All right."

When the cab pulled up in front of the guesthouse, a slender dark-haired young man was closing the front gate behind him. The taxi had barely stopped when she flung the door open and called, "Charles!"

He turned, smiled and started toward her.

"Grace! You're here! Good to see you. And Willem, too. What a fine surprise!"

"I can't stay," Willem said. "I just came to see Grace safely into your hands."

"I'm on my way out for a bite to eat. Won't you join me?"

Willem, who was holding the taxi, said he couldn't. He seized Grace's hand and kissed it.

"*Adieu*," he said and then he was gone.

Charles picked up her suitcase.

"What was that all about?" he asked.

She shrugged. Charles touched her shoulder.

"Are you all right?"

She swallowed. "Of course."

"Let's go in and you can tell me what happened."

She shook her head. "Nothing happened."

"Are you hungry?"

"No, but I can keep you company."

Chapter Fifteen

Charles didn't press Grace for information because he was caught up in plans for seeing Heidelburg and then taking a Rhine River cruise. The weather was gorgeous for their sightseeing, and on the cruise they saw Frankfurt, Wiesbaden, Mainz and Koln. In Brussells they parted company, she to return to Paris, he to join friends and go back to London. They had made plans for Belva's visit. She would arrive in England the first week of May and would join Grace in Paris. After some travelling with Gunvar, the sisters would meet Charles in England and take a train north to Edinburgh, which they all wanted to see. Then in early August Grace would sail home from Southampton.

Grace sealed William into a compartment of her mind so that she could enjoy travelling, but on the train trip from Brussells to Paris, issues that had loomed large in their relationship manifested themselves in a crude form. She found herself in a compartment full of men. The one sitting beside her, who was young, blond and handsome, struck up a conversation, starting with the weather and moving on to other innocuous subjects. Then he began paying her extravagant compliments straight out of a romance novel. As he kept up this barrage he was, all the while, inching closer and closer to her until she was pinned in a corner against the wall. She knew he was showing off to the other men who regarded his efforts with grins and mocking looks. For two hours, Grace fought off his attempts to put his arm around her waist and his head on her shoulder. He kissed her hand and would have kissed more if she'd let him. By the time she got back to rue Cler she was angry, exhausted and contemptuous of all men.

Back in Paris, she found a note from one of the Kays saying that she should go around and see Julia. She set out in beautiful weather, April in Paris, feeling angry and foolish. Why was it that one girl could lose herself in unwedded bliss with her jazz musician while another girl of the same generation fizzled out so foolishly with the man of her dreams? On arriving at the apartment she was greeted, not by Julia, but by the wife of the apartment owner, who had been in the south for the winter. When Grace explained that she was Julia's friend, the middle-aged woman ushered her into the salon and explained in hushed tones that Julia was ill; she'd tried to kill herself. By a miracle they'd happened to arrive back in Paris the evening of her attempt. They'd called an ambulance, then wired her parents, who were now on an ocean liner coming to take her home to America.

Thoroughly shaken, Grace went in to see Julia and found her in bed, haggard and pale. When Grace hugged her, Julia began to cry. Then she told Grace what had happened. She'd dropped in to Luc's place unexpectedly to talk about their moving in together, because he'd been dragging his feet. There she saw a photo of a young woman on his dresser – his ex-girlfriend from Montreal. Julia had believed that romance was all in the past. Luc had claimed he had the photo on display only because a relative of the Montreal girl was coming to visit. This explanation only underlined his ties to this girlfriend; he hadn't told her people that he was with Julia now. In total despair, Julia had gone home and drunk iodine.

"Your life is precious," Grace told her. "Far too important to lose over Luc. It was Fate, or God that brought back your friends in time to save you."

She was happy to see Julia brightening a little. How could someone so modern in her ideas turn out to be so vulnerable? When Julia asked about Willem, Grace told her where things stood.

"What is wrong with men that they can't be faithful!" Julia cried. "And they call women the weaker sex!"

Grace hoped that Julia's spirits would rise at the thought that she was one of many broken-hearted girls. In case they didn't see each other again before Julia went home, they promised to write to each other when Grace was back in Canada.

Grace walked home in a fog of thought. Julia's story was a cautionary tale about the sad consequences of sex without commitment. Yet she couldn't help but admire Julia's courage in giving everything she had to the relationship with Luc. Her love hadn't been half-hearted.

Willem wrote to Grace from Berlin, a friendly letter with no reference to what hadn't happened, and no mention of getting together. Would it do any harm to keep the lines of communication open? She replied with a carefully casual letter, in French, using the formal "vous" instead of the intimate "tu". She told him about Julia, then about her train journey back to Paris.

"Now, Herr Doktor," she wrote. *"isn't my frankness admirable, even a bit interesting to a man of your experience? It's you, you know, who have put me on the track of writing about such things."* She joked that he would find American midwesterners naive. *"We North Americans are all naive; we can't lose this trait and we enjoy providing amusement to those in the old world who have need of it."* She signed it, *"Au revoir. As always. Grace."*

When Belva arrived, Grace stepped back into the familiar world of family and put Willem out of her mind. This was possible by day when she, Belva and Gunvar went out sightseeing in Paris. Since they had no reason to go to rue de Verneuil they never ran into Willem. For all Grace knew he was still in Germany. Sitting out at the *Dôme* with the girls, watching Batia sketch some of the other patrons, she could manage her emotions. When she, Belva and Gunvar went to Nîmes to see Roman artifacts, and then on to Marseilles and Nice, and finally, to Geneva, she focused on the beauty of her surroundings and tried not to wish she was seeing them with him.

At night, however, she relived every moment, every conversation, every touch. Pain turned to anger; anger turned to introspection. How little she knew about human nature – specifically, about men. She hoped Willem would not reply to her letter, because it would be so hard to sustain the casual tone that was demanded now that they were "just friends." She knew she had to forget about him, but it was agony to think that she would never again see those mischievous blue eyes, never again laugh or argue with him, or walk with him along the Seine with him. She wept into her pillow so as not to disturb her sister in the twin bed across the room. Belva wouldn't understand. She'd be shattered that Grace had almost given herself to someone who didn't love her.

Mother, if she knew, would praise her for having changed her mind, but would Mother know what to do with the terrible feeling of loss? It was galling to have to return home as her mother's virtuous daughter again, the one who played by the rules because she was too weak to do otherwise.

What would an objective modern woman say about the debacle with Willem? Agnes Macphail, for instance? In recent years, the press had quit mocking Agnes's appearance, for she had become chic. Reporters now praised her slim black dresses and black cape with the red satin lining which she wore on dates to go dancing at the Chateau Laurier ballroom.

Grace remembered coming home from Ottawa Normal School one day to find Agnes, her mother, and Ella, the wife of another M.P., in the parlour laughing like schoolgirls.

"Agnes, you're supposed to be an example to the young women of Canada!" Ella exclaimed. When Grace entered, they looked up and greeted her warmly.

"What's new?" she asked.

"Nothing much," her mother said, still smiling. "How was your day?"

Later, Grace coaxed the story out of her mother. Apparently the bachelor Prime Minister Mackenzie King had made his way to Miss Macphail's office after an evening sitting of the House, to offer her a cabinet position if she would switch from the Progressive Party to the Liberals. To his chagrin, he found that she was already entertaining one of his colleagues, and beat a hasty retreat. Since then, Agnes had formed a settled, longterm relationship with her Alberta colleague, Robert Gardiner.

Regarding Grace's failed love affair, Agnes would probably shrug.

"Men are like street cars," she'd say. "If you miss one, another comes along in twenty minutes. Don't worry about finding a man. Find your life's work instead and throw yourself into it."

* * *

Standing on the deck of an ocean liner at Southampton, England, waving goodbye to Charles and Belva, Grace wasn't sorry to be leaving Europe. After a calm ocean voyage and a long train trip, she arrived back in Winnipeg in August. She was greeted with hugs, laughter, congratulations on her certificate from the Sorbonne, and many questions about France. Grace showed her photos and theatre programs, talked about the places she'd been, and asked after the family's activities. Ralph was working up north with a survey crew, Bruce on an Alberta ranch, and Howard on a Manitoba farm.

One evening, when they were alone on the verandah, her mother asked about the young man she'd written about in her letters.

"Andrew Hallett? He came first in our course. I imagine he's at sea right now, literally, on his way back to Australia."

"What about the other one, the historian?"

"I imagine he has found a teaching position somewhere."

"Your father and I conducted much of our courtship by correspondence," her mother mused aloud.

"Oh, I broke it off with him," Grace said airily. "We were just ships that passed in the night. Right now, I look forward to earning some money. I'm down to my last sou."

After a few days of rest, Grace contacted the offices of the Winnipeg school board and made an appointment to meet the principal of the school to which she was assigned. She took the street car, wearing her Chanel-style suit from a Paris department store, eager to create a good impression and start the next phase of her life. The principal was a pleasant middle-aged man who greeted her in very basic French, and after a stilted exchange, reverted to English. He nodded approvingly at her curriculum vitae; she was just what he needed for six classes of French with first year high school students.

With great enthusiasm, Grace returned home with the textbook and Ministry of Education guidelines and began preparing lessons. Mother was happy to talk about her own experiences and techniques in language teaching. It was like having a colleague under the same roof. With their knowledge and experience combined, what could go wrong? If there was one thing Grace had learned from being the eldest child, it was how to handle boisterous kids. And, after juggling eight grades in the one room Dunrobin school, she felt confident about handling just one subject and one grade level.

In quiet, rural Dunrobin, however, the children had been eager to learn. The thirty-five students in each of her Winnipeg classes regarded school, and French, as unnecessary evils. Many were marking time until they were old enough to leave school forever.

It took the first ten minutes of every class to get them settled, and in every fifty minute period someone created an incident, ranging from spitballs and spilled ink to a humming undercurrent of disrespect and inattention. Every class had a core of mischief-makers who distracted, drowned out and bullied those who wanted to learn.

Grace began the year with a pep talk about the value of knowing French as a second language. She told the students that proficiency in French helped bridge the gap between English and French cultures and made Canada a stronger country. She mentioned the satisfaction of visiting the French-speaking villages near Winnipeg and being able to communicate in the residents' mother tongue.

"Who wants to talk to a bunch of half-breeds?" one of the boys muttered. The murmur of agreement shocked Grace. Clearly the children of English ancestry associated the French language with the 19th century Métis uprisings. Old hatreds died hard. As well, some of her students were new Canadians who had learned English as a second language and weren't in a hurry to learn a third one.

Grace emphasized the value of knowing French when you visited Quebec, or France, but her words were received with blank looks. She realized she might as well have suggested visiting the moon. A few of her pupils might continue with French throughout high school, and one or two might do so in university, but most would be quitting school and looking for work. They were in her class to pick up a course credit, nothing more.

Grace and her mother believed in teaching French as a living language, rather than having the students write out endless conjugations of verbs. Grace's approach was to greet the class in French, then pose easy, everyday questions that would lead to short conversations. It was learning by practice and listening. To her disappointment, many of her students refused to respond, and those who participated were sneered at, pinched and poked. Grace grew eyes in the back of her head, and was constantly on guard.

"Get some fun into your classroom," her mother said, when Grace discussed her troubles with her. "Let them act out plays. Teach them some songs. Have spelling bees."

Grace tried these things, but the core of troublemakers mocked the songs and skits and bullied those who made an effort. One day the principal popped in on an especially unruly class, and at recess told Grace to get tough with them.

"Let them know who's boss," he advised.

To survive, Grace made herself into the kind of teacher she hated. She wielded a pointer, snapped her fingers, raised her voice and used sarcasm. She gave up on French conversation and instead, drilled the students on vocabulary. She required them to write out vocabulary lists and verb conjugations in class, and woe awaited anyone who omitted an accent.

Whenever she raised her voice she felt like a terrible person. It hurt her that she couldn't get through to these students, who were normal average kids from families struggling from payday to payday or from one relief payment to the next. Their salt-of-the-earth working-class parents might well have voted for her father.

Having spent the past four years as a university student, she had forgotten how exhausting teaching was at the best of times. A teacher was always on-stage, constantly communicating, trying to be patient, positive and encouraging, or at the very least, pleasant. It was draining. On arriving home each day she didn't want to speak to anyone. When the cat ventured into her room she found its demands for attention too much, and shooed it out.

She was evasive when her mother or Belva asked how things were going. Mother had other things on her mind, such as Father's health and Charles's plans to visit their uncle in Japan in the new year and also see something of China. Grace missed him already though he hadn't even left yet. His company was a welcome diversion from school.

She also missed some of her Paris friends. If only she could meet with the two Kays, or Brandy, or Batia and sit at a sidewalk café, chatting and enjoying the passing scene. But Winnipeg had no sidewalk cafés, only hotel dining rooms, family restaurants and beer parlours that decent women didn't enter.

In October, she was the guest speaker at the monthly meeting of Winnipeg's Alliance Française. She wore her Chanel-style suit, though it was getting too big for her now, because she never felt like eating, and she brightened her wan appearance with powder and lipstick.

At the lectern, she extolled the beauty of France's countryside, the wonders of her architecture, historic sites and museums; the lacy structure of the Eiffel Tower against a sunset; and the precision and clarity of French thought. When she bowed to their applause and answered their questions she felt like a fraud. If she'd been truthful, she would have said that much of her time in France she'd been afraid, and that her Paris experiences had been an emotional roller-coaster, but no one wanted to hear that. She gave her mother a copy of the speech as her contribution to the Christmas family annual.

Along with personal worries, the news added to her concerns. After months of volatility, the New York stock market crashed on October 30, 1929. Throughout the past decade business had been booming in the United States and the price of shares had been rising. In a euphoria of speculation, everyone acted as if there would be an endless increase in the value of stocks and an endless demand for goods, and there had been widespread borrowing of money to gamble on the stockmarket. Then, after ominous fluctuations, there came a great rush to sell shares before they got any lower. People lost their life savings. Business tycoons committed suicide by jumping from skyscrapers.

Grace's colleagues saw the economic crisis as an illustration of the evils of speculation – buying stocks "on margin" and hoping to pay up when the stock increased in value. They saw the situation as an example of American excess which wouldn't affect Canada. Canadian business and political leaders said the "fluctuation" was a normal adjustment in the system, and would soon right itself.

Grace, like others on the left, thought it might be the collapse of capitalism. Unregulated, with no planning or coordination among various economic sectors, capitalism operated in an ongoing cycle of boom and recession. It inevitably created a super-abundance of goods – an over-supply. Wages and salaries hadn't risen enough to allow consumers to keep the system booming. To put it simply, there was a limit to the number of cars, refrigerators and radios that a person could afford.

This looming recession looked big. Canada, which relied on exports of grain and forest products, might find it hard to sell these staples as the U.S. and other countries raised tariff walls to protect their own industries. Production would stagnate, and as unemployment grew, there would be strikes and other civil unrest. If that happened, the forces of the state might well descend in brutal repression, wiping out hard-won rights and freedoms.

Section 98 of the Criminal Code would be invoked to suppress dissent.

Clearly it was a time to hang onto your job if you had one. Grace, however, had reached the end of her rope. She went to the principal and told him that she had failed as a teacher. She was thinking of resigning. He listened gravely.

"Just keep order and go through the motions," he advised.

As she shook her head, his brow furrowed in thought.

"I know of a local elementary school principal who is looking for a teacher," he said. "Maybe you'll do better with younger children."

Grace thanked him profusely.

Christmas 1929 was an uneasy time for the family, because Father was ill. He had high blood pressure and the doctor ordered him to stay in bed. Mother wrote brightly in the Christmas annual about the joy of having all her children home for the festive season, but privately she was terrified that James would have a stroke, and she confided her fears to Grace. The family set up the tree in Father's bedroom, and kept the noise down so that he could get some rest.

During the holidays, several girls who had graduated with Grace in the Class of '28 invited her to parties in their homes. One was married, two engaged, and all were eager to matchmake. Through them, Grace met several worthy, eligible men, who had no conversational skills and ignited no excitement in her. She went out on a couple of dates to the movies, but when her suitors asked for a second date, she pleaded the pressures of work. It wasn't fair to string them along when she had no feelings for them.

In January, when Grace started teaching primary children, all the songs and rhymes her mother had taught her came into play. She made school fun, and the children loved her, and were eager to please her. Occasionally one would call her "Mummy", then blush with embarrassment.

As the winter wore on, however, Grace sometimes thought of her studies at the Sorbonne, of all the challenging assignments, and the phonetics professor who was a stickler for correct pronunciation. What had all that been for? Her French was rusting. And, to be honest, although the younger children were charming and endearing, she wasn't making full use of her abilities and she was bored.

She knew better than to share these feelings with her mother, who adored the company of young children. Were other elementary school teachers bored too? During her first four hectic months Grace hadn't had the time or energy to get to know her colleagues. The staff at the high school had been made up mostly of older, single women who had looked disapprovingly at Grace's bobbed hair and remarked that Winnipeg must be awfully mundane compared to Paris. Grace had merely smiled and said that Paris seemed as far away as a kingdom in a storybook.

After Christmas, however, she struck up a friendship with a kindergarten teacher in her early thirties. Lily Carter was always rushing in on the dot of 8:45 a.m. with an armful of newspapers and catalogues for the children to cut up. After teaching for twelve years in one-room rural schools, Mrs. Carter felt fortunate to have been hired in Winnipeg. She and her husband, a millwright, and their three year old daughter lived in Fort Rouge, where, with their combined incomes they could afford the mortgage payments on their house. But at Christmas Mr. Carter had been laid off, and had been in a foul mood ever since. He didn't like being at home minding the child, and was thinking of going to British Columbia to find work. Mrs. Carter was afraid of losing both her husband and her home.

One recess, passing Mrs. Carter's classroom, Grace noticed her friend staring at a letter and wiping her eyes. The letter was a notice to all married women teachers employed by the Winnipeg school division, requiring them to provide concrete evidence as to why they ought to keep their jobs.

"This is unfair!" Grace exclaimed. "The men aren't being asked to justify keeping their jobs."

Mrs. Carter sighed. "Supposedly they're the breadwinners and need their jobs – but I'm the breadwinner in my family."

"You must tell that to the administration."

"I will. It's just so humiliating to have to explain my personal situation. Apparently my twelve years of successful teaching count for nothing. You're lucky you're single."

Grace wished there was something she could do, but what? She'd attended a couple of meetings of the Manitoba Teachers' Society but had found the organization dominated by men in love with the sound of their own voices. None of them seemed likely to go to bat for the married women teachers; naturally they would want to protect their own jobs.

When Grace told her mother about Lily's predicament, Mother sighed and said she would mention it at the next women's labour Group meeting, not that they could do anything. She suggested that Lily appeal personally to one of the left-wing school trustees.

"I'm so thankful that you're a specialist in French," she told Grace. "You'll be needed."

Chapter Sixteen

At Labour party meetings with her mother, Grace found the discussions sobering. Everyone was concerned about layoffs and growing unemployment. The western premiers (all Conservatives) had approached Prime Minister King to provide them with federal funds to help with relief payments, but to no avail. Mr. King and the Liberal Party claimed that Canada was enjoying record prosperity and that those who were out of work didn't want to work. When pressed by the opposition in the House of Commons to increase payments to the provinces for relief of the poor, King declared that he would not give so much as a five cent piece to any provincial government that opposed the Canadian government.

"The Tories will use that in the upcoming election," Father wrote from Ottawa.

As the robins returned and the snow melted, Grace yearned to go to Vancouver and Gibson's Landing, where the fruit trees would be in bloom and her childhood friends would welcome her. By the time school got out in June, however, a general election had been called for July 28, 1930, three days after her twenty-fifth birthday, so she postponed her holiday plans to help her father get re-elected. In a Conservative landslide, he might lose Winnipeg North Centre, and what would their family do then?

As the campaign brought the family together as a team, Grace was buoyed up by the excitement and activity. She and her younger brothers, except for Charles, who was in Japan, stuffed envelopes, canvassed and attended rallies. Mother spoke at several meetings in the constituency when Father was out of town helping other Labour candidates. Grace was optimistic because the old parties had no creative ideas for dealing with the economic crisis, while Labour wanted to stimulate the economy and provide for the needy with increased direct relief and public works programs.

When the election results came in, Canada had moved out of the frying pan into the fire. The Conservatives, led by Richard Bedford Bennett, a millionaire from the Maritimes, won the most seats. Mr. King was out of office, but Mr. Bennett seemed as deep in denial of the depression as Mr. King had been.

Grace's father won Winnipeg North Centre, and one new Labour candidate got elected, bringing the total to three. The new Labour M.P. was a Mr. MacInnis from Vancouver South. Father said he had a strong trade union background as a streetcar conductor, and in public office as a Vancouver school trustee and then as a Vancouver city councillor. He was expected to be a valuable asset to the Ginger Group in Parliament – the coalition of Labour and radical Progressive M.P.s led by Father and Bob Gardiner.

In August, Grace went with her mother and some of her siblings to the west coast to visit old friends. Belva had accepted a position to teach home economics in a Vancouver school, and Grace helped her to get settled. Then she and the others visited Gibson's Landing, the site of some of her happiest memories and the place where her political consciousness was raised.

She spent a few days with Kathy, her best friend from Gibson's days. Kathy had found her soulmate and had married him soon after graduating from university. They were very much in love, and their home radiated goodwill. Some years earlier, when Kathy had written to say she was getting married, Grace had felt sad, as if she were losing a friend, but after meeting Kathy's husband she saw that she had gained one.

On the two day train journey home, she wondered if she should try harder to meet someone. In a workplace full of children, largely staffed by women, she met few men, and she was too tired and too busy with school work to go out in the evenings. The kindly principal was a man, but he lived with his elderly mother and was reputedly "not the marrying kind."

What would Agnes Macphail advise her to do?

"If you're not happy in Winnipeg," she might say, "find a rural school, another Dunrobin, where you can make a difference and enjoy life while doing it. In my teaching days in Grey County I had a whale of a time going to dances, sleighing parties, card parties and so on. Rural communities make their own fun."

Actually, Miss Macphail, like Father, was swamped with letters from desperate constituents with real problems; she'd have no patience with Grace's discontent. In fact, Grace realized she was fortunate to be in an urban school system. Many rural communities, faced with crop failures, couldn't collect enough school taxes to pay their teachers, so some rural teachers were working for room and board.

The week before Labour Day, Grace was summoned by a new principal, who informed her that in September she would be teaching high school students again.

"There must be some mistake!" she blurted.

He shook his head.

"You're overqualified to teach young children," he told her. "And now you've had a year of experience teaching French, so it should be easier."

Alas, it wasn't. Grace found herself with many of the troublemakers from the previous year, who were repeating the grade. Once again, she tried once again to be firm but fair, to emphasize spoken French over written French, and to introduce folk songs and activities to make it interesting. But by October she felt like Captain Bligh on the *Bounty*, and it was a horrible feeling. One morning on the streetcar she watched the wind whipping the last leaves from the trees, and felt a terrible surge of homesickness, as she had in Paris. Homesick for what? She *was* at home.

She guessed she was homesick for the summer just past: the sense of purpose she'd found in campaigning, and the pleasure of having her father home. He was so full of the strength of conviction that whenever she listened to him speak, her spirit soared. Canvassing with her brother, Ralph, going door to door, hearing people's troubles, and trying to help seemed so worthwhile.

But Father was gone now. He'd left for Ottawa at the beginning of September when Parliament was called, only to find that after a startlingly brief session, it was recessed until the new year. Many were shocked and angered that the new government didn't want to hear from the people's representatives at a time of national crisis. Meanwhile, her father was making use of his railway pass to travel around the country building support for a federation of socialists, trade unionists and progressives, to offer the voters an alternative.

In the evenings, when the boys had finished their homework and were in the kitchen having snacks and chatting, their mother often read them excerpts the letters she'd received from their father. Though Grace longed to join them, she usually stayed in her room marking papers and preparing lessons.

The night of the first snowfall she looked out her window at the street light shining through a curtain of falling flakes, and wondered where her bright future had gone. She'd been proud of her accomplishments and shouldn't have been. From the mists of her churchgoing past surfaced a Bible verse from *Proverbs:* *"Pride goeth before destruction; and a haughty spirit before a fall."*

She wasn't sleeping well, in part because the leg pains that she'd suffered during her first year of university had flared up again. She was seeing an osteopath, who helped to some extent, but still her joints ached. It occurred to her that her illnesses might be partly psychological in origin. To get to sleep, she tried to guide her thoughts to happier teaching days: her year at the Dunrobin School near Ottawa, with its cooperative farm kids, and her spring at the Poplarville School with Ukrainian children eager to learn English. These memories only made her wish that she could recover the sense of purpose and achievement that she'd felt there.

Counting sheep didn't work for her so she tried making lists. Popular songs stirred too many memories. When she listed the American states she always reached the one in the mid-west where she thought Willem might be teaching. Listing all the rivers she knew started out well, with the Assiniboine and the Red, but eventually went on to the Loire and the Seine, and made her want to cry.

When she finally slept, she sometimes dreamed of Willem. Often they were entwined as one and she awoke in bliss; then reality dawned and she realized it had only been in her imagination. Again she began to dissect the relationship. Where had her life taken a wrong turn? On that train to Germany.

Certainly a casual affair went against her upbringing and her nature. But to grow as a person it was necessary to take chances and confidently proceed into the unknown. Timidity and uncertainty had made her pass up an experience that might have been wonderful. She might have won his heart with her body. He might have decided he could never let her go. She'd told him at the time that if they made love and then parted, it would destroy her. But something was destroying her now. If she'd acted in a more mature fashion, she might now be with him on a campus somewhere, perhaps on her way from the French department to meet him in the History building and then go with him for coffee.

Telling herself that the experience would have been awkward, that it probably wouldn't have convinced him to commit to her, didn't help; it just made her feel worthless. Some part of her realized that by now he probably had another girl, or girls, in love with him, so captivated by his personality and achievements that they'd throw their own aspirations to the wind.

But pursuit of her own aspiration, to teach, was a nightmare. If teaching was the right choice for her, then why did she feel sick every morning when she came in sight of the school? Why did the thought of teaching, on and on, in years to come, make her weak?

She had a permanent headache and upset stomach, and ordinary everyday things filled her with sadness. The blue shadows on the snow made her think of Willem's blue eyes, his blue sweater and the beautiful windows of Chartres Cathedral. She would never see any of these things again, and never again feel alive the way she had in Paris.

Her nightmares were torment. One recurred: a host of slimy worms slunk around the roots of feeble plants struggling toward the light. Pitiful, blind, the plants groped upward, but the clever worms curved among their roots, sapping their strength, killing them.

Doggedly she went to school each day until one morning it was as if her body had grown roots to the mattress and she couldn't get out of bed. When her mother came up to see why she was so late, Grace asked her to call the principal and say that she was sick.

When her mother brought her breakfast up on a tray, Grace tried the tea.

Her mother sat on the bed, and put her arm around her.

"How can I help you?"

Grace's hand shook and she spilled a few drops of tea on the quilt. Her eyes filled with tears.

"Grace, don't worry, it's only a few drops. I wish you'd talk to me."

Grace shook her head, handed her the cup, curled up and closed her eyes.

After Grace had spent another day in bed, her mother called the doctor. He came to the house, listened to her heartbeat, took her temperature, and asked her why she hadn't been eating. She said she wasn't hungry.

"If you were a veteran, I'd diagnose battle fatigue. What's wrong?"

"I don't want to teach anymore. I'm letting everyone down but I can't go back."

"Teaching isn't for everyone. I'll sign you out until December 31st. Get some rest."

She thanked him. At the end of November, effective December 31st, a teacher could break her contract. She would write her letter of resignation as soon as she had the energy.

The younger "children" knocked on her door and peeked into her room with worried faces. They brought her gifts – a novel, scented soap, an embroidered handkerchief. Near tears, she thanked them, and when they left she wept for having been so bossy with them in years gone by. Somewhere in her mind she knew her guilt was way out of proportion, but the feeling haunted her.

One afternoon when her mother came in she asked Grace if she would like her to read to her. "When your father comes home exhausted he finds that my reading aloud calms him."

Grace always felt better in her mother's presence. "All right," she said.

"Let's see." Her mother glanced at the crowded book case. "Ah, here's one you and Kathy read as girls. How about *Daddy Longlegs*?"

Grace nodded. As her mother began reading, Grace tried to let herself be caught up in the story. It was written in epistolary form, and the letters gave it an air of authenticity and intimacy. She liked the humour and the subtext, which suggested a need for social equality.

The novel was about an orphan who has reached "graduation" age from the orphanage and faces a life of domestic service. She's saved by a university scholarship offered by an anonymous philanthropist, whose only requirement is that she write to him regularly about her progress. The young woman addresses her unknown benefactor as "Daddy Longlegs" because all she has seen of him is his shadow, long-legged and skinny. At college she falls in love with the wealthy uncle of one of her classmates, and then, after many letters – surprise! – he turns out to be her benefactor and they live happily ever after. Grace had loved the novel ten years earlier. Now, however, she was long past Cinderella stories.

"Mother, please stop," she said urgently.

Her mother closed the book and reached for Grace's hand.

"Tell me what's bothering you?" she coaxed.

Tears were coursing down Grace's cheeks. Oh, it would be so nice to be fifteen again, believing in happy endings.

"I can't lose myself in a story like that," she sobbed. "Life isn't like that."

Her mother handed her a handkerchief.

"Talk to me, please," she urged. "I know about your problems in the classroom, but I sense there's something more."

"There's no happily ever after," Grace blurted. "Not for a coward like me."

Then, out spilled everything about Willem.

"I could have tried harder to make him love me, but I was timid and old-fashioned and I lost him. I know you're shocked."

Mother shook her head. "I'm just concerned about you. It's hard to find the right one, I know. I was thirty when your father and I were married."

"Please, please promise me you won't tell Father about this!"

"Not if you don't want me to. Have you heard from Willem?"

"No, and I won't and I don't want to. It's all in the past, only I can't get it out of my mind. I was worthless then and I'm useless as a teacher as well."

Mother gasped. "Don't say that. You're a normal young woman and a wonderful person and someday you'll find a man who will appreciate you."

"I doubt it. What will become of me, Mother? I've reached a dead end."

Her mother took her hand. "You'll find your calling in time."

"I can't see a way forward."

Downstairs, a door slammed. Someone was home from school.

Mother sighed and rose. "I should go down before they come looking for me. Now, Grace, I'll keep everything you've told me in strictest confidence, but I'll have to tell your father that you've quit teaching for good. Maybe he'll have something to suggest."

She kissed Grace's forehead, started for the door, then paused.

"Why don't you write everything that's bothering you and get it out of your system?"

Grace slept until Ralph knocked on her door with a tray of dinner for her. She ate a bit, then put the tray aside and got out a notebook and pencil. Where to begin? Slowly, she wrote the word "Apologia".

"In the past, it was always easy for me to write, especially for our family annual, known as Father's Book," she began. *"Starting when we were little, we've drawn pictures or written compositions to tell Father what we've been doing while he was away, until gradually the book has evolved into a family report on our year."*

In Gibson's Landing days her contributions had been mostly poetry, derivative verses about nature and native legends. After the General Strike, she'd penned political polemics. During her Ottawa years she contributed romantic fantasies. At university, her writings were mostly self-assessments and resolutions.

"Then came Europe, and the full revelation of my amusing naiveté and utter uselessness. Starting then, I became reluctant to claim authority on any subject. That Christmas and the following one I contributed a few innocuous pages from my Paris diary. And then came the first sobering touch of work, spelled in hard, angular letters that in certain lights appear to be tentacles alive with destruction. Avoiding annihilation at the hands of the monster seems to take up most of my time and energy. Thinking has become an unnecessary waste for me, and as for writing, it's a lost art. This must be what is known as the burden and the heat of the day."

The following morning Grace came down to breakfast after her brothers had left and her mother was at the table drinking tea and reading a letter.

"Hello, dear," she said, as if Grace's presence at the table was normal. "I have a letter from Charles here. I'll pass it on to you in a minute."

Grace poured herself some tea and sat down. She wished Charles were here. Optimistic by nature, he would have boosted her spirits.

"Look what he has sent us for Father's Book," her mother exclaimed. "An article on *A Day in the Life of a Japanese City*. He's having a grand time there."

Grace pulled a wadded paper out of the pocket of her robe.

"I've written something for the family annual, too." she said, handing it over. Mother put it in a folder up in the cupboard where she was saving all the contributions.

"I'm making the Christmas cake today," she announced. "The boys helped me chop the nuts and peel last night, but I could use your strong arms to help stir it."

As Grace helped her mother mix the ingredients, she remembered long-ago days when she and her siblings had taken turns attempting to stir the thick batter. The work gave her a sense of accomplishment, as her mother had probably intended.

Back upstairs, she lay down and went to sleep. She woke to the sound of knocking on her door. It was dark; she'd slept away much of the day.

"Grace, may I come in?"

"Father?"

She crawled out of bed, turned on the light and opened the door.

"I didn't know you were coming home today."

She saw, with a pang of sorrow, that his hair and beard were more white than grey, and that his threadbare suit was in need of pressing.

"I didn't know it myself," he said, "but a meeting in Moose Jaw got cancelled. Come and give your old father a kiss."

In his embrace she felt like a child again, and her eyes filled with tears. She sniffed.

"Let's sit down," he said. He took the chair and she perched on the bed.

"Your mother showed me your essay," he continued, "and told me that you're through with teaching. May we talk about it?"

"There's nothing to talk about because I'm never going back." Her words sounded sullen and defensive, and she didn't want to be like that to her father. "I know you're disappointed that I'm a failure but school is making me sick."

"How could I be disappointed in you when I've changed paths so many times? I read your *Apologia* and know you're being too hard on yourself. I was struck by your reference to '*the burden and the heat of the day.*'"

"It's from the parable about the vineyard owner who hired some labourers late in the day and paid them the same as those who had worked since sun-up. "It ends with*: The last shall be first and the first last, for many be called but few chosen.*"

He smiled. "I know it well." Of course he did. She was an idiot.

"I think that parable was directed at people like me. I thought I was first and now I'm last and it feels awful."

"You're misinterpreting it," her father said. "That parable shows that everyone deserves God's grace and mercy, that everybody deserves the good things in life. It's something like the old socialist principle: *From each according to his abilities, to each according to his needs*. Stop berating yourself, Grace. Your mother and I don't compare our children to each other. We love you all and we never expected you to be perfect."

She wiped her eyes. "I'm far from perfect. I'm a failure. Useless."

"Everyone fails. I fail all the time in Ottawa when I try to press for social reforms as a first step to changing the system. And anybody who has worked in an actual grape harvest isn't a useless person."

"It means a lot to hear that." She blinked back a tear.

"I have a proposal. Would you come to Ottawa and work with me?"

She stared at him. "In your office? On Parliament Hill?"

"Yes, to help me out. To answer my letters, type my speeches, do research."

"But I never took typing in school."

"It's a skill anyone can learn. Now, you won't be on the government payroll. You'll get an allowance from me."

Images whirled in Grace's head. Ottawa's familiar streets. The majestic Peace Tower. The Parliamentary Gallery where one could watch the debates. The deep blue of the Gatineau Hills. Remarkable people to admire and respect, like Miss Macphail, Mr. Heaps and the other "Ginger Group" members.

"Your fluency in French, alone, would be a great help to me," her father added.

"I'd be glad to do something useful, if you think I can. Or are you just being kind?"

"I do. Tomorrow we'll buy you a typewriter and a book on the touch system."

Chapter Seventeen

The Peace Tower looming through a fog of snow was a beautiful sight to Grace on the February day her train arrived in downtown Ottawa. She'd spent six weeks taking a French course at the University of British Columbia and reconnecting with people she knew in B.C., and now felt renewed and eager to earn her keep.

Her boarding house downtown was near her father's, and often they walked to Parliament Hill together. There, he and the other Labour and United Farmer M.P.s had offices on the sixth floor, in a corridor that members of other parties nicknamed "Socialist Alley". On her first day, at lunch with her father in the Parliamentary cafeteria, people came over to say hello and to be introduced to his "pretty young lady friend", an experience that was gratifying but embarrassing. Earlier, Agnes Macphail had greeted her like a long-lost pal.

"One of these days you'll join me on the floor of the House of Commons as the second woman ever elected to Parliament in Canada," she'd said, a ridiculous but flattering remark. Agnes told Father he was lucky to have a private secretary; no longer would he have to rely on the secretarial pool as most other backbenchers did. She couldn't get along without Lilla Bell, whom she'd hired as her assistant. She promptly introduced Grace to Miss Bell, a gracious, middle-aged woman who was a fountain of information about Parliamentary rules and routines, and went out of her way to orient newcomers to "Socialist Alley". Miss Bell took time to sit down with Grace and provide advice. She warned Grace to beware of a certain former cabinet minister who periodically got drunk and tried to take liberties with the female secretaries, often chasing them down the corridors.

The highest legislature in the land seemed to be full of *amour*. A number of dignified, well-respected members had an Ottawa girlfriend – often a secretary – in addition to a wife back home in the constituency raising the children and keeping the home fires burning. Interesting relationships abounded. Gossips surreptitiously analyzed Mr. King, now Opposition leader, who had a close personal friendship with a married lady and often took evening strolls along the Rideau Canal with her and their Scottish terriers. Was her husband oblivious to their fondness for one another? Was he too lazy to care? Had he accepted the situation because of the perks that accompanied friendship with an important man? Apparently it was Mr. King's second such involvement. Ottawa readers of Freud and Jung claimed that the pattern was formed in his early family life. Apparently his mother had regarded his father as a failure and had looked to "Willy" to have a brilliant career and make her proud. His triangular relationships replicated, psychologically, his situation with his parents.

Grace wasn't especially interested in the workings of the former prime minister's psyche, but she enjoyed watching the people on Parliament Hill – the ancient senators tottering on their canes, the smartly dressed ladies, stout government ministers, eager journalists, and aloof, purposeful secretaries. In her father's office, she had a little desk in one corner, where she typed his letters slowly but accurately. She strived to learn fast and not get in the way of his work.

One of her first tasks was to mail out copies of his latest speech. Members of Parliament had free mailing privileges for the nation's business and Father made good use of them. As she was typing the envelopes he came over and asked how it was going.

"Fine, but are you sure you gave me the right list? I'm addressing these envelopes to all the Methodist ministers in the

Maritime provinces. How many of them are going to become socialists from reading your speech?"

"Some of them probably are already," he said, "and all of them are concerned about suffering people in their communities. But leave it for now. The Ginger Group is meeting here in a quarter of an hour, and I'll need you to take notes."

Grace had met several members of the "Ginger Group". She already knew Abraham A. Heaps, a longtime family friend. British born, an upholsterer by trade, he had joined with the workers in the Winnipeg General Strike, had served some jail time and subsequently was elected to Parliament. A family man and a hardworking representative, Mr. Heaps was one of the few Jewish members of Parliament. The Ginger Group included the three Labour M.P.s and ten United Farmer/Progressive members – the survivors of the United Farmers/Progressive movement elected in 1921. The others had gone down to defeat or had joined the Liberals. The Ginger Group usually voted as a bloc and tried to introduce progressive legislation, such as old age pensions, minimum wage laws and unemployment insurance, in private members' bills.

As the caucus gathered, Grace studied the new Labour M.P. from Vancouver. Tall, skinny, with sticking-out ears, he towered over the others with an awkward air. His blue three-piece suit was so obviously new that it might as well have the price tag on it, and he seemed uncomfortable in it.

The main area of discussion was, predictably, the economic crisis, with everyone advocating pressuring the federal government to invest public funds in job creation. The Liberals hadn't done so, and it seemed unlikely that Prime Minister Bennett and his Conservatives would. The independents discussed tactics to spur the government to action, as well as alternative economic approaches. Mr. Irvine and Mr. Spencer thought that taking Canada off the gold standard would put more purchasing power in the hands of ordinary people, thus stimulating the economy. Miss Macphail insisted that concern for urban workers should not be priorized over help for farm families, who had lost markets for their products and were struggling to feed themselves off the land.

Then Mr. MacInnis cleared his throat. In a raspy voice he spoke of the flood of young men pouring into Vancouver to look for work. They were straining Vancouver's relief resources and something had to be done immediately. Above and beyond that problem was the tragedy of a lost generation of young people who ought to be earning money, getting established, buying homes and contributing to the economy.

"At forty-six, I'm no youth," he said, in his gravelly voice, "but it breaks my heart to see young people's lives stalled and their prospects bleak."

Then his eyes came to rest on Grace, who was sitting in a corner taking notes.

"Let's have the young person in the room tell us how it feels to be young in these times," he said.

All eyes turned to Grace. Although their gaze was friendly, she had a moment of panic at being singled out.

"Yes, Grace, give us your perspective," coaxed Agnes Macphail.

Grace took a deep breath.

"Well, I don't know how typical I am, but I do know that many young people are just treading water, not getting anywhere, and some of them are drowning. The group I know most about are young women teachers in Manitoba."

She began to tell the group what she knew.

Many school boards had cut teachers' salaries and laid teachers off, and the first to be fired were young women just starting out. Teachers were desperate for employment; she'd heard of a rural school district in which thirty young women had applied to teach in what was, essentially, an ill-equipped one-room shack, for the immense sum of $450 a year. Whoever was hired probably didn't receive this salary in cash, either, but had to take it in the form of room and board, because rural school boards were broke; people couldn't pay their taxes.

She mentioned the Winnipeg school board directive of the previous year that all married women teachers, regardless of their years of experience, had to justify to the board why they should retain their jobs, even though some of them were the sole supporter of a household. In her view, men and women should be treated equally and receive the same salaries for equal qualifications and experience.

Although she had loved her year in an Ontario country school, in a relatively prosperous farm community near Ottawa, she knew that many rural schools were short on books, poorly heated and ventilated, with inadequate sanitation. Having forty pupils in eight different grade levels was not unusual. Some rural Ontario schools went beyond Grades One to Eight, and offered the first two years of high school, but most Ontario teachers had just a high school education plus a year of Normal School, and weren't qualified to teach high school.

As she paused for breath she noticed that Miss Macphail was nodding emphatically.

Since the three Labour M.P.s were probably wondering: "What about the union?" she spoke of the ten year old Manitoba Teachers' Society, founded to elevate the status of the teaching profession and help teachers become more actively involved in decision-making with regard to their profession. The organization, she said, was heavily male-dominated, with older men firmly entrenched in supervisory careers and younger men eager to gain any advantage that might keep them employed. They did not particularly care if women teachers lost jobs. Also, the two dollar annual membership fee was beyond the means of many young women teachers.

The difficulties facing teachers in general, and young women teachers in particular, would affect the young people they were trying to educate. Meanwhile, many young men rode the rails in search of employment or relief while many young women stayed home. Glancing at her father, she said she was fortunate to have parents who were willing to help her out financially.

When she stopped speaking, there was silence for a few seconds. Then Mr. MacInnis began clapping his hands, and the others joined in.

"Thank you for spelling out the situation so clearly," he said.

"It's all too true," Agnes Macphail agreed, with a sigh.

Grace felt her cheeks burning. She was glad her remarks were well taken, but embarrassed to have been the focus of attention. It wasn't her place to talk in caucus. Also, though she knew about the economic problems teachers faced, she wasn't one anymore.

When the meeting ended, Mr. MacInnis came over to Grace, thrust out his hand for her to shake, and introduced himself.

"Angus MacInnis. We first met years ago at one of your father's lectures at the Columbia Theatre in Vancouver. I learned a lot from J.S.'s talks. I believe your mother spoke once or twice, too."

Grace couldn't remember. If she'd met him he hadn't made much of an impression. She decided to be amused at his eagerness to establish a connection.

"Mother will be pleased to be remembered," she said. "I'll mention it in my next letter home."

Another M.P. wanted to speak to her, so she said "Excuse me," to Mr. MacInnis and turned to the newcomer.

Later, alone in the office, typing her envelopes, she thought about Mr. MacInnis, and felt sorry for him. He seemed intimidated by his surroundings. She knew what it was like to be uncomfortable in a new role. Though he was unpolished, he had a sound record of public service, and could have a commanding presence if he stood tall. It was sad to see someone so remarkable being cowed by Ottawa.

That evening over dinner at a small family restaurant, her father said he had a request. Would she help Mr. MacInnis with his correspondence?

"I don't just mean typing," he added. "His grammar and spelling need correcting too. Mac is the salt of the earth but he's self-taught. As a boy he had to work on the family farm in Prince Edward Island and he missed a lot of schooling."

She nodded. "Sure, I'll put his letters into standard English. What's his story? How did he get from P.E.I. to British Columbia?"

"He went west on a harvest train some twenty years ago and continued on to Vancouver, where he had some relatives."

"Does he have a family?"

"No wife, but a family, yes. He lives with his mother, sister and a teenaged niece. I gather that, for years, he hadn't enough money to support a wife and children."

"What is he like as a person?"

"Shy. A great reader: he's read Marx and Engels, the Webbs – all the standard texts. He's a union man but not the pugnacious flamboyant type. He had the reputation of cutting to the heart of the matter at Vancouver school board and council meetings. Unfortunately his performance in the House hasn't been impressive."

"How so?"

Her father looked pained. "He made a poor job of his first speech, which was supposed to end in a motion in reply to the Throne speech. He used his forty minutes to lambaste the government and then ran out of time and never proposed the motion. The Speaker cut him off."

Grace giggled. "He sounds like a diamond in the rough."

The following day she looked through back copies of Father's *B.C. Labour Statesman* to see what she could find on Angus MacInnis. Both he and her father contributed columns to this publication, though Angus had only written two. His first, published back in the fall right after the election, poked heavy-handed fun at the pomp and circumstance surrounding the opening of Parliament. In his next column he complained about Members of Parliament rigidly voting their party affiliation on every bill.

Grace frowned as she read his columns. She remembered an experience she'd had, back in 1922 just after the family had joined Father in Ottawa. There had been a luncheon for the daughters of Members of Parliament, which her parents thought she should attend. A rebellious seventeen at the time, she'd balked, claiming the other girls would be elitist snobs. Her parents insisted, however, and once there, she'd enjoyed the occasion because she was seated beside the friendly, down-to-earth daughter of a United Farmer/Progressive member from Alberta. Not all formal occasions were pointless.

She recalled a teasing poem she and her friend Kathy had written back in 1921 when her father, packing to go to Ottawa, dug out the formal evening attire which he hadn't worn since his university days. Amazingly, it still fit, though the swallow-tailed coat had smelled of mothballs.

"Come forth my dress suit from thy long repose [they wrote]

Tonight I dance with Lady Maud

Where's back? Where's front? Oh, goodness knows!

I would not be a clod."

Father had laughed at the poem, but he'd taken the formal clothes to Ottawa, because formal attire was proper etiquette for the opening of Parliament. Although he disliked some of Parliament's archaic traditions, he respected the institution and was willing to comply. In contrast, Mr. MacInnis's complaints about these traditions made him sound like a hick who might not be able to settle in and effectively represent his constituents.

On the matter of members voting their consciences rather than the party line, she had mixed feelings. The left criticized "partyism" and wanted the people to have more of a voice in government. Yet, when labour, socialists and progressives formed a federation, and ran candidates under its banner, those elected would have to vote as a bloc to get social legislation passed.

Grace was often in the House of Commons Gallery taking notes, as she had taken over her father's task of writing a weekly column of Parliamentary news for several farm, labour and socialist papers. One afternoon she heard Mr. MacInnis speak. As he rose, she noted that he was a commanding, almost Lincolnesque presence, and that his voice, while not melodious, was audible. But he spoke off the cuff, and got off on a tangent, differentiating between peaceful democratic socialists like himself, and revolutionary communists. He used an analogy – hatching eggs in an incubator. It took twenty-one days. That, he said, was the Labour way. The communists, in contrast, believed that if you turned up the heat in the incubator you would get chicks in just fifteen days, but in reality you would cook the eggs.

Grace cringed at the poultry references. Chickens? Eggs? Homespun wisdom was all right in its place, maybe, but the House of Commons was not the place. Some honourable members, those who had looked up from their newspapers, were clucking and crowing with laughter. She left the Gallery shaking her head. Later, her father asked if she'd heard "Mac's" speech.

"Yes." She rolled her eyes.

"Then you saw that he needs help. I can't offer it because if I did it would hurt his pride. Besides, I don't have time. Could you work with him on his next speech? It will be in reply to the budget if the Tories ever get around to presenting one."

Grace gasped.

"How can I waltz into his office and announce that I want to help him write his next speech? He'd be insulted."

Father shook his head. "An offer of help from a colleague would humiliate him, but from you it would be different, because you're just a girl..."

She laughed. "Just a girl? I'll tell Mother you said that! I may report you to the Women's International League for Peace and Freedom."

Her father smiled.

"I only mean that he won't be threatened by a young woman. You could offer to type his next speech, and then clarify and reorganize it."

Grace sighed. "I'll try, but I can't guarantee results."

The following day she knocked on Mr. MacInnis's office door.

"Come in," he called.

He sat at his desk which was covered with papers. His hair was rumpled, as if he'd dragged his fingers through it in frustration.

"Hello," she said, standing in the doorway. "If you have anything that needs typing I'd be happy to do it."

He smoothed his hair and straightened his tie.

"That's generous of you, but don't you have enough to do for J.S.?"

She put on her friendliest smile.

"Nothing pressing at the moment. I also wanted to say that I was most interested in your columns in the *Labour Statesman*."

He looked surprised. "It's kind of you to say so."

"I also came across a laudatory article about you in the *Vancouver Sun*, of all places. The title was, *Angus MacInnis Wins his Spurs*."

He smiled. "I was surprised too, but pleased. Come in, won't you?"

She sat down and looked at him across the desk.

"I miss Vancouver," she said. "What do you hear from home?"

He groaned. "The unemployment situation is worse than ever. I'm drafting a speech to give during the Budget debate and having one hell – one devil of a time with it."

"Oh?"

"Well, it's a foregone conclusion that the Bennett budget will fall short of the funding needed for relief, let alone to stimulate the economy. I want to talk about the economic plight we're in, but don't know where to begin. I thought of starting with a history of capitalism, drawing on Marx, and then getting into specifics, about world markets drying up, no profit in further production, plant closures and the like."

Grace suppressed a shudder. She agreed that the cycles of boom and recession were characteristic of capitalism, but what he'd just said sounded boring even to her. The House full of Tories and Liberals wouldn't want to be lectured on socialist theory. They'd either doze or heckle unless they were presented with concrete issues.

"How many unemployed are there in Vancouver?" she asked.

"Ten per cent of all the unemployed in Canada have flocked there to find work, and there is none." He reeled off a list of mines, forestry operations and secondary industries that had either cut their work force dramatically or closed down.

"You should say that in your speech," she told him. "That would get the attention of the House. I'd like to know more about the situation in British Columbia. Do you have time to fill me in? And may I take notes?"

He looked surprised.

"Sure, if you want to. Have a seat."

She got out her pen and pencil, and as he talked, she scribbled the gist of what he said.

"You paint a vivid and grim picture," she commented, when he paused.

"I'm not exaggerating. I get letters every day from constituents who are broke and trying to survive. One backbench M.P. who is part of a tiny group can do little for them. I'm letting them down and I know it."

"You can publicize their plight. If you quoted from some of their letters it might be very effective."

"That's a thought."

"Why don't I type what you've told me, and see if it could form part of your speech?"

"Would you do that?" His eyes widened. "That would be very helpful."

"Of course. I'll type my notes and you can correct them and expand upon them."

He looked pleased. "That's really good of you."

"It's no problem at all."

By the following day she had shaped his remarks into the core of a coherent speech, leaving a space marked "For quotes from constituents' letters." She also wrote an introduction and conclusion, labelled "DRAFT" in upper case letters, as a signal that she wanted his input.

Her father looked over her shoulder while she was typing.

"A speech for Mac? Good."

Later that afternoon she knocked on Mr. MacInnis's door. Other M.P.s often had cronies hanging around at that time of day, having a drink, shooting the breeze, but he was alone at his desk reading.

"I have the notes typed," she said.

"Already? You're a wonder. Come, let me see."

Looking over his shoulder while he read, she inhaled the faint lemon-lime fragrance of his soap, or perhaps his hair oil.

"I'm going to read it aloud," he said. "Tell me how it sounds."

She sat opposite him, clasped her hands and looked attentive. He read smoothly; she had caught the rhythm of his voice.

"You've made me sound like myself, only better." He grinned.

"Then you think it's a start?"

"I won't change a word of it."

"What about the introduction and ending?"

"They're fine as they are."

Grace liked his smile. She decided that he was not really ugly, but rather, boyish, and endearing.

"When you choose the letters you want to quote from, I'll retype the speech and include them."

"Would you take the letters and decide which to include? I trust your judgment."

"All right. I'd be interested in reading them."

He looked through the files on his desk, picked up a thick one and handed it to her.

"Some of these will break your heart," he said.

On Saturday, when she and Father went in to work, Grace put the finishing touches on Mr. MacInnis's speech, making three carbon copies. Father asked to read it, and since he was the caucus leader, she saw no reason why he shouldn't.

"You write well, Grace," he said. "Why don't you type what you said about teachers in the Depression and send it to a labour publication?"

On Sunday, she and her father were invited to dinner at the home of Ella and Hank, a couple who had been friends with her parents for ten years. First elected in 1921 as a Progressive/United Farmers candidate, Hank was now one of the Ginger Group members and supported the concept of a federation of the left. He and Ella were a delightful couple whose western friendliness was a welcome antidote to Ottawa pretentiousness. Their door had always been open to Father; their children called him "Uncle James." After the meal, their two daughters entertained with an impromptu piano recital. They were taking lessons at the Sacred Heart convent where, years earlier, Grace had studied French.

"When we're back in Alberta I encourage the girls to be vague about where they're taking their lessons," Ella remarked. "There's a lot of anti-Catholicism back home."

The after-dinner conversation covered a range of topics, and at some point Ella asked Father how Mr. MacInnis was adjusting to his new role as Member of Parliament. Grace was pretty sure that she already knew, from Hank. Father said, diplomatically, that "Mac" was learning quickly.

"His socialist rhetoric won't go down well with the farmers back home," Hank remarked. "It won't help attract them to our proposed federation."

"All shades of the left use Marxist terms," Father said, "but Mac is staunchly anti-communist."

Many on the left were fed up with the revolutionary rhetoric of the communists, who claimed that social democrats were "social fascists" propping up capitalism through their reforms. Grace agreed with her father that, while democratic socialism could succeed in Canada, a Bolshevik style revolution wouldn't. In Canada there was no collapse of institutions, no power vacuum, as there had been in Russia at the end of the Great War, when Lenin had found power "lying in the dust" and had picked it up and used it.

Father was saying that the left in British Columbia was fragmented and sectarian, and that Mac was better positioned than anyone else to bring the small socialist parties under the big umbrella of a left-wing democratic federation.

"Why isn't Mr. MacInnis married?" Ella inquired.

"I believe he was engaged some years ago but that it didn't work out," said Father, looking pained. He didn't approve of personal questions about colleagues.

"Mac is the sole supporter of his elderly mother, single sister and a young niece around the age of our girls," Hank told his wife.

Ella looked interested. "A niece? Is that a euphemism for something else?"

"The niece is his dead brother's child," Father said.

"Pardon me. It's just that streetcar conductors are notorious flirts."

"I believe the parents died in the flu epidemic when the child was quite young," Father told Ella. "Mac and his mother and sister took her in. They're humanitarians."

"I've been doing some typing for him and the other Ginger Group members," Grace remarked, to fill the uncomfortable pause.

"Editing, too, I imagine," said Ella.

"Yes, but his lack of formal education shouldn't be held against him," Grace replied. "He had to go to work at an early age. After years of listening to professors, I find his clear straightforward thinking a refreshing change."

"I'm sure." Ella poured more coffee.

Grace worried that she'd come across too strongly as Mr. MacInnis's champion. Ella might think she had a crush on him.

"Speaking of professors," Hank interjected, "what do you hear, James, from the fellows who want to start a Canadian version of the British Fabian Society?"

He was referring to some academics from McGill University and the University of Toronto who supported the plans for a cooperative commonwealth federation and wanted to bring artists, scholars and professionals into it. Some labour people were reluctant to accept non-working class people into the movement, on the grounds that they couldn't fully understand workers' struggles. Ella, Hank and Father hoped that the new federation of the left would be a big tent, including all sorts of people who wanted democratic change.

Walking home, Grace thanked her father for bringing her into a stimulating milieu.

"I'm glad you're yourself again," he said.

"I am," she said.

Lately she'd greeted each day with enthusiasm. She was also sleeping well, no longer plagued by nightmares. For the last couple of months she hadn't dreamt at all, at least, not that she could remember.

But that night she had a dream, a delightful erotic fantasy, and on waking from it, she felt shaken and embarrassed. Shocked by the goings-on of her unconscious, she could hardly look herself in the mirror. It was so inappropriate, so mortifying, so ridiculous to dream of *him*! What did such a dream say about her?

The unconscious mind was a garbage can, full of flotsam and jetsam from daily life. New people, new circumstances, new things to learn had coalesced to disturb her rest in the most preposterous way. It meant nothing.

As she got ready for work she couldn't get it out of her mind, and she kept blushing about it. She couldn't believe she'd dreamed in such a way about Angus MacInnis. Why, she hardly knew him! She wasn't even sure that she liked him! He wasn't handsome, though his black hair was glossy, his hazel eyes were warm and there was something attractive about him. But there was such a disparity in their ages, their educational levels, their social skills. Her natural sympathy for the underdog was to blame for this wild flight of fancy – this hallucination.

The thought of running into him in "Socialist Alley" troubled her – what if he could read her mind? At the office she ran into Miss Bell, who told her that he was tied up in a committee. Good, she thought, though why was Miss Bell telling her that? Could Miss Bell read her mind? All morning she felt flustered. Maybe she should get away from Parliament Hill for a complete change of scene. Maybe an afternoon at the movies would help. It would feed new images into her mind, give her a handsome male actor as fodder for her fantasies.

Everybody was raving about a new movie, *Anna Christie*, because Greta Garbo starred in it, and she talked! It was her debut in a talking picture. Taking the afternoon off would be more fun with company. Father? No. He wouldn't play hooky and probably didn't know who Greta Garbo was, let alone care what she sounded like. On impulse, she went into Miss Macphail's office where Lilla Bell was rapidly typing. She looked up with her usual friendly smile and asked how things were going.

"Very well." After some small talk, Grace asked her if she'd seen *Anna Christie*.

"Oh, yes, and it's excellent! I went last week with Mr. MacInnis."

"Oh." To hide her confusion, Grace quickly asked what Garbo's voice was like.

"Low. Husky. The plot is very advanced. Grittily realistic. You'll like it."

"It sounds worth seeing. Maybe on the weekend."

Walking down the hall, Grace gave Mr. MacInnis's office a wide berth. Evidently he wasn't as snowed under with work as he'd seemed to be, if he had time to go to the movies. Grace resolved not to think about him any more. In fact, she might suggest to her father that Miss Bell, with her superb organizational skills and fund of useful information, should take over the revision and typing of Mr. MacInnis's work.

Chapter Eighteen

That afternoon, when she was mailing a bulletin on Fisheries to an elderly woman in the Saskatchewan dust-bowl, Grace heard a knock, and looked up to see Mr. MacInnis in the doorway. He was holding a blue box tied up with a ribbon.

"This is a little gift to thank you for helping me with my speech."

He approached awkwardly and set it down on her desk.

"That's so kind of you," she said, "but quite unnecessary. Thank you, though."

He waited for her to open it. She untied the bow, lifted the lid and found, nestled in tissue paper, a delicate cream-coloured china cup dotted with yellow roses. She could see by the hallmark that it was the finest English bone china.

"It's lovely," she exclaimed.

He looked pleased. "When I saw it I thought of you."

"It's almost too pretty to use. Whoever helped you pick it out knows a lot about china. This is the best."

"Oh, I chose it myself. I collect china. I'm sure you're thinking *bull in a china shop*, but..."

"Oh, no!" she exclaimed. "I'm thinking that you're very courageous."

He looked mystified. She forged ahead to cover her confusion.

"It's brave to have a hobby like china collecting in a crazy broken world like ours. It's an act of faith that the fragile beautiful things will survive."

"I never thought of it like that. I got started – well, you wouldn't be interested."

"I would. Please have a seat."

"Well, growing up on the farm in Prince Edward Island we barely had dishes, let alone china. Then I saw a china cabinet in a wealthy neighbour's home, the kind of home I wished for. To me, china means life with a few luxuries. When I've had money to spare, I've bought bits and pieces – a plate, a pitcher, often a cup and saucer. It probably seems a funny kind of interest for a man to have."

She shook her head. "Not at all. And wasn't it Claude Renoir who began his career handpainting china?" That was a non-sequitur; she was babbling.

"I'll take your word for it," he said. "Actually I came here with a request, for your company at dinner tomorrow evening at the Café Henry Burger in Hull. It's French; I thought you'd like it."

"Oh, my goodness. That would be very nice. But these expressions of gratitude aren't necessary, you know. I'm typing for several M.P.s in the Ginger Group."

"It's not gratitude, it's selfishness," he said earnestly. "I enjoy your company and want to know you better. You're an unusual young woman."

"Well, thank you. And so are you – an unusual man, I mean."

They laughed, then he seemed at a loss as to what to say next.

"I've finished the final draft of your speech," she said. "Would you read it aloud to me now, so we can see how it sounds?"

"All right. Shall I stand?"

"Yes. You'll be standing in the House."

She got up and closed the door. He rose and began to read, the paper vibrating slightly in his hand. When he'd finished she clapped her hands.

"Bravo! It sounds very natural."

He turned red. Footsteps sounded outside the door.

"Shall we leave around seven tomorrow evening?" he whispered.

"Yes. Why don't we meet on the steps of Notre Dame Basilica?"

The door opened and her father came in.

"Thank you, Mr. MacInnis," she said.

"Hello, Mac," Father said. "Are you just leaving? Grace, please find me the file on Section 98."

After Mr. MacInnis left, Grace threw herself into her work but didn't get finished until 7:30 p.m. She had missed dinner at her boarding house, but when her father suggested supper out, she said she was tired and would have a snack from her stash of food in her room. She needed to be alone to sort out her feelings.

As she walked to her boarding house, rain began to fall, first a sprinkling, then a downpour that plastered down her hair but cleared her head. Why lie to herself? She was gone on Angus MacInnis. Her feelings for him were ridiculous, inappropriate, unsuitable, but they were there, and you couldn't argue away a feeling.

As she lay on her bed with the rain beating softly on the roof, her imagination played like a film. In some scenes she was in his arms. In another, he was being applauded for a speech he had just given. He held out his hand, drew her up on the platform beside him, and told the crowd: "I owe so much to Grace."

She had chosen the steps of Notre Dame Basilica as a rendezvous because if they left Parliament Hill together, people would talk. Also, the cathedral was not far from the Alexandra Bridge which connected Ottawa with Hull, Quebec. From the Hill, she had a half-hour walk along Wellington Street and Sussex Drive, so the following evening she left early to give herself ample time.

Approaching the basilica, she saw no sign of Angus, so she went up the steps and in through the open doors. Slipping into a back pew, she closed her eyes and wished with all her heart that this evening would be a success. A breeze wafted through the open doors and felt like a good omen. After five minutes, she checked her watch and went out to the top of the steps. Mr. MacInnis was on the sidewalk, looking around uncertainly.

"I'm here!" she called.

He looked up. "There you are!" Then he hailed a passing taxi.

In a twinkling they were across the bridge to Quebec, pulling up in front of a Georgian limestone house with blue canopies over the entrance and garden. Mr. MacInnis sprang out, opened doors, and moments later they were in the foyer, being welcomed by the maitre d'hotel. Automatically Grace switched to French and asked for a table for two.

The dining room felt like home, but an elegant home with tiny lamps on the tables and ornamental china plates on a rail around the room. She translated the menu for Angus and suggested the *coq au vin*. The Burgundy she ordered to go with it was delicious, and calmed her.

"You're a mental acrobat, the way you switch back and forth from French to English," Mr. MacInnis told her.

"Thank you, Mr. MacInnis. I imagine you are too, with English and Gaelic."

"Ah, you've been checking up on me. And please call me Angus."

"And I'm Grace. Angus, I heard somewhere that Gaelic is your mother tongue."

"I only use it now to talk to my mother. She speaks only Gaelic. She never learned English."

"That's fascinating. I'm glad you still speak it. It's easy to lose a language. My French has improved from being in Ottawa talking with grown-ups."

"You must miss France," he said.

"Not really, though I'd like to go back sometime. While I was there, not a day passed that I didn't miss my family. Do you miss P.E.I.?"

He shook his head. "Not the poverty and endless work. There was always something to plant or pick. It's a wonder I don't have a permanent stoop. In the spring we planted potatoes, all summer we picked potato bugs, and in the fall we dug the potatoes. Picking berries was better. The worst was picking stones. Our farm was rich in them."

Angus had attended school sporadically for four years, then had to quit at age twelve because his older brother had died and his help was needed on the farm. He enjoyed reading, but the only books at home were a Bible, a Farmer's Almanac, and a volume of Robert Burns's poetry. One of the neighbours took the Charlottetown *Guardian*, which serialized novels, and Angus used to walk five miles to the neighbour's home to read the latest episode. His favourite was *The Man from Glengarry*.

Grace raised a glass. "An end to poverty," she proposed, with a grin. "A chicken in every pot. May everyone in Canada dine as well as we will tonight."

He smiled and they touched glasses and drank.

Grace's mother had encouraged her children not to hog conversations and to encourage shy people to talk, and Grace followed this advice now. She wanted to *get* an impression, rather than to *make* one, and she sensed that Angus was starved for an opportunity to talk about himself. She understood. Plunked into a new environment, one could easily have an identity crisis. So she listened, periodically saying, "Do go on."

Angus's story touched her heart. He'd left P.E.I. in his early twenties to work in a chandlery in Boston, then he returned home, but left again in 1908, this time on a harvest train to the prairies. After the harvest he continued west to British Columbia and worked on his uncle's dairy farm on Lulu Island. For a while he delivered milk; then got hired by the B.C. Electric Company as a streetcar motorman, and subsequently, a conductor. He'd left this job just last year on being elected to Parliament. Though he'd served as a school board trustee and a city councillor in Vancouver, these positions were unpaid.

"My family was Conservative and Presbyterian," he told her, "but when I came to B.C., everyone was talking about socialism, so I read up on it and became active in the Street Railway Workers Union."

The radicalizing event in his life was the 1912 Nanaimo coal miners' strike. The brutal suppression of this strike, over dangerous working conditions, had shocked him to his core and affirmed everything he felt about the need for a strong Labour party. That same year, his elderly mother and his sister moved to Vancouver, where they and Angus pooled their resources to buy a house. Later, his little niece came to live with them.

"Around 1919 I started attending your father's classes at the Columbia Theatre," he said. "And a couple of years later, when your family moved from Gibson's to Vancouver, I met you. You were around sixteen, just starting at the University of British Columbia."

"I wish I could remember. I was probably wrapped up in myself."

"I knew then you were a remarkable girl, and you still are," he said, with a twinkle in his eye. "Tiny and efficient, like a honeybee, always busy. The Hill seems to be your natural environment."

"I'm happy to be working in Ottawa even though it isn't a real job."

His eyebrows shot up. "Why do you say that? The work you do is certainly real."

"Well, thank you, but I'm not self-supporting: I get an allowance from Father."

"Do you miss teaching?"

"No. This work seems more important. You see, the radicalizing experience of my life was my father being jailed during the Winnipeg General strike. Sometimes it has been daunting to be my parents' child, but I'm used to it now and I'm their staunchest supporter. I'm not sure if I can contribute in any way to the new socialist federation, but I would like to. I suppose Milton was right in saying: *They also serve who only sit and type.*"

John Milton's famous sonnet actually ended: "*only stand and wait.*" She'd expected a smile, but Angus just looked puzzled. Shame on me, she thought, for mentioning a poem he probably hasn't read.

"There will be plenty for you to do for the new party, and not just typing and filing," he said. "You can build the movement by speaking at meetings."

"I'd be terrified."

"A teacher who has faced a classroom can address a crowd. You state your ideas clearly; you did in caucus the other day. I'm the one who founders in the House in front of all those lawyers trained in the gift of the gab. My first two speeches were terrible flops. I've been thinking of resigning and seeing if I can get hired back by B.C. Electric."

She was stunned to see that he wasn't joking. Her fork came down with a clang.

"Oh, Angus, you can't quit! Don't even think of it. Listen, I've spent years listening to professors and politicians in love with their own voices. Parliament needs genuine honest people with progressive ideas. The speech you're working on now is excellent, and it will hold the attention of the House. We both know that."

"I appreciate your vote of confidence," he said.

After dessert, coffee and a warm "au revoir" from the host, they stepped out into a fine spring night. The faint pink and gold streaks in the west had vanished; everything was deep blue, with the moon and stars clearly visible. The lights of the Parliament Buildings across the river were reflected in the water. She felt as if she had stepped into the Milky Way.

"Let's walk," she suggested, to prolong the evening. Angus took her arm and they strolled in comfortable silence. It felt right, the two of them arm in arm. Obviously he liked her, and that was a start, but in her heart she wanted more. She would have to proceed carefully. She had to try.

Pausing, she looked across at the Parliamentary library which glowed like a little round jewel on the cliff above the river.

"In Paris I walked by the Seine," she told him, "but this is just as beautiful."

"Very beautiful."

Looking up at him, she found that his eyes were on her, not the cityscape across the river. She reached for his hand and they continued across the bridge.

"Let's rest on the cathedral steps," she suggested, so they sat down with the great church looming above them. He put his arm around her.

"Another nice place to walk is along the Rideau Canal," he said. "Perhaps we could go for an evening stroll there."

"I'd like that."

"How about tomorrow evening at seven? We could meet at the Laurier Avenue bridge."

"That would be nice."

As they continued to her boarding house, she drank in the fresh air of almost-spring and felt as if she and the spring were one, she was so happy.

"Then I must be Indian summer," he joked, and she realized, to her embarrassment, that she had spoken her thoughts out loud.

Chapter Nineteen

The following evening as she approached the canal she saw him on a bench, and had a strong urge to steal up behind him and kiss his cheek. Instead, she called out, softly, "There you are!"

He turned and rose. "Hello!" he said, his face lighting up.

"I was afraid you might not show up. The House is sitting late tonight."

"I'd much rather walk with you in the fresh air than listen to a lot of hot air," he said. "Shall we aim to walk to the Hog's Back locks tonight?"

They were way out of the city. "Maybe not that far."

They set out along the path away from the city centre. Walking beside him, she wished he'd hold her hand, but he didn't. The last of the sunset was echoed in the water and the spring air had that hopeful feeling. She was pleased that he had the same ideas about walking as she did. They strolled along, talking, then both paused at a tree, not yet in leaf, its golden branches arching toward the ground. Once this weeping willow was filled out with foliage it would make the perfect secluded shelter where they could steal a kiss or two.

Then a gust of wind came along, plastering her coat to her body, and he put his arm around her and led her to a park bench sheltered by a clump of evergreens. She liked the sheltering arm, but it was withdrawn. Never mind. First they had to get to know each other, and she had endless questions. So they talked about their work and the personalities they'd encountered. She'd listened to a speech by Henri Bourassa, who had been her father's first seat mate in the House ten years earlier. Mr. Bourassa's excellent French and his strong ideas on the folly of the Great War and the need for Canadian neutrality in the modern world had impressed her. He and Father were of one mind on matters of war and peace, and had become good friends. To her dismay, however, she'd observed that Mr. Bourassa had retrograde ideas about the role of women; he believed their place was in the home.

"I've always believed," said Angus, "that social progress can be measured by the social position of the female sex." Music to Grace's ears.

They spoke of the Independent Labour Party conference in Montreal, coming up in a few weeks, which they both would be attending. She asked him what she should wear. Would the banquet require a long dress or would a street length one be appropriate?

Angus thought a street length one would be fine. "It's a workers' conference and a lot of women won't have long dresses to wear. I'm not taking my tuxedo; I'll wear the suit I have on now."

As sunset became twilight they rose and walked some more. Then the sky became indigo with the moon and stars shining. There was something unreal about the beauty of their reflections in the water, and the shadows of the trees in the street lights. She'd thought this kind of magic had died two years ago, but here it was, spring again, and the same kind of hopeful excitement was bubbling inside her.

She thought of a passage she'd read in a book by George Meredith about two levels of conversation going on simultaneously, the one that was aloud, and the other conversation, or interior monologue, going on in the conversationalists' thoughts. She looked up at him, hoping to read in his eyes his feelings about her. She wished on all the stars that he would want to see more of her. And, at midnight, when he saw her to her boarding house on Nepean Street, she hoped for a goodnight kiss.

Instead, he thanked her for her company and said he hoped it was the first of many such strolls. From the doorstep she watched his tall figure getting farther and farther away. Then, before he turned the corner he looked back and waved at her.

Next day he came into her father's office where she was typing, and asked her if she wanted to go for a walk that evening.

"I'd love to."

"I'll meet you outside your house at ten."

Evidently theirs was to be a late-evening, night-owl friendship – the best kind for now. Parliament Hill pulsed with gossip. Why stir up speculation about what was going on between them until they themselves knew?

They were walking along, deep in conversation that evening, when her foot caught a crack in the pavement, and she tripped – not strategically, but accidentally. Then she felt his hand on her elbow, steadying her. When they resumed walking she felt her hand enclosed by his large cool one.

At work, they were formal with each other, addressing each other as "Miss" and "Mr.", but they exchanged smiles and glances when no one was looking. Their evening walks were now a regular thing every night. Sitting on the bench that they called theirs, they shared their thoughts and feelings with each other. To her amazement and joy, she recognized Angus as her ideal friend, the one person who seemed to accept her completely. His approving attitude was a lot like her mother's unconditional love. Grace wondered if he could feel the admiration and affection – and desire – radiating out from her toward him.

One evening he asked if she intended to return to teaching or stay on helping her father and the Ginger Group. Impulsively, she decided to make a clean breast of what had happened to her career. She'd been avoiding all thoughts of the events that had brought her here to Ottawa for fear of conjuring up pessimism and futility. But now, in the twilight, holding his hand, she felt brave enough to revisit that awful time.

He listened without comment as she told him how ashamed she felt, for she had coped with difficult people and tough challenges before.

"If you don't mind my opinion," he said quietly, "it seems to me that you took on a job that put too great a burden on you. You had the training but not the experience. You'd studied hard for years and were exhausted. Intellectually you were qualified for the work, but not physically or emotionally."

What he was saying wasn't quite accurate, for she had taught successfully before her failure with French. It wasn't just the teaching that had laid her low, but she was so grateful for his calm sympathy that she decided not to elaborate.

"Probably many factors combined to make you break down," he continued, "and because you're sensitive and high-spirited you consider it a failure. But you were just in the wrong place. The change of scene and different work will make all the difference. It will be all onward and upward from now on."

"I hope so. Sometimes I feel worthless."

"No one in the Woodsworth family should have an inferiority complex," he said. "When you come up in the world from nothing, as I did, you always feel inferior in spite of any success. I feel awkward much of the time. I'm afraid of meeting people for the first time but I pretend otherwise and often come across as a know-it-all."

She squeezed his hand. "Friends can improve each other's outlook. Look what you're doing for mine."

"And vice versa."

She thought he was going to kiss her, but the moment passed.

In another conversation she admitted to feeling ashamed at being financially dependent on her parents at her age. They never complained, though only two of their six children were self-supporting and they still had three to educate. She felt especially guilty because her father scrimped and saved to support them. He also managed to donate a tenth of his income to the Independent Labour Party. When he travelled around giving speeches about the need for democratic socialism, he never paid for a sleeping berth but sat up in the tourist class coach all night, taking his food with him in brown paper bags to save money.

Angus pointed out that, in these hard times, many young women and men had to fall back on their families. As a former school trustee, he knew that teachers really worked hard for their money, and since she had buckled under the strain, nobody would expect her to go back to teaching. He admitted that he was no stranger to guilt. He sometimes felt badly about leaving the burden of the P.E.I. farm to his brother and heading west. He assured Grace that her experience on the Hill could lead to other work in Ottawa.

Grace then shared another secret. Although she loved her father, she sometimes didn't like him. He had always been driven, a man on a mission. He was exacting about how he wanted things done, and often impatient. Their home life always chugged along well under her mother's benevolent leadership, but when he came home, the atmosphere got tense, as he was always exhausted and needed quiet when he was working or sleeping, and it was hard on her younger brothers who were naturally boisterous.

Angus said he worried about Grace getting scolded for dropping into his office so often, though he was always delighted when she did.

"Father thinks I'm helping you with your work."

"And you are."

Grace believed that she was of help to her father, but wished her mother were here to keep him to a schedule of nutritious food and sufficient rest. For now, though, her mother had to stay in Winnipeg while the boys were still in school. Her parents couldn't afford to educate their children and maintain homes in both Winnipeg and Ottawa. Also, it was important that they live, if not right in his constituency, then near it.

"Your father's a saint," Angus said firmly, "and from what I've read, saints aren't usually easy people to get along with, although J.S. has been very good to me."

Grace told Angus that her parents were going to Europe in mid-August for about three months, because her father had been seconded to work for the League of Nations Secretariat for the fall session, and her mother was accompanying him. They intended to see contacts in Britain and France, and hoped to go to the Soviet Union to observe the embryonic workers' state being organized there. They'd asked Grace to take charge of the home in their absence, since Belva, the other possibility, would be leaving to teach in Vancouver. Angus thought a change of scene and some time together would do her parents good. Then he spoke of his own plans when Parliament recessed.

"I'm not boasting when I say that I'm the only man who can bring the B.C. branch of the Socialist Party, and the other small left-wing parties in B.C. into a new federation of the left," he said. "Your father can't. He's known nationally, but some of the more doctrinaire British Columbia socialists consider him too middle class."

As a member of the Socialist Party (which was under the Independent Labour umbrella) Angus planned to travel around the province speaking to labour groups and to anyone who wanted to hear about democratic socialism being the only way out of the capitalist morass.

"Sometimes I feel caught in the middle," he confided. "Some of the Ginger Group members, like Miss MacPhail, consider me a Bolshevik because I criticize the capitalist system and speak for labour. Some of the British Columbia socialists, like Mr. Winch, think I'm too moderate in my critique of capitalism. Meanwhile the depression keeps getting worse. The non-communist left needs a viable party to give Canadians an alternative to the status quo."

"But you have the respect of a lot of people in both factions," she insisted. His chances as a mediator would be enhanced by a ringing good speech on the budget, which would then be published in the western labour papers. The following day at work she persuaded him to rehearse his speech again. While in his office she produced a draft of her article for the *Labour Annual*, and asked for his opinion, and he grinned ear to ear. He read it on the spot, said it was first rate, then asked if their evening walks were keeping her out too late.

"Not at all," she assured him.

"I've always been a night owl. Also, while we're getting to know each other we should have some privacy. Walking out together late in the evening is the only way I can think of for us to develop our friendship away from prying eyes."

"Tonight, then, at 10:00?"

That evening, as he was bending his head down to her, to better hear her voice over the spring piping of the frogs, she kissed his cheek. He hesitated for a moment, then put his arms around her and she tasted his soft lips and his minty breath, and it was thrilling.

The following day, when she came into his office with some letters for him to sign, she stood beside him, and after he'd scrawled his signature, she touched his silky dark hair. His face was that of a surprised boy. Then he stood and took her in his arms and kissed her until footsteps in the corridor made them ease apart.

"We're tempting fate," he murmured. The door was unlocked; anyone could walk in. "Later," she whispered, and left the office. Then, out in the corridor she paused, then opened the door again. From behind his desk he looked up, smiling and bewildered.

She approached him, smiling. "I want more."

So did he, but again they drew away reluctantly when they heard footsteps outside. Grace smoothed down her hair and picked up her letters. Just as she opened her father's door, Mr. Heaps came out of her father's office.

"Hello, Grace." He strode down the hall and knocked on Angus's door. A narrow escape, she thought. They laughed about it that night when they were sitting on their bench, and agreed to be more cautious.

One morning when her father was dictating a letter to her as she typed, there was a knock on the door frame.

"Mac!" her father greeted him. Grace turned to see Angus in the doorway.

"I want to introduce Miss P., a friend of mine from Vancouver. She's a strong labour supporter and an admirer of yours."

Beside Angus was a tall, smartly dressed woman, possibly in her mid-thirties, her eyes wide with anticipation.

"Oh, Mr. Woodsworth, it's such an honour!" She stepped forward and held out both her arms to Father, as if for an embrace. "I heard you speak the last time you were in Vancouver, and I was spell-bound, simply in awe."

Father looked pleased as he shook her hand. Who would not enjoy such effusiveness? It was only human to like praise. Grace was used to women gushing over her father, but she still found it annoying, even though she knew that her mother was the only one for him. Sometimes at social gatherings a little crowd of ladies would sit around him, hanging on his every word, and afterwards, he sometimes remarked that some little Miss Information, some dumb Dora, had a keen grasp of socialist principles. When this happened, Grace and her siblings would exchange glances and giggle.

"I'm always happy to meet supporters of our movement. This is my daughter, Grace, who is also my assistant."

Grace greeted Miss P. with her best company manners. Miss P. glanced at her as if she were the coat stand.

"Do sit down." Her father indicated the sofa and chairs. "Tea? Yes? Grace, could you arrange that, please."

"Certainly."

When she carried in the tray, Father, Angus and Miss P. were talking about the Vancouver political scene.

"Angus is sorely missed," Miss P. was saying, with a slight Scottish lilt. "He's such a commanding presence when he addresses an audience. Education is my field, and when I first heard him speak at a school board meeting, I thought, *This gentleman is going places*. And you certainly have, Angus!" She smiled fondly at him.

Grace poured the tea, including a cup for herself, and asked Miss P. if she had toured the Parliamentary Library, the only part of the original building which had survived the fire of 1916. Miss P. seemed startled at the question, as if a mouse had crept out from under the desk and spoken.

"No, not yet."

As the visitor chattered on, Grace fought down the impulse to chip in and correct some of the things she said. She restrained herself and sipped her tea. Finally the telephone rang, a cue for tea-time to end.

"Mac, are you showing Miss P. the sights of Ottawa?" Father inquired.

"He has been wonderful!" She beamed at Angus. "This morning we took a street car out to the Experimental Farm to see the glorious blossoms. After lunch today – in the Parliamentary Restaurant – he's going to show me some other beauty spots in the city."

"How long can you stay?" Father asked the question Grace had been dying to ask.

"Today and tomorrow. Then we're off to Montreal."

"I hope you have a fine time."

"Oh, how could I not with a big strong man like Angus to show me around." She tucked her arm around Angus's and they left the office.

Grace and her father went back to work. He was dictating a letter as she typed it. After making three mistakes she ripped the paper out of the typewriter and said that if he was going to go so fast, she'd better take it down in longhand, which she did. Her father suggested that she spend the afternoon in the Gallery watching the proceedings of Parliament and gathering information for her next article.

The next interruption was the arrival of some new photographs. Father had wanted a new picture of himself to reflect the way he looked now; his old campaign photo dated from before he'd gone grey. He'd insisted that Grace have pictures taken, too, as she would need them to accompany her articles.

"Very distinguished looking," she told him. "Let's send one to Mother today."

He studied hers. "You look very grown up."

Mr. Karsh had insisted on lipstick and a dark outfit for good contrast. Her lips were full and sensuous, her black silk blouse shining. She looked mature, self-confident, even sultry. She liked this unfamiliar self that the photographer had somehow seen in her.

That evening after dinner her father went back to the office, but insisted that she go home and get some rest. It was a soft spring evening, ideal for "walking out" with a lover. Did she still have one?

"Nothing lasts," she thought. Up in her room she lay down and tried to lose herself in a book. She was about to put on her nightgown when her landlady rapped on the door.

"A gentleman to see you," she puffed. "I asked him if he knew what time it is and he said he did, but it was important."

Grace flew downstairs and found Angus in the front hall.

"Can you come out for a while, so we can talk?"

"Let me get my coat and key."

Back upstairs, as she put on her coat, she opened the envelope of pictures and put one in her pocket, just in case.

They walked past the Edwardian houses on Nepean Street.

"I won't keep you out long," he said. "I want to explain."

Miss P. was on her way to Scotland to teach in Glasgow, indefinitely, perhaps permanently. Her mother was one of the Labour women who had worked on Angus's campaigns. He had taken Miss P. to several functions but they hadn't been "going together". When she'd written that she was stopping off in Ottawa, he could hardly refuse to see her and show her around. She'd asked him to accompany her to Montreal and see her aboard her ship to Scotland, and he couldn't decently refuse.

"I understand," Grace told him. "You don't want to alienate a supporter and campaign worker. Did you take Miss P. walking along the Driveway?"

"Yes, but I didn't sit with her on *our* bench."

Grace had to laugh. "Are you sure she's not an old girlfriend?"

"She's not. I was engaged to be married a while back, though. Not any more."

Grace stopped in her tracks. "Oh?"

"Not any more. The woman, Miss Em, broke it off because she said our differences in education and background wouldn't make for a happy marriage. In other words, I was too ignorant and working class for her."

Grace was stricken.

"She was a fool," she blurted. "Are you over her?"

"Absolutely. She's just a friend now, and so is Miss P. While I'm showing her around and taking her to Montreal I'll be thinking of you all the time."

Grace took out her photograph. "You'll need this to remember me by."

He peered at it under a street light.

"It's beautiful, a perfect likeness. May I kiss you?"

"I insist."

The approaching labour convention in Montreal gave Grace and Angus a reason for working closely together. He was nervous about speaking for the first time to a large labour gathering in the East, and wanted to do well. She felt a twinge of apprehension as she helped him organize his speech, not only for him, but for herself. She had been asked to address the audience too, on the subject of women in the Independent Labour Party, and was determined to do a good job.

Her greatest challenge at the convention, however, would be to stand on the platform beside her father, translating as he spoke. Then in the question and answer period she would have to listen closely to the questions posed to him in French, translate them into English for him, then translate his replies into French again for the audience. She had done this before, but not at such a large meeting.

In years to come she would look back on this convention as a unique experience for many reasons. First of all, she found that when she was interpreting for her father on stage she was too busy concentrating to be afraid, though afterwards when she sat down she was clammy with sweat.

Her father's talk focused on the economic plight of Canadians and what should be done. Nationalization of the banks and railways was essential. Speaking of the gap between rich and poor, he got an outburst of applause when he said, "If it is a case of high dividends for the shareholders or a decent living for the workers, let a decent living for the workers come first."

When Angus was called upon to speak, Grace sat with her hands clasped and her nails digging into her palms. At first hesitant, he soon found his voice, and it was as if he were among family. Abandoning his notes, he spoke from the heart and did well. He focused on the need both to improve existing conditions for workers and to reorganize the entire economy along fairer lines. He emphasized the importance of including people of all races and creeds in both the union movement and the labour party.

Watching him, Grace understood why he'd risen in politics. Outside the House of Commons, among his fellow workers, he came across as the knowledgeable and experienced man that he was. She was in awe of him, she adored him and admired him. In a world where the economic system was collapsing, he grasped the magnitude of the situation and had ideas about what should be done.

Then: "Who am I," she thought, "to imagine myself as the woman he needs for his life?"

If he ever married, he'd want someone more like him, someone strong, who had struggled against the odds to make something of herself and who knew firsthand the harsh realities of workers' lives. Grace felt small and unworthy.

When it was her turn to address the crowd, though, she put aside these self-doubts and gave a speech that generated a wave of applause. She was presented with roses, and, as she sat down, Angus gave her a big smile and an enthusiastic thumbs-up.

After speeches by Mr. Heaps and several union leaders, when people came up to speak to them informally, she sought Angus out in the crush and told him that his speech had been superb.

"You're a little flatterer," he said, but he looked delighted.

When she entered the banquet room that evening she saw him standing alone and went over and took his hand. Then they found themselves seated side by side. It was impolite, as well as too obvious, to direct all her attention to him, so she turned to the person seated on her other side, the secretary of the Montreal District Labour Council. His name was Dave Lewis.

They exchanged compliments on their speeches.

"And your Welsh accent made it a pleasure to listen to," she added.

He laughed and shook his head.

"I'm not Welsh," he said. "I'm a member of another chosen people. One of my teachers was Welsh."

Soon she was hearing about his life. His father, a socialist in Poland, had immigrated to Canada with his wife and children when Dave was twelve. He'd been put into a beginners' class at school, which hurt his pride, so he'd buckled down and learned English in record time. He was now a law student and an applicant for a Rhodes Scholarship to Oxford University. Grace spoke of the glimpse of Britain she'd seen back in 1928-29.

"That year abroad was an amazing experience," she remarked, "but a challenge in many ways and sometimes a lonely one."

Mr. Lewis wasn't worried about loneliness because his girlfriend was going with him. She wouldn't be allowed to live with him, or even to live in Oxford; the university was strict about that, but she would find secretarial work in London and he would go and see her on weekends.

Grace admired them for being a thoroughly modern young couple and hoped he'd be awarded the Rhodes Scholarship.

Back in Ottawa, she found Angus in his office reading an account of the convention in the *Montreal Gazette*.

"Listen to this," he said, with a big smile.

"Although not a 'rabid feminist', Miss Woodsworth nevertheless feels that women are as prominent as men and are using their franchise to better advantage. She said that there is no pink tea atmosphere to any of the women's labour group meetings. She finds working with her father a – 'recreation'."

She gasped. Had she actually used the words "rabid feminist?" Surely that was the journalist's interpretation. And she was sure she'd said "capable", not "prominent."

"Well, my work *is* a recreation, at least in one respect." Her mouth twitched.

"There's more." Angus picked up the paper. *"Of medium height and decidedly attractive in appearance, with black hair and expressive eyes, she has the gift of holding the attention of her audience with her well modulated voice and effective gestures."*

"The reporter certainly got that right," he commented.

She peered over his shoulder at the article.

"The reporter didn't say anything about your physical appearance and voice. It isn't fair that what I look like should be made as important as what I have to say."

"I agree, but the reporter did give you three paragraphs," he pointed out.

"Probably when more women get into politics the press won't be so interested in our looks. But how would you like it if you read something like this: *Tall and decidedly handsome in appearance, with dark hair and expressive hazel eyes, Angus MacInnis holds audiences spellbound with his resonant voice and the movements of his capable-looking hands.?"*

He began to laugh.

"I'd be delighted. Speaking of hands, I was awfully pleased when you came up to me before the banquet and slipped your little hand into mine."

Then Mr. Heaps came into the office and they complimented him on his talk.

The lilacs were in bud; it was definitely spring, but the session of Parliament showed no signs of coming to an end. She anticipated more walks on successive evenings, and thought about where they might lead. Then, inadvertently, she did a terrible thing. In one of the handwritten letters Angus gave her to type, he'd written "quiet" when it should have been "quite." When she took the typed letter and the original back to him, she'd made a joke about being "quite quiet", intending to draw his attention to it in a lighthearted way so that he would remember for the future. Instead of laughing, he looked like a slapped child, and for the rest of the day he avoided her. When he didn't show up at 10:30 that night to go walking, nor at 11:00, she realized she'd rubbed salt into an open wound of inferiority. From now on – if she had a future with him – she'd walk on eggshells and just make the corrections quite quietly.

The next day at work when she found him alone in his office, she apologized and he told her to think no more about it. That night, much to her relief, they went walking, and their kissing, as usual, never seemed to be enough.

Love made them reckless. One afternoon, after watching Question Period from the gallery, she was returning to Socialist Alley when Angus caught up with her. He opened his office door and held out his hand. As soon as they were inside he closed the door and took her in his arms. Then she heard a faint noise. Was it a snore? He'd heard it too, for he released her and stood transfixed. It seemed to be coming from the sofa. They tiptoed over and found, fast asleep, the wife of another Ginger Group

Member of Parliament. Her coat was over her knees; her purse and shopping bag were on the floor. It was general custom for the Ginger Group members to pop into each other's offices quite freely and obviously she'd made herself at home.

Angus grabbed Grace's hand and together they crept to the door, praying it wouldn't creak as they opened it. Back in the hall they struggled to control their laughter. She led him into her father's office, but the mood was broken. Since they were together, Grace told him it was an opportunity to rehearse his budget speech again. Recently the speaker had ruled a member out of order for reading a speech, and she didn't want that to happen to Angus.

The day he gave the speech in the House she sat white-knuckling in the Gallery with her eyes glued to him. He stood up very straight and appeared to be looking the finance minister in the eye, though actually, as she had advised, he had chosen a point in the air just above the man's head. He began in a strong voice and continued in a well-paced manner. When he came to the quotes from constituents' letters, his voice cracked, but he soon recovered, and, anyway, some authentic emotion was not a bad thing. He ended within his allocated time period and received vigorous applause from the Ginger Group and from some Liberals, too.

That night, on their bench, they relived every nuance of his performance. He looked the happiest she had ever seen him, particularly when she said they should not delay in sending his speech to the *Labour Statesman*.

"I couldn't have done it without you," he told her.

"Sure you could have."

One June night she realized with a sinking heart that these evening walks that she lived for would soon be coming to an end. When the session came to a close he would be travelling to the coal and steel towns of Nova Scotia where conditions were driving the miners to militancy. After that, he had some speeches to give in Ontario, and then he'd be heading back to Vancouver. Her plans were to visit her relatives at Cavan, near Peterborough, Ontario, for a week or so, then go home to take charge of the house and her younger brothers. She wouldn't see Angus for months, until Parliament was called again and that might not be until January of 1932. Absence didn't always make the heart grow fonder; there was another saying, "Out of sight, out of mind."

On their bench, she drew as close to him as possible and cherished every affectionate word he spoke to her.

"When I first came to Ottawa," he told her one evening, "I had no idea that I would find a friend like you. I'm continually astonished that a pretty, talented young thing like yourself wants to spend time with me."

"I value your company above everything." She sounded like a character in a Jane Austen novel, so she elaborated. "Your kindness has a good effect on me. Since you've come into my life I feel more steady and self-confident."

They kissed. She wanted more. She let her hand creep up his arm, then feel its way between the buttons of his coat to touch his chest. He didn't object, but he never took any liberties with her, and she began to wonder why. The night they'd had supper at an out-of-the way café in Hull where the E.B. Eddy workers ate, their knees had brushed under the table, and he'd shifted away.

She finally decided to speak up and clarify things.

"I'll miss you when the session ends," she said one evening when they were sitting on their bench. "Will you have time to write to me?"

"Of course, if you'll write to me too."

"I'd like to. But some things are easier to say in person than in a letter." She met his eyes. "For instance: I need to know if you have special feelings for me, or if I'm just one of many women you like."

"You're special to me," he said in his gravelly voice, "and it terrifies me."

She snuggled close. "Why am I so frightening?"

"You're not. You're everything a man could want. But I'm so old and you're so young and lovely and educated, with your whole life in front of you. I want to keep on seeing you but I'm not sure it's fair to you."

"It's what I would like, because I'm in love with you."

He studied her face. "Are you sure? You have to be really sure."

"I am."

Then his arms were around her and his lips on hers with a new intensity. When they came apart for air, he said he worried about taking unfair advantage of her. "I've sometimes thought it's inexperience that makes you lavish your love on me. You've been too busy studying to meet many other men."

This was no moment to admit that she'd been in love before.

"I'm old enough to understand my feelings," she said. "I'm twenty-six."

"All of twenty-six!" He laughed. "As old as that?"

"These past months with you have been the happiest in my life. You've changed me for the better, whether you think so or not, and I don't want this to end."

"I don't either, but for now I should get you home."

As they left the seclusion of the Driveway, a policeman patrolling his beat approached them. "It's past midnight," he informed them. "Close to 1 a.m."

"We're on our way home, officer," Angus told them.

"What should we do now?" he asked, when they reached her door.

"Keep on with what we've started. But maybe not tell anyone we love each other, not just yet. And when the session ends, we'll write."

"And I'll come to see you in Winnipeg on my way back home. How's that?"

"That would be lovely."

Chapter Twenty

The session went on into July, and they enjoyed many a hot, floral scented evening together. Then Parliament recessed. Her second-last evening in Ottawa she worked late, tying up loose ends for her father, while Angus, just down the hall, packed up the papers he'd need. They left the Parliament Buildings separately but when she got to the wrought-iron gates that led from Parliament Hill to Wellington Street, he was waiting for her to set out on their evening ramble. She tried not to think about the following evening, when they would part. When they reached their bench and he bent to kiss her, tears crept out of her eyes.

"I'm sorry." She searched for her handkerchief but couldn't find it, so he took out his and gently wiped her cheeks. Then he gathered her in his arms and asked if she knew any poems by Robert Burns.

"The first verse of *My Love is Like a Red Red Rose*."

"The other verses are important too." He recited the poem, which ended: *"And I will come again, my love, though it were ten thousand miles."*

"That's how I feel about you," he said. "I'll come to see you in Winnipeg. And when we're married, if I go on any speaking tours, ten thousand miles or less, I'll want you with me."

"Married?" Their eyes met. He nodded, and she covered his face with kisses.

The following evening he saw her off at the station. Her destination was Port Hope, on Lake Ontario, where her cousin would meet her and drive her to the family farm at Cavan, the first lap of her return to Winnipeg. She'd given Angus her Cavan address, and would send her letters to his Parliamentary address because he'd be stopping there after his eastern tour.

"Pardon me, sir, ma'am, could you spare some change?"

A stubble-cheeked, threadbare man, leaning on a cane, hobbled toward them.

"Anything you can spare. I've been out of work for a year now."

Angus handed him a dollar.

"God bless you, sir."

"Vote Labour," Angus told him.

When she was about to board Angus handed her the brown paper bag he was carrying. She peeked inside and found oranges.

"Thank you," she said. "Thank you for so many things."

"I'll see you in a few weeks." He squeezed her hand.

It hadn't seemed worthwhile to pay for a berth for a five hour trip, especially as she was too filled with emotion to sleep anyway. Lulled by the motion of the train, however, she nodded off, and next thing she knew the conductor was calling "Port Hope." It was sunrise when she disembarked, and since there was no sign of her cousin, she went for a stroll along the lakeshore. As she ate an orange, watching a fishing boat bob up and down, she wished Angus were with her to share in the perfection of the morning. Then she heard, "Grace!" and there was tall, strapping Cousin Ralph waving at her.

After Gibson's Landing, B.C., the farm at Cavan was the place she loved most. "Sylvan Sward", a thriving mixed farm, had been in her mother's family for generations; here her mother had grown up, and here her parents had been married. When the big farmhouse set against rolling green hills came into view, she felt at home.

Her parents had brought her here first when she was a year old, and she remembered her father carrying her outdoors one morning to see the horses, with their velvet noses and enormous teeth. When he'd set her down on the grass she'd felt dew on her feet for the first time. That summer her parents had left her in her grandmother's care when they travelled to Europe. Mother, however, came back early, and when Father returned and took a pastorate in British Columbia, she'd stayed in Cavan with Grace until Belva was born.

Later, when Father was moving from the Stella Avenue Mission to the Bureau of Social Research, Mother and the children, four of them then, had come east again for an extended stay. Much later, during the family's Ottawa years, they used to visit the farm. Grace remembered picking wild raspberries, sitting in "the armchair", a big rock with a U shaped cleft in it and visiting the Tallman sweet apple tree at the foot of the orchard that Grace's mother, as a child, considered "her tree." There was a maple on the front lawn where orioles built their nest every year. Here, Grace always had a sense of belonging and continuity. The morning of her arrival was fragrant with new mown hay, reminding her of the summer when she and Charles visited for a month. She'd worn overalls and helped her cousins, four boys, with the haying.

When they reached the house, Aunt Ethel greeted her at the door, embraced her and led her into the kitchen, redolent with the aromas of coffee and sizzling bacon. There were eight at the table: Aunt Ethel, Uncle Sandfield, herself, three of the four cousins, a hired man and a hired girl, Gretchen, about Grace's age.

Everyone was glad to see Grace and eager to catch up on family news and the latest in Ottawa. She entertained them with stories about the important people she'd seen, omitting the most important one. Later, when she offered to lend a hand with anything that needed doing, she was taken at her word. Her first afternoon chore was ironing, and when the evening meal came around – known as "tea" – she was glad. After a game of bridge, they went to bed at 9:30, the earliest Grace had retired for months.

As she started upstairs, Cousin Ralph said he was taking a load of veal calves into Peterborough the next morning, early, and that she was welcome to come along for the ride. "Yes," she said, for here was an opportunity to mail a letter to Angus. Upstairs, she got out pencil and paper and wrote:

"I want to send you just a word to say that I miss you tonight. It's cool and fragrant with clover, and very quiet, with a new moon. It's everything the heart could wish for, except you. As a first love letter this can hardly be called a success, but farms and writing don't go well together. What more is there to say except that I am thinking of you always. Your Grace."

Grace wasn't the only person in the household who was in love. One day when she was gathering eggs, Gretchen, the hired girl, asked her in lightly-accented English, how she was related to the family. When Grace explained that she was a first cousin, Gretchen seemed relieved, then asked if Ralph had ever mentioned her. As Grace shook her head, Gretchen blushed, then blurted that she really liked him, he was so tall and handsome, with curly hair and a dimpled chin. She hated the thought of leaving in the fall to study nursing. Grace had observed that, while he was kind and polite to Gretchen, he didn't seem interested in her; his heart was elsewhere. Grace told Gretchen that it was always good for a woman to have some sort of special training.

Cousin Ralph declared at suppertime that he needed a break from farm work. Would Grace like to take a road trip to celebrate her birthday on July 25th? As Gretchen looked downcast, he proposed a jaunt to Toronto to pick up his brother, then a drive to Niagara Falls. Then they'd cross into the States, drive around Lake Ontario, and cross back into Canada near Kingston. Grace said she'd love to.

On the drive to Toronto, her cousin divulged that he'd wanted to get away from Gretchen, who fancied him, though he hadn't encouraged her. Feeling like a matchmaker, Grace pointed out that Gretchen was very pretty, with pale blonde hair, and certainly capable of a farm wife's duties.

"She's nice," he said, "but I don't have those feelings for her, and even if I did, it's no time to marry, with the economy as it is."

It's no time to marry thudded on Grace's eardrums. She'd been thinking of telling this childhood pal about Angus, but decided not to. Instead, she asked Ralph if he'd ever been in love. Turning red, he said there was a girl he liked a lot, but she didn't live anywhere nearby and he hardly ever saw her.

"When I see her," Grace told him, "I'll ask her to write to you more often."

His mouth flew open and his face turned tomato-red. For many years, Grace had suspected him of having a crush on her sister; whenever Belva visited the farm he never took his eyes off her. Though Belva claimed that she had no romantic feelings toward him, she and Ralph had been corresponding since they started high school, addressing each other as "Curly" and "Bubbles."

In Toronto Grace and Ralph met up with Ralph's older brother and the three of them proceeded to Niagara. Grace found the falls breathtaking and wished she were seeing them with Angus. It was exciting, though, to sail along American highways at sixty miles an hour with the windows open and the wind in her hair. On arriving in Rochester, New York, they found that the relatives they were planning to stay with were away, and found a tourist cabin at eleven o'clock that night. The following day they crossed back into Canada on the ferry at Gananoque. This carefree trip had been a welcome change.

Back at the farm a letter was waiting. Grace read it in a secluded corner of the lawn, smiling at the birthday card, signed with "love".

"Ever since you left, the bells in the Peace Tower have sounded awfully mournful," he wrote. *"I never noticed that about them before."*

He'd be speaking in Hamilton one weekend soon and wondered if she could meet him there. It killed her to say no, but Cousin Ralph couldn't take time off again so soon to chauffeur her to Hamilton, and besides, there would be questions.

She took her pen and paper out to the lawn and sat under the tree with the oriole's nest to answer Angus.

"Let me know your plans for the west," she wrote. *"If you can keep me abreast of your travels, we can meet in Toronto, and if you're not too proud and plutocratic to travel tourist with me, we could have a good trip together."*

A letter came from Mother saying that she and Father would be leaving on their travels on August 19th. It was time to get home and touch base with them before they left. Eagerly she awaited Angus's reply.

His next letter said nothing about travelling west, but was full of his experiences in Atlantic Canada. He said he missed her and looked forward to seeing her again, but nothing about meeting her at the station in Toronto. Was he afraid that, when travelling together they would meet someone they knew and their secret engagement would become public knowledge? Would that be so bad?

They'd rarely gone out in the daytime; the last occasion had been to an Ottawa department store, where she'd helped him choose a dress for his niece. He'd claimed he was hopeless at shopping, except for china, and needed her advice. It had been fun. Grace was ready to take their relationship into the light of day. Why wasn't he?

A letter came from her father, mentioning that he'd had lunch with "Mac" in the Parliamentary restaurant, but not what they'd talked about. Presumably it was the economy, not Angus's intentions.

Finally she wrote to Angus, informing him that there was a CNR train leaving Toronto at 10 p.m. the following Tuesday, and that she would be on it, tourist class, upper berth as usual. *"If you find it convenient to be along, so much the better,"* she wrote. *"If not, I shall understand. Love, your Grace."*

Chapter Twenty-one

Angus was there, also travelling tourist class, but they had only time to exchange a few words before they were shown to their berths, just enough time to arrange to meet for breakfast in the dining car at 8 a.m. That night, despite the gentle rocking of the train, she slept poorly because she was brimming over with anticipation.

At 8 a.m. when she entered the dining care, he was there, reading the *Globe and Mail* and sipping coffee. When he saw her, smiled, and rose to pull out her chair, all nervousness vanished. While acres of evergreen forest sped past, she ate her preferred breakfast: coffee and a grapefruit. He'd been reading about the Governor of New York, a reformer, who might be seeking the Democratic presidential nomination next year.

"Just another plutocrat living on inherited wealth," he remarked, but Grace was not so sure. She'd read about the governor's wife and her work for the poor and thought she might influence Governor Roosevelt.

"You know a lot about politics," Angus remarked. "You must be a quick study to have learned so much since you came to Ottawa, or else you were interested long before that."

With a pang of alarm that he knew so little about her after four months, she said that no one could have grown up with parents like hers and not be interested in world affairs and the class struggle. At the time of the Winnipeg General Strike, she was thirteen and living with her mother and the other kids at Gibson's Landing, B.C. while her father was on a speaking tour for the labour movement. When he heard about the strike in his home town, he was aboard a train in Northern B.C., and he continued on to Winnipeg, hoping he could get both sides talking to each other. The two sides were too firmly entrenched for that, so he helped the workers' committee which ran the city for six weeks and ensured good order and the necessities of life. The business elite, however, backed by all three levels of government, was determined to break the strike and eventually succeeded. Her father, who was working on the strikers' newspaper with Fred Dixon, was arrested and charged with seditious libel.

Grace had been frightened, but tried not to show it for fear of alarming the younger children. Her mother had been magnificent. She'd asked Grace to take all her father's socialist books and hide them, in case the North West Mounted Police came searching for evidence of sedition. Grace had done so, and although the police never came, she'd felt better for being able to do something to help her family.

"You'll like my mother," she told Angus. "At the time of the General Strike she wrote to my aunt in Winnipeg, saying that she didn't want a life of comfort and security, not even for us children, while others lacked these things. She has always been as one with my father in wanting a world of equality, especially economic equality."

In recent years, now that the children were older, her mother had become more active in the peace and socialist movements. In Vancouver, back in 1921, she helped found a branch of the Women's International League for Peace and Freedom, and in 1924 she and Agnes MacPhail attended the organization's international conference in Washington, D.C.

"She and Agnes are good friends, but on that trip she found Agnes a little hard to take," she added. "Agnes asked the hotel management to change them to another room because she found the wallpaper too overpowering."

Angus said it sounded like Miss MacPhail all right. Back in the almost empty coach they continued their conversation. When he asked if she hoped for a life like her mother's – the heart of the home, making time for causes she believed in, Grace hesitated. While her mother was happy in her choices, and an expert in juggling several projects at the same time, Grace didn't want to duplicate that life exactly.

"My parents are still in love with each other after all these years, and regard each other as equal partners, and I want that with you," she began. "But I'd like to be active in the world more than she's been. When she got married at thirty she'd already had a professional career. I haven't. She has always seemed delighted with us children, but I doubt that I could keep up that level of enthusiasm. I'm at my best when working on a project, like getting a student through his entrance exams or writing an article. Politics may be a man's world at present, but it interests me."

He reached for her hand under cover of his newspaper.

"I like the way you speak your mind."

"Oh-oh. Do I shock you?"

"Oh, no. From the first time we met you impressed me as a woman who, if she cared for the company of men at all, wanted it on a basis of equality."

His words disturbed her. Surely he didn't think...

"It's my hair, isn't it!' she exclaimed. "I know it's short, but the hairdresser assured me that it's the latest style for women. It's called an 'Eton crop' and it's easy to take care of. It isn't a sign that I dislike the company of men, because I do like men, one man in particular."

"I wasn't implying anything. I only meant that I like a woman with ideas and opinions." Angus was grinning widely.

"Even Miss MacPhail?" she teased.

"I respect her opinions even when they don't coincide with mine."

They talked about the unfortunate political divide between farmers and urban workers which would make it hard to draw both groups into a federation of the democratic left. Farmers, who worked from sun-up to sun-down, thought that urban workers, with a ten-hour day, had it easy. Farmers' incomes depended on the weather and the crops; to them, anyone who got a regular wage was fortunate and should be too grateful to go on strike. Saskatchewan grain farmers, however, were the exception. Bankrupted by drought, they were desperate, angry at the two old political parties, and ripe for change.

Thinking of the United Farmers in the Ginger Group, Angus mentioned hearing that Bob Gardiner, Agnes's intimate friend, was ill and thinking of retiring to his Alberta farm. He'd also heard that Bob had proposed to Agnes – again – and that she'd turned him down again.

"Bob hasn't interfered in her career so far," he observed, "so why would he if they were married? Agnes is such a strong character; if ever a woman would insist on equality in marriage, she would."

"She considers matrimony a trap for women, because, once a woman marries, society expects her to retire to the home. And maybe she's afraid that, once legally tied to him, she might fall out of love with him."

Angus fell silent. Oh, dear. She should have realized that the subtext of this conversation was their own future. Perish the thought that they might fall out of love after they were married. She wished she'd bitten her tongue.

Then Angus smiled at her the way an adult does at a child who is afraid of getting into trouble, and her discomfort evaporated. He offered her the news section of his paper, and they read in comfortable silence. She felt very happy being so close to him, their arms brushing, his shoulder sometimes touching her cheek because of the motion of the train. Then her eyes closed, and she awoke four hours later with her head on his shoulder. She quickly straightened up, hoping she hadn't drooled, snored or cried out.

He smiled. "You looked so peaceful. I dozed off too for a little while."

It was on the tip of her tongue to joke that this was the first time they'd slept together, but she refrained. The train must have stopped several times, for there were more passengers in the car. Down the aisle, a mother with three young children was offering bread and jam to the older two, while the baby slept on one of the seats. The toddler dropped his piece of bread and jam face down in the aisle, and began to cry when his mother wouldn't let him eat it. She shushed him and gave him her bread and jam.

In Grace's overhead luggage was an orange she'd brought from Cavan. She got it out and offered it to the mother, who was very grateful. Grace watched as the woman spread out her handkerchief, carefully peeled and sectioned the orange, then divided the pieces equally between the toddler and the preschooler. The mother nibbled the peel.

When Angus went out to the club car for a cigarette, Grace opened her book.

"Excuse me, Miss, could I ask a favour?" The young mother was standing in the aisle near Grace, the two older kids clinging to her skirt. "Would you keep an eye on the baby while I take these two to the washroom and clean them up?"

"Certainly."

As the mother shepherded her sticky children down the aisle, Grace moved opposite the infant asleep on the seat. Six months old, she guessed. Was it still breast-fed? The mother kept it well; its clothes were well-worn but clean and it looked healthy.

When Angus returned to the car, having forgotten his tobacco, the noise and draft from the door woke the baby. As its brown eyes searched for its mother, it wrinkled up its face to cry. Then the train lurched. Its mouth fell open but it was too startled to squall as it rolled toward Grace. She scooped it up, held it against her and patted its back. Its little hands clung to her. She hoped it wouldn't spit up. To her relief, the child merely whimpered, then closed its eyes. The mother and children, who were taking their own sweet time, finally returned and she handed it over.

"Well done," murmured Angus, as she returned to her seat beside him. He began talking about his young niece, who had come as a toddler to live with him and his sister. He'd felt completely at a loss when she used to cry at the top of her lungs, and would leave her to Christine or his mother, who would rock her and talk to her until she calmed down.

"You have a way with babies," he added.

"I had a lot of practice with Bruce and Howard when they were little. Tell me more about your niece."

"She's a delight in many ways. She's growing up pretty, and talented in music. It will be quite a while, though, before she's out on her own."

"Clearly you've been like a father to her."

His eyes met Grace's.

"I know what you're getting at, Grace, so I'll be as direct as you usually are. I don't want us to have a child right away. We'll want to enjoy each other's company. And in these uncertain times..."

"I feel the same way."

"You do?"

"Yes."

He took her hand in his. She wished he would put his arm around her but the coach was nearly full and it was always possible that someone they knew would pass through and recognize him.

He asked her about her younger years, so she told him about living in Vancouver in 1920-21, in a grey wood frame house with chickens in the back yard. Howard, then five, the baby of the family, loved to torment the hens. If she didn't watch him he would grab a stick and chase them, shouting, "I'll give you a taste of my sword!"

"I guess he liked to have power over something," Angus remarked. He mentioned that he owned a hobby farm outside Vancouver where he hoped to raise poultry some day. Grace listened, hoping this notion would fade as time passed.

Angus wanted to know more about that Vancouver year, so she told himself about her first year at the University of British Columbia. Kathy, her best friend from Gibson's, had attended too, boarding with Grace's family, and her company had been the best part of a difficult year. Grace had missed classes because of aching limbs, and without her mother's help, couldn't have kept up. As it turned out, she did well in all her subjects except the one she'd considered her best – English.

"The professor had conventional ideas about composition and my essays were too informal for him, too much like articles, I guess. I'd had stories and poems published and probably needed to be taken down a peg, but I hated his class."

Then she remembered a letter her father had written to her that February from Cavan, on his way to Ottawa, a kind letter full of encouragement at the time when she was raging over the professor's obtuseness. Father wrote that he understood how she felt, but added that it only led to unhappiness to expect that one's path would be free of obstacles. We should realize that we are responsible for our own happiness and instead of blaming others for making us unhappy we should regard them merely as part of the environment, and find our way around them.

His words came back to Grace now:

"I know something of the struggle you're having. Don't let formal composition ideas spoil you. I'd rather have you fail in exams than have that happen. There's a big world ahead of you – much bigger than the UBC classroom."

"I shouldn't complain about Father," she told Angus. "He can be cross and exacting, but at heart he's very kind and very wise."

Angus smiled.

"I know. I'm so pleased you can share your thoughts with me."

Grace was sorry the train journey was coming to an end. That evening it was hard to say goodnight. When she was in her upper berth she left the curtains open, hoping to see him on his way to his bed, and when he came along the aisle she impulsively held out her hand to him. If only he would climb up and join her. Instead, he kissed her hand and whispered, "Goodnight."

Chapter Twenty-two

When their train arrived in Winnipeg at 9 a.m., Father, Belva and Howard were waiting at the station to greet them. While the greetings were going on, Grace glimpsed a man in overalls watching them, then approaching them.

"I want to thank both of you," the man said, "for standing up for the working man." Two or three other people recognized Father and Angus and clustered around them, offering their hands, commending them for standing up to that S.O.B. Bennett.

"Keep them on their toes in Ottawa!" one man urged.

A man with a little boy on his shoulders wanted the child to meet Father. A woman pulled out a paper from her purse and wanted his autograph, and Angus's. Grace had been at meetings where her father's speeches received standing ovations, but hadn't seen such a spontaneous show of appreciation in an ordinary setting. She felt proud to be connected to both men.

Since it was early for Angus to check into his hotel, Father invited him to come home with them for a late breakfast/early lunch.

"Mr. MacInnis is very popular in Vancouver," Belva whispered to Grace as the men looked after the luggage. "And I know he's not here to consult with Father."

Her smile showed her approval.

Home, at 60 Maryland Street, was a mess. Her parents' trunks were open in the front room, and the dining room furniture was under sheets because Bruce was painting the walls. Grace had hoped that Charles and Ralph would be there, but they were at work, Charles as a reporter at the *Winnipeg Tribune*. Seeing that Angus was nervous and shy, Grace's mother took him under her wing. She had him sit beside her, and apologized for serving their meal in the kitchen because of the muddle in the dining room. Angus relaxed.

Bruce and Howard didn't think it was especially notable to have a guest, for they were accustomed to having people from all walks of life turn up at the table at any meal. Mother steered the conversation onto one of Angus's topics, sectarianism in the B.C. socialist movement. Grace didn't contribute much; she was too busy trying to contain her joy and excitement at having him there. At one point she noticed Howard looking at her, then at Angus. Did Howard suspect?

After Angus left to check into his hotel, Father reminded Grace that before he and her mother left, he'd need to go over money and constituency matters with her.

"James, that can wait," said Mother. So Grace went upstairs to bathe and have a nap. In mid-afternoon she was sitting on the front veranda, trying to keep calm, but when she saw a tall lean figure coming up the street, her heart quickened.

"Would you like to go walking in Assiniboine Park?" she asked. He said yes. He was carrying his suit jacket because of the heat, and she offered to put it inside for him.

"First, I have something for you." He took from his coat pocket a silver-framed photograph of himself.

"I have your picture in a frame identical to this one," he said. "If we set the two together we'd have Beauty and the Beast."

"And here I thought I'd cleaned up so well!"

Angus looked confused for a moment, then laughed.

"You look so handsome," she told him, "and I'm so happy to have it. Thank you."

After she'd taken his coat and photograph upstairs to her room, and they were leaving the house, they saw a woman and a boy of perhaps ten years old opening the front gate.

"Miss Woodsworth?" said the woman. She was painfully thin, with shadows under her eyes. The boy wore a faded shirt, too-big trousers held up with a belt, and shoes with the soles coming off.

Grace studied her face. Had they met? No, but she knew her; she was one of the millions living in poverty.

The woman coughed. Tuberculosis? Grace wondered. The radical Montreal doctor, Norman Bethune, had recently spoken out about the spread of TB, due to exhaustion, undernourishment and overcrowding.

"May I speak to your father – or your mother?" the woman asked.

"Of course." Grace led them up the steps and opened the door. Her mother appeared and invited them into the kitchen, where, Grace knew, she would feed them. If they were in difficulties with the relief authorities, Father would take the time to make a phone call or write a letter and straighten it out.

"It's hard to imagine there won't be a revolution, with so many people down and out," she remarked to Angus as they walked down the street.

Angus said no, that most Canadians were like that mother and son, too ground-down to think of anything but where their next meal was coming from. They'd stay quiet, fearing to lose the little that they had.

"Every encounter like that one reinforces in my mind that the system must be changed," she declared.

Angus squeezed her hand. "That's what we're working for. In the meantime, if you get requests for help that you can't sort out, just phone Abe Heaps, or even write to me and we'll see what we can do."

His calm practicality reassured her. It was good to be outdoors in the bright afternoon, away from Ottawa eyes. When they were seated on a shaded bench, she was hungry to get close to him and eager to feel his arm around her shoulders. When no other strollers were nearby, she nestled close and put her hand on his chest. Then her fingers crept between the buttons of his shirt and made contact with his skin. She touched his breast bone, then one of his nipples, and felt the soft moist hair on his chest.

"No," he said.

She withdrew her hand. "I'm sorry. I'm being too forward."

"We must come back here when the stars are out," he said. "I'll appreciate your attentions all the more from having to wait."

"We'll pretend the Assiniboine is the Rideau Canal, and there will probably be the odd mosquito here too, to make us feel at home."

"It's nice here but very flat," Angus remarked. "When you come to Vancouver, Clinker and I will take you hiking in Little Mountain Park and Stanley Park."

Clinker? Oh, yes, that was his collie. Grace hoped Clinker was friendly. Ever since a German shepherd had barked in her face when she was two, she'd been afraid of dogs.

She urged him to tell her more about his life in Vancouver. He happily painted a domestic picture of his eighty-four year old mother in her rocking chair; his strong, plain sister, Christine, who kept the house spic and span and was the best cook in the world; and his little niece, Violet, who played the piano. Grace imagined her as being like little Edith de Bussy in Paris, or like Hank and Ella's daughters in Ottawa.

The household sounded like the one in the novel *Anne of Green Gables*, with Angus as Matthew and Christine as Marilla, the brother and sister living on the old home farm, and Violet as Anne, the charming orphan who comes to Green Gables and becomes a light in everyone's life. It was a delightful picture, except for one thing – Matthew didn't have a wife.

In the months to come, looking back over her time with Angus in Winnipeg, she saw in her mind's eye a series of snapshots or short bits of film. One was of Angus helping Bruce paint the railings despite her mother's protests that he wasn't there to work. Grace also vividly recalled him at the table, talking about the plight of Nova Scotia miners and the strength of the communists there. She would never forget the evening he took her to the movies to see *Daddy Long Legs*. The film was based on the novel she'd loved as a girl – the book she'd rejected last winter because of its impossibly happy ending. But with Angus beside her, with his arm around her, it didn't seem impossible after all.

Another day she met him downtown for lunch. The family restaurant near his hotel was bright with red-checkered table cloths and offered a basic menu of plain foods. When he suggested the roast beef, the most expensive item, she urged him to have it, but said she couldn't eat so much for lunch.

"Are you afraid I'm going to spend too much," he joked, "or that too much food will interfere with our conversation?"

"Both."

"It's nice to meet a girl who is careful with money."

"I'm like the girl in *My Baby Just Cares for Me*."

He blinked and looked confused.

"You know, that song by Eddie Cantor."

"I don't know it. Where money is concerned, I'm your typical Scot, but today I'd like to spend some on a ring for you. In Ottawa I thought of going to Birks Jewellers to buy you the biggest diamond I could afford, but then I thought maybe you'd like to choose one for yourself. Shall we shop for one this afternoon?"

"Oh, Angus, you're so generous! But I wouldn't feel right about having a diamond ring when so many people are going hungry. Knowing we're promised to each other is enough for me. If you like, you can buy me some jewellery for Christmas."

"All right. When will you tell your parents about us?"

"I think they've guessed. Love may be blind, but Father isn't. I'll tell them before they leave, but ask them to keep it a secret for now. I won't tell my brothers because they might broadcast it, and I know you don't want reporters asking you about our plans before we've made any. When will you tell your family?"

"Once I get home and settle in a bit. I haven't seen them for five months. I'll let them get used to me again first."

That afternoon, as they walked and talked, she learned more about his friends and associates in Vancouver. She recognized some names, like Ernest Winch, prominent in the trades and labour council, who had befriended her father years ago. She'd also heard of Lyle Telford, the radical physician who had a radio show on which he advocated innovative ideas, many of which stirred great controversy, such as "companionate" or "trial" marriage. Dr. Telford was convinced that the law should permit people to marry on a temporary basis for three years, and practise birth control. Then, if they decided not to stay married, they could go their separate ways with no legal penalties or requirements.

Angus also mentioned various women in connection with progressive projects. One woman was going to help Dr. Telford establish a women's clinic, the first in B.C. Several other women friends had been to the Soviet Union or were currently there, taking a look at the new workers' society being built in that country. Many had helped Angus in his election campaigns. All seemed to be a credit to their gender – experienced, courageous and *capable de tout*. Grace felt like Thumbelina in comparison.

In the midst of praising Miss Somebody for speaking so well at some meeting, Angus broke off.

"I'm sorry. I wasn't thinking. I guess I'm being unkind."

There was a long pause as Grace wondered how to reply.

"Surely you're not jealous! In politics you have to be friendly with a lot of people, and I am, but I'm not intimate with all of them."

"That's good to know."

Probably he had been intimate with some of them. Of course he had. He was forty-six, going on forty-seven. She reminded herself that jealousy was childish, counter-productive and unworthy of a socialist; it was a character flaw to be overcome.

"You're not the only one who likes to be petted," he added, "but you are the only one I want to pet at the moment."

At the moment. She laughed.

"I've heard it said that Members of Parliament are like sailors, with a girl in every port," she said. "Or is it *any port in a storm*?"

He took her hand. "All my love is yours. Don't be jealous. You have no reason to be."

"All right, I won't." If only saying so could make it so. "How can I be jealous when I'm so happy? I'll miss you terribly."

"And I'll miss you," he said. "We must write to each other often."

"Passionate letters?" she teased.

He blushed. "Within reason. I like some things to be left to the imagination."

Among the memories of his visit, which she would go over in the months to come, were the two meetings he'd addressed on his last day in Winnipeg. Grace was eager to hear him speak, though she would have preferred time alone with him. It seemed that everyone was leaving, first Angus, then her parents, then Belva, and then the two older boys, though only for a holiday.

The morning of August 12, Angus's his last day in town, Grace and her parents met in the study to go over the details of home and constituency management.

"You'll have no trouble," her mother assured her. "You can handle anything that comes up if you keep calm and use your head."

"Any final questions?" her father asked.

"I have something to tell you," she said. "Angus and I are engaged."

"Oh, Grace, I am so happy for you!" Her mother threw her arms around her. "He's such a nice man. I sensed romance in the air."

Grace turned to her father. "You suspected too, I think."

"I did." He looked less than ecstatic. "Now, Grace, I know you're a grown woman and that you make your own decisions, but I have to ask if you're sure about this. Have you thought things through?"

Well, no, she hadn't thought through every detail and neither had Angus, but they both had faith in each other.

"I'm sure of my feelings for him. I thought you liked Angus," she said reproachfully.

"I do, but it seems to me that this romance has blossomed rather suddenly. This time last year you didn't know his name."

"Oh, but I did! When a third Labour member got elected it was national news."

"Now, James," her mother said. "Cupid's arrow always takes people by surprise. I was in love with you for years before you considered me as a possible wife, and when it finally occurred to you it struck you quite suddenly."

"My dear Lucy, I admired you from the moment we met. Now, Grace, I don't want to be a nay-sayer, but..."

"It's the age difference, isn't it?" Grace demanded. "Age is just a number. In our souls, Angus and I are the same age. "

"His age is a point in his favour, James," Mother said. "A younger man insecure in his life's work might feel threatened by a woman as talented and accomplished as Grace, and he might thwart her ambitions. Angus is a mature person who has achieved a great many things. He'll support and encourage her. And the two of them are dedicated to a common cause, just as you and I are."

"It's not so much the age difference as the disparity in your education and backgrounds," her father insisted. "You've helped Mac with his letters and speeches and you know his limitations. He has only about four years of formal education. You're a university graduate and have learned excellent manners and social skills from your mother. I doubt that Mac understands any of your literary references, for example."

"Oh, Father, our life together isn't going to be a literary quiz or a lesson on which fork to use. Angus is well-read and educated in the school of life. He's an original thinker and the smartest man I've ever met."

Mother asked if they'd set a date.

"Not yet. I wanted to let you know before you leave, but we aren't telling other people yet. Angus and I will write to each other every day, like you and Father do when you're apart. When you get back he wants me to go to Vancouver to meet his family."

"Well, that sounds reasonable," her father said. "You'll get to know each other through your letters."

"I'm so happy for you both," her mother said, "and we won't tell a soul until you're ready to announce your engagement."

Grace kissed each of them in turn and said she had to get ready to meet Angus for lunch downtown. As she closed the study door, she heard her mother's soft, amused tone.

"James, you're still the smartest man I've ever met."

Over lunch, Angus apologized again for being tactless the previous day about his women friends, and he and Grace held hands across the table.

That afternoon, in the Labour Hall, she saw again that in front of a workers' audience he was more relaxed and effective, more himself, than in the House. Today he was talking about deportation, an issue particularly relevant in a city like Winnipeg with a large working class population of non-British origin.

All over Canada, city relief departments were working hand in hand with the federal Department of Immigration to reduce the number of people on the dole by conspiring to deport them to their country of origin. It had become regular practice for relief departments to provide the local immigration officer the names of anyone on relief who had been in Canada less than five years. The propertied classes who dominated city governments wanted to keep the relief budget as low as possible to keep their taxes low. In 1927-8, Winnipeg had paid out $31,000 for relief, but in 1930 its relief payments had soared to 1,600,000 dollars.

Immigration claimed that only "undesirables" – meaning criminals – were being shipped back to their native lands, but in fact, people who were not in conflict with the law were being sent back to Europe simply because they were unemployed. In past decades, Canada had advertised in Eastern Europe for people to come to Canada and build a better life in exchange for hard work. With the capitalist system gone belly-up, who could find a job?

Grace had grown up with newcomers at her father's mission in the north end. In Gibson's Landing, she had friends in the Finnish community. Since these friends had been in Canada more than five years. they were safe, but others like them were being victimized because of the economic crisis. Listening to Angus speak out against the deportation policy, she felt proud and honoured to have his love, and reflected that, in a world with such huge problems, a socialist had no business indulging in petty personal jealousies.

After the meeting, he was surrounded by an enthusiastic mob, and when they finally stole away to have a quick bite for supper before the evening meeting, he looked exhausted. Over the meal she repeated all the nice things she'd overheard about him from where she sat. Before the evening gathering, they strolled along the railroad tracks and sat on a pile of ties in the setting sun. When it was time to face the crowd, he seemed refreshed and ready.

This meeting was not just for the ILP faithful, but for the public, and there were hecklers present, who accused reformist socialists of propping up capitalism. Angus countered by accusing them of promoting violence. Democratic socialists, he said, believed that a modern intelligent community could organize its economy rationally, without resorting to revolutionary dictatorship to do it.

Afterwards he was again surrounded by well-wishers; then it was time for him to catch his train. At the station, he looked woebegone and she fought back tears to give him a cheerful "au revoir". She yearned for an embrace but he made no move. Once he was aboard she stayed on the platform and waved to him until the train pulled away. That night she had the uneasy feeling that his visit had been a dream.

The following morning everyone was up early to say goodbye to Mother and Father, who had insisted on saying goodbye at home, not at the station.

"Remember, Grace is *in loco parentis*," her father told the boys, "but that doesn't mean she'll be doing all the work around here. The rotating chore schedule is still in effect."

Mother kissed them all and said that Grace had a list of the places in Europe where they would be picking up mail. She knew all would be well.

"And remember, Howard, an hour a day with Grace, working on your French."

Chapter Twenty-three

After they left, Grace felt overwhelmed. Housework, shopping, meal preparation and moral support for four young men, not to mention work for her father – how would she ever manage it all? As the day progressed, though, as she helped Bruce and Howard with the painting, and tuned in to their activities and plans, she felt calmer. That evening, regardless of the schedule, everyone pitched in to prepare a meal and clean up, and afterwards they sat around and talked about the immediate future. Belva announced that tomorrow she would take Howard and his best friend on a picnic, a generous gesture considering that she was leaving soon for British Columbia. Then, in the evening, Belva, Charles and Ralph had been invited to join thirty of their friends at a corn roast. They wanted Grace to go, but she said no, as Bruce also had plans with his friends and she didn't want to leave Howard all alone.

That evening, when Howard had gone to bed after several games of cards, she picked up her pen and wrote to Angus:

"I shut my eyes and picture you addressing meetings," she wrote, *"so forceful and tough in criticizing the status quo, and nobody there realizes how human and lovable you are."* She had been about to say "vulnerable" but thought better of it. *"How lovely it would be to see you open our gate and come up the walk. We would sit together on the veranda and you would forget about being reserved and dignified, and I would forget about being grown up and I'd muss up your hair."*

For the next couple of days she immersed herself in domestic duties and tried not to think about him. Then a letter arrived, written on the train.

"I said I'd write to you when I arrived home, but here I am, just twelve hours out of Winnipeg, wishing I were with you, missing your voice, your soft little hands and your lovely self entirely. I never loved you so much or wanted you so much as I did last night. There now. That's more love by 99% than I have ever put in a letter before. I am almost afraid to drop it in a letter box. All my love is yours until we meet again."

She put the letter in the drawer where his picture stayed during the day.

Again, from the train, he wrote:

"I am wishing again that I were talking to you rather than writing, and that I could feel your little hand on my arm, that little hand that was hardly ever still, but kept feeling its way like a little blind creature for a more intimate resting place. I am sorry that my sensitive temperament, as you call it, would not allow me to stay longer in Winnipeg. The visit told me one thing that I'd never been quite sure of before, that you love me. I never loved or wanted you so much as I did that night when you were on the platform and I in the coach looking out."

Grace sighed. A lot of drudgery lay ahead before the handsome prince would return to claim Cinderella. Actually, housework was a change from office work, and, as well, there was a certain heady feeling about being chatelaine of the domain. She was pleased that her brothers did their chores without being nagged, and even happier when they hung around in the evenings wanting to talk to her. Charles and Ralph were going on a hiking-fishing-hunting holiday in British Columbia before university began, and their conversation was mostly about outdoor equipment. They were no longer boys, but men.

Bruce and Howard, whom she'd minded as babies, were the two most likely to cause her trouble. As a kid, Howard had been prone to fits of the giggles, and Bruce had enjoyed setting him off by whispering certain "secret words." When Grace once asked him what the secret words were, he said if he told her they wouldn't be secret any more. Their fighting used to drive her crazy, but so far, except for occasional friendly jostling and mock-wrestling, they were getting along. Either they had matured or she was less on edge than formerly.

By Labour Day Belva, Charles and Ralph had all left for British Columbia, and Howard announced that he was spending the day biking with friends. Grace planned to keep busy so she wouldn't miss Angus so much. Then, to her surprise, Bruce asked her if she'd like to come with him out to the country for a day of swimming and shooting. Amazed that he wanted her company, she immediately accepted the invitation. They packed up knapsacks and took the street car to the end of the line about ten miles out of the city, to a flat stretch of prairie where there was an oak hummock beside the Assiniboine River. They had worn their bathing suits under their knee breeches, and found the water refreshingly cool, though muddy.

"Remember the summer in Ottawa when we rented that cottage in the Gatineau Hills?" Bruce inquired, as he floated alongside her. "Remember how Father taught you to swim?"

"That was at an earlier cottage near Kenora, but yes, I remember."

At the time, Grace had known the fundamentals of swimming but was afraid to take the plunge, and her father, losing patience, had thrown her off the dock.

"Sometimes he uses that sink-or-swim approach when he assigns me a task in the office," she added.

"Was it in the Gatineau that we had Betty the chipmunk who lived under the porch?" Grace laughed "Ah, yes. Betty. When we saw Betty with another chipmunk we realized his real name was Bertie."

They swam until they were hungry, and when it came time to cook a midday meal, Bruce wouldn't let Grace help. She lay under a tree observing the methodical way he did everything. He served fried eggs, bacon and tomatoes on tin plates, with pears and cake for dessert. Over lunch, he asked if she would help him with Latin as their mother had, seeing as how she was tutoring Howard in French.

"Sure. It's nice you and Howard are getting along so well."

"We promised Mother we wouldn't do anything to upset you."

"Thank you." Good heavens, did she seem that fragile?

"Howard has grown up a lot in the last year," Bruce informed her."He was a giddy child the year you were in France."

He began an anecdote to illustrate Howard's former immaturity, unaware of any irony in doing so. Grace fought back a smile. One evening two years earlier their parents had invited to dinner two elementary school teachers who knew the boys from former days. These pleasant, middle-aged ladies praised the boys for having developed into fine young men. The evening began on a high plane. After the meal, Bruce and Howard entertained the ladies with *Flow Gently Sweet Afton* and other selections on piano and violin. Then talk turned to Grace in Paris and the ladies exclaimed that it must be wonderful to be there, visiting famous museums and art galleries. The conversation reminded Father of the trip he and Mother had made to Europe in 1906 and the art books they'd brought home.

"When he asked me to get those books," said Bruce, "I could have told him he was making a big mistake."

Soon everyone had gathered around the tea table to look at great paintings, like Gainsborough's "Blue Boy" and Turner's "The Fighting Temerare." Then one of the ladies opened the book of Greek and Roman statues.

"We heard a giggle, no, a whinny," Bruce recounted. "The nudity set Howard off. Father was so angry that his face turned a deep wine colour. I thought he might explode. But what could he say or do with company there? Mother ordered Howard to bed and after a while the teachers left. By morning Father had cooled down and there were no consequences. But Howard is still very childish."

"I'll bear that in mind," Grace said solemnly.

After more reminiscing and more swimming, Bruce lined up some rusty cans on a log for target practice. Grace remembered to focus on the sights, not the target, and to exhale before pulling the trigger, and was pleased that her marksmanship hadn't deteriorated, but she was not as sure a shot as Bruce. Then, noticing the time, they had to run to catch the last streetcar, and when they got home they discovered that neither had a key, so Bruce had to enter via a window. Still, it had been a great day and she thanked him.

Last year she'd found the boys annoying, but now they were interesting, especially Howard, with one foot in childhood and the other in his teens. One evening he was invited to a birthday party and transformed himself from an unkempt boy into a dapper young man. He came down at 7 p.m., fresh from his bath, looking like a dandy in his suit, with his hair slicked back, and asked for a piece of cake so that he wouldn't be too hungry for the refreshments and act greedy. When an automobile pulled up for him, he told Grace not to wait up. He was back, looking proud, at 11 p.m.

Bruce, who had not yet attended a high school dance, was planning to take this big step, One evening, he and one of his buddies discussed etiquette for this event while Grace ironed in one corner of the kitchen and listened. Instead of going stag and having to dance with wallflowers, it was better to invite the best looking, most popular girl you could find, the prettier the better, so that she would inspire envy and make you look good. It was important to act sophisticated and never admit that it was your first dance. Above all, it was vital to fit in and follow the crowd. Grace stifled a giggle. They were so superficial and so afraid of being unconventional.

The following Saturday Bruce and Howard went with friends back to the spot by the Assiniboine, and by the time night had fallen, they still weren't home. Grace paced by the window. Now she knew how her mother had felt when they'd stayed out late. They had taken the .22 and their bathing suits. Had there been a drowning? A shooting? Just when she was thinking of telephoning the mother of one of the other boys, she heard her brothers' tread on the steps. She exhaled.

After saying goodnight, she went up to her room and took Angus's photo out of the drawer. As was her custom, she set it on her bedside table for company in the night. She had just curled up on the bed with his letters when there was a knock at the door.

"We haven't worked on my French yet." It was Howard.

She sighed. "Come in."

She was determined to bring him up to a passing grade, not only for his sake but also for hers, to prove that she was capable of teaching the language to a young person. Languages had been Mother's area of concentration at university, and she'd been horrified to think that one of her children would fail French.

He came in and dropped his books on her desk before she had time to tuck Angus's photo and letters away in the drawer.

"That's the man who was here a couple of weeks ago – Mr. MacInnis. Is he your sweetheart?" His voice dripped incredulity.

"Yes. He's my fiancé. That's a French word. Do you know what it means?"

He shook his head.

"It means he's the man I'm engaged to marry."

His eyes rounded. "Do Mother and Father know?"

"Yes, but no one else does, except you. We aren't telling people right yet. Can you keep it a secret for now?"

A conspiratorial smile crossed his face. "Absolutely. When is the wedding?"

"We haven't set a date yet."

He looked at her left hand. "Is he going to give you an engagement ring?"

"He wanted to, but rings are expensive and I don't need one. Now, let's get started."

She explained reflexive verbs. He wrote out some declensions, then turned to her.

"Who will be Father's secretary when you get married?"

"I will. I'll be married, Howard, not incapacitated."

He giggled. "But...?" Then he clamped his mouth shut.

"What?" she asked.

"After a few months, won't you have to quit because of the baby?"

"What baby? A baby doesn't automatically follow marriage, you know."

He looked confused. "But they usually do."

"Often but not always."

"Oh."

He considered, then turned pink and hastily went back to his book.

She squirmed. How much did a boy his age know about such things? She'd said more than she was comfortable with.

As he worked his way through the verbs, she realized something. Her vision of the future with Angus included meetings, and Parliament, and dinner dates and moonlight walks, and coming home to bed instead of going to their separate lodgings. She pictured more train trips, shared sleeping berths. There was no baby in any of these pictures. He'd said he didn't want a child now and maybe that meant never. In three years he would be fifty; in twenty years he would be almost seventy.

But Howard was right about a baby usually coming along shortly after marriage, unless steps were taken, and she and Angus had never discussed what they were going to do about that. When he was her age, nice girls wouldn't have discussed such things. What would he think of her when she broached the subject?

Chapter Twenty-four

Whenever a letter came from Angus, as one did every second or third day, she was on Cloud Nine. His third letter, dated August 15, had been sent from Kamloops, British Columbia, where he'd stopped over to address meetings. Kamloops had between five and six thousand full-time residents and about five hundred transient unemployed men who were living in a tent city in the park known as "the jungle."

"*I saw some of them yesterday*," he wrote, "*and they were real fine young fellows. They were bathing in the river, washing their clothes and hanging them on trees to dry.*" The unemployed men were running the camp by themselves and doing it well, making rules about sanitation and choosing a magistrate. From Kamloops, Angus's hosts drove him the sixty-five miles to Magna Bay, where he addressed a packed meeting. One of the men present had driven fifty miles to attend. Angus also spoke to a meeting in Kelowna where he answered a lot of questions.

His next letter, from Vancouver, reported that friends had met him at the station and that when he got home, his dog, Clinker, greeted him in a frenzy and licked his face. When he unpacked, he put Grace's photograph on his dresser, and his mother asked who the lady was. "Someone you haven't met yet," he told her. "She looks nice," his mother said. His sister Christine recognized Grace as one of the Woodsworth girls. "I have not told them yet," he wrote.

He'd been on a family picnic with a number of relatives Grace hadn't heard of. His niece Violet was spending time with her other grandmother and enjoying the summer.

"*The best thing about getting home,*" he wrote, "*was having a letter from a sweet little girl waiting for me.*" For a moment, Grace wondered who this sweet little girl was – another niece? – then realized he meant her. He wrote that she was his greatest inspiration, that he missed her, and that all his love was hers. She felt very happy.

But later, while mopping the kitchen floor, she began to feel the way she used to when faced with an exam – worried that she wouldn't measure up to a beloved teacher's high standards. What had brought this on? Wringing out the mop, she realized that it was Angus's letter, especially the "sweet little girl" part. Earlier when they'd talked about her French teaching fiasco, he'd interpreted her breakdown in a way that was kindly but inaccurate. He thought she'd been in an ivory tower with her books for too long and hadn't experienced life, so had found the working world too much of a jolt. But it wasn't quite like that. Teaching tough students had been only part of the reason for her *crise de nerfs*.

"Sweet little girl" implied such innocence. And when he said she was his greatest inspiration, he was placing her on a pedestal as if she were a statue, when she was very much flesh and blood. She wrung out the mop, went into the study, and began a letter in which she poured out her heart.

Their months together, she told him, had been the happiest of her life. As a teenager, as a young teacher and as a university student she'd longed physically and spiritually for her "basherter", the one who would complete her. For years she'd been saving her passion for that special man, and in Paris she'd thought she'd found him. But they'd been on different paths in life, and at the last minute, she'd decided she couldn't fully express her love for him because they had no future together. The end of this affair, flawed and unconsummated though it had been, had shaken and undermined her and had contributed to her inability to cope a year ago. Then, as if by a miracle, Angus had come into her life and had become her redemption and her destiny. She wanted to put everything she had into their relationship.

When she reread it she blanched and murmured, "I can't send this."

Someone in his family might read it – but that was just a small part of her concern.

The letter was so raw that it would frighten him. If he knew her as well as she knew herself he would be afraid to trust his happiness with her. At best he would worry that she was getting too wrought up. At worst, he would think less of her for having loved someone else. After all, she didn't want to hear about his former fiancée, except to know that the attachment was over.

Although she'd boldly told her parents that age was just a number, and although she and Angus were so in tune with each other on most things that they seemed like contemporaries, they weren't. He'd come of age in horse-and-buggy days; his ideas of women had been formed in the Victorian era. Perhaps he felt, deep down, as many Victorians had, that decent women had no erotic feelings, but submitted to sexual intercourse only to have children. Although he was a socialist and an agnostic, he'd been raised a Presbyterian and probably had the traditional Christian suspicion of the body.

She tore up the letter and began again.

"I wrote you a letter but I didn't send it, because it reminded me too much of a little girl who says everything and doesn't leave anything to the imagination. These days I feel restless as a Manitoba wind. I wish you were here with me so we could continue our great adventure together. If you were here, first I'd want you to spoil me and then I'd want to mother you."

"Mother" wasn't quite what she felt, but he would find it more acceptable than if she'd written, "I want to smother you with kisses and have you caress me to ecstasy."

"There are many things I'd like to tell you that I can't write. Of course I couldn't say them either, but you'd guess them. Sometimes when I'm imagining our life together I feel, in the

middle of my happiness, a sensation of panic. How I wish you would come to see me. Talking face to face is so much better than by letter."

He replied, urging her to write anything she wanted, no matter how childish; he would love it. He wrote:

"I too am almost unnerved at times by the immensity of the project in front of us. I think mostly of you. You are young and you have a right to demand so much of life. Do not think I have any misgivings about your worth. If anything I might wish that it were not so great. You are so frank and open, you seem to do things with such utter abandon. Do not worry, dear, you are such a friend as I could hope for and you will add much to my life. What makes me fearful, will I fill up your life to the same extent that you will fill up mine?"

Grace was glad she'd ripped up and burned the emotional outpouring. Instead, she would write about their shared social concerns. She told him about a visit from a family friend, a social worker who was very concerned about the plight of the poor in the coming winter. The Canadian Pacific Railway shops in Winnipeg had closed indefinitely, and the relief work that had begun in the city was a drop in the bucket.

Grace wrote of the Romanian man who came to 60 Maryland to see Father, who had officiated at his wedding some twenty-five years earlier. A roofer by trade, he wondered if her father could direct him toward some work. "Work, not relief!" he'd insisted. Grace knew of no jobs, and neither did Mr. Heaps when she telephoned him. *"I told this nice man that there was no shame in going on the dole; that he was one of millions in the same situation and that it was not their fault, but I don't think I convinced him."*

She wrote, too, about the Labour Party situation in England, which she'd read about. The Prime Minister, Ramsay MacDonald, who was Labour, had split his party by forming a coalition with the Liberals and Conservatives to deal with the depression. It seemed to her that the situation didn't augur well for any labour government that might be elected in future, say, in Canada. If it tried to please the free market establishment it would alienate its supporters, and if it remained true to its principles it would be defeated, crushed, or co-opted. What was Angus's opinion?

She mentioned a talk she'd given to a Winnipeg area branch of the Independent Labour Party, about the Bennett government's failure to recognize the growing unemployment in Canada. She mentioned seeing in the *Labour Statesman* that Angus MacInnis was speaking somewhere every night.

"Talk about knowing a celebrity!" she wrote.

Her parents, she reported, had reached Geneva, where Canadian diplomat Dr. Riddell had found them a nice place to stay. Father's letter had praised the beauty of Geneva, but expressed his frustration as a member of the British delegation. Britain saw the League of Nations not as a vehicle for world peace but as one to push her national imperial interests.

Mother had written that they were enjoying each other's company in a lovely setting. *"The other day we began to talk of the richness of living, and then about our six precious friends – children, I suppose we call them – across the big water."*

Clearly her parents were not ready to come home, and her Vancouver trip would have to wait.

Sometimes it was hard to be good-humoured. Whenever she felt good about her role as maternal presence in the household, an incident would occur, like the morning Howard woke late. He came down dressed like an unmade bed, wanting breakfast and demanding that she find his French assignment for him.

She exploded. "I'm not your servant! You're old enough to look after your own things."

Then he drew himself up to his full height and said, "Control yourself."

Grace sat down, sipped her coffee and ignored him. Afterwards she felt amused by the incident. Howard and she were usually good friends. He spent most of his time in sports, except for piano practice and French. One day he came home from school waving a test on which he'd scored 90%, fifth highest in the class. His fifteenth birthday was approaching, and in the days leading up to it, he mentioned, ever so casually, that his fountain pen had quit working, that all his friends owned a specific type of flask and that it was still the family custom to have birthday cakes. Grace took the hints.

One evening at supper, after Howard told an amusing tale about school, Bruce said, "You're fooling away your time and not applying yourself."

"I suppose you act like a saint all the time." Howard clasped his hands and looked heavenward with a pious expression, Bruce and Grace laughed.

Her morale depended upon Angus's letters. He'd started addressing her as "Dearie" or "my own dear Grace" which she especially liked because her father always began his letters to her mother, "My own dear Lucy." She was pleasantly surprised, too, to find his letters well-composed with a wide vocabulary. He could type, too, a skill he'd kept a secret in Ottawa. She would spend less time typing for him in future and concentrate on getting him better organized.

She took his latest letter with her for company when she went shopping, and was delighted to hear he had taken her most recent note with him when he went to his small farm outside Vancouver. A young couple was living there and managing to feed themselves off the land, but they couldn't afford to pay rent and he wasn't asking them for any.

So as not to be lonely, she accepted invitations to afternoon tea or evenings at friends' homes. One evening she joined other guests at the Heaps's home and enjoyed its atmosphere of culture, particularly the real oil paintings on the walls, and the tea served from a silver service. Angus wasn't mentioned; otherwise Grace might have blushed and given away the secret. Still, she wondered if Bessie Heaps suspected anything.

She was happy when Charles and Ralph got home from holidays. They brought with them a letter from Belva, who'd had a good time entertaining them. "*But it's you, Grace, not I, who should be in Vancouver,*" she wrote.

Ralph, the brother who most resembled their father in physical appearance, had a heavy course load in math and science, but was never too busy to get out his violin and join Grace at the piano. Charles's hours were irregular, as he was taking an extension course as well as working at the *Trib*, but she was always buoyed up by his cheerfulness. He seemed to appreciate anything she did for him, like packing him a lunch or making his favourite soup. Were her brothers going out of their way to be good to her, on account of last year? Maybe so, or maybe they genuinely liked her. They were growing up to be nice men.

One suppertime, feeling guilty about leaving them to make their own supper, she rushed out to the Agnes Street Labour Forum where she was speaking. The crowd was larger than usual, no doubt curious to hear J.S. Woodsworth's daughter. *"Won't it be fun,"* she wrote later to Angus, *"when people come out of curiosity to hear Angus MacInnis's wife?"* And maybe someday people would come out to hear her for her own sake.

Advocating a fairer economic system made her feel more useful than trying to alleviate human misery on a personal level. One day a man came around the house with a bouquet of bittersweet, which he had cut in the woods, hoping to trade it for clothes or food. Tired-looking, shabby but dignified, he told her in broken English that he and his wife had three sons in their teens, with no job prospects, and a younger girl. Grace gave him tea and cookies, then located some clothing she'd put aside – a woollen sweater, a couple of her old dresses, and mittens. She wished there were more but her brothers were already wearing hand-me-downs. The man was delighted with the clothing, and also with a loaf of bread and tin of salmon she'd intended for Saturday lunch. He insisted that she take the bittersweet.

"Aptly named," she thought, breaking off a sprig to send to Angus. She began baking soda biscuits every morning to give the needy who turned up at the door. One day, while shopping, she came upon some grapes, past their prime and on sale, and bought them for grape jelly. Having never made it before, she looked for instructions in the family recipes, and found an old cookbook that had belonged to her Grandmother Woodsworth, written by a Methodist women's group and published before the turn of the century. Reverently she opened it – then read on the frontispiece the words: *"Let me feed the nation. I care not who makes its laws."*

Grace cared very much who made its laws. Shortly after that, when she was asked to speak at the Fort Rouge Labour Hall, she accepted without hesitation.

Chapter Twenty-five

Grace's Fort Rouge speech and the publication of her article in the *Alberta Labour News* attracted attention, and she was asked to speak to a group of Independent Labour women about tariffs, a subject that seemed challenging until she did some research.

Canada depended on sources outside the country for raw materials and manufactured products, and could pay for these things only if she could export her major products from agriculture, forestry and mining. Currently this export trade was being strangled by the protectionist policies of other countries. Canada needed to negotiate agreements with other countries and to set up public boards to organize imports and exports and to regulate the flow of other commodities through licensing. A little planning and reorganization would end the exploitation of producers and consumers, establish stable prices for exports, and coordinate the processing, transportation and marketing of products.

The audience listened closely, but seemed to like best her impersonation of Mr. Bennett promising to "blast" Canada into the markets of the world. One woman in the audience asked what point there was in her father and the other labour members playing the Parliamentary game of trying to influence the old parties and hold them to account. Real change, she said, came from outside the legislatures, from the people. Grace suspected that the woman was a communist; they never got tired of dogging the democratic socialists. Calmly she said that working people needed to be heard both in the legislatures of the land and in extra-parliamentary movements and organizations, such as trade unions. The two worked hand in hand. Extra-parliamentary actions that failed, however, could lead to state repression. Most of the women nodded, remembering the General Strike twelve years earlier. The questioner walked out during Grace's reply, but others applauded, and she felt that she'd been clear and strong.

The following week she was making pies and listening to the radio when she heard a knock at the front door. She found two old friends on the doorstep.

"Mr. Heaps! Mr. Ivens!"

She had known them for years. Mr. Ivens was a former Methodist minister who, like her father, had broken with the church over its support for the Great War. Like Father and Mr. Heaps, Mr. Ivens had served time in jail for supporting the General Strike in 1919 and subsequently had been elected to the Manitoba legislature.

She welcomed them into the front room, then went to the kitchen and put the kettle on. She tore off her apron, put shortbread cookies on a plate, made tea, and carried in the tray, wondering what they wanted. Did Mr. Heaps need some typing done? Did they want her to relay a message of some sort to her father?

Pouring the tea, she mentioned that her parents would shortly be leaving Geneva for the Soviet Union.

"Actually, we're here about you, Grace."

Mr. Ivens glanced at Mr. Heaps, who began praising her assistance to the Ginger Group in Parliament. He'd heard that her recent speeches had gone over well, and that many were impressed by her *Labour Statesman* piece.

"You're embarrassing me!" She laughed and passed the shortbread. "Ottawa has been an education; mostly it has taught me how much I have to learn."

"You already have a firm grounding in socialism," Mr. Heaps told her. "You're well aware of the issues of our time. You're well-educated, fluent in French, an excellent speaker and writer, and last but not least, you're a woman and J.S.'s daughter. Will and I think you'd make an ideal candidate in the upcoming Manitoba election."

Grace's jaw dropped.

"I'm honoured that you think so highly of me, but I'm not ready. Not yet. Maybe in a few years."   Her last words surprised her.

"Think it over and let us know," Mr. Ivens said. They talked of local issues for a while, then departed, urging her again to give serious consideration to their idea.

Back in the kitchen, she peeled apples and mulled things over.

There was no way that she would run in the next Manitoba election. Turn her back on love to contest a seat that she'd probably lose? There was nothing to consider. But how flattering to be seriously considered as a candidate by two men of such stature in the movement. Maybe, when a larger federation of the left was formed, and when she had more experience, she'd run. Someday.

"Their idea was flattering", she wrote to Angus, *"and made me realize that it is something I might want to do, down the road, when I am a great deal more knowledgeable and experienced. But their visit brings up in my mind the question of the sort of life I ought to plan to live with you. Do you think I should plan to get into politics in a public way, always supposing that I had the ability? Or should I write, or do organizational work in a small way? Or should I continue with the secretarial line, or go for something different, like tutoring? We never really discussed this matter seriously. I would be happiest making the fullest and best contribution to our partnership, whatever that happens to be."*

Angus's reply enclosed a clipping from the *Vancouver Sun*, headlined, "Daughter of M.P. assails Bennett at ILP Meeting."

"It's simply wonderful," he wrote. *"If I could see you tonight I would give you a good hug, not one but many, and kisses without*

number. How pleased your father will be! All of the family noticed it too, even Violet. With your personality and talent, not to mention family background, you might indeed win a seat in Winnipeg or possibly Vancouver."

He went on to say what he'd been doing. He'd gone hiking with his dog in Little Mountain and Stanley Parks. He addressed meetings almost every evening and was received with a lot of enthusiasm.

"I haven't yet told Christine of our affair," he wrote.

"Affair?" The term startled Grace. Not "engagement"? She read on.

Angus was concerned that Christine would be hurt. *"I do not mean that she would make a fuss about our engagement, because she wouldn't,"* he wrote. *"In a way, I've meant a lot to Christine in her life, which has been otherwise hard. We have been working together for a long time to have our home, and she has been a brick in many ways. Now, my dear, do not feel bad about this. I would be extremely sorry if I were to disturb you. It is just one of my difficulties. I thought I would share it with you."*

He added that Violet had loved the dress Grace had selected for her, though Christine said he ought to be shot for spending so much money on it. Thinking of shopping, he'd bought some new shirts, all white, because Christine said he looked better in white than in colours. A green shirt that Grace particularly liked wouldn't be replaced.

He'd recently learned that another niece of his, his brother's daughter, had been unhappy at home and had moved to a rooming house near the restaurant where she was waitressing. She had a fiancé but they couldn't marry yet because he couldn't support a wife. Angus thought she looked worn-out and that she ought to have a home, so he'd invited her to come and join the family on Prince Edward Street.

That night Grace dreamed that a tall, dour woman in an apron was scolding her because she hadn't rinsed the dishpan properly. She woke in a sweat. She'd never had a strip torn off her like that. She wrote to Angus to let her know if she could do anything to make it easier to break the news to Christine: *"If it would make it easier for her to see me before the wedding, perhaps we could be married in Vancouver."* Her parents would probably like her to be married from their home, but since they already knew of the engagement they wouldn't experience the sense of loss that his family might feel.

"I think Christine suspects something," he wrote in his next letter. A friend of his telephoned to say that he was getting married. When Angus got off the line he said to Christine, "Guess who's getting married?" and she said "Yourself?"

"I said: Not just now, but afterwards I thought it was a good opportunity missed."

Indeed, thought Grace.

Angus didn't think that where they got married would matter much to Christine, and that they should probably get married in Winnipeg because the bride's parents had rights and *"things should be considered in their proper relation."*

He wrote of his upcoming trip to Washington state to visit his other two sisters and their husbands. Recently, when his sister Jennie had been in Vancouver, he'd intended to tell her of their "affair", but had lost his nerve. He would tell Jennie when he next saw her. Meanwhile, he had a number of speaking engagements and meetings with friends. He was invited to the home of a widow who was a secretary to a key figure in municipal administration, but was "not a socialist". He also had an appointment with "Miss Em," his former fiancée, who was recently back from Russia. He wasn't particularly anxious to see her, he said, but she'd phoned him twice since his return and he'd run into her at Dr. Telford's office.

"I shall tell her I am engaged but I don't think I will tell her who to," he wrote. *"It will percolate through in due course. Gossip will get busy when I leave Vancouver to go east."*

If "going east" meant a visit to Winnipeg, Grace hoped it would be soon. It sounded to her as if Miss Em wanted to rekindle things with him, and it was high time he told her he was taken.

She read on. A woman in the ILP had phoned him to ask if there was any truth to the rumour that he was to be married. He said "Maybe", and when she asked if it was the Woodsworth girl, he said he wasn't saying anything about it.

He closed by praising Grace's many talents. *"The one thing you do better than all is to be a loveable artless little girl."*

Chapter Twenty-six

As she peeled potatoes and hung out the wash, Grace mulled over Angus's letters. He had a life that was all worked out, one that he'd built over the years with effort and patience. Instead of marrying and creating a new family for himself, he'd uplifted his birth family. His financial and domestic partnership with Christine provided a roof for the two of them and his mother and Violet, and now for another niece who was down on her luck. After years of patience and hard work he was finally getting the respect and honour he deserved, and enjoying a stable domestic life where he was appreciated. As for other needs, he apparently had a host of women friends who were ready, willing and able.

Grace thought of the beginning of *Pride and Prejudice*: *"It is a truth universally acknowledged that a single man in possession of a good fortune must be in need of a wife."* Jane Austen was joking, of course, and the idea that Angus needed a wife was also a joke. Grace believed that he loved her, or his idea of her, but who was she to disturb his settled life?

His subconscious must be telling him not to marry her; otherwise he wouldn't be so reluctant to speak of their engagement. What should she do? She loved him with all her heart. One form of the marriage service said "with my body I thee honour", and she wanted that, too. If he decided he wanted her to be "just a friend", could she handle that? She'd have to; she couldn't imagine life without him. If only they could talk directly.

Apart from these anxieties there was much that she wanted to discuss with him. In Toronto, the leaders of the Communist Party of Canada had been arrested and jailed, their party outlawed. Who would be next? The Independent Labour Party? Had the ILP made clear enough its commitment to non-violence and parliamentary methods?

While heartily sick of the communists' attitude toward democratic socialists, Grace didn't think it was right, in a democracy, to outlaw the Communist Party. Also, democratic socialists and communists were sort of like cousins. They shared an analysis of capitalism and agreed that it had failed and was ruining lives. Where they differed was that communists supported direct actions that often led to violence, in the expectation of precipitating a Russian-style revolution, while democratic socialists wanted change through the ballot box and the legal system. They wanted social welfare measures, not to prop up capitalism, but to alleviate human misery.

The situation in Bienfait, Saskatchewan, which was much in the news, showed the turbulence of the times. Coal miners there had been on strike over wages and working conditions since September 7th. Charles, who hoped the *Tribune* would send him to Bienfait and Estevan to report on the situation, heard from colleagues on the scene and discussed the news with Grace.

Coal mining in Saskatchewan was a shaky industry. The price of Saskatchewan coal was low because it served a limited domestic market and faced competition from Albertan and American coal. The mine-owners provided winter work and laid off miners in the spring, expecting them to find employment as farm hands, but with the drought and the consequent collapse of agriculture, farmers weren't hiring. The mine owners, enjoying the labour surplus, picked and chose who would work, and lowered wages to $1.60 a day. A year earlier, one company had introduced mechanized strip mining, which yielded more coal than underground mining and threatened the miners' future. Meanwhile, the miners complained of dangerous conditions underground, like broken timbers and blocked air passages in the tunnels. Miners hated their bosses' pressure to deal at the company stores, where prices far exceeded those of Estevan merchants. Another issue was company housing, which was substandard and overcrowded. Charles had heard of a family of eleven living in a bedbug-infested three bedroom wooden shanty with a leaking roof. The teenaged daughter had told reporters that on winter mornings the floor was always covered with frost. Yet miners in company houses were advantaged in that they were considered permanent employees and got first chance at what jobs there were.

Although the miners had been organized by the Workers' Unity League, a branch of the Communist Party of Canada, it seemed obvious to Grace that the strike was no mere inflammatory gesture but the result of desperation; the miners had little to lose.

To call attention to their plight, several hundred planned to go to Estevan, the nearest large town, to parade and call attention to their plight. Annie Buller, a well-known Workers' Unity League organizer in Winnipeg, was supposed to speak.

Charles was eager to cover the story, but Grace hoped he wouldn't be sent. In such a volatile situation, an innocent junior reporter might get clubbed or shot.When two hundred miners and their wives turned up on the outskirts of Estevan they were met by the Estevan fire department and a troop of Royal Canadian Mounted Police armed with rifles and revolvers. When fire hoses blasted the strikers, they surrounded the fire engine and cut off its water power. Then the Mounties moved in. The miners' bricks and stones were no match for their guns; the police fired on the crowd, wounding many and killing three.

Charles wasn't there; much to his disappointment, he wasn't sent. He'd heard that a young Baptist minister from Weyburn, someone named Tommy Douglas, and his wife, Irma, had collected food and clothing and had driven to Bienfait and Taylorton to deliver it to the miners' families. Charles thought Mother and Father knew the Douglas family from the days when Father ran the Stella Avenue mission in the north end of Winnipeg. Grace said she'd mention Mr. Douglas in her next letter to them.

Meanwhile, in the latest *Labour Statesman*, Grace found an article Angus had written about Ramsay MacDonald's coalition government with the Conservatives. The article wasn't in his usual style. Who had helped him with it?

Angus's reaction to the Estevan tragedy jarred her a little.

"What happened there," he wrote, *"is the inevitable result of communist policy. They foment trouble, get the men to go out on strike under adverse conditions, then ask for an impossible settlement. The leaders always clear out when the police come. Where capitalism is as strong as it is, here on the North American continent, their approach is sheer lunacy."*

Grace wished she could discuss the matter with him, and when she reached the end of the letter, discovered, with great joy, that she would soon be able to. He would be leaving for Winnipeg on October 26th, and had given 60 Maryland Street as the address where the British Columbia ILP could reach him if necessary.

He was coming!

Chapter Twenty-seven

He would be here in her house! There were so many things she wanted to ask him, or get a sense of.

"To think of seeing you again!" she wrote. *"It seems almost too good to be true. If it were anyone else but you I would be far too frightened to undertake such an adventure as we are embarked upon, but the memory of your gentleness and understanding reassures me. Come by the morning train just like Father does, by surprise. You will come up to the house when all the boys have gone to school and I am here alone. I'm only pretending – of course I want to meet your train. Only please don't arrive on Monday, wash day, for once the laundry is started it simply must be finished."*

She wanted him all to herself, she wrote, but she was aware that once Labour people knew he was in town they would swoop down upon him and make him speak at meetings. She invited him to stay at the house, and told him to bring a winter coat.

It turned out that Angus had a solution to the problem of being monopolized by the ILP during his short visit; he'd told Mr. Ivens and Mayor John Queen that he was arriving two days later than he actually was. Grace was delighted, until her eyes moved down the page and read that *"it would not be possible"* for him to stay at 60 Maryland. No doubt he thought it would be improper with her parents away.

"We shall have to take it for granted that our engagement will become public property when your visit is known," she wrote.

"So many people are telling me that I am quite changed since my return from Ottawa and it would not take much to get gossip going."

One evening when her brothers were all at the dinner table, she told them that Angus MacInnis was coming to Winnipeg again for a week. He would be at the house for meals and in the evenings would help her with some work matters that had arisen in Father's absence. She would also be attending some evening meetings with him and on those nights they would have to feed themselves.

"Is this the man who was here in August?" Bruce's inquiry sounded innocent, but a smirk twitched at his mouth.

"Yes, he's the one."

"He seemed nice," Ralph put in.

Howard began singing softly:

"My cutie's due at two to two/he's coming through on a big choo-choo"

He stopped abruptly under Charles's glare.

"There's something more," she said. "You may have guessed. Angus and I are engaged to be married."

"I suspected it," said Charles, with a big grin. "Congratulations, Grace!"

"I guessed too," Bruce added.

"So did I," said Ralph.

"I knew officially way back in August," Howard declared. "Grace told me just after she told Mother and Father."

"When is the wedding?" Bruce inquired.

"We haven't set a date yet. It's one of the things we'll talk about when he's here."

* * *

As passengers slowly emerged from the train, she trembled. Then they saw each other. She wanted to throw herself into his arms but knew he didn't like public displays of affection, so she and Ralph, who was with her, saw him to his hotel. When she invited him to lunch at the house the following day, he accepted without hesitation.

Next morning, Howard tried to plead illness and stay home, but when she told him firmly that he was going to school, he didn't put up much resistance. That morning she waited at the window, and when Angus came up the walk her heart leapt up. She flung open the door, pulled him inside and stood on tiptoe to kiss him. He looked very happy.

"I've missed your smiling face," he said. "I don't think you've changed much. You're still the impulsive little girl as well as the grown woman."

"And you're still your wonderful self."

They couldn't count on complete privacy at the house, as Charles's hours were irregular, and there were always telephone calls and friendly neighbours and needy people coming to the door. She served Angus an early lunch, a chicken cooked according to one of Madame Fuch's recipes, with crème caramel for dessert, and was glad to see him eat with good appetite.

She asked about his sisters in Washington state. Both were married, one to a man who had lost their life savings in the Crash; they were barely making ends meet. The other sister, Jennie, was the one he thought would be the happiest about the engagement, and he intended to tell her, soon.

Hm. He hadn't told her yet. Grace said she was sure his family had guessed.

"Do you think a strong, able-bodied man like yourself, who receives letters twice a week from the same woman, and has her picture in his room, wouldn't arouse suspicion?"

He laughed and said he guessed he was waiting for someone to ask.

"You Scots are so restrained, much more so than my family. Howard asked, the other brothers guessed and Belva knew there was something between us last summer when we got off the train together."

She praised his letters, so well written. She thought both of them had revealed things about themselves, and that their time apart had allowed some necessary reflection.

"And I've learned so much from you about the labour movement in B.C." she said, and they slid into the political realm.

Angus had been taking the social democratic message to a variety of groups ranging from the Unitarian ladies to the Vancouver Trades and Labour Council. Every day, desperate people had come to him seeking his help. Inevitably the economic system would have to change, but he didn't know what form it would take. In spite of developments like the Bienfait strike, it was hard to imagine a violent revolution in Canada. Big business and government had allied many times to put down labour actions with force and Section 98 of the Criminal Code was a vehicle of state repression. Instead of a truly democratic government of workers and for workers, the country might go in the direction of Mussolini's Italy. It was a frightening thought.

Angus looked tired, so after the meal she suggested that he take his coffee into the living room while she tidied up in the kitchen. Ten minutes later, she crept in, eager to press kisses upon him and perhaps tickle him, and found him fast asleep with his head on the back of the sofa. Tiptoeing out, she fetched the darning basket, and returned to sit by the window. She put the china egg into the toe of Howard's sock and set about weaving a patch on the hole. As Angus breathed deeply and regularly, she smiled, anticipating a time when they would be sharing their slumbers.

When she got tired of darning she read, and then she heard feet on the veranda, the door flung open and Howard's call, "Anybody home?"

Angus woke with a start and was flustered until she kissed him and then went to ask Howard into the study. Her youngest brother was the perfect gentleman. He greeted Angus warmly, asked about his trip and talked about hiking, grouse hunting and hockey. When the other brothers arrived, Grace found herself alone in the kitchen like a farm wife about to feed a threshing gang and was perfectly happy. Dinner went well, with no awkward lulls in the conversation.

After the meal, when Howard and Bruce cleared the table, Angus suggested a walk, and soon he and Grace were out in the cold starry night. His gloved hand grasped her mittened one. With breath that came out in clouds, he asked her when she could come to Vancouver, and she told him she'd written to friends in Gibson's Landing to see if she could come and stay with them sometime in the next month. A visit to the coast depended on her parents' plans, though. She hadn't heard from them for a while but wasn't worried; they were probably in the Soviet Union.

Angus hoped she could come. On the deserted street, in the shelter of a clump of spruce trees he put his arms around her. His lips were warm but his cheeks were chilly.

"Let's go home," she said. "We'll sit in the study. Everyone will soon be upstairs doing homework."

Back at 60 Maryland everyone had cleared out of the ground floor. The upstairs was quiet except for the brief sound of feet padding across a room. Grace put the kettle on for tea, and when it was made, Angus carried the tray into the study, the cosiest room downstairs. The green desk lamp illuminated a rectangle on the blotter where her typewriter sat, but the rest of the room was shadowy. They sat on the sofa drinking tea.

"This is the first time we've been alone together in a comfortable place," she remarked. "I can hardly believe you're really here. Over the past few months I had moments of wondering if our love might have been a fantasy."

Angus put down his cup and reached for her. After awhile when they separated for air, he asked her if his kisses had felt real and she said yes, very much so. She took the two throw pillows on the sofa, arranged them both against one arm, and whispered, "Let's lie down."

"You're sure?"

"Very sure."

The difference in their heights didn't matter when they were lying down. It was thrilling yet somehow natural to be pressed against him, separated only by their clothes. As he kissed her mouth and then her throat she tingled with excitement and wanted him to unbutton her blouse. She put her hands under his shirt. Then they tensed. Something was on the veranda just outside the window. They stayed perfectly still as a key turned in the lock.

"Charles," she whispered.

Angus swung his feet to the floor as the study door clicked and the doorknob turned. Grace could feel her hair sticking up every which way. She sat up and straightened her blouse just as Charles appeared in the doorway.

"Oops," he said. "I saw a light on. I'm sorry. Carry on."

He withdrew and closed the door.

Angus fastened the top button on her blouse and smoothed her hair.

"I'm sorry," he whispered. "I got carried away and forgot who was in my care."

"I'm the naughty one. I suggested it. It's fine, Angus. We're engaged to be married."

"Your parents would have me tarred and feathered."

"Oh, I don't think so, and besides, they aren't here and there's no harm done. If this old sofa could talk it could probably tell many a tale."

He chuckled. "Maybe the older generation was no more dignified at times than we are now."

"You look dignified enough. Your hair isn't mussed up. Mine must have given Charles a fright."

"You look lovely. Now, I should go. Just one more kiss to say goodnight."

He invited her to meet him for lunch the following day and then he was gone.

When they met the next day both wore silly grins.

"Am I forgiven for last night?" he asked.

"There's nothing to forgive."

"That's just like you to say that, Dearie."

"Charles informed me this morning that he'll be working late again, and I'm sure when he comes home he won't go around checking for lights left on."

The waitress appeared, and when Grace chose a sandwich and salad, Angus ordered the same, saying that she was a good influence on him.

"I often go without meals and then eat too much and the wrong things. I have other bad habits, too."

"None that I've noticed so far. And I have my flaws, too. I'm opinionated."

"No!" he joked. "Give me an example."

She told him about one recent social gathering where she'd argued with a professor who didn't perceive the depression as the result of capitalism run amok.

"I can be impatient and demanding, and sometimes forget other people's limitations. In fact," she added, "I'm a lot like Father. When we children were growing up, Mother tried to train us out of certain behaviours and at some point I realized that these were the same traits that Father had. But when I said as much to her, she denied that he was like that."

Angus smiled. "She loves him and can't see his faults, or else his good points outnumber them. I hope we'll be like that to each other. As long as you love me and are nice to me, you'll find you can do anything with me."

In the pale afternoon sun they strolled in Assiniboine Park and talked about many things. Discussing the domino effect of economic collapse that had followed the Crash, Grace referred to a company as "putting the screws" to its employees. Angus stared at her.

"What?" she inquired.

He grinned. "I never imagined my little girl using an expression like that."

"Everybody says *put the screws to....* It's from the gangster movies, and it's accurate in this instance, wouldn't you say?"

"Yes. You just surprised me."

"Another of my faults. I use crude modern expressions."

They found a bench where they kissed until she felt as if she were about to melt, in spite of the cold.

"What are you thinking, Dearie?" he whispered, during a lull.

She laughed and pointed to a leafless maple. "I was thinking that if you kissed that tree you'd get its sap running. Do I shock you?"

"No. I'm getting used to the frank way you express your feelings."

"But deep down, do you disapprove?"

"No. I understand that it's because of your youth and inexperience, my darling. I know of no other girl of your station and background who would be so free in expressing her love."

She winced at the "station and background".

"Times have changed, Angus. In the years since the Great War, all the old rules about proper behaviour have been overturned. I love you and you love me, so why would I pretend to be a shy delicate flower – even though in one way I still am?"

He looked at her with devotion.

"I love you so much," he said. "I just hope I can keep up with you."

That afternoon, as they prepared dinner, he peeled and chopped vegetables and spoke of his friend from socialist circles, Wallis Lefeaux, who had recently married a younger woman. Angus had sent them a wedding present and had received a thank you note saying, "Go thou and do likewise."

"I guess rumours are afoot. A man like yourself with cooking skills was bound to be snapped up sooner or later."

"When we're married, I intend to help with all the household chores," he informed her. "I don't expect you to keep house for me. We'll keep house together."

At dinnertime that evening Grace casually remarked that she and Angus were going to be working late in the study that evening and hoped not to be disturbed. The boys assured her that they were swamped with homework.

She actually did want to consult Angus about a letter she was composing to make sure she was referring the recipient to the right government department. She also wanted to show him an article by John Maynard Keynes on the need for governments to spend their way out of the depression. They discussed these matters, aware of the radio playing in another room, but then it was shut off and the stairs creaked and all was still.

Soon they were in each other's arms and kissing, but it did not seem like enough, so again they lay down, fully clothed but blissfully close. Then, cautiously, Grace's "little mute hands" as he called them, took on a life of their own, and his hands, too, went exploring. Instinct took over and although they didn't cross the line, they came close.

"Oh, Grace," he whispered.

"Oh, what a foretaste of glories divine," she murmured.

They laughed together in the dark.

Chapter Twenty-eight

The following day when they went walking they were a little shy with each other at first. She was afraid he would retreat to oldfashioned, hands-off, courtly love before she could broach a necessary subject.

"The first night you kissed me, back in the spring," she began, "I didn't want to wash my face the next morning and wipe that kiss away."

"Silly little girl, when you knew I'd give you another."

"When I went into the study this morning, I saw the two cushions with the imprints of our heads. I'm sentimental enough to leave them just like that, at least until my parents come home. Last night I saw more fully than ever before what marriage is going to be. But I have only instinct to guide me. You have instinct and experience. You've taught me some things, but...well, I want our life together to get off to a good start, and..."

She faltered, hoping he would chime in.

"You should read Dr. Marie Stopes," he said.

"All right." She didn't tell him she had already read *Wise Parenthood*, which was actually about avoiding parenthood, or rather, about spacing children. She had a good theoretical knowledge of spermicides, suppositories and sponges, as well as the diaphragm and the condom, and had been working up to asking what he thought they should use. Now she felt too embarrassed to continue, for fear he'd think such a discussion was inappropriate for a girl "from her station and background." The moment passed.

Perhaps this discussion could wait, for, sadly, there would be no more intimacies in the study for a while. For the rest of his visit Angus had evening meetings that would run very late.

Sitting with friends and acquaintances in the meeting halls, she kept a poker face when those around her praised him for being so clear and down-to-earth. The last evening, when she entered the hall, Mrs. Heaps spotted her and beckoned to her to join her in the front row. Vibrant and outgoing, Bessie Heaps was a keen observer of human nature, so again Grace struggled to give nothing away and was particularly careful not to laugh too hard at Angus's jokes. Afterwards, when the Heaps invited them out for coffee, she addressed her conversation mainly to them, talking mostly about her parents' travels. Even so, she thought she noticed Mr. and Mrs. Heaps exchanging knowing looks. Angus finished his coffee in a surprisingly short time and declared that he was exhausted and was heading back to the Maclaren Hotel for a good night's sleep. Mr. and Mrs. Heaps wanted to see Grace home, but since they were going in opposite directions, she assured them that she would be fine. When they were out of sight, she went back to the hotel, where she found Angus reading a newspaper in the lobby.

"You look sensational just now, your face all aglow," he told her as he got up to walk her home.

"It's nervous excitement. I think Mrs. Heaps knows, but she's too polite to ask."

When they said goodnight on her front porch, she fought back tears, because her proposed trip to the coast was indefinite. She might not be seeing him again until February.

"Whatever the future holds," she whispered, holding his hands, "we'll always have the memory of these past few days. You've been lovely with me."

"I love you more than ever."

He kissed her and left.

Next morning as she got her brood out of the house for the day, she thought of him boarding the train all alone. She would have to get used to these partings; a life in politics was sure to have a great many of them. That morning, as she tried to get on with some housework, the phone kept ringing with requests for help, and when the doorbell rang she thought that another soul in need would reduce her to tears. To her great delight, however, she found a florist's deliveryman, who presented her with a bouquet of cream and red roses. As she put them in water, she stroked their satin petals and smiled.

That night, when the house was asleep, she got up and found Marie Stopes's books in her mother's bottom bureau drawer. A refresher glance through *Wise Parenthood* convinced her that she would have to talk to her mother about the best precautions to take until she'd had enough experience to be fitted with a diaphragm. Or maybe Angus would use a condom.

She'd never read *Married Love* because, until recently, marriage hadn't been on her horizon. Also, she'd thought the book might be a 20th century version of the old Victorian advice books, like *Mrs. Beeton's Book of Household Management*, claiming that the way to a man's heart was through his stomach. *Married Love* was about pleasing a husband, all right, but it was about erotic pleasure, and actually more about the wife's than the husband's. Once she started reading it, Grace couldn't put it down, because it gave her insight into what Angus knew but was too shy to articulate.

She skipped the parts where Stopes expressed opinions about who shouldn't have children, and about the need to space pregnancies to produce healthy offspring and strengthen the human race. Grace's concerns were personal.

To her great joy, she realized that Angus must have an understanding of a woman's physiology, and be aware that women felt erotic desire as well as romantic love. He had undoubtedly read the passage where Stopes said that a man shouldn't use a woman as a "passive instrument" and that he must "woo" her before "every separate act." *Married Love* was technical and explicit where necessary, but was written in sweet, gentle language. Couples, said Stopes, must get to know each other and learn the intricacies of each other's hearts and bodies, "with the tenderest and most delicate touches."

Stopes had ideas, as well, for preventing marriage from becoming dull. Both partners should have their own independent projects, and when these interests took them into association with other people, the spouses should not be jealous of each other, because these interests made them more interesting people and gave them something to talk about. There should be trust on both sides. Reading this, Grace understood that Angus would encourage her interest in politics and that she should fight down her jealousy of his women friends in the socialist movement.

The passage that resonated most with her was Stopes's statement that the union of a man and woman was a "new and wondrous thing" that surpassed what they were separately. She wasn't talking about children, but instead, about the "superphysical entity" created by a man and woman in love.

Grace thought that, in a future letter, she might quote this passage before sharing with Angus a concern that she'd never confided to a soul.

Chapter Twenty-nine

Angus's first letter, from the train, provided addresses in Cranbrook and Nelson if she wanted to write to him there. He would be back in Vancouver on November 12th.

"I miss your ardent warm kisses," he wrote. *"Now more than ever I want you. I hope you will be able to come to the coast, although I feel that, under the circumstances, I will not see much of you."*

What circumstances? His busy schedule, or the new phase of their relationship?

These days Grace was much in demand socially, for everything from bridge to public speaking. At one bridge evening a professor asked her to go dancing, and she said maybe sometime. She was surprised to be asked by the Theosophist Society to give a talk. Were they interested in socialism? She gave the talk – badly, she thought – but everyone was very nice, and one gentleman walked her part of the way home. The fifteen young people in the socialist discussion group which met Wednesdays at her house treated her like the resident expert. And one evening she met a celebrity.

Friends of her parents had invited her over to meet a young YWCA social worker working with unemployed girls. The celebrity guest, however, was Dr. Charles W. Gordon. Now in his early seventies, he was highly respected as a former Great War chaplain and Presbyterian Church moderator. Under the pseudonym "Ralph Connor", he'd written many novels, including the famous *Glengarry School Days.* Grace had read his novel,

To Whom That Hath, about a strike, and had not been impressed, because he implied that labour problems could be solved by virtuous individuals, not through workers' rights. That evening, when Dr. Gordon remarked that Ramsay MacDonald had been wise to shelve his socialism until a more suitable season, Grace declared that if there ever was a time for socialism, it was now. He seemed taken aback, and she felt astonished at her nerve in publicly disagreeing with this great man. The social worker was more interesting, so Grace invited her to the Wednesday group.

She wrote of these experiences to Angus, hoping they didn't bore him. His letters about his tour of the B.C. interior fascinated her. In Cranbrook he spoke for an hour about the Independent Labour Party to an attentive audience who suddenly became strangely mute when he asked for questions. The following evening, at Kimberley, a zinc and lead mining town of about 5,500 people, forty people showed up to hear him – a larger audience than Grace's father had attracted there a few years earlier. Once again everyone listened intently, but later had nothing to ask. The price of metals had fallen and miners were working only three or four days a week; obviously, they were afraid to show too much interest in socialism for fear the managers would fire them.

"All I'm doing is making contact," he wrote. *"If your father or Abe Heaps came here in the next couple of months to build on my visit, they might establish a branch of the ILP here, because I think the people are fed up with the Liberals and Tories. So said Mr. S. who put me up at his house. His family made me very welcome, and he entertained us one evening by singing in a good bass voice. I told him he should run for Labour here. He's very bright and would fit in well with your father, Heaps and myself. Grace, darling, so far this letter might as well have been written to your father and not to my love, but I had to unburden myself to somebody and who is the more logical choice than yourself?"*

He next wrote from Nelson. He'd left Cranbrook expecting to arrive in Nelson at 7:40 p.m., but a wreck on the line delayed the train and he got there at 4:30 a.m.

"I'm staying with the Turner family," he wrote. *"Mrs. Turner reminds me of you in that she is petite and slender, with dark hair. But her features are not like yours and she differed in other respects, too. When I was sitting in the front room, alone, she did not come in and tickle me under the chin or stroke my hair or give me a kiss. It's the kisses I miss most. Habits form quickly."*

Someone then drove him to New Denver, forty miles from Nelson, to stay with a Mr. and Mrs. Harris at their farm on beautiful Slocan Lake. *"Mrs. Harris is not a socialist,"* he wrote, *"but very nice in spite of that."* In the evening he spoke at Silverton, where a branch of the ILP had been organized, and had a good audience.

Next day he went by train to Sandon, twelve miles from New Denver, where he had dinner with an Italian family he'd met at the Silverton meeting. He returned to the Harrises in a truck on a mountain road a foot deep in snow with a drop of a thousand feet.

"I rather wished you were with me in the truck," he said. *"The element of danger would add to the pleasure. I'll be back in Vancouver tomorrow, and hope for a letter from you saying that your parents are home and that you're coming to B.C. Then the sun will shine once more."*

Evidently he was no longer brooding about the "circumstances".

His next letter was from Vancouver.

"My stay in Winnipeg was surely a pleasure and the best part is that neither of us has a trace of regret," he wrote. *"You are so free in showing your love and I am still enough of a boy to love you for it. You are a great mixture of childhood and maturity, the maturity that expresses itself in logical reasoning."*

"The tables in my room have been tidied in my absence. The one at the head of my bed has your picture on it, but an old one of me had been added, with a vase of flowers between us. So your picture was well looked after when I was away. They have been so accustomed to me having lady friends who were nothing but friends that I am sure they will get a big surprise. However, when they see you I am sure everything will be all right."

Grace thought it obvious that Christine had set up the table that way to show that she was aware of their romance and wanted to be informed. Why hadn't he told her yet?

He'd had a letter from Miss P. in Glasgow, containing some heather. Grace, who had sent him bittersweet, wanted to be the only woman sending him plant sprigs. She reminded herself that Miss P. was far away in Scotland.

But what of this?

"Wednesday night I have an invitation to visit a widow, who, I am afraid, has designs on my freedom."

Then maybe he should have declined and stayed home. He'd also had a letter from a woman friend saying she was engaged to be married. Apparently she'd felt that Angus deserved to be informed in a personal note. Angus had replied, saying that he too was engaged, but asking the woman friend not to broadcast the news for a while yet.

Grace reminded herself of Marie Stopes's advice against jealousy. The fact that he was mentioning these women suggested that none of them was competition for his love. Maybe he'd gone out with each of them a couple of times but had never had strong feelings for them. She didn't trust the widow, though.

When Charles poked his head into the study that evening and asked her if she'd like to come with him to the theatre, she said yes, that a change of scene would be good.

On returning home that night they were chilled, and sat with hot chocolate in the kitchen for a while.

"If you want to go to Vancouver," Charles said, out of the blue, "then go and sort out what's bothering you."

"Bothering me?"

"I'm a journalist with keen powers of observation." He grinned. "I'm also the oldest man in the house, so I can handle things here."

"Oh, Charles, you're so kind! But I can't. For one thing, I promised Mother and Father that I'd manage our home and I can't fail them. Another thing – you're run ragged as it is, and soon everyone will be having exams. And Angus is so busy, speaking at one or two meetings every day, that he wouldn't have time for me. And staying at Gibson's Landing I'd be inaccessible anyway. It isn't worth the cost of going."

"I'll bet he'd find time once you got there."

"Maybe I'll go after our parents get home, if there's time before Christmas."

Angus's reluctance to tell people they were engaged bothered her. She wanted to be introduced to his family and his Labour friends as his fiancée, especially to the women who flocked after him. But he hadn't told people of their engagement. And would they get any time alone? Going for walks was pleasant but it wasn't enough any more.

She had too much pride to go to assert her claim, especially as he seemed to be seeing other women, and not just in public. She wasn't dating. If she occasionally talked to a man other than her brothers, it was at a meeting or at the home of friends, always in public. His letters were full of love and longing but contained no specifics as to when they should be married, nor plans for their life together. She imagined that if they married before the new session, they'd rent an apartment in Ottawa. But sometime next year, when Parliament recessed, she might be going to Vancouver to live with people she'd never met and who might regard her as an interloper.

Maybe he didn't intend for them to get married any time soon. Perhaps he was still on the fence about marriage and couldn't admit it to himself.

She looked across the table at Charles.

"I need a male opinion on something," she began. "Suppose you were engaged to be married..."

He looked startled.

"Just hearing you say that, Grace, sends a shiver up my spine. The last time I went out with a girl it was a double-date, absolutely not serious."

"No one special?" she asked mischievously.

"They're all special, but I have a lot of living to do, and even if I were ready to settle on one, in this economy..." He broke off abruptly. "I'm sorry, Grace. I didn't mean you. I know Angus makes enough to support you."

"No offence taken. Now, here's my hypothetical question. If you were engaged, but the engagement hadn't been officially announced, nor a wedding date set, would you still go out with women other than your fiancée?"

"I don't think so, unless, say, my old high school teacher, Miss Smith, who is sixty, needed an escort to the theatre or somewhere."

Grace smiled.

"Another hypothetical question. If you were engaged, at what stage would you tell our family?"

He considered.

"After the girl said yes? Oh, Grace, I'm afraid I'm no help. These aren't my concerns right now. But I'll mind the home fires if you decide to go to Vancouver."

Before she went to bed, Grace wrote to Angus that her parents seemed to be having a wonderful time in Europe and showed not the slightest intention of coming home. She guessed they wouldn't return much before Christmas.

"So I don't think I can come to the coast, even though I'd like to come and kidnap you, just to prove that I have the ability to be unconventional."

When she finally did meet his family she would try very hard to make them like her. *"Perhaps they can forgive me for coming in and disturbing your life if they see that I love you."*

She couldn't bring herself to ask if he was having second thoughts, so she turned to their shared cause. His difficulties in getting a response from the workers in the B.C. interior was a common one. Mr. Heaps, the guest speaker at the Wednesday group, had told them of his difficulties trying to organize a meeting in Guelph on his way west. The mayor had refused the use of the town hall, so the ILP had to find another venue. No local ILP supporter wanted to chair the meeting so they'd had to bring in someone from Hamilton. A lot of spade work would have to be done before the movement would glean any results. Right now, more university types than workers were showing an interest in the ILP, probably because they were less fearful of losing their jobs.

She also wrote to him of a local matter. Although the Communist Party of Canada had been declared illegal, individual communists still continued to slam the ILP, and one prominent Independent Labour man in Winnipeg had enough. He'd gone to a magistrate and charged one such communist with libel. Grace thought it was pretty drastic of him to go to the law. Her father was often verbally attacked by communists, but always ignored them, saying that to respond in any public way was to give them the attention they wanted.

Another reason for not over-reacting was that the communists shared an economic analysis with democratic socialists. Both wanted capitalism replaced by a planned social order that guaranteed the economic equality of all people. The difference was in method, in violent revolution versus change through the electoral system. Labour M.P.s were representing workers within legislatures; communists were organizing workers at a grass roots level; to an extent they reinforced each other. She wanted Angus's opinion.

Meanwhile, her time with her brothers was drawing to a close, and it was unlikely they'd ever all be together like this again. The following evening at dinner when everyone was digging into ham and scalloped potatoes, Grace clinked her knife against her glass to get everyone's attention.

"There's something we must do before our parents get back," she announced.

"Oh-oh," murmured Bruce.

"I have a very full schedule," Ralph informed her.

"We should have a party," Grace said.

Howard looked astonished.

"Absolutely!" Charles exclaimed.

"With girls?" Howard inquired.

"It wouldn't be much of a party without them," said Bruce.

Together they began making plans for an evening that would start out high-toned and cultural and end with dancing. They invited twenty-five guests including several of their parents' generation who had entertained them. The Wednesday group, Charles's friends from the *Tribune* and the younger boys' chums were included. The evening began with music, with a pianist friend accompanying Charles on his violin. When she played some solo classics, including Beethoven's "Moonlight Sonata", Grace was transported to some faraway place, a place of blossoming trees, like Ottawa, or Gibson's, with Angus near. His face, which she could not always call up in memory, was now very clear.

After the music they served refreshments, got out their records and wound up the Victrola. Some of the older guests departed before the dancing, but it was a Saturday night and the younger guests had no intentions of leaving early.

As Grace circulated, carrying a tray and taking in the scene, she smiled. Ralph was dancing sedately to *Mood Indigo* with their social worker friend. The girl next door, the former homework buddy of both Ralph and Bruce, was dancing with Howard, who looked proud. Bruce was in a corner talking earnestly to a young woman. Charles and his *Tribune* friends were in the kitchen laughing at each other's jokes.

When she came out of the pantry with more sandwiches, Charles took the platter from her and handed her a glass of wine. It was delicious. Then she felt a hand on her shoulder and turned to see one of Charles's colleagues beside her, a matinee-idol of a man with curly dark hair and eyes like chocolate.

"I'm Jack Gold," he said, "and you must be Grace. I've been wanting to dance with you all evening."

He led her into the front room where *Dream a Little Dream of Me* was playing, a slow song about separated lovers craving each other's company. Jack asked her about her work in Ottawa and when the song ended they found a quiet corner and continued their conversation, mostly about his work on the paper. Wandering to other subjects, they found that they had read many of the same things and shared many of the same ideas. It was amazing to run into someone on the same wave length.

When Howard came over to say that he was seeing the girl next door to her home, Grace looked at her watch and saw that it was 3:00 a.m. Quite a few people had left, but several couples were in each other's arms, swaying to dance music on the radio. The aroma of coffee wafted from the kitchen, where a noisy card game was going on. It sounded as if Charles was winning.

"Time has just flown!" she said.

"It has. We have so much to talk about. How about dinner some evening?"

"Oh, Jack, I wish I could, but I can't. I've enjoyed our conversation, though."

He looked hurt. "Don't you date fellows of my persuasion?"

"Oh, it's not that. It's because I'm engaged to be married."

He glanced at her left hand. "Where is your ring?"

"I don't have one. He offered but I thought it was too ostentatious. But soon I'll be wearing a wedding ring."

He smiled. "Well, you can't blame a guy for trying, and it has been a fine evening."

"It has."

Grace said goodnight, left Charles to see the remaining guests out, and went up to bed.

"*Last night we had a party,*" she wrote to Angus the following afternoon, as freezing rain pelted down outside. "*It was a great success and the proof of that is that we didn't get to bed until around 4:00 a.m. We all emerged around noon, none of us terribly the worse for wear, and we tidied up, and now we're all here in the kitchen, except for Charles, who is upstairs working on constitutional history. Ralph is sitting on the counter doing some* wood carving. Bruce is at the end of the table with a hunting knife in his hand, skinning the grouse that Howard shot on Friday in the woods with the .22. Howard is looking over Bruce's shoulder reading aloud from an instruction book.

"I'm pleased at how well we're getting along. Nobody has accused me of being bossy. Maybe we've all matured. They all pitched in to make the party a success.

"The highlight of my evening was my conversation with a young reporter friend of Charles. Talking to him, I felt that electric current that happens when two minds meet. To me that's almost the most thrilling experience there is. I say 'almost' because when two people understand each other body and soul, that has to be the supreme experience."

Chapter Thirty

In mid-November, when Grace was outdoors planting bulbs in a pail she realized that ten days had passed since she'd last heard from Angus. The sun was shining, the sky intensely blue and her fingers also blue from the cold. Had something happened to him? Had he changed his mind and didn't know how to tell her?

She buried her anxiety in work, attending ILP meetings in support of civic election candidates, often with Charles, who was covering them for the *Tribune*. One evening at a meeting of the International League for Peace and Freedom, a woman asked her if she knew the new Labour M.P. from Vancouver. "His speeches in *Hansard* read so well!" she gushed. She was fishing, Grace knew. With a poker face she said that he was indeed an effective member of the Ginger Group.

"I *think* I know him," she said to herself.

One Wednesday evening after the young socialists had dispersed, a young woman from the group, Delores, lingered to help tidy up, but really to talk. As she dried plates, she told Grace her story. She was eighteen and lived in a rooming house with her widowed mother, who couldn't seem to shake a persistent cough. Her father, a self-employed carpenter, had died of a heart attack a year earlier, leaving no insurance and no pension. Without him they could no longer keep up payments on their house; they'd sold it to cover the mortgage and had nothing. For the past year, Delores had been working as a salesclerk for a downtown department store, but had recently been laid off, with not much hope of part-time work. The management preferred a part-time staff but gave priority to women who had worked there for many years. The idea of going on relief horrified Delores.

Grace said there was no shame in being on relief; one out of four Canadians was.

"Could you go with me to apply?"

Grace agreed, and arranged to meet her at her home the following day. She set out on the cold brightness and found Delores's rooming house in a neighbourhood of large houses that had once been middle class. No one responded to her knock and she was debating whether or not she should walk right in, when an elderly man answered, and directed her up the stairs to the first door on the right. Passing through the hall, Grace noticed that what had once been a large parlour was now partitioned off.

Upstairs, Delores opened the door at Grace's first rap. As she pulled a man's wool sweater over her dress, the skirt rode up and her woollen over-pants showed below her hem. Her worn tweed coat lay over a chair. The former master bedroom was now functioning as a studio apartment, with much of the space taken up by two beds. In one, Delores's mother lay coughing. On a kitchen table in a corner there was an electric hot plate where an egg was boiling. With a dresser crammed in as well, there was barely space to turn around and no place to put anything.

Delores helped her mother into an easy chair, arranged a quilt over her and served her the egg and some tea. When Grace handed over the bag of oatmeal cookies that she'd brought for them, the mother's eyes welled up with tears. She thanked Grace profusely until her words were lost in a bone-racking cough.

"I'll be back in an hour," Delores promised. Grace thought this estimate was optimistic, and it proved to be so. When they arrived at the Elgin Avenue relief office they found a line-up of applicants extending out the office door and into the wood yard on the adjoining city block. They joined the line.

While they waited, rubbing their hands together and stamping their feet to keep their blood circulating, Delores asked Grace about medical assistance from the city. She had no money to take her mother to a doctor. Grace said there was a doctor for relief recipients but the wait was impossibly long. She advised her to take her mother to the emergency department at one of the hospitals, where she would not be turned away.

The line moved at a snail's pace, but eventually Delores and Grace entered the waiting room. Happy to be in out of the cold, they didn't mind the smell of wet wool, sweat, garlic and smoke from the heater stove. They took a number and found seats.

"It looks like a long wait," Delores told Grace. "You don't have to stay."

"I'll stay for a while."

There were three doors leading to the inner office, one marked "Applications", another for "Rent and Fuel" and another for "Groceries." All three queues were long, the one for new applications the longest.

An hour later, Grace and Delores saw a clerk, who said Delores could apply for relief for herself, but not for her mother, who would have to come down. At that point, Grace introduced herself as J.S. Woodsworth's secretary, and said that the mother was too ill to leave the house. Finally the clerk agreed that Delores could apply for both. An investigator would be coming to their home to see if they qualified.

Grace again stepped in to say that Delores and her mother needed food vouchers right away, so the clerk filled out a requisition and sent them out to wait in the "Groceries" line. By the time Delores was given the vouchers, Grace felt like a dishrag, and was sure Delores did too, so she took her to a lunch counter for coffee and a doughnut. When she accompanied Delores home she pressed a dollar into the girl's hand.

Back home she found two letters from Angus, and, still wearing her coat, sank down to read them. He was incredibly busy, at a meeting every day, most recently an Independent Labour Party organizational one in Grandview. He'd been invited to speak to the Vancouver South Liberal Association, of all things, where he'd said that capitalism was on its way out and that the ILP wanted a peaceful transition to a more equitable system and an improvement in living standards. If the Liberals didn't put the needs of the poor at the forefront of their program, their party would soon wither away. He didn't say how this opinion was received.

He'd written to the Vancouver Relief Department on behalf of a mother and son who had come around to his home begging for help. *"The soles of the young man's shoes were almost worn through,"* he wrote, *"so I gave him a good pair of heavy shoes I'd bought for hiking some years ago but hardly ever wore."* He'd also bought shoes for his elder niece's birthday; he'd taken Christine to an ILP social, and he'd attended a banquet of the St. Andrews and Caledonian Society.

Grace found these details of his daily life interesting and endearing, but also saw how full his life was and how necessary he was to his family. He wrote that Jennie and her husband from Washington were visiting, and that he'd told her of the engagement.

"Yes!" Grace breathed, and read on.

Jennie had urged him to tell the whole family while she and her husband were there, and he intended to *"take some time to think it over."*

He'd heard that Parliament would be called earlier than usual, probably in February rather than in March. *"I'm afraid I have no idea,"* he wrote, *"as to the best thing for us to do."* It was up to her whether they got married in Winnipeg or in Vancouver. *"I do not think my family will mind in the least what I do, and they do not know you."*

If they wouldn't care, then why couldn't he tell them?

She read on.

"I went to the theatre Friday night with Mrs Q. Except for books, she and I are on opposite sides of the world. She doesn't see the unfairness of the present social order. She's interested in the royal family."

Was this the widow who had designs on his freedom? He mentioned as well that he had seen Miss F. at the home of a friend and that she had been very impressed with Russia. Grace couldn't quite place Miss F. in the harem.

"Oh, by the way," he wrote in a postscript, *"when I was in a Chinese restaurant having a bite to eat with Miss V of the women's labour group the other day, Mr. J of the B.C. Socialist Party noticed us and came over to say hello. He wanted to know when your father would be back and I told him mid-December. I thought I should let you know.*

Love, Angus.

Grace shook her head. Clearly one side of him loved her and wanted to marry her, but another side wanted to stay as he was – the good son, brother and uncle, the mainstay of the family, the bachelor who could always find some willing lady friend. "The reserve army of the unemployed" was a term she knew well. Was there also a reserve army of seasoned, available women? It seemed so. His failure to tell the family about his engagement, and his refrain that their future marriage was unfair to her, were indications that he was wavering. The last thing she wanted was for him to marry her out of a sense of obligation, thinking they'd gone too far to turn back now.

She had no right to be angry with him, though. Several years ago she'd agreed to a course of action and then at the last minute couldn't follow through.

She didn't want to lose him as a friend; he was essential to her life, closer to her than anyone else had ever been. Yet she couldn't be "just a friend", either. She guessed if she wanted to spend time by his side, she might have to join a queue and take turns.

In the study she rolled a paper into the typewriter.

Dear Angus,

If you feel, even now, that marriage is an unwise step for you, then you must say so. It would be so easy to postpone it indefinitely and just let it slide. Perhaps you don't think you can adapt to married life, for whatever reasons. The last thing I want to do is to take away your freedom; I love you too much for that.

I have no regrets about the week you came to visit. It will always be one of my most precious memories. I think that I have become mature enough and modern enough to consider another type of relationship with you. I cannot say that I would prefer it, yet, in time, I might. We know of people who have worked out an alternative to marriage which appears to suit them, and perhaps we can do likewise. I know you will take this idea in the spirit in which it is meant, and will feel how sincerely I mean every word of it. I think I love you enough to mean it.

"Please, Angus dear, do consider carefully what I have just said. A great fear comes over me that you may be taking this important step feeling that it would make me unhappy if you did not do so. I would be terribly unhappy if I thought that was why you married me, and such a thing would be bound to come out sooner or later. I love you almost enough to be unselfish about it."

Chapter Thirty-one

It was hard waiting for his reply. When the letter came she read it alone in the study.

"My dear Grace," he wrote:

I feel proud to have you as a friend, let alone to have your love. As far as I am concerned I am making no sacrifice. I wish I could feel as easy in my mind about you. To be bound with you would be the essence of freedom.

As for the alternative relationship, at one time that might have been possible before I knew you well enough to appreciate what a lovely nature yours is. Now I do not wish it, although I forget myself when I am with you. It is not the morality of the situation that would prevent me, but my love for you.

I am not unmindful of the physical basis of love and I know that attracts me to you, but I love you so much that to have you on a basis other than permanence would be unworthy. With a relationship of that kind one is never the same again, and you might be sorry. As Burns wrote: I waive the quantum of the sin/ the hazard of concealing/ But oh, it hardens all within and petrifies the feeling.

I won't have it that way. I would rather leave you to some other fellow, not out of consideration for him, but out of regard for you. If we are to forget each other, I want your memories of me to be pleasant, as mine would be of you. But I want to marry you."

"He wants the highest level relationship with me," she thought.

"You have answered my doubt," she wrote to him. *"I think you have tried to, many times, but this is the first time it has sunk in. I have no doubts now and if they recur I will reread your letters. I am so happy to be experiencing the kind of love I've longed for. It may seem strange to be going down to Ottawa in such a new relationship, but Darling, I will love it. If we weren't going to be married we'd find it so dull. I'll have the right to feel proud of you as my own, and also the right to come into your office whenever I like without being afraid that a certain parliamentarian's wife will wake up from her nap on your couch and find us kissing. Now, don't leave this letter lying around for if it became public it could wreck the Ginger Group caucus."*

She was glad he'd told Jennie of their engagement and imagined that by now he had told Christine.

"I am longing for you tonight," she said in conclusion, *"but I suppose it is best that you are not here for if you were I should not let you get away."*

Winter had set in. Blizzards alternated with cold sunny days when, if your skin was exposed for more than ten minutes you'd get frostbite. In the evenings, Grace often sat in the yellow lamplight, darning socks, with Howard at the table drowsing over his homework, sleepy from his battle with the wind on the way home from school. On such nights, with everyone quietly studying, the house felt like a sanctuary. She longed for such a place with Angus, a place of peace, with firelight and warmth.

In his last letter he said that the *Vancouver Sun* predicted that Parliament would resume on January 28th, and had said, *"Dearie, it will not be long now."*

In spite of the weather and the tedium of marking time until they could be together, Grace had two experiences that stood out for her. One was her conversation with Judge Stubbs. The judge and his wife, Mary, held a holiday party, and since Charles was friends with one of their sons, he and Grace were invited.

Judge Stubbs had been a friend of her father ever since the Winnipeg General Strike in 1919, when Stubbs, then practising law, had helped Fred Dixon (now a city councillor) prepare his defence. The judge's impressive full name was Lewis St. George Stubbs. West Indies born, Cambridge-educated, he'd come to Canada to practise law. In the 1917 election he'd run as a Laurier Liberal, and out of gratitude he'd been appointed judge in 1923 by then-Prime Minister King. Though not physically attractive, he had great fire and energy.

The year Grace was abroad, 1928-29, the judge had been at the centre of a controversy involving a millionaire Winnipeg grocer who had willed his fortune to several charities. His will was presented to Judge Stubbs for probate. Then two relatives produced a more recent will, signed by the millionaire on his death bed, which left all his money to them. Suspicious, Judge Stubbs had held a trial to investigate the circumstances surrounding the new will, and had found it to be void because its presentation and execution had involved deception and fraud.

The relatives then took the matter over Judge Stubbs' head to the Manitoba Court of Appeal, where the judge granted probate without even reading Stubbs' written judgment or the trial transcript. Declaring himself the champion of the out-of-luck charities, Judge Stubbs had organized a public demonstration before the legislature to protest the decision. Since it was now apparent that there was one law for the rich and another for the poor, he sought to rectify the imbalance by giving light sentences to those brought before him.

His nerve took Grace's breath away. Was he trying to get himself disbarred? Was he planning on running for public office? If so, would he run for Independent Labour?

The first part of the evening featured musical performances. Later, when the dancing began, the judge came over and held out his hand to Grace. After they'd danced they found a quiet corner to talk, and she asked him about the prominent ILP man who had charged a communist with libel. Should he have done so?

Judge Stubbs felt that the conservative establishment was using the ILP man as a cat's paw to put down the communists. In his view, Labour should never align itself with big business against any group that championed the poor. From a purely tactical point of view, said Stubbs, the ILP man had probably lost the communist vote, which had made up a substantial part of his support, with the result that he might not be re-elected.

Though Angus had disagreed with her on this case, Grace now felt vindicated. She and the judge agreed that Labour should ignore the communists and concentrate on appealing to the voters.

She asked the judge if he had ever officiated at a wedding held at a private home rather than at the courthouse.

"No, but I would as a favour to a friend." His eyes twinkled. "Is someone we know getting married?"

She laughed and said, "Someone might be."

The second experience was seeing a stage production of *The Barretts of Wimpole Street*, about the romance between two nineteenth century British poets, Elizabeth Barrett and Robert Browning. Based on their love letters, it showed how Robert Browning had persuaded Elizabeth Barrett to defy her tyrannical father and elope with him from rainy England to sunny Italy. Grace found it deeply moving and saw herself in Elizabeth.

"It was wonderful," she told her brothers at supper, "especially when Robert says to Elizabeth: *We are risking unutterable disaster to gain unutterable happiness*."

Bruce's brow furrowed. "Tell me again who these people are."

"Poets. You know them from English class. Browning wrote *My Last Duchess*, among other things. Elizabeth is most famous for the sonnet that begins: '*How do I love thee/let me count the ways*.'"

Bruce rolled his eyes.

"It sounds awfully mushy," said Howard.

Charles and Ralph exchanged amused glances.

"Philistines!" she scolded.

Later, as she and Charles were doing the dishes, he remarked that she was very romantic these days.

"It's only natural," she said.

"Did the play mention Elizabeth's addiction to opiates?"

Grace dropped the pan she was washing. "What do you mean?"

"She took laudanum. When married she weaned off it – for a while."

"How do you know this?"

He shrugged. "I read widely. So you see there is little similarity between the Brownings and you and Angus."

Despite her brothers' lack of interest in the play, Grace got out her mother's copy of Browning's poems that night and saw something she'd never noticed before. Certain passages about love had been marked lightly with a line in the margin, and a faintly pencilled "J." "J"? Then she realized it was for "James", and smiled.

In Angus's next letter he remarked on Winnipeg temperatures, hovering around 18 below zero, Fahrenheit.

"When I read how cold it is there I thought of a little girl with soft caressing hands and wished she were here in Vancouver where the cold is not so intense, or perhaps for other reasons, maybe to feel the touch of her hands."

Jennie had gone back to Washington, he wrote. She'd wanted him to tell Christine of his engagement while she was in Vancouver so the two of them could go in together on a wedding present. Angus told her that he and Grace didn't want presents.

"Jennie hopes you will be one of us and not hold yourself aloof," he continued, *"and I said you were very anxious to please and would feel very badly if you were not gladly received. The conversation ended there. I did not tell Christine yet. I will do so when the holidays are over."*

With Christmas approaching, he wanted to send Grace a gift but didn't know what she would like. *"Please, dear,"* he wrote, *"help me."*

Chapter Thirty-two

In her next letter, Grace suggested that if it would make Jennie happy to give them some little souvenir, perhaps they should accept it.

"You mean a lot to your family and they will want to show it in some material way," she wrote, adding that of course she wouldn't be aloof, but would try her best to make herself likeable. As for a Christmas present, although she didn't need one, she would like a keepsake to keep her company.

"I might even be vain enough to show it to my friends. I shall love it, whatever it is, because it comes from you. You leave me to make so many decisions; this time I want you to make one."

She finished writing an article, which took the better part of one Sunday, and started getting the house shipshape for her parents' return. While downtown shopping at Eatons, she met the Heaps, whose little boy had demanded to be taken to see Santa Claus. Abe told her that Parliament would resume around February 2nd. A wedding date the last week of January seemed a good plan, and she would suggest it to Angus and her parents. There was plenty of time to organize a simple wedding.

By daylight she kept nervousness at bay, but at night she slept poorly and couldn't quite identify what was bothering her. It wasn't her parents' arrival; she looked forward to that. And Angus's letters were filled with love.

One night it dawned on her what the problem was. It was the same one as in Paris. She got up, wrapped herself in her quilt and got out pen and paper.

"*Dear Angus,*

With my parents coming home, January seems very close, and I have a strong need to talk to you. I have been worrying about something even though I promised not to. Thinking about what married life is going to mean to both of us, I realize I am still quite ignorant about some things. I have read Marie Stopes, but the whole psychological realm of men and women is practically unexplored and I must tell you of a fear, a "complex" I have that could endanger our happiness."

She told him how, as a girl, she'd become curious about the series of young unmarried women from the mission who had stayed with her family, doing light housekeeping and some child care until they left, usually quite suddenly, to have babies of their own. Her mother had sympathized with these girls in a society that blamed them for their predicament, but had also made clear to Grace the social consequences they faced.

Then, at around fourteen, Grace had read Upton Sinclair novel, *The Jungle*, a grittily realistic novel of slum life, which included a horrific scene of a woman and baby who died in the agonies of childbirth.

"*No book that I have ever read made a deeper impression on me,*" she wrote. "*For years the fear of having a child was the greatest of all my fears, so great I have never spoken of it to a soul until now. It has underlain what the boys call my Puritanism.*"

Nowadays the risk of dying in childbirth was small, and modern medicine had eliminated much of the pain, but her fear remained. Physically, she was quite capable of having children, probably with less suffering than average, and possibly, sometime in the future, she might want the experience of having a child. But not yet and maybe not ever.

Now came what she'd tried to ask when he was in Winnipeg.

"As yet I am ignorant," she said, *"of how far it is possible to have a satisfactory sex life without the constant risk of conception. I know you do not want a child now and neither do I. I know perfectly well that women do not discuss this question ahead of time because frankness is distasteful to them and their husbands-to-be. But you, Angus seem to have more understanding than a man – to be a compound of both men's and women's understanding. I am not afraid of you and mostly I am not afraid of what you will think of me for being so frank and bothersome. If you want me you will have to take the doubting, weak side of me as well as the other, which is there too. I want to do everything I can to make our life together get away to a good start."*

Grace's parents arrived on December 19th at 9 a.m. and sat down to a combined breakfast and lunch that lasted all morning. Both parents looked rested and invigorated, but Father had already made the transition from vacation mode to work-a-day mode, and in the afternoon he called Grace into the study to go over the household accounts and to answer some correspondence. He had more typing for her, too, because he was writing about his Soviet Union trip for the *Toronto Star*.

Then he wanted to talk about her and Angus. Were they still in love? When she said yes, he said he saw no reason why they should wait to get married. Angus was a lucky man, and he hoped Grace would be as happy in her marriage as her mother and he were in theirs.

"And Angus will have to write to the Secretary of the Department of Railways and Canals in Ottawa to arrange transportation for his wife," her father said.

The words "his wife" thrilled her.

She watched the mail over the next few days for a letter from Angus, and when it came she rushed to her room to read it.

"My dear Grace," he wrote. *"Any man would indeed be proud to receive a letter such as the one I received from you. I am replying without delay, although I have other important things to do, because I would rather write to you than anything else. I well realize how excited you must be with the homecoming of your mother and father and then our own approaching affair too. You must not allow yourself to become unduly excited. However, with your mother home, she will take care of you.*

The matter you referred to in your letter need not be discussed now. I appreciate so much your confiding in me. There are one or two precautions that a man may take, but satisfactory relations are not possible. Such precautions as a woman may take I am not familiar with. I have read about them but they did not leave enough impression on my mind that I can remember now. But do not be afraid, dear. With love and understanding we can overcome all our little troubles.

For now, at any rate, it would be better not to have a baby and if you want to be as sure as possible you could get information from someone qualified to give it, but whatever you do, do not worry over it. I shall understand.

Thanks again for confiding in me your hopes and fears. I hope you will always feel free to do so.

All my love, Angus.

She reread the letter several times. Though he meant to be reassuring, it was clear that he considered this aspect of their life together to be her responsibility. Very well, then. She put the letter away, went downstairs and asked her mother to come for a walk. Mother was only too pleased to drop what she was doing. As they walked past the snowbanks that mild afternoon, Grace once again marvelled at her mother's capabilities. She provided useful information and even a contact, an Ottawa social worker whom Grace could consult in due course about a diaphragm. Meanwhile, mother and daughter would visit a pharmacy together.

Riding home on the street car, holding on her lap a shopping bag full of useful products, Grace felt as if she'd received the best Christmas present ever, and she felt proud to be making this contribution towards their married happiness. She had no way of knowing, that, many years later, in the mid-1960s, she would serve on a House of Commons committee holding hearings on the advertising of family planning products. When her support for open advertising provoked sniggers and asides from the other Honourable Members, all male, her response made the national news.

"I am not talking as a feminist," she said, *"but let me tell you that women are far more accustomed to the physical appearances of foams, jellies, douches and all that sort of thing than you men are. It shocks men to think of these things depicted in a magazine or newspaper, but women are used to them. Why force women to bootleg these things? After all, men do not have to suffer the inconvenience of using them, so I think they should suffer the embarrassment of seeing them, until they get used to them."*

But all that was far in the future. In 1931, she was grateful that, whatever happened, Angus would be standing by her *"Nothing, and I mean literally nothing, is bothering me these days,"* she wrote to him. *"I think of that night on the sofa when we came the closest to each other. All I could think of was the soft warmth of you and the delight of knowing it again. You too, I hope, think often of that side of things."*

She urged him to tell Christine of their engagement at Christmas, for if he left it much later she would be hurt that they hadn't confided in her earlier. Also, Christmas was a time of love and sentimental feelings, more so than any other time. *"And why keep it a secret longer? For the first time I would almost like to have an engagement ring to let the whole world know about it."*

These days, the whole world seemed to be coming to 60 Maryland to ask her father to sort out their difficulties and to invite him to speak at meetings. As well, her parents were planning a party for fifty of their Labour friends on December 22nd. Bruce had been assigned to go through the old art books, which they usually put out at parties, to see which were in good enough repair, and was excluding the one on Greek and Roman statuary. Her mother had hired a household helper for the next six weeks to help her manage the festive season and then the wedding.

Grace and Angus settled on Saturday, January 23 as the date. The wedding reception would be in the afternoon, and then they would catch the train to Ottawa which left around 6 p.m. When her father heard of these plans, he frowned and said he had to be in the Swan River area around the 23rd and didn't know if he could get back.

"I really hope you can," Grace said.

Having typed his January schedule, she knew he had far too many speaking engagements scheduled before Parliament resumed. He was full of enthusiastic plans, but had taken on so much work that he would soon lose the benefit of his time away. This past winter and spring he'd been good to her, always taking her out to eat, and giving her time off when she looked tired. In Ottawa she and Angus would try to look after him.

From Kathy, her best friend from Gibson's days, she received effusive best wishes on her engagement. Kathy and her husband lived in Burns Lake, B.C., where they ran a newspaper, and they were well aware of the new, outspoken, socialist M.P. representing Vancouver. If he and Grace should happen to be in B.C. on their honeymoon trip, they must come and visit.

On Christmas Eve Angus's gift arrived, a magnificent pendant, jade in a gold setting, on a gold chain. Thrilled by its elegance and beauty, sobered by its evident cost, she put it away to wear on their wedding day.

So much was happening, and so quickly. Angus liked the cuff links and tie clip she'd sent him for Christmas and was saving them for the wedding. He had finally told his family about the engagement, and they were happy for him and eager to meet Grace. Christine was glad that he would have a wife to accompany him to official events; she'd found them a social ordeal and was happy to bow out.

In their letters, Angus and Grace consulted each other about new clothes. What would she need as the wife of a Member of Parliament? She didn't have an extensive wardrobe. He replied that he knew that, adding, *"But you didn't seem to mind and I am sure I didn't. You are always lovely to me in whatever you wear."* What she'd need would depend on whether they'd be attending Ottawa functions. *"I'll leave it to you to decide that, but I hope you decide not to."*

Should he buy a new suit for the wedding, as he had only his blue suit and his tux? Grace said yes, and told him about her wedding dress being made by a neighbourhood seamstress. It was made of *peau de soie*, a silk fabric of medium weight and the texture of satin without the shine, the best fabric for a winter wedding. It would be a two-piece garment, more of a suit than a dress, and she hoped he would like it. *"She has also made me a silk camisole and bloomers. I'm sure you will like them,"* she added.

They also discussed practicalities. Angus didn't think they should buy furniture in Ottawa, but instead, should rent a furnished apartment. In between sessions of Parliament, as long as he was a Member, they would have to live half the year in Vancouver.

"We should try to find a place large enough to have a few friends in occasionally, but one in which we can live as simply as possible so that we can be as free as possible."

Once their engagement was announced, plans got more complicated. Grace wrote to warn Angus that the "informal reception" would involve thirty to forty guests.

"I know this goes against our original idea of a very quiet wedding, but people are so interested in it, because of Mother and Father, of course, and I haven't the heart not to have them here for a little celebration. We don't want to hurt people by neglect, but we will try to keep it as simple as possible."

Grace was determined to keep calm and not get upset by little details, but when Belva wrote to say that she couldn't get enough time off school to attend the wedding, she could have wept. Then came a letter to Mother from Agnes Macphail. When it arrived, Mother's hands were covered with flour and she asked Grace to open it.

Miss Macphail regretted that she could not come to the wedding, but asked Mother to convey to Grace her best wishes. She looked forward to seeing her back in Ottawa. She was sorry, however, that Grace's promising future in politics was being nipped in the bud.

How disappointing to hear this assumption from someone she respected and admired! Agnes had broken new ground as the first woman in Parliament; why couldn't the next step in the advancement of women be a married woman who also had a career in politics?

She wrote to Angus that there was nothing on her mind but the certainty of their love, but it wasn't quite so. With the best of intentions, some of her friends were making her feel that their plans were flawed and make-shift. Her parents approved of her having Judge Stubbs perform the marriage ceremony, but some people expressed surprise that a minister's daughter wasn't having a religious ceremony – even though Father was no longer associated with any church. *"Bless your heart, Grace,"* wrote Angus, *"for choosing a civil ceremony. Stick to your guns."*

Although she adored the pendant he'd sent her for Christmas, she wished now that she had an engagement ring. When people wished her well on her engagement, their eyes automatically went to the third finger of her left hand and found it bare. She had only herself to blame; back in the summer she'd told Angus that a ring was unnecessary. She still felt that way, but when people asked her where her ring was, and she said she didn't have one, that a ring was an extravagance when people were going hungry, she sounded like an awful prig.

When asked where she and Angus were going to live, and she said a rented furnished apartment in Ottawa, she often saw raised eyebrows. Apparently she was supposed to want a little cottage with roses at the door.

Mother suggested that Grace devote her time to her secretarial duties and leave the wedding plans to her, and Grace agreed. She always felt better when she had a specific, interesting assignment. Then she caught a cold, and spent her time wiping her nose and rubbing vaseline on her chapped lips. Going for walks always brightened her mood, but the weather now alternated between bitter cold and blinding snow.

The arrival of a letter from Angus cheered her, at first. It began with love, then went on to family news. His mother, who had turned eighty-five on Christmas Day, had fallen and sprained her wrist, and although he had treated it with cold compresses, he was afraid it would drag her downhill, as she was frail. Violet was full of vim. His older niece had told him that he was nicer to get along with than she had expected. He had gone hiking with Clinker.

He hesitated to write for a free railway pass for his wife, even though he knew other M.P.s accepted them as a matter of course, because he disliked all favours and perks. Grace frowned. Did he want Father to pay her way? Or did he expect her to stowaway in a boxcar? Then:

"Last night I invited Miss Em out to dinner," he wrote. *"She gave me a small photo of herself as a Christmas present, so I thought I had better tell her about our plans for marriage. We were sitting in the restaurant talking about your father's articles on the Soviet Union, when the radio, which had been playing in the background, suddenly blared out the announcement of our engagement. I turned red, and Miss Em, who hadn't been paying attention, wanted to know what was wrong. She'd caught your father's name and mine, but nothing more. I wouldn't tell her until we finished our meal. Then I did. She is pleased and is looking forward to meeting you when you come to Vancouver. Our engagement announcement is also in the Sun. I was hoping to be safely out of Vancouver before the news broke."*

He signed "with love."

Alone in her room, Grace stared at the letter, shaking her head. She was too angry to cry. Miss Em was the woman he'd been engaged to, the one who had broken it off because of his working class background and lack of education. Maybe his election to Parliament had elevated him in Em's eyes, making him socially acceptable – husband material. Grace had believed this affair was far in the past, but it sounded as if it had been recent, within the last couple of years, and it certainly seemed as if Miss Em wanted to rekindle it, if she'd given him her picture at Christmas. Evidently Angus felt that he had to break the news to her in a public place, and even then, wouldn't tell her until after the meal, no doubt for fear that she'd make a scene and walk out in the middle.

And what was this business about hoping to get out of Vancouver before people learned of their engagement? Was he ashamed of it?

If he was having second thoughts, he wasn't the only one. Maybe it was time to call the whole thing off. She'd gladly pass up the experience of being cordial to Miss Em and Angus's other lady friends. The thought of never meeting his family, though, gave her a pang of sadness.

It would cause a lot of talk if she cancelled the wedding, but the people she cared about most wouldn't blame her a bit. They'd assume that the age and educational gap was just too wide. Certainly Father wouldn't mind. His remark about Swan River suggested that he still had his doubts about her choice. If she bailed out, he'd think she'd finally come to her senses.

Working in Ottawa with Angus nearby might be strained, at first, but she could handle it. She knew how to use frosty politeness to maintain a distance. Though it would be hard to part with the jade pendant, she'd dump it on his desk and if it got lost in his confusion of papers, who cared? The presents could be returned. She'd wear the silk suit to a gala occasion in Ottawa, perhaps to a reception following the opening of Parliament.

In the midst of her anger, some part of her realized that if Miss Em still meant anything to Angus, he wouldn't have shared the restaurant incident in his letter. Rereading the letter, she perceived that he'd wanted to make a final break with the woman in a way that would be clear to her, yet in a gentlemanly way, without hurting her feelings.

"But what about my feelings?" she asked the ceiling, as she lay back on her bed. Weariness swept over her. The rational thing would be to sit down and make a list of pros and cons – reasons to go ahead with the wedding and reasons to call it off – and see which was longer. Right now her hands were too shaky to hold a pencil. Maybe later she would ask Mother what she thought.

She felt as if the last ten months of her life had been erased. Here she was, back in her old room, where the weight of her failure as a woman and as a teacher had come down on her. She'd written to Angus that 1931 had begun as a year of failure and had ended with the beginning of a glorious success, thanks to him. Maybe that was an illusion.

The old worthlessness started to possess her. She told herself that, no matter what happened, she would be in Ottawa soon, doing important work for her father, and after that, well, she could join Mr. Ivens in planning a campaign to win her a seat in the Manitoba legislature. She could make a future for herself on her own. With that thought in mind, she gave in to exhaustion and slept.

She couldn't know, then, that Angus's lady friends would become a standing joke between them. A decade or so into the future, when she was in Victoria as a member of the British Columbia legislature and Angus was in Ottawa serving his constituents, he occasionally mentioned having taken Miss Bell or some other woman of a certain age out to lunch or dinner.

"All this dining out must be getting expensive," Grace wrote to him. *"Can't you get one of your lady friends to cook you a meal at her place? It would be better for your digestion and our budget."*

Meanwhile, in Victoria, the premier and other MLAs were sending Grace flirtatious notes to which she did not respond.

Grace had no way of knowing, either, that when she eventually met Miss Em in the summer of 1932, she would feel completely secure in Angus's affections, especially after accompanying him on a cross-country speaking tour. Aware that it was important to get along with socialist colleagues, she made friends with Miss Em, a tall elegant woman slightly younger than Angus, who planned to run in the next provincial election. That fall, however, Grace learned that Miss Em was having an affair with a prominent married politician, an intimate relationship which had been going on for the past ten years. Her brief engagement to Angus had been within this time frame. Because of the potential scandal in the socialist movement, Grace and Angus withdrew their support for her candidacy. Soon after that, Miss Em became pregnant, had a baby, convinced her lover to divorce his wife and marry her, and was no longer politically active, except as a rose in her husband's lapel at official ceremonies. Grace and Angus saw her occasionally at social events but were not close.

That January day in 1932, Grace slept for four hours and awoke in a better frame of mind. She reread the letter and reminded herself that she and Angus had agreed to share their experiences and feelings. Hadn't she mentioned her stimulating conversations with Jack Gold and Judge Stubbs? They'd meant nothing, and Angus had recognized that, and hadn't been jealous – or hadn't said so if he was.

Rereading his letters, she felt confident that she had replaced all others in his heart. She abandoned all thought of a pro and con list. The wedding was definitely on.

"What a joy I have had in reading your letters and writing to you," he wrote, in a letter that arrived on the heels of the previous one. *"I have enjoyed love before but have never been as happy in the love of anyone else than I am now. I've often felt I had no one to love me, so you can imagine what it meant to me to have your love, so true and kind, like a gift from heaven, and how I have appreciated it! And Oh, God, Grace, how I hope I can keep it.*

From now on I'll be returning to my house in Vancouver as a visitor, because my real home will be with you."

Grace replied:

"Sometimes our love seems like a dream. At other times I feel a throbbing real sense of wanting you. I once thought I knew what love is, but it was never intense like this. A marriage in winter may seem dreary to some, but to us it will mean cosiness and warmth. I love the cold purity of the snow, for by contrast our love seems rich and warm."

Chapter Thirty-three

The morning of the wedding, Grace's mother was checking on a dozen things at once and humming *By Killarney's Lakes and Fells*, when Grace caught up with her.

"Mother, where will the judge stand? And am I on Angus's right, or his left? And who will hold my bouquet when the ring goes on? Oh, who would have thought a simple wedding could be so complicated."

"Oh, Grace," her mother sighed. "You act as if you've never been married before."

Grace began to laugh, and when her mother realized what she'd said, she laughed until tears came to her eyes.

"I'm happy for you, dear," she said, reaching for her handkerchief, "but I'll miss your company."

"Oh, you haven't seen the last of me!" Grace exclaimed, and hugged her.

The wedding was perfect. Grace wore her silk suit, a gold lace cap and the gold and jade pendant. Her bouquet was golden roses; her ring was a thick gold band. Angus looked proud and dapper in his new suit as he stood beside Charles, the best man. Father had rearranged his schedule to be there. Judge Stubbs performed the ceremony and everyone enjoyed the reception, particularly Mrs. Heaps, who said she'd known for months that love was in the air.

Late that afternoon Angus and Grace bundled up and caught their train. In the coach they held hands and gazed at each other with a happy sense of achievement. That night, in her upper berth, with the curtains open, Grace waited for Angus to come down the aisle, and reached out her hand to him. This time he took her hand and climbed up to join her.

"*Come east as soon as possible and we will have another honeymoon,*" he wrote to Grace years later. "*We've had a number of lovely ones since that first one in 1932.*" And, years later, Grace remarked in a letter to her sister that she and Angus had a "*lovely five days together in Winnipeg, our umpteenth honeymoon,*" which they'd enjoyed even better than the first, "*just as one is more comfortable when the first newness is off a pair of shoes.*" Every reunion was a "honeymoon", and they had many, as they both began to travel, often separately, to build support for her father's dream.

The new socialist party, of which her father was a key founder, brought together under a big tent a wide range of people and groups: trade union councils; the Independent Labour Party; other socialist parties; academics and professionals, and ordinary working people who wanted a just, egalitarian society. Thanks mainly to Angus, the B.C. branch of the Socialist Party of Canada came into this umbrella party, which was called the Cooperative Commonwealth Federation, (CCF) at its founding convention in Regina, Saskatchewan in 1933.

Grace, who corresponded with some of her Paris friends, wrote to them of her marriage and received warmest wishes. None of the girls lived in Paris any more. Gunvar, back in Norway, urged Grace to bring her new husband to Europe to look at innovative social democratic developments in Scandinavia. The American girls, including Julia, were back in the States.

When Julia's parents had come to Paris in May 1929, to bring her home, the young stockbroker they'd wanted her to marry had come with them. Full of love and concern for her, he'd proposed on the return voyage. They'd married in September 1929, just before the Crash. Though her parents and husband had been almost wiped out financially, Julia sounded happy. Her father had managed to retain a small farm in Pennsylvania where all four of them were living. The men had thrown themselves into mixed farming, her mother was learning to cook and keep house, and Julia was the household wage-earner – teaching French at the local high school.

In 1935, in a belated Yuletide greeting, Julia wrote that the new history teacher at her school knew a Paris friend of Grace's. The new teacher had recently graduated from a midwestern university, and had mentioned that his favourite professor had been the brilliant, popular Dr. Willem Van Aarden. Willem was married and the father of a young child.

Grace's eyes lingered on this sentence. The missing last page of a book had turned up and completed the story. She wished Willem well. How could she not, when she was so happy?

Angus looked up from his newspaper.

"You're smiling," he said. "Who's your letter from?"

"Julia." She handed him the letter and got up to do some ironing.

In the fall of 1936, Angus and Grace had a honeymoon in the sense of a "wedding trip" to Europe for three months. One of the forms they filled out required them to state their occupations. When Angus glanced at what Grace had written he laughed and said, "How could you tell a big lie like that?"

Under "occupation", Grace had written "housewife." As the Depression wore on, a married woman who worked for pay outside the home received much social disapproval, if her husband could support the household. Grace was the secretary for the CCF caucus, an assistant in the party office on Wellington Street, the organizer of the youth section and a campaign organizer, and was not paid for any of this work; she was strictly a volunteer. She laughed and said maybe she should have said "jack of all trades".

On the *Duchess of Richmond*, bound for Liverpool, they relaxed and had fun; Angus even danced with her, once, – a waltz. After disembarking, however, they were so struck by the poverty all around them that they felt even more committed to their cause. After meeting with their contacts in the British Labour Party, they went on to the Scandinavian countries, where fellow socialists showed them innovative public housing developments and child care centres. In Norway, they contacted Gunvar and were welcomed into the bosom of her family and entertained at several dinner parties.

In Finland, they found that their visas to the Soviet Union, for which they'd applied in Canada, were not waiting at the Soviet Consulate in Helsinki as they had hoped. Word came that their entry was refused. Evidently Moscow knew about the Cooperative Commonwealth Federation's refusal to cooperate in a common front with the communists. They went from Finland to Copenhagen, Denmark, where they again were welcomed by democratic-socialist connections.

Their journey through Germany en route to Paris was disquieting, with so many soldiers and so many huge posters of Hitler around. A German businessman with a swastika lapel pin sat across from them on the train and monologued about the alleged superiority of the Nordic race. It was an effort not to argue with him, but the last thing they wanted was to get into any trouble that would keep them in Germany. They were glad to get to Switzerland and change trains.

Approaching Paris, Grace tingled with anticipation. She could hardly wait to show Angus the "City of Light" and make new memories there with him. They settled into a small hotel near the Sorbonne, and Grace, delighted to be near her old haunts, took him sightseeing, including a visit to colourful Montmartre. After a couple of days she noticed that Angus, though cooperative, was quiet. When pressed, he said that big noisy cities didn't appeal to him, that the night life was low and degraded, and that his stomach was upset from too much rich food and wine.

Shocked, Grace said she was sorry. She hadn't realized he wasn't enjoying himself. She had been particularly careful in her menu suggestions, avoiding escargots, frogs' legs, eel and especially *cheval*. That night, in each other's arms, he apologized for being a wet blanket and said he was pleased to see her so happy. He was just tired, he said.

Watching him sleep, Grace realized that he felt isolated in Paris, even with her there to interpret for him. In the Scandinavian countries, conversation had been in English, which their contacts had learned as school children; in France he was a fish out of water.

She sensed that something more was bothering him. Surely a person couldn't be jealous of a city! But maybe he was jealous of an old love who never crossed her mind anymore. She'd intended a romantic walk by the Seine in the velvet evening light, perhaps a kiss in the shelter of the pont Neuf, but decided that the charm might be lost on him. Instead, tomorrow afternoon might be better spent visiting the Fuchs.

She had been corresponding with the old couple off and on over the past eight years, and had made it a point to contact them before leaving for Europe. They said they would be delighted to see her again and meet her husband, but the exact date of their rendez-vous hadn't been set. They had moved to Paris, so there would be no need to travel to Cinq-Mars-La-Pile to see them. A family evening with the old couple might be just what Angus needed.

The following afternoon, when Grace and Angus turned up at their flat, the old couple were beside themselves with joy. They embraced Grace like a long-lost granddaughter and hugged and kissed Angus too. In their shabby apartment they talked for hours, with Grace as interpreter. They were impressed that Angus was a "deputy" in the Canadian Parliament, and discussed the deteriorating political situation in Europe with him. When Monsieur actually had a good word to say for Leon Blum, the socialist party leader, Grace was amused and touched. She suspected the old man had adopted this uncharacteristic attitude for her sake and Angus's.

Grace had intended to invite the Fuchs out for dinner, but when she noticed Madame's swollen ankles and Monsieur's difficulty in getting around the apartment, even with his cane, she abandoned that plan. Obviously they hadn't much money and wouldn't have food in the house for an evening meal for four, so

Grace asked if Madame would roast a chicken with herbs the way she used to, if she went out and bought one. This request made Madame very happy.

So Grace and Angus went out and brought back a chicken, pastries and wine, and they had a banquet. After the meal, when Madame served coffee, Monsieur brought out his Courvoisier. Grace silently implored Angus not to refuse and hurt the old man's feelings, and to her relief, he accepted a glass and joined them in a toast to good times.

At midnight they reluctantly said "adieu", and Grace and Angus set out hand in hand toward their hotel.

"I liked them," he said.

Grace started to say she was glad, but her voice failed her. They were so old and fragile. She knew she would never see them again, and she hated partings. The dream of world peace was fading too. War clouds were gathering. Grief choked her.

Then Angus, ordinarily so shy about public displays of affection, took her in his arms and stroked her head.

"I know," he said.

AUTHOR'S NOTE

Grace in Love is a novel about a young Canadian woman in search of a life's work and a love to last a lifetime, in an era of great social, economic and political change – the late 1920s and early 1930s.

Grace Woodsworth MacInnis (1905-1991) was a Canadian parliamentarian who was a strong advocate on social issues, particularly those pertaining to women. For many years she worked behind the scenes in the party her father, J.S. Woodsworth, helped to found – the Cooperative Commonwealth Federation (CCF), a party of the democratic left and the forerunner of the New Democratic Party. Grace served as a member of the British Columbia legislature during the Second World War years, and as a federal member of Parliament from 1965 to 1974. For several years, she was the only woman in the New Democratic Party caucus and in the House of Commons, and took on the role of woman's advocate with energy and enthusiasm.

Like her father, who served in Parliament from 1921 to 1942, and her husband, Angus MacInnis, who served from 1930 to 1957, Grace was a strong proponent of social equality and civil liberties. She was also inspired by her mother, Lucy Woodsworth, a teacher and peace advocate. Yet her road to personal happiness and a Parliamentary career was neither fore-ordained nor easy. As this story shows, she struggled to find the best focus for her talents, like many young people of any era.

The fact that she left to Canadian archives not just her papers from her Parliamentary career, but also letters, diaries and interviews about her formative years, indicates that she hoped her life experiences would interest future generations.

In historical novels, invented characters often mingle with those based on actual persons. Some minor characters in *Grace in Love* are purely fictional creations.

In writing fiction about real people, I have tried to be true to their personalities and views as revealed in primary source materials.   Some of the real people in this novel have been given fictional names because the sources of information about their motives and intentions are limited. Though based on actual people, they are, to a large extent, the products of my imagination, so I gave them new names.

I hope readers will find Grace and the other characters as interesting as I have.

Bibliography

Archival materials:

Cornelius de Kiewiet Papers, 1923-30, Carl A. Kroch Library, Cornell University, Ithaca, NY, 3-7-372, Box 2 (1928-9)

Grace and Angus MacInnis papers, Irving Barber Learning Centre, Special Collections, University of British Columbia. (This collection includes several diaries: Grace's Paris diary in French; the diary of their 1936 trip to Europe; a joint diary begun in 1939.)

Grace MacInnis Papers, Library and Archives Canada, Ottawa, MG32C12, Col. 1-24

The Ralph Sharpe Staples and Belva Woodsworth Staples Fonds, Peterborough Centennial Museum and Archives, Peterborough, Ontario, 1997-029, Boxes 1 and 2.

The J.S. and Lucy Woodsworth Fonds, Simon Fraser University, British Columbia. (Grace and Angus's courtship letters are in this collection.)

The J.S. Woodsworth Papers, Library and Archives Canada, Ottawa, MG27 III c7, Vol. 15, 16

Interviews with Grace MacInnis:

Covernton, Jane, Interview with Grace MacInnis, April 23, 1973, British Columbia Provincial Archives, Victoria, B.C.

Mills, Allan, Interview with Grace MacInnis, October 1983, *Manitoba History*, Number 7, Spring 1984

Scotton, Anne, Interview with Grace MacInnis, April 1978. University of British Columbia, Special Collections.

Stursberg, Peter, Transcript of a Series of Nine Interviews with Grace MacInnis, Vancouver, November 17, 1979, Oral History Project, Parliamentary Library and Public Archives of Canada.

Trott, E. Joy, Interview with Grace MacInnis, Vancouver, B.C., October 24-26, 1986, used with permission of the late E. Joy Trott

BOOKS:

Allen, Frederick Lewis, *Only Yesterday, An Informal History of the 1920s*, NY, HarperCollins, © 1931, 1964.

Bouvet, Vincent, and Durozoi, Gerard, *Paris Between the Wars, 1919-1939*, NY, Vendome Press, 2010

Crowley, Terry, *Agnes Macphail and the Politics of Equality*, Toronto, Lorimer, 1990

Endicott, James, *Raising the Workers' Flag, The Workers' Unity League of Canada 1930-1936,* Toronto, University of Toronto Press, 2013

Fass, Paula E., *The Damned and the Beautiful: American Youth in the 1920s*. NY, Oxford University Press, 1977

Gray, James H., *The Winter Years*, Toronto, Macmillan, 1966.

Guidluck, Lynn, *Visionaries, Crusaders, Firebrands*, Toronto, Lorimer, 2012

Heaps, Leo, *The Rebel in the House: The Life and Times of A.A. Heaps*, Toronto, Fitzhenry and Whiteside, 1970, 1984

Hemingway, Ernest, *A Moveable Feast*, NY, Bantam, 1964

Howard, Irene, *The Struggle for Social Justice in British Columbia: Helena Gutteridge, the Unknown Reformer*, Vancouver, University of British Columbia Press, 1992

Latta, Ruth and Trott, E. Joy, *Grace MacInnis: A woman to remember*, Philadelphia, X-libris, 2000

Lewis, David, *The Good Fight: Political Memoirs 19019-1958*, Toronto, MacMillan, 1981

MacCarthy, Mary, *The Group*, New York, Harcourt Brace & World, 1963

MacInnis, Grace, *J.S. Woodsworth: A man to remember*, Toronto, Macmillan, 1953

McNaught, Kenneth, *A Prophet in Politics: A Biography of J.S. Woodsworth*, Toronto, University of Toronto Press, 1959

Mills, Allen, *A Fool for Christ: the political thought of J.S. Woodsworth*, Toronto, University of Toronto Press, 1991

Naylor, James, *The Fate of Labour Socialism: The Cooperative Commonwealth Federation and the Dream of a Working-Class Future*, (University of Toronto Press, 2016)

Stopes, Marie, *Married Love* (first published 1918), Oxford University Press, 2004

Stopes, Marie, *Wise Parenthood* (first published 1918) various editions

Robertson, Heather, *More than Just a Rose: Prime Ministers, wives and other women*. (Toronto, Seal, 1991)

Woodsworth, Bruce, *African Adventures* (Madeira Park, B.C., Bruce Woodsworth, 1997)

Woodsworth, Charles J., *A Prophet at Home: An intimate memoir of J.S. Woodsworth with three of his previously unpublished letters*. (Vancouver, Tricouni Press, 2005)

ARTICLES/THESES

Ashby, Suzanne, "The History of Women Educators in Manitoba between the years 1880-1940," October 19, 2009, awmp.athabascau.ca/documents/History_of_WomenEducators.pdf

Bishop, Mary F., "The Early Birth Controllers of B.C." *B.C. Studies*, No. 61, Spring 1984

Brutin, Batya, "Batia Lichansky", Jewish Women's Archives, http://jwa.org/encyclopedia/article/lichansky-batia

Dodd, Diane, "The Canadian Birth Control Movement on Trial, 1936-7", *Social History*, Vol. XVI, No. 32, 1983

MacInnis, Grace, "J.S. Woodsworth – Personal Recollections", *Manitoba Historical Society Transactions*, Series 3, Number 24, 1967-68

Montreal Gazette, "Labor Conference in Montreal", *Montreal Gazette*, Vol. CLX, No.11, April 27, 1931

Stewart, Richard Grey, "The Early Political Career of Angus MacInnis", B.A. thesis, History, University of Manitoba, 1967